# MIKE EⅤANꙄ

# FRIENDS OF ZION:

## JOHN HENRY PATTERSON + ORDE CHARLES WINGATE

*a Novel*

TimeWorthy
BOOKS

P.O. Box 30000, Phoenix, AZ 85046

*Friends of Zion: John Henry Patter & Orde Charles Wingate*

Copyright 2015 by Time Worthy Books
P. O. Box 30000
Phoenix, AZ 85046

Design: Peter Gloege | LOOK Design Studio

Hardcover:   978-1-62961-073-3
Paperback:   978-1-62961-074-0
   Canada:   978-1-62961-075-7

This book is dedicated to
my dear friend, the International Chair
of the Friends of Zion Heritage Center,

**President Shimon Peres.**

# PRINCIPAL CHARACTERS & ORGANIZATIONS

*Yoel Horev:* Son of Jewish immigrants to Palestine. Fourteen years old as the story begins. As an adult, served with Patterson in the Zion Mule Corps and Jewish Legion, and with Wingate in Haganah

*Amos Horev:* Yoel's older brother

*Joseph Trumpeldor:* Former Russian soldier. Instrumental in founding of Zion Mule Corps

*Ze'ev Jabotinsky:* Russian journalist turned Zionist activist. Instrumental in founding of Jewish Legion

*Chaim Weizmann:* Russian scientist turned Zionist activist. Became president of the World Zionist Organization

*John Henry Patterson:* Colonel in the British army during World War I. Led both the Zion Mule Corps and the Jewish Legion. Zionist activist

*General John Maxwell:* British general. Commanded the Egyptian Expeditionary Force during World War I

*Zion Mule Corps:* Transportation unit comprised of Jewish volunteers, primarily from refugee camps in Egypt. Served the British army during the Gallipoli Campaign

*General Edmund Allenby:* British general. Commanded the Egyptian Expeditionary Force during the Palestine Campaign of 1917–1918

*Jewish Legion:* Infantry unit of the British army comprised of Jewish volunteers, first from Palestinian refugees, later with volunteers from the United States. Fought with General Allenby in the Palestine Campaign

*Orde Charles Wingate:* British officer detailed to Palestine after World War I as an intelligence officer. Developed strategy of addressing Arab uprising using Special Night Squads

*Special Night Squads:* Small groups of Haganah volunteers trained and deployed by Orde Wingate to combat Arab gangs

*Haganah:* Jewish paramilitary organization created by the Jewish Council during the British Mandate period to provide security for Jewish settlements against Arab attacks. Became Israel Defense Forces after statehood

# FOREWORD

foz

IN NOVEMBER 1914, the Ottoman Empire entered World War I. The decision was announced by Sheikh ul-Islam, who called it a holy war. He urged Muslims everywhere to take up arms against England, France, and Russia.

We were Jews living in Palestine and the news of that decision disturbed many of us. My brother and I, though still teenagers—he was seventeen, I was fourteen—were very upset by the news. Our father, however, seemed to be not the least bit concerned and assured us the war meant nothing to us. We should concern ourselves, he suggested, with the work at hand in maintaining our farm, which was located not far from Kinneret, in the section of northern Palestine known as the Galilee.

In spite of the sheikh's pronouncement, not much changed for us at first. We rose early in the morning, worked until dark, and collapsed in bed shortly after supper—as we had since we moved to the farm years before. But that December, the mayor of Jaffa expelled all Jews from the city. News of that order sent shock waves through the Jewish settlements near our home. Still, our father seemed unfazed. Then the violence started, with roaming gangs of Arabs and Ottoman soldiers attacking Jews who dared to remain on the land.

Over the next few months the expulsion of Jews from Palestine intensified and became official Ottoman policy throughout much of the region. By the end of 1915, many Jewish settlers in Palestine had been driven from their homes. Eleven thousand of us fled to Egypt where we sought refuge under British protection, hoping one day to return to the land we'd come to know and love.

It was a difficult life for us, particularly those first few months in the refugee camp, but in the struggle that followed we met two men who changed us from terrified youths to confident adults. Men who proved to be true friends not only to us but to Jews throughout the world and to the dream of a Jewish state in Palestine. This is our story.

—Joel Horev

HOOFBEATS POUNDED the ground outside our house with a thunderous *thump, thump, thump* so hard and heavy they rattled the panes in our bedroom window and jarred me from a dreamless sleep. As the animals pranced and pawed and darted back and forth, I felt the weight of their every step against my chest. Startled and scared, I lay motionless on my bed, my eyes wide open and alert while the veins in my neck throbbed.

The room I shared with Amos, my older brother, was dark except for a thin shaft of moonlight that shone through a tiny gap in the curtains. When I stole a glance in that direction, I saw his bed was empty, the blanket thrown aside to reveal the bare sheets and pillow. I lay there a moment longer, wondering where Amos was.

As I listened, the sound of the hoofbeats moved away, toward the end of the house, circled around, faded to the opposite side, then grew loud again as they made the turn and started back toward us. They went around once—their hooves pounding the earth with the sound of rumbling thunder—then circled back again, then fell silent.

Amos called to me from across the room. "Get up," he said in a whisper almost as loud and demanding as a shout. "Get up and get over here," he ordered.

I glanced in the direction of his voice and saw him crouched in the corner by the wall near the end of his bed. He was always telling me what to do, so my first instinct was to lie right where I was and do nothing, then shots rang out. Panes in the window shattered, sending chards of glass across the room. Pieces of it rained down on me, stinging my cheeks and lips. A salty flavor filled my mouth, but before I could swallow, there was a loud *whap! whap! whap!* and bullets whizzed overhead. They struck the wall beside my bed, creating a row of pockmarks in the plaster less than a meter above my head.

Knowing what I know now, I should have been off the bed and out the door to the front room, but right then time seemed to slow and an unhurried sense of deliberateness swept over me. As if the row of marks on the wall gave me a strange sense of relief. They were shooting at me, I surely knew that, but if they meant to kill me they would have aimed lower. Wouldn't they?

Instead of running like a frightened child, I glanced around once more and saw the floor beside me was littered with glass. It shimmered in the moonlight that now streamed through the window. I wondered why the light was so bright but then I noticed the curtain was torn from its rod on one side, leaving a gaping hole where the bullets had ripped through.

Through the opening I saw two horses standing outside the window. They were big, muscular animals and atop them were men dressed in white robes with turbans on their heads and rifles slung over their shoulders. In the moonlight, with the night sky behind them for a backdrop, they looked magnificent, like an image straight from a fine piece of literature about Arabian horses and daring Bedouins.

Still, I did not feel rushed. My shoes were tucked beneath the bed and after a moment I felt for them, drew them out, and slipped them on. "Hurry up," Amos snarled. "They can see you through the window."

As my feet slipped into the shoes, I looked up in time to see one of the men outside raise a rifle to his shoulder and point it in my direction. At first the barrel was aimed high, but slowly it descended until the sights lined up and I was staring straight into the gunman's face.

Instinctively I sensed the danger I'd ignored before and dove to the right. Two shots rang out and I heard them hit behind me. The first one struck the frame of the bed, right where I'd been seated. The second hit the pillow. But by then I was in the corner crouched at Amos' side, my arms around his waist, squeezing him as tightly as my fourteen-year-old muscles allowed—the brave and stoic boy reduced to a sniveling child in a matter of seconds.

◆ ◆ ◆

We'd come to that farm in Galilee ten years earlier, when I was four and Amos was seven. Back then it seemed like a grand adventure. I did not know until much later that we'd left our native Novhorod-Siverskyi, a Russian city on the banks of the Desna River, after a mob burned the synagogue where our grandparents, Abraham and Esther Davidoff, attended. No one wanted us to leave. Grandfather wanted us to stay and fight. But our father would have none of it and so we came to Palestine.

We were offered a place at Kvutzat Kinneret, a farming collective near Tiberias at the southern end of the Sea of Galilee, but our mother did not like the communal lifestyle. She insisted on rearing her own children, washing her own clothes, and wearing what she wished. At the kibbutz, most people wore the same thing—gray work shirts and pants with heavy boots. Even the underwear was shared. Mama didn't care for that.

Instead, we purchased a small farm to the north of the settlement. Still within easy walking distance if we needed help or wanted to see a friendly face but far enough away to be on our own. We grew vegetables—tomatoes, melons, peppers, and zucchini—which we sold at the market in Tiberias.

Our nearest neighbors were the Riskins—David and Tzipi. Like us, they'd come to Palestine to avoid European persecution and, also like us, they eschewed the farming settlement, preferring to make a go of it on their own. They had two sons, both of them a little older than us, and one daughter, Dalia.

✦ ✦ ✦

More bullets zipped through the window and whizzed past us, but we were tucked in the corner, out of the line of fire and so they went past us without doing harm. Then Amos nudged me and said, "Come on. Let's go."

I shook my head. "No, let's stay right here."

But he would not be dissuaded. "We have to see about Mama and Papa."

Amos shoved me aside and crawled to the door, then reached up to open it and pushed it aside, too. As the door swung out of the way I saw Papa in the front room, crouched at an open window, loading his rifle. He glanced over his shoulder in our direction. "You boys all right?" he asked as he cocked the hammer on the gun.

"Yes, sir," Amos replied.

"What are they doing?" I wailed.

Instead of answering my question, Papa raised up from his hiding position, poked the barrel of the rifle through the window, and squeezed off a shot. From the shouting that followed outside, I supposed that he hit whatever he was aiming for.

Just then, the door opened from a room to the right and Mama appeared. Dressed in a nightgown, she walked fully upright and confident. Head high, shoulders back, a smile on her face. In one hand she held a rifle and in the other a small sack of ammunition. Papa saw her and his eyes were wide with fear. "Sonya!" he snapped in an angry tone. "Get down. They'll see you."

"Elad," she said as she continued toward him. "This is my home. I will not cower to a gang of thugs in my own home. They can do as they—"

*Whap! Whap! Whap!*

A burst of gunfire interrupted her in midsentence. The panes of glass that remained in the window shattered.

One bullet struck a vase that sat on a table near the corner by the door Mama had just opened. It had belonged to our grandmother, and Mama had insisted she had to bring it with us. The bullet shattered the vase in an instant, splintering it into a thousand pieces.

The second shot whizzed past my head and lodged in the frame of our bedroom door. The third made no sound at all and as I glanced around I saw not a stray mark from it. I was about to ask Amos where it hit when I noticed Mama.

She was standing in the center of the room, directly opposite the window. Her body fully erect with her chin in a regal pose. Her eyes were fixed on an unknown point in the middle distance and on her face was the strangest look—as if she were listening to a distant conversation, straining to hear every word.

Without warning, the rifle slipped from her hand and clattered to the floor. The ammunition bag dropped at her side and her knees buckled as she collapsed in a heap beside it, her head landing only inches from my feet.

Papa, still across the room, stared at her a moment, then turned back quickly to the window and fired a shot from his rifle. While the report echoed through the night, he tossed the gun aside and crawled quickly to where Mama lay. He lifted her gently from the floor and cradled her head in his lap, one hand beneath her and the other gently stroking her cheek. That's when I saw the blood dripping from his fingers and noticed the gaping hole near Mama's ear.

Suddenly all the air was sucked from my lungs. I gasped for breath but none would come and then the room started to spin. Papa must have noticed the look on my face because he slapped me on the chest and shouted, "Yoel!"

Startled by the impact of his hand, I looked over at him but I must have appeared as dazed and confused as I felt, because in the next instant he glanced past me to Amos and said, "Take your brother and get out of here."

Amos protested. "We can stay and help."

"No, you can't," Papa replied. "Now take your brother and go."

"Where?"

"Go to the Riskins. Tell them what's happened. Tell them to be ready because they may be next."

"But what about you?" Amos continued. "What about Mama?"

Papa shook his head. "Your mother is dead," he said in a solemn voice. "She's gone now. And I'll take care of myself." Then he gave Amos a shove. "But you have to go. So do as I say. Take your brother and go."

From out front, two more shots passed through the window. They landed harmlessly against the rear wall of the house. At the sound of them, Papa glanced toward the window with an angry glare. The horsemen were still outside and I could see them preparing to fire at us again.

Papa laid Mama on the floor and crawled toward the window. I sat there, watching, trying to make sense of it all, trying not to pass out, while Amos hurried back to our room and returned with our pants.

"Here," he said in a tone that sounded just like Papa. "Put these on." When I didn't move, he snapped at me. "Do it now, Yoel. We have to hurry." I slipped the pants on and stood, just like Mama.

Amos screamed at me, "Get down, you idiot!" But I paid him no attention and walked calmly to the back door.

Papa shouted over his shoulder in our direction, "Amos, take care of your brother!" Then he looked me in the eye, "Yoel, do as he says."

As I stared back at Papa—wanting with all my heart to run to him, to wrap my arms around his neck, to feel his wrapped around mine—I heard a noise from our bedroom. Amos was at my side by then and heard it, too.

"They're in our room. Come on." Then he opened the back door and pushed me outside.

As we stumbled from the house, the Arabs were nowhere to be seen. Their horses, riderless and abandoned, loitered near our bedroom window. Today, after all that happened to us and all we saw and did, I would run to the nearest one, climb onto its back, and ride away. Amos would do the same, giving us the advantage of speed and leaving our attackers to travel on foot—if they could escape Papa's marksmanship. But back then, we were young and scared. Seeing the horses riderless and unattended told us the gunmen were inside the house, so instead of maximizing even the smallest opportunity to inflict some harm on our opponents, we ran away on foot as fast as our legs would carry us.

AS WE RAN AWAY from the house I heard gunfire behind us and turned to look over my shoulder. Amos grabbed me by the arm and tugged to turn me around. "Don't look back," he said with a grim tone.

"But what about Papa?"

"He said for us to run. That's what we're supposed to do."

"But what will happen to him?"

Amos looked even more determined. "I don't know. But our job is to get to the Riskins' farm and warn them." He glanced over at me. "And keep you alive in the process."

"And keep *you* alive," I replied.

"I'll take care of that," Amos said, once again sounding just like Papa. "You concentrate on doing what I tell you."

As we came from behind the barn I smelled smoke, and from the direction of the Riskins' house I saw a large amber ball glowing behind the stand of cedar trees that shielded the back side of their house. "What's that?" I asked, though I knew full well what it was.

"Fire," Amos muttered.

I came to a dead stop. Amos' hand slipped free of my arm and I stood there staring as the glow turned into flames that rose into the sky. "I'm going back," I announced.

"No, you're not," Amos retorted and in an instant he shoved me to the ground and fell on top of me. "You can't go back! I won't let you go back." He pointed his index finger at me and jabbed me in the chest. "It's my job to keep you alive." Tears filled his eyes. "That's what Papa told me. 'Take care of your brother.' And that's exactly what I intend to do. We are going to do what he told us whether you like it or not."

Amos wiped the tears from his eyes with the back of his hand but they kept coming, flowing down both cheeks in a continuous stream. And that's when I knew we would never see Papa again. "They're going to kill him, aren't they?" I cried. "They're going to kill him and burn the house, just like they're doing to the Riskins."

We lay there staring at each other, then Amos took a deep breath. "I don't know what will happen to Papa," he said calmly. "But I know what he told us to do. And if he is dead, he died giving us time to do it." He climbed off me and we stood together. Then he took me by the hand, "Let's go. We have to see about the Riskins."

✦ ✦ ✦

We ran as far as the stand of cedar trees and took cover there. Kneeling on the ground, doing my best to stay out of sight, I felt the heat of the flames as it consumed the Riskins' house. "Where are they?" I asked.

"I don't know. I don't see anyone."

Just then, a man approached sitting atop a large horse like the ones I'd seen outside our bedroom window. He jerked back on the reins as he came near us, bringing the horse to a stop, then the rider stared in our direction, his eyes focused and intent as if he'd heard something that caught his attention. I ducked my head and lay as flat and still as possible, my head turned sideways with my cheek pressed against the ground. Finally I heard the jingle of the horse's rigging followed by the gentle clop of its hooves as it moved away from us. I raised my head enough to steal a glance in that direction and saw the horse galloping toward the opposite side of the house. I watched as it disappeared behind the glow of the flames.

Just then, a hand touched my back. I knew in an instant it wasn't Amos' and I glanced to the left to see David Riskin beside me. "You must be quiet," he said in a whisper that was barely audible. As I nodded in response I looked over his shoulder and saw his family hiding just a short way from us. His boys looked as scared as I felt. Then I noticed Dalia lying next to her mother. Our eyes met and she tried to force a smile, but even from that distance I could see she had been crying.

We hid among the cedars for what seemed a long time. Amos told me later it was less than an hour, but to me it seemed like the remainder of the night. The men atop their horses galloped around, shouting and yelling phrases in Arabic, but eventually they grew tired of it and after a while they set off into the night, leaving us alone with only each other for company. We waited a few minutes more, then David pushed himself up from the ground and stood. Amos did also and I stood next to him.

As the others gathered with us, David turned to Amos. "Where are your parents?"

"Mama is dead," Amos replied. Tzipi gasped in anguish but Amos kept going. "Papa was at the house when we left, still fighting back with his rifle. I'm not sure what happened after that. After they shot Mama, he made us leave."

Tzipi reached for me and squeezed me close, muttering something in Russian I couldn't quite understand—a prayer, I think, but I'm not sure. While she hugged me and stroked my hair, David turned to one of the older boys. "Go to their house," he ordered. "And see if Elad is there."

"Do you think that is a good idea?" Tzipi asked.

David glanced at the boy. "Be careful. Approach quietly. Make sure the way is clear before you move toward the house." Then he looked back at Tzipi. "They are our neighbors and our friends. We cannot simply abandon them."

When the boy was gone, Tzipi let go of me and turned back to Dalia. Amos and I followed David and the others toward the fire and stood with them, watching as the remnants of their home slowly disappeared in the flames.

In a little while, the boy who'd been sent to check on Papa returned. "Mrs. Horev's body is there," he said, breathless from the run. "Mr. Horev was not."

"Any sign of what happened to him?"

The boy shook his head, "None."

David thought for a moment, "We should bury her."

Tzipi touched him lightly on the forearm. "We should get going."

Without turning to her, David shook his head. "We cannot leave her body."

One of the boys found two shovels in the barn, which was left unharmed, and we trekked back to our house. It was standing and intact, though the windows were broken and much of the furniture destroyed. Amos and I chose a place behind the barn for the grave and set to work digging a hole, while David and his sons retrieved Mama's body.

A few minutes later, they appeared with her wrapped in the sheets from our beds. We took turns digging and in a few hours the hole was deep enough for a grave. Then we lowered her body into it and stood there staring down at her. It was all very...strange to me. Just the day before she'd been laughing at something I said, now here she was, her lifeless body about to be covered in dirt forever. Then David began to pray the Kaddish.

"Exalted and hallowed be His great Name."

"Amen," we responded in unison.

"Throughout the world which He has created according to His Will. May He establish His kingship, bring forth His redemption and hasten the coming of His Moshiach."

"Amen."

"In your lifetime and in your days and in the lifetime of the entire House of Israel, sword, famine and death shall cease from us and from the entire Jewish nation, speedily and soon, and say, Amen."

"Amen."

"May His great Name be blessed forever and to all eternity. Blessed and praised, glorified, exalted and extolled, honored, adored and lauded be the Name of the Holy One, blessed be He."

"Amen."

"Beyond all the blessings, hymns, praises and consolations that are uttered in the world; and say, Amen."

"Amen."

"Upon Israel, and upon our sages, and upon their disciples, and upon all the disciples of their disciples, and upon all those who occupy themselves with the Torah, here or in any other place, upon them and upon you, may there be abundant peace, grace, kindness, compassion, long life, ample sustenance and deliverance, from their Father in heaven; and say, Amen."

"Amen."

"May there be abundant peace from heaven, and a good life for us and for all Israel; and say, Amen."

"Amen."

"He who makes peace in His heavens, may He make peace for us and for all Israel; and say, Amen."

When we finished, Tzipi touched me on the elbow and gestured with a nod of her head for me to come with her. I followed after her a few steps, then thought of Amos and turned to glance back at him. She grasped my arm more firmly, and Dalia took the opposite hand. The touch of her palm against mine felt strange but in a good way and I did not let go of her hand as we moved away from the grave.

Tzipi led us to a bench near the house. As we approached it, Dalia let go of my hand and moved ahead of us to take a seat on the far end of the bench. Tzipi sat in the middle and I sat next to her. We waited there, Tzipi staring into the night. My feet did not quite touch the ground and I swung them forward and back as we passed the time. In a few minutes I noticed Dalia was propped against her mother's shoulders, eyes closed and lips parted. I glanced up at Tzipi, who gestured with a finger to her lips for me to be quiet.

In a little while, Amos and David came from behind the barn, followed by the older boys. When they reached the bench where we were sitting, Dalia roused from her nap and we looked up at them. David's eyes met mine. "We buried your mother," he said in a kind voice. "Near the corner of the barn. We didn't have anything to mark the grave and I'm not sure we should."

"The Arabs," Amos offered by way of explanation. "They might return and dig her up."

The thought of that unsettled me and for an instant images of her dead body flashed through my mind. "Why would they do that?"

"Because they're mean," one of the boys replied.

"I think it's best," David added. There was nothing else for me to say so I stared down at the ground, wondering what life would be like

FRIENDS OF ZION: PATTERSON & WINGATE

without her and worrying about when Papa would return to take care of us.

"We should stay here tonight," David said.

I looked up at him and saw he was talking to Tzipi. "You sure about that?" and she gave him a knowing look in my direction.

"It's late," he said. "And I'm not sure how we'll get to Haifa. There's no one out there now except Arab gangs."

"And the Turks," one of the boys added.

David gave an approving nod and waited for Tzipi to respond. "Well, I suppose," she sighed. "But these boys can't sleep in the house."

I jumped up from the bench. "I'm not sleeping in there."

Amos stepped toward me and slipped his arm around my shoulder. "We'll sleep in the barn. We've done it before. We know how to make a bed."

Before anyone could respond he steered me away from the bench and we started toward the barn. When we reached the door, I glanced over my shoulder and saw the others following after us.

✦ ✦ ✦

Sometime later I felt a nudge against my side. I forced my eyes open to the glare of the morning sun to see Amos standing over me. "Time to get up."

"What for?" I grumbled.

"They're leaving." His voice had a matter-of-fact tone and I knew without asking that something was wrong.

David appeared behind him. "We're all going," he said. "You two have to come with us. You can't stay here by yourselves."

I pushed myself up from the hay where I'd spent the night and glanced around, trying to make sense of it. "But what about Papa?" I blurted out finally.

David stared at me a moment, then said, "I don't think he's coming back."

"He wouldn't leave us," I protested. "He'll be back."

"They don't think he's alive," Amos added.

The truth of what they said was obvious—Amos and I knew that the night before—but I'd convinced myself that he was just down the road and would come walking up soon. Now, seeing the looks on their faces and hearing the tone in their voices, I knew that was just a dream I'd forced myself to believe. Papa was gone and he was never coming back, but that was more than I wanted to admit.

Tears filled my eyes. "Of course he's alive!" I tried my best to believe the words I said. "I know he's alive." Amos put his arm around my shoulder and I leaned forward, resting my head against his chest. "He has to be alive," I sobbed.

Amos knew I knew the truth, but for once he remembered we were brothers and instead of arguing back he just held me. I even felt his fingers rub against my hair once or twice, the way Mama used to do it when we were little.

We stood there awhile and I wondered why Tzipi didn't come to my rescue, but she never did. Dalia was nowhere to be seen, either, and after a few minutes Amos gently pushed me away. "They found some bread in the house," he said. "I saved a piece for you." He reached inside his pocket and took it out. "Here, eat it." I took the bread from him and began to chew but the taste of it reminded me of Mama and I began to cry again.

When I'd eaten the bread, I looked over at David, who still was nearby. "Where will we go?" I asked.

"Haifa."

"What's there?"

"A ship."

My eyes grew wide at the realization of what that meant. "A ship? You mean to leave?"

"Everyone is leaving," he answered. "Going to Egypt until it is safe to return."

The thought of leaving was beyond my young mind's ability to conceive. Papa and Mama had saved and gone without to get that farm. Then we all did without to keep it. And now the Riskins wanted us to just up and leave it for the Arabs to trample, pillage, and destroy? "I don't want to leave," I said, squaring my shoulders in a determined pose.

"None of us do," David said. "But if we stay here, we will die."

"But how would we get all the way to Haifa?"

"We'll walk to the main road," David explained. "Someone will come along and give us a ride. We won't have to walk far."

The thought of leaving the farm was almost more than I could bear, but David was right. Staying there alone was impossible and the truth of it was clear, even to my young mind. Amos didn't want to go either but seemed to think it was the best we could do. "We will return," he said bravely. "One day we'll come back. And then we will make it the best farm in Galilee." I knew he was only trying to make me feel better, but I didn't argue with him.

FRIENDS OF ZION: *Patterson & Wingate*

# CHAPTER 3

foz

WE FOLLOWED THE RISKINS out to the main road and, sure enough, not long after that a truck came by and picked us up. The driver gave us a ride to Kafar Ata, near the coast. From there we rode with a family who had been attacked by an Arab gang a few days earlier but managed to escape before the shooting started. They took us the rest of the way to Haifa. In Haifa, a friend of the Riskins gave us a place to stay. Amos and I were glad to finally sleep in a bed, though we had to share it.

A few days later, we walked to the docks where we found a ship moored there—the USS *North Carolina*, an American warship. It had arrived several days earlier with a cargo of food for settlements still holding out against Arab gangs and the Ottoman army. After the food was unloaded, they took as many aboard as they could manage. We were among them and not long before sunset we sailed for Egypt.

The following day, we arrived in Alexandria. British soldiers met us as we came down the gangway. They lined a path through the crowd that had come to meet the ship, some of whom were not glad to see us or have us in their country. They shouted at us to leave but the soldiers kept them away and directed us to a large warehouse not far from the water.

As we entered the building, I noticed tables at the opposite end with clerks seated at them. Already long lines had formed and I followed Amos to the nearest one as we queued up with the others to wait.

Air inside the building was stiflingly hot and I could hardly breathe. Amos noticed me fidgeting and frowned at me. "Be still."

"It's hot in here," I complained.

"At least we're in the shade."

"We're in an oven," I grumbled.

A guard passed by and scowled at us. "No talking in line," he grunted.

Amos glared at me and I knew what he was thinking. We were in trouble and it was all my fault. I turned my head and looked in the opposite direction.

The Riskins were in a line next to us and I stared at them, trying to get their attention, but they didn't seem to notice us at first. Finally, though, Dalia looked in our direction and I thought she saw me, but then I realized she was looking at Amos. He smiled at her, and she smiled back but in an odd sort of way. Which struck me as even more strange to see that she would look at him and not at me, especially after that night when she took my hand as we were walking with her mother...and then we sat together on the bench outside our house... now she was staring at Amos with that...look.

And that was the moment I realized the Riskins wouldn't be around to look after us anymore. I should have realized many things then, too, but that's what I remember noticing. The distance from our line to theirs wasn't just the physical space between us. We were in Egypt now. That's what they'd said before, after the Arabs burned them out and killed Mama. They told us they were going to Egypt. That we couldn't stay at the house alone. We had to go with them.

They never said anything about taking us to raise as their own children, or anything like that. Just, "Go with us. We're going to Egypt. You can't stay here alone." And now we were there. In Egypt. They'd done all they were going to do to help us.

It was scary to think we really were on our own, but not altogether surprising. Even before we reached Haifa I could feel the distance growing between us and them. The more time passed, the more they kept to themselves, and I could see they were too worried about their own survival to worry about us. I sensed it then—instinctively I guess—before we got to Egypt and I realized it with my mind. Without even thinking about it, I followed Amos everywhere he went, never letting him out of my sight, never letting him get more than an arm's length away. Always keeping my hand on his elbow or forearm and when we were in a crowd I hooked my fingers in the waistband of his trousers. Even now, as we stood in line waiting on the clerks in that building near the docks in Alexandria, my fingers were curled around the waistband of his trousers. He didn't complain about it, though. Just about my fidgeting.

After an hour or two, we finally reached one of the tables. The clerk, a glum-looking man with a British accent, barely glanced at us. "Name?" he asked in a flat, affectless voice.

Amos answered his questions as he took down our responses. After that, he wanted to know our ages and birth dates. The place where we were born and the place where we lived. Then he asked about our parents and whether they were alive. Amos told him what happened, but the clerk seemed not the least bit interested or concerned.

It didn't seem to bother Amos much, either, but hearing him talk about it brought back memories of Mama lying on the floor, the blood oozing from her head and trickling from Papa's hand as he held her. I did my best to push the images from my mind and gripped the waist-band of Amos' trousers tighter.

When we finished at the table, a soldier directed us toward a door that led outside. Others were headed in the same direction and we followed them. As we approached the opening, the air was noticeably cooler and I took a deep breath, letting the air fill my lungs. Then we came from the shadow of the building into the sunshine and I felt the searing heat on the back of my neck. Amos was right. Being inside was better, but by then we were around the corner of the building and there was no going back.

We were on the shady side of the building and found a place to sit near the far corner. I sat with my knees scrunched against my chest and my heels pressed against my thighs. When I grew tired of sitting, I leaned forward, folded my arms atop my knees and used them for a pillow to rest my head.

Before long, however, boredom set in and I glanced around, look-ing for a familiar face. The Riskins were nowhere to be seen and I wasn't even thinking about them, but we had met other people on the ship and I wondered where they were. Before long, I wondered if we'd ever see them again, too. Only a few days from when Mama died and Papa disappeared, and already we were gathering a collection of people we *used* to know.

✦ ✦ ✦

Later that day, the soldiers loaded us onto trucks. We climbed into the nearest one. It was already almost full, so we squeezed into a spot near the back. I didn't like the way we were jammed up against every-one else on one side and all but hanging over the edge on the other. But Amos said it would be okay. I didn't want to be separated from him so I kept quiet.

A solider banged the tailgate of the truck in place and I stared out at the crowd below us. They stared back and seemed to make eye contact with us, but their eyes were listless and dull with a look I would later know as bone-weary fear—the way people stare when they're too tired to move and too afraid to think. I didn't know it then but I would see that look again, too many times.

A moment later the truck's engine roared to life and then we started to move. As we did, I caught sight of the Riskins and was certain Dalia caught sight of me, but she only stared after us as we rode away.

From the warehouse near the waterfront, we rode slowly through the streets of Alexandria. The pavement was rough and the truck jostled from side to side. The motion of it, together with the heat, made me drowsy. Once again, Amos was right. It really was much cooler there than farther up toward the truck's cab, but still it was all I could do to keep my eyes open and my head flopped from side to side. Finally I gave up trying to stay awake and rested my cheek against Amos' shoulder.

✦ ✦ ✦

In a little while the truck slowed and I opened my eyes. Through the slats on the side of the truck I saw a fence that stood higher than the truck. It had seven strands of barbed wire that ran along the top, and armed soldiers manned towers at the corners. The truck slowed some more, then lurched to a stop and I heard loud voices as someone talked to the driver. A soldier appeared at the corner by the tailgate latch and glanced in at us. After a moment, he shook his head in disgust and disappeared back the way he'd come. I heard him shout to the driver, then we started forward again.

That's when I saw there was a gate in the fence. It was open and we rolled through to the opposite side. Someone said we were in Gabbari, a refugee camp on the south side of the city. I had no way of knowing for certain, but I knew we were near the sea. I could smell it in the air and took a deep breath to enjoy it. Then as we moved slowly away, I watched out the back of the truck as the soldier I'd seen before pushed the gate closed behind us. All at once, it seemed like a long time since that night at the house when the Arabs killed Mama. I longed for the scent of newly plowed dirt on our farm and the hint of cedar that wafted from the trees near our home. A sense of sadness settled over me and I wondered whether we'd ever get back there—and if we did, whether there'd be anything left of what we once knew.

Beyond the gate, the truck made its way past rows and rows of wooden barracks. Grayed and weathered from the blistering heat and brilliant sun, they looked like relics from the past, though they'd been constructed by the British only a short time before we arrived. People along the way looked much the same—tired, haggard, dirty, and listless. I knew they'd not been there very long but they appeared as those who'd lost the will to move forward. The smell of the sea I'd enjoyed moments earlier was gone, too, overwhelmed by the stench of humans packed into a space never meant to accommodate so many.

Not long after we passed the gate, we came to a stop. More guards appeared at the back of the truck and ordered us to get out. Amos and I climbed down to the ground and a soldier directed us to a table where we once again stood in line—this time in the open, unprotected from the sun and heat. I remembered the sweltering warehouse earlier that day and thought of it with nostalgic fondness, though just a few hours earlier I had complained about being confined there.

Even though we'd already given the clerks at the warehouse our names and everything else we remembered about ourselves, clerks at the tables in Gabbari asked for it again. The process was slow and tedious but when we finished, a soldier led us with a group of five or six others to a barracks several rows away. A man with a clipboard met us there and led us inside.

Beyond the doorway, the building was filled with wooden bunks, each of them three beds high. All of them with a number stenciled in white paint on the end. Designed for two, many were filled with three and four people to a bed. I found one on top in the corner and claimed it for us, glad to find it available. It didn't take long to find out why. The corner received almost no circulation and being on the top level we were trapped in stale, hot air. Amos didn't like it, but he didn't complain. I would have preferred a cooler location, as well, but not if it meant being separated from him.

The man who led us through the building noted our choice on his chart and I smiled with satisfaction. We were safe and together. That was all I cared about.

✦ ✦ ✦

In the afternoon we followed the others from our building to the canteen where we ate supper. By most standards, it wasn't much—a watery stew made from potatoes and served with a large hunk of bread—but that day it tasted good and I would have eaten three bowls if they let me. We ate there twice each day, once in the morning and once in the afternoon. Mornings were my favorite. They served bread with butter and jam and a hot, dark drink they called coffee but I'm still not sure that's what it was. We could get a second piece of bread if we wanted, and jam was never in short supply.

Mealtimes were also the time in the day when we saw people from all over the camp. Several people who'd come down with us on the ship were there and a boy I met once at the kibbutz in Kinneret, when Papa went there on business. At last, familiar faces in the sea of strangers. And the Riskins appeared again, not as friendly as they once had been but more interested in us than they'd been when we arrived at the docks that day.

It was easy to see why people in the camp were unmotivated. Nothing was expected of us except to act in an orderly manner, and most days that's about all that happened. We awoke in the morning and trudged from our barracks, stopped at the latrine, then continued on to the canteen for breakfast. After that, we found a shady place to sit and waited for the afternoon meal. Time passed slowly. A few other boys my age lived in our section of the camp, but I didn't want to get too far away from Amos so I mostly stayed with him, though he did slip off alone once in a while and I never knew where he went.

A few weeks after we arrived, I noticed a big kid staring at me when we were in line at the canteen. I found out later his name was Yitzhak Gitai, but at first I only knew him as the Big Kid. That day when I first saw him he was with a group of boys about his age standing in line behind us. They kept nodding toward me and laughing. It made me uncomfortable but there wasn't much I could do about it, so I did my best to ignore them. Yitzhak and his friends looked like trouble and the last thing I wanted was trouble.

A week or two later, as I was leaving the line with a bowl of stew, a hand reached over my shoulder and a voice said, "I'll take that." When I looked up I saw Yitzhak walking away with my bread. He glanced at me over his shoulder with a cheesy smile and took a bite from the bread just for spite.

Amos saw what happened and I expected him to go after the guy, but instead he just nudged me to keep moving. "Let it go," he said quietly. "You can have some of mine." I didn't want to let it go, but Yitzhak was taller than I was and fifty pounds heavier. The thought of fighting him frightened me. Still, I considered doing something anyway and watched as he joined his friends. Then Amos grabbed me by the elbow. "Come on," he said impatiently. "Let's just eat and not have any trouble."

Just then, one of Yitzhak's pals slammed into me as he moved past. The force of it sloshed half the stew from my bowl, and he snarled, "Better listen to your brother, little boy." Then he reached for Amos' bread, but Amos turned away at the last moment and the kid missed.

"Over here," Amos said, nodding toward a place outside where we could squat in the lee of the building. I followed him but didn't like it.

As we ate, Nisei Rosenberg took the spot beside me. He was an older guy with a narrow face, deep-set eyes, and craggy lines near his mouth and across his forehead. His bunk was across from ours but on a lower level and next to the window. At first he didn't say anything. Just sat there with us, sipping the stew and eating his bread. Then he said, "You have to do it, you know." I gave him a puzzled frown, and he said, "You have to fight back."

"Me?"

"Can't let the big kid push you around. You let him push you around now, he'll do it from now on."

"But he's bigger than I am."

"Then you'll have to find a way to get the advantage."

"He can beat me up."

"Yes," Rosenberg nodded. "And it might hurt. But even if he beats you up, he'll leave you alone next time."

I was intrigued and I guess Amos noticed it, because he leaned closer and said, "Don't listen to him. He's spent too much time in the sun." But in my heart I knew Rosenberg was right. This thing with Yitzhak wasn't going away on its own.

After we'd finished eating, Yitzhak and his friends left the canteen together. By then I had decided to follow Rosenberg's advice, but when I started after them Amos once again grabbed my arm. "Don't. That old man doesn't know what he's talking about. He should mind his own business. We should, too."

"This *is* my business," I replied and shrugged free of his grasp. "I just want to see where they go."

"No you don't," Amos argued. "You want to follow them and get into a fight."

"I'll be okay."

By then, Yitzhak and his friends were out of sight. I hurried up the alley past the rows of barracks, checking after each one with a glance as I passed. Finally, four rows later, I saw them moving away from me to the left. I continued past the next row of barracks, then turned left and ran along the alley parallel to their position.

In a while they came to a stop and stood together, talking and laughing. Then they parted company, each one going his separate way. Yitzhak continued in the same direction as before, only now he was alone. I hurried past the next building and sprinted down the opposite side, hoping Yitzhak didn't appear at the corner before I reached it.

I was almost to the next alley when suddenly he emerged, walking with his head down and his hands in his pockets. Without slowing, I lowered my shoulder and plowed into him from the side, knocking him to the ground. Before he could react I climbed on top of him and pummeled him in the face with my fists, hitting him as hard and as fast as my arms would move.

Within seconds, Yitzhak's cheeks were red and already beginning to swell. After a few more punches, blood trickled from his nose, ran along the ridge of his upper lip, and collected at the corner of his mouth. When the taste of it reached his tongue, his eyes opened wide with a look of realization and he began to buck and heave with all his might.

He managed to twist onto his side, then pushed himself up from the ground, sending me for a tumble. I scrambled to get to my feet, but when I turned to face him he was already reaching for me. Then the thrashing began and I took a beating.

But before Yitzhak could do much damage, David Riskin appeared and wedged himself between us. "Break it up!" he barked. "Break it up!" Yitzhak tried to reach over him to get to me, but David was quick and strong and kept him away. Holding Yitzhak at bay, he looked back at me and said, "Are you all right?"

"Yeah," I nodded as I wiped my nose with my hand. My fingers were red with blood but I didn't care. It felt good to stand up for myself and I was glad I did.

"He started it," Yitzhak shouted and pointed at me. "I was just defending myself."

David gave him a knowing look. "I think we all know what this was about."

Hearing him say that sent a warm feeling over me, to know that he'd been watching in the canteen. I thought the Riskins were long gone, but all the while he'd kept an eye on us, and to know that made me glad.

Yitzhak shrugged from David's grip and backed away. "I'm not through with you," he warned.

"You know where to find me," I replied. Then Yitzhak moved up the alley, dusting off his trousers as he went.

When he was gone, David turned to me. "Sure you're all right?"

"Yes, sir," I replied. "Thank you."

"Well," he sighed. "Life here is different from what you knew before. You gotta do whatever you have to do to survive."

Dalia was standing nearby and in her eyes I saw a hint of admiration. Not exactly the look she gave Amos but one that was different from before, and a flushed feeling swept over me. It felt strange. Even more strange than seeing her look at Amos and him at her. This was different. This was me. And I wondered if she felt the same.

The next morning I arrived at the canteen looking bruised and feeling sore. My left eye was blue and I had abrasions on both cheeks. Yitzhak looked even worse. And he no longer laughed and joked with his friends as we stood in line. In fact, he no longer stood with them at all but kept to himself, and for some reason I felt sorry for him. He'd had friends before. Now it seemed he didn't and I thought how bad that was—to have had them and then lost them. And then it all seemed hollow and worse still—to know that his friends were only his friends because they thought he was tough, and when he proved vulnerable they no longer wanted to associate with him. As if being with him now acknowledged their own vulnerability. No one in the camp wanted to admit how vulnerable we all really were.

Amos and I took our bread outside and sat again in the lee of the building. Before long Rosenberg joined us and took a squatting position next to me. "I see that kid did not take your bread this time."

"No," I replied. "He didn't."

Rosenberg grinned, then leaned around me and caught Amos' attention. "The fight will come to you, too."

"I don't have to fight," Amos said with a shake of his head.

"None of us enjoy it," Rosenberg acknowledged. "But we all have to, sooner or later. Maybe not here, but somewhere, somehow, it will come to you. The fight comes to all of us. That is our lot in life. To struggle. That is how we survive."

As we talked, a man appeared. He was taller than most, with muscular features and a lean, hard look that seemed like that of a soldier, but when I looked more closely I saw he had only one arm. I was sure he couldn't be a soldier with just one arm. I discovered his name was Joseph Trumpeldor. "Rosenberg," he said with a friendly voice, "who's your friend?" and he gestured over at me. We exchanged names and he said, "I heard about that fight you had yesterday. Must have been something."

Rosenberg spoke up. "The big kid had it coming."

"Yes." Trumpeldor smiled and looked at me once more. "And you are the one who gave him his due." He paused to take a bite of bread, then asked, "How old are you?"

"Sixteen," I replied with newfound confidence.

"Ha," Trumpeldor laughed. "Not a day over twelve."

My shoulders sagged as I mumbled, "Fourteen."

He glanced in Amos' direction and continued, "You look to be about sixteen."

Amos nodded, "Seventeen, to be exact. Why do you ask?"

"Some of us are interested in going back to our farms. But we need able-bodied men to do it."

Mention of returning home sent a tingle up my spine. "I'm able," I said with an eager grin.

"Yes," Trumpeldor smiled. "I know. But you are young."

"I'm not that young."

"It's just talk now," Trumpeldor added with a shrug. "Just an idea. No one is sure what to do about it yet. But I am asking around to get an idea of how people feel about it and whether anyone is interested."

"Many are too afraid to try," Rosenberg commented.

"I'm not afraid," I said, taking every opportunity to impress on them my readiness to leave. More than anything, I wanted to get back home to our farm in Galilee. We never should have left.

After we ate, I followed Trumpeldor from the canteen, hoping to talk with him more about returning to Palestine. He was a dozen paces ahead of me and I hurried to catch up with him, but just before I reached him I realized Amos wasn't with me and my hand wasn't latched to the waistband of his trousers. It was the first time I'd been separated from him since we left the farm that night and the thought of him not being there sent a wave of panic over me. I turned to check over my shoulder, but he wasn't there. Then I looked to the right and saw him standing by a rain barrel at the corner of the next barracks with Dalia Riskin.

All at once the panic I'd felt at not having Amos with me turned to anger at seeing them together. The way they looked at each other and how close they were. Almost touching. And she took his hand, the same way she'd taken mine. It was...

Then I remembered Trumpeldor and when I turned back to look I saw him turn down the alley, two rows up from where I stood. If Amos could leave me to talk to her, I could leave him to talk to Trumpeldor, and I sprinted toward the alley after him.

Moments later, I caught up and Trumpeldor glanced down at me with an amused smile. "Something you wanted to say?"

"Your arm," I said boldly between gasps to catch my breath.

"Which one?"

"The one that's missing."

"Ah, that's the one I ask about, too."

"You ask about your own arm?"

"I miss it sometimes."

"I'm sorry. Maybe I shouldn't have said anything."

"It's okay."

We walked in silence a few steps farther but curiosity quickly got the better of me. "So," I began slowly, "what happened to it?"

"I lost it in the war."

"Which war?"

"Ah, yes," he nodded. "Which war was it? It was known to most of the world as the Russo-Japanese War."

"You are Russian?"

"Very much. And you?"

"Yes."

"Where from?"

"Novhorod-Siverskyi."

"Ah, yes," he said with a nod. "A beautiful city on the Desna River."

"And then we moved to Galilee."

"You and your family."

"Right."

"And where are they now?"

"There's just me and my brother left."

"Your brother?"

"Amos."

"Oh. Yes. The seventeen-year-old." He gestured over his shoulder. "The one who didn't want you to fight the big kid and is standing back there with that girl."

"Yes," I chuckled. "That's him." We walked a little farther and I was still curious about his arm, so I said, "Was it as bad in the fighting as they say?"

"In the fighting?"

"The war. In Manchuria."

A cloud seemed to settle over him. "Worse, much worse than anyone could know."

"Papa said it was awful."

"He was there?"

"No. But he knew people who went."

As we continued to talk, Trumpeldor told me about learning to fight with just one arm. He even taught himself to shoot a rifle and became as good with one arm as most were with two. I found that hard to believe. I shot Papa's rifle a few times and it was all I could do to keep the barrel from flying up against my nose when I fired it.

Trumpeldor seemed not to mind my questions. So I asked and he answered, telling me about his father, who served in the Caucasian War. Trumpeldor had wanted to follow his father into the army, but his father sent him to school instead, where Trumpeldor studied to become a dentist. But when trouble broke out in Manchuria, he left school, joined the army, and went off to fight. The wound he received put him in the hospital and he was advised never to return to battle, but he did anyway, and when the Russians lost control of Manchuria, Trumpeldor became a prisoner of war.

"That must have been horrible," I gasped. "Being a prisoner of the Japanese."

"It wasn't as bad as it sounds. They had more respect for those of us who were Jews than they did for the others. It wasn't fun, but that's where I first met people who were interested in coming to Palestine."

"So if you hadn't been taken prisoner, you might not be here?"

"Maybe. But I wouldn't have made it to Degania, either."

"You were in Degania?"

"Yes."

"That's only a short distance from where we live."

Trumpeldor paused and turned to me. "And this is where you live now." He pointed to the barracks, and I glanced over at it to see that he was right. It was our barracks. I wondered how he knew but when

I turned back to ask him, he was already headed up the alley away from me.

As he walked away, I thought of how things had changed for us. Just a few weeks earlier we'd been on the farm with Mama and Papa. Then the Arabs attacked and we'd been forced to run for our lives. With nothing except each other—feeling very much alone, forsaken, abandoned—we'd arrived at the camp in Egypt because it was the only thing left to do. And then we met Trumpeldor. After only a few hours with him, things changed. He'd noticed us. Noticed me. In less time than it took to eat our evening meal, the measure of friendship he offered transformed the way I saw our circumstances, our world, our identity. Maybe we weren't as alone as I first thought. Maybe there were friends in the world—true friends who would come alongside us and with whom we could join.

Trumpeldor continued on his way that evening, and I turned aside to enter the barracks. But as I did my heart felt lighter, my step moved quicker. I didn't know what lay ahead for us, but that day I found a sense of hope that we had turned a corner in our journey and that something good was beginning to unfold.

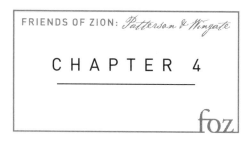

# CHAPTER 4

IN EUROPE, John Henry Patterson, a colonel in the British army, boarded a ship at Calais, France, and sailed across the English Channel toward the naval dock at Gravesend; not far from London. Tall, slender, and dignified, he stood at the rail watching as the sea passed by beneath him. The gray water, whipped into whitecaps by a northerly wind, might have appeared ominous and foreboding, but Patterson hardly noticed.

In his imagination Patterson was back at the Western Front, a line of trenches that stretched across Europe from the Belgium coast down to Alsace and over to the Swiss border—scene of the most horrendous fighting of the war—the Great War, they already were calling it. But Patterson had been there. He'd seen it with his own eyes and there wasn't anything great about it, except for the loss of life and the rampant destruction.

Gathered along that line of demarcation were the military forces of Europe positioned against each other in the most recent version of an historic conflict that had marked the region's history since the time of the Romans. To the north and east of the line were the armies of the Central Powers—primarily German units. To the west and south were the Allies—mostly British and French. All of them ensconced in fortified trenches that snaked across the once lush and serene countryside.

Between them lay no-man's-land—a treeless, desolate expanse of death and destruction stripped bare of vegetation by the constant and withering barrage of gunfire between the two sides. Anyone who ventured beyond the protection of the trenches or even poked his head up to look around was likely to die an immediate and painful death, as already many had. So many, in fact, that the nations of Europe were rapidly depleting the ranks of draft-age men available to carry on the carnage. And that's the thing that bothered Patterson the most—the men reaching the age of conscription—forced service in the nation's army.

Patterson had a son of his own and, though he was still quite young, as the war dragged on the day drew nearer and nearer when he would be called upon to join the men in the trenches. The thought of that—his own son slogging through the mud, the wounded groaning and crying in agony around him, bodies mangled and shredded by artillery attacks, thousands of men scattered upon the ground from the gas...

A shudder went through Patterson at the memory of what he'd seen on the field.

And then there were the hospitals. The artillery and gas killed many immediately but those who survived weren't much better off. An arm missing from that one. A leg from the one next to him. Another with sores and burns over his face, neck, and hands. Throat and lungs destroyed from inhaling that awful concoction. Most of them waiting to die with little hope of ever seeing home or family again.

"There has to be a better way," Patterson mumbled to himself. "There has to be a better way."

Traveling with Patterson on the trip was Edward Davis, a captain and friend who had accompanied him as his aide. They met in Africa where Davis served as his chief of staff. Now in between postings, Patterson had prevailed on the War Office to send him along, and they had obliged.

Davis appeared at Patterson's side by the rail. "You were saying something?"

"Just thinking aloud," Patterson replied.

"We've seen a lot these past few weeks."

"Yes, indeed," Patterson sighed. "There must be a better way to solve our troubles."

"You mean Cremer's Inter-Parliamentary Union?"

"Huh," Patterson grunted in response. "Perhaps something more along the lines of Goldsworthy Dickinson's League of Nations."

"That would be something, wouldn't it? All the nations of the world, gathering to arbitrate their disputes instead of killing each other's brightest and best."

"Instead of politicians sending other people's sons to do their bidding?"

"Touchy subject."

"I suppose so." Patterson shifted his position and leaned against the rail. "I doubt the nations of the world would agree to submit their fate to the decision of others, but we need something better than what we've just witnessed."

"I agree with that." Davis looked over at him. "But for now, this is all we have."

"What do you mean?"

"I mean, this is the war at hand. I don't think you or I can change that."

Patterson looked away. "No, I don't suppose we could."

"Do you think you could find a place to fit in? At least a place to serve?"

For Patterson, that had been the unstated question. He'd traveled to the European front to review Allied forces on assignment from the War Secretary. In reality, Patterson was looking for a place to join the effort.

Something of an enigma, no one knew much of Patterson's past—not even Davis, one of his closest friends. They only knew that he was Irish and in his youth his father regaled him with stories from the Old Testament, which he found fascinating as a boy and captivating as an adult. When not attending to official duties, he spent most of his time reading Hebrew literature and studying Jewish history, particularly the parts about ancient Jewish commanders—Joshua, Gideon, David, and the Maccabees. Saying often that he found in them a model of leadership and unerring faith he hoped to emulate. But he accounted for very little of his life prior to the age of seventeen, when he joined the British army. Before then, his life was shrouded in a veil of self-imposed silence.

As a young private, he'd trained at Canterbury Barracks. After an initial posting to South Africa, he was sent to India where he found favor with his commanding officer, William Robertson, and was promoted to sergeant. While in India he met Frances Gray, the woman who would become his wife. When not at work in the field, he studied engineering and developed a proficiency in Hindi. Because of his engineering expertise, the British Colonial Office selected him to take charge of a railroad project in East Africa. Many of the laborers on that job were Indian, and Patterson's knowledge of the language made him perfect for the task.

At the outbreak of the Boer War, Patterson returned to South Africa, where he fought with distinction. Not long after the war ended, he was appointed chief game warden for East Africa, a position he loved and enjoyed.

As 1914 approached, and with war on the horizon in Europe, he'd expected to be called into service. Something important, he'd assumed. After all, he'd risen from private to lieutenant, then jumped from lieutenant to colonel—not many had moved up so fast—in an already successful career that seemed destined for more. Yet, even as lines were drawn and forces squared off against each other, no new assignment came.

Finally Patterson took matters into his own hands and wrangled a trip to Europe to survey the troops, the fighting, and the prospects for victory. What he saw there was the world's first industrialized war. A war of unparalleled horror made possible by the application of new industrial technology as a means of killing. Yet, as horrible as it was, he needed a place to serve. He wanted a place to serve. He'd trained all his life for moments like this, but, as Davis had asked, where could he fit in? Where could he find that place?

✦ ✦ ✦

Frances was waiting with Bryan, their son, when Patterson's ship arrived at Gravesend. After an emotional reunion, they rode home together and spent the evening catching up. The following morning, while Bryan slept, Patterson and Frances sat at the table in the kitchen and talked. Finally, he opened up to her about what he'd seen and how he'd felt.

"This has to end," he said, after a vivid account of the trip. "Before Bryan comes of age."

Frances reached across the table and took his hand. "Jack," she said softly, "do you really think it will last that long?"

"I worry it will."

"But it seems so unlikely we could all hold out that long."

"We've gotten very good at these things. Both at building and tearing down, and this one is...beyond imagining." They were silent a moment before he said, "Really, this war is not like the others."

"What makes it so different?"

"Machines."

Frances had a perplexed look. "Machines?"

"Machines on the battlefield and industrial production have made it a thousand times what it was when Henry V met Charles VI at Agincourt. Maybe even worse than that."

"What could make it less...?"

"Destructive?"

"Painful is the word I would have chosen," she said. "But destructive is appropriate."

"I don't know." Patterson shrugged as he picked up his cup to take a sip of coffee. He swallowed and looked over at her. "One of the worst things about it is, I want to join this fight."

"But you just described how horrible it is."

"I know," he said with a sheepish smile. "But I was trained for this. And we need to stop the Germans."

"We need to stop the Turks," she offered.

"You are right," he nodded in agreement. "And on top of it all, my career needs the experience of having served in combat. Of having served in *this* war. Soldiers who let a war pass them by are soon passed over and ridden out. I just need somewhere else to serve besides the Western Front." He looked away. "Such a waste."

Frances watched him a moment before saying softly, "Jack, is there something we need to discuss?"

He jerked his head around to look at her. "What do you mean?" he asked with an aggravated frown.

"Has this..." She seemed to search for the right word. "Has this... shaken your...confidence?"

"Oh my, no," he blurted and dismissed the question with a wave of his hand. "I'm horrified by what I've *seen*, but not by the possibility of my own death. I dealt with that issue a long time ago. No, the thing that troubles me is the senseless waste of human life—shooting each other from trench to trench of all things—and for no real purpose." He scooted his chair back from the table. "They have those boys slogging around in the mud. In the heat of battle, the wounded are everywhere. Men stepping over the bodies of their fallen comrades to get to a more advantageous position to kill the poor fellow on the opposite side...or the poor fellow on the opposite side's friend." He gave her a knowing look. "They're all in the same position. Neighbor and friend, shoulder to shoulder, shooting neighbor and friend. Those who don't get shot catch some dreadful disease."

Frances grimaced. "That's not a pretty picture."

"No, it's not. And if the shooting and the artillery doesn't kill them, then the gas comes in and finishes them off."

Frances glanced down at her cup. "I read about that." She didn't know enough about the situation to engage him like many of his army friends did, but she always knew when he needed to talk and this was one of those times. So she did her best to keep him talking. "Do they really use it as often as they say?"

"I don't think so. At least not while we were there. But the thing of it is, this fighting—the way they're doing it—is such a waste. Not really fighting at all, only the slaughter or maiming of human beings who ought to be doing something else. Some of them should still be in school, flirting with the girls."

"I agree," Frances said. "It terrifies me to think our son might one day face that, but I'm not sure what we can do about it."

"There must be other ways to settle our differences. Man has come so far in other areas. Why can't we share the same continent without always going to war?" Patterson moved his chair farther from the table. "And there must be a way I could contribute to the effort without spending my time on the Western Front, preoccupied with surviving rather than destroying our enemy. Something that could produce actual, meaningful results."

If Frances knew when her Jack needed to talk, she also knew when he needed to move on. As he continued to talk, she stood and picked up the plates. "Well, perhaps a walk will do you good. That always seems to clear your head."

"A walk might be just the thing." He gulped the last sips of coffee from his cup and stood to move past the table. Frances was at the counter, her back turned toward him, and he reached over her to set the cup with the dirty dishes. Then he kissed Frances gently on the lips and started toward the door.

+ + +

While Patterson was out for a walk, Frances washed the dishes and straightened up the kitchen. When she finished, she started up the hall toward Bryan's room to check on him. As she passed the telephone table near the bathroom door, she saw the morning newspaper. Patterson had gone out early to get it, eager to catch up on the *real* news as he called it, but in the fun of being at home together, with Bryan sleeping and a morning to themselves...they'd forgotten all about it. Now she picked it up to take it back to the kitchen. *Jack will want to read this,* she thought.

At the table, she unfolded the newspaper to lay it flat and an article above the fold caught her attention—the Turks were calling for Jihad against all foreigners living in Palestine. And not just the British, but the Jews, too. She wanted to read more but Bryan called to her, so she laid aside the paper to tend to him.

An hour later, Patterson returned from his walk and took a seat at the table. Bryan waddled in to join him, and Patterson lifted him onto his lap. They laughed and giggled together, playing first one game then another, but after a while Bryan wanted down and a moment later was busy playing on the floor. While he played at Patterson's feet, Frances stood beside him and pointed to the paper. "There's an article you might be interested in."

"Oh? I meant to read that earlier, didn't I?" He gave Frances a playful look. "But someone distracted me."

She smiled coyly, "You didn't seem to mind."

"Not at all." He reached over to pull her closer. "Perhaps you could distract me again when Bryan takes a nap."

"I might." She leaned down and kissed him, then pointed back to the paper. "But you should look at that article. It mentions your friend Maxwell."

"John Maxwell?"

"How many friends named Maxwell do you have?" Frances crossed the room. "Look at the article about Palestine," she called from the pantry doorway.

Patterson found the article and quickly read the opening paragraph. "We heard about this call for Jihad the other day," he said, pointing. "Some don't think there's much to it. The Turks might be Muslim but they don't carry much weight with the Arabs."

"Maybe it won't matter for the British army," Frances answered as she came back to the room. "But read a little further. They've ordered all the Jews to leave Palestine."

Patterson's eyes opened wide. "All of them?"

She reached over his shoulder and pointed to a paragraph near the bottom of the page. "'...ordered them all to leave,'" she read, "'even those who purchased their farms through the available legal process.'"

"Hmm," Patterson groaned. "That can't be good. John Maxwell is commanding our forces in Egypt. I wonder if he plans to do anything about this." Patterson glanced over at Frances. "If so, he might have a place for me. I would enjoy serving with him."

"You could ask the people you know in London," Frances suggested. "See what they can tell you about plans for the region."

Patterson shook his head, "No, I don't think so."

"Why not?"

"The folks in London are interested in protecting the Suez Canal but that's about the extent of it in the Middle East right now. All the big effort is in Europe."

"Makes it all the more attractive to me then," Frances said. "Less chance of you getting shot at if you're in Egypt."

"Right," Patterson nodded. "But that defeats the purpose of finding a place to actually contribute."

"Well," she said as she moved back to the counter. "It was a thought."

"Yes, and a good one, at that."

Something in his tone caught Frances attention and brought her up short. She'd heard that voice before and she'd come to know it as the point when an idea ceased to be merely an idea. He tried on many ideas, rolling them around in his mind to see how they felt. Using his imagination to project himself into countless situations as a way of testing the thought before acting on it. That's what he was doing now and she knew it. Asking himself, could he serve in Egypt? Would it be legitimate war service, or merely a place to hide? He'd never accept a place to hide, she knew that. As much as she might want it, he'd never take it. But if it was legitimate, real service, he'd be willing to give it a go.

"What are you thinking?"

"I'm wondering if I should pay a visit to General Sir John Maxwell."

"You mean travel to Egypt on your own? Just like that?"

Still seated at the table, Patterson turned in the chair to face her. "Why not? That might be just the thing to do."

"Just show up? Unannounced? Uninvited? Without posting or assignment?"

"Yes."

"Wouldn't that be against the rules?"

"Not at all. I'm on leave for the next three weeks. I can do whatever I like." He turned back to the table. "I could go there and offer to help. See if Maxwell has a place where I could be of use."

"London wouldn't object?"

"They might not like it—and if I asked they'd probably say no—but if I go there, and if Maxwell wanted me to stay, no one in London would order me back."

Patterson pushed back his chair from the table and stood. "I think I'll make some calls."

"Are you sure about this?" Frances asked.

He shrugged, "Well...I don't know. But it won't hurt to phone a few people. See what I can do with it."

Frances watched with an amused smile as Patterson started up the hall toward his study. He'd be gone in a few weeks. She could tell by the way he walked, the slight tilt of his head, and the movement of his arms at his side. He was into it now and he'd find a way to get to Egypt, as surely as she knew that, she realized what lay ahead for him there would be nothing like what he imagined right now. Reality always turned out different from the dream. But whatever awaited him, she wasn't afraid.

# CHAPTER 5

ABOUT THAT SAME TIME, Ze'ev Jabotinsky rode in a taxi through the streets of Odessa, a beautiful Russian city along the northwestern shore of the Black Sea, opposite the Crimean Peninsula. Though founded by the Tartars in the thirteenth century, the area had once been a Roman colony. It was seized by Russian troops in the eighteenth century during the Russo-Turkish War and officially chartered as an imperial city by Catherine the Great. Since that time, it had been the Russian Empire's primary warm-water port. More recently, it had been transformed into a resort location with new hotels and restaurants that attracted tourists and vacationers from around the world.

Jabotinsky, a journalist, knew the city well, having been born and reared there. His father, a wheat merchant who was fully assimilated into Russian life, made certain Jabotinsky attended the best schools the city had to offer. Later, when Jabotinsky became interested in journalism, he found his first job as a reporter writing for the *Odesskiya Novosti* (*Odessa News*). Though he lived in Moscow now and wrote for *Russkiya Vedomosti*, the city's largest newspaper, many members of his family still resided in the city. Indeed, it was family business that brought him there on this occasion, but while attending to that he received a message from Alexander Torkunov, an assistant to Pyotr

Rostovsky, the Russian foreign ministry's attaché for Ottoman affairs, asking if they could meet. Torkunov was on his way to Moscow and stopped over in Odessa. A mutual friend mentioned Jabotinsky was in town. Torkunov wanted to talk. Jabotinsky, always eager to see an old friend and work a source, readily agreed.

The taxi turned onto Pushkinska Street and came to a stop in front of the Bristol Hotel. One of the city's lavish new hotels, it stood across from the Odessa Philharmonic Theater. After paying the fare, Jabotinsky pushed open the door, stepped out to the sidewalk, and made his way toward the front entrance.

As he came through the doorway, Jabotinsky glanced around and saw Torkunov seated at a table in a coffee shop just off the main lobby. Jabotinsky made his way in that direction and took a seat across from him.

Over a cup of coffee, Torkunov handed Jabotinsky an envelope. "You should read this dispatch. I can't leave it with you, but you should know the contents."

Jabotinsky opened the envelope and took out a two-page memo. He read it with grave concern.

According to Russian sources in Jerusalem, as a further response to Sheikh ul-Islam's call for a holy war against the West, Ahmed Jamal Pasha, the Ottoman governor of Palestine, was set to issue a decree expanding the general order expelling all foreigners that included confiscation of their property. In the case of land, the property would be returned to its original owner or distributed among deserving Arabs at the governor's discretion.

Jabotinsky looked over at Torkunov. "We heard of this already. I wrote a story about it last week."

"Read the second page," Torkunov instructed.

Jabotinsky turned the page to find a single sentence that read simply, "Political elements associated with British expeditionary forces in Egypt have indicated their support for Ottoman policy in Palestine and the governor's decision."

Muscles in Jabotinsky's neck grew tense. "Can this be true?"

"I'm afraid so."

"They should resist," Jabotinsky said tersely.

"Who?"

"The Jews of Palestine. They should fight back."

"They have nothing with which to fight."

"One can always find the means of defense." Jabotinsky handed the memo to Torkunov. "They will never be free unless they fight."

"They will die."

"Some, perhaps." Jabotinsky nodded as if casualties were a fore-gone conclusion. "But not all. If they fight, the Arabs will leave them alone."

"You say that as if you know it for a fact."

Jabotinsky's eyes were piercing. "That is how we survived here in Odessa. It is why the pogroms have been one-tenth what they are in other areas."

Torkunov looked startled. "You were part of the resistance?"

"I would not call what happened *resistance*." Jabotinsky had a faint smiled. "One must first survive before he can resist."

Torkunov shook his head. "I never knew you were part of that."

Jabotinsky looked away. "Some things are better left unsaid, even among friends."

✦ ✦ ✦

When he returned to Moscow, Jabotinsky met with Nikolai Vyazemsky, his editor at *Russkiya Vedomosti*. Vyazemsky, a heavyset man with thick jowls and a pale complexion, was seated at his desk and looked up with a skeptical smile as Jabotinsky entered the office. "What grand scheme are you bringing me today?"

Jabotinsky closed the door behind him and made his way to a chair in front of the desk. He reached it quickly and took a seat, then said in a hushed voice, "I had a meeting with a contact the other day."

"A contact?" Vyazemsky feigned skepticism but already Jabotinsky could see he was interested. "You're always so secretive. Speak up." He gestured with his hand. "I can barely hear you. What source? What lies have they told you this time?"

Jabotinsky raised his voice only slightly. "I fear these are not lies."

"Nonsense. Sources always lie."

"This source has contacts within the foreign ministry."

Vyazemsky frowned. "The *Russian* foreign ministry?"

"Yes."

"I've told you before," Vyazemsky cautioned, "you must be careful when inquiring about the czar's business."

"I didn't inquire. The source contacted me."

"And what did this source have to say?"

"He showed me a memo addressed to our attaché for Ottoman affairs." Jabotinsky slid forward in his chair and leaned over the desk. "The source says that not only is the governor of Palestine forcing the Jews to leave, he's ordered the confiscation of their property."

"Nothing new in that, is there?" Vyazemsky gave a dismissive flip with the back of his hand. "Certainly nothing unexpected. We knew they were forcing the Jews to leave. You wrote about it."

"Yes, but we didn't know that elements within the British government were in agreement with the policy."

Vyazemsky raised an eyebrow. "They knew about this before it happened?"

"Apparently."

"And how does your source know this?"

"The document I read was a memo summarizing recent meetings in Istanbul. It was written because the governor of Palestine's latest order addressing property of the evacuees was a new development. So someone in the foreign ministry generated a new memo. But the memo went on to say that elements within British expeditionary forces in Egypt knew about the policy, apparently before it went into effect, and they approved of the policy."

Vyazemsky stroked his chin. "That *is* interesting." He looked over at Jabotinsky. "What do you want to do with this?"

"I want to go there."

"To Jerusalem?"

"To Jerusalem, to the entire region. Travel through Palestine, Transjordan, Egypt. Find out if the Ottoman call for Jihad means anything to the Arabs. And find out the true position of the British."

Vyazemsky was interested, but not quite convinced. "And this is relevant to our readers because...?"

"Many would like to see us get out of this conflict as quickly as possible. No one trusts the British, and perhaps with good reason. If they are cutting a deal with the Arabs in Palestine, they might be reaching an agreement that covers the entire region. Are they going behind our backs, getting us to fight and die in Europe while they gain control of the entire Middle East? To their benefit and at our expense?"

"Yes," Vyazemsky nodded thoughtfully. "I see your point. The British have been working hard to convince the Muslims to throw in with the Allies. They have that man—Lawrence—making big promises to gain their allegiance."

"Exactly," Jabotinsky said. "But if the Muslims respond to the Turk call for Jihad, it would disrupt those plans. This is potentially a major problem, and a major story, from two or three perspectives."

"How long would this trip take?"

"Two months...three tops."

"I'll give you one."

"Six weeks," Jabotinsky countered.

"Done," Vyazemsky snapped. "But keep your expenses to a minimum."

"Certainly." Jabotinsky rose from his chair, aggravated with himself for not insisting on seven, but by then the moment had passed. He started toward the door but before he could open it, Vyazemsky called after him. "And report to me before you report to anyone else."

Jabotinsky glanced over his shoulder and smiled mischievously. "Of course."

✦ ✦ ✦

That evening over dinner, Jabotinsky told Hannah, his wife, of his plans to travel to the Middle East. "Is that what you'll really be doing?" she asked with playful skepticism.

"What do you mean?"

"The call for Jihad. The British. Is that what you really want to find out?"

"Well..." he shrugged. "I *am* interested in many things."

"More of your Zionist work," she said, unconvinced.

For years, Jabotinsky had been involved in the promotion of the Zionist cause—the historic migration of Jews to Palestine—often using his credentials as a journalist to insinuate himself into contentious situations. "There are many things I want to know. Like why the Arabs hate us. Why the Europeans hate us. Why the Russians hate us."

"And?"

"And what we can do about it."

She looked up at him without lifting her head. "That's the part that worries me."

"Look, this isn't just a Turk problem," Jabotinsky put down his fork. "It's a problem everywhere. Even in the U.S."

"And the only way to survive is to fight," she said in a singsong fashion and with a wag of her head.

"Well, it's true," he responded forcefully. "And you know it. So don't belittle the notion."

She looked him squarely in the eye. "I would never belittle anything you say or think or do," she said defensively. "But I don't want to lose my husband to a war in the desert over some *cause* we can't possibly win."

"I'm not going off to support *some cause*. I just want to find out what's really happening."

"But you think the Jews of Palestine should fight, rather than flee."

"Yes," he said insistently. "They should fight. They bought that land. They own it. The Turks sold it to them. The Turks should be protecting and defending Jews in Palestine instead of ordering them to leave and seizing their property."

"Aren't the Turks also opposed to the British?"

"I'm not sure." Jabotinsky picked up his fork and began to eat again. "That's another thing I want to find out."

"What do you mean you're not sure? The Ottoman Empire has joined the Central Powers, no? And the Central Powers are still at war with the Allies, right?"

"Officially, yes," Jabotinsky nodded. "But I am not so certain the British are with us in the Middle East. Or with the Allies." He had an ironic smile. "They might just be in the region solely for themselves."

"Why do you say these things?"

"I have sources."

"Sources?" Hannah rolled her eyes. "Always with the sources. Is that why you slipped off by yourself when we were in Odessa? To meet with one of your *sources*?"

Jabotinsky's eyes darted away. "I can't say."

"Yet you expect me to support you without question."

"As I give you my support." He smiled at her. "But I love your questions."

She grinned. "You're a madman, Jabo."

He turned again to the topic at hand. "Look, we support the czar and yet he turns the mobs loose on our people everywhere." He tapped the table with his index finger for emphasis. "But not in Odessa."

"Because you fought back."

Jabotinsky nodded his head vigorously. "Because we fought back."

"And now you want the Palestinian Jews to do the same. To fight back." She looked him in the eye. "Part Zionist, part journalist. Which is the cover and which is the real you?"

The smile on Jabotinsky's face became a grin. "You ask too many questions."

They stared at each other a moment, then she asked, "How long will you be gone?"

"Vyazemsky gave me six weeks."

"So you will be gone eight."

He had a playful look. "Unless I need more."

✦ ✦ ✦

Ten days later, Jabotinsky boarded a ship at Petrograd and sailed for England. After four days in London, he took a freighter to Gibraltar, then caught another to Tangier, and began a slow trek eastward across the northern coast of Africa.

Along the way, he visited friends and contacts he'd developed through years of travel and reporting and talked with acquaintances he made on his journey. They assured him that no one took the Ottoman call for Jihad seriously. "Not from the Turks," they explained. "Turks call for Jihad all the time, but they are Turks. They think only like Turks. They act only like Turks. They are not Arab. When they needed money, they sold land to the Jews and did so against our will. Now that the Jews have shown their true colors and sided with the British, the Turks don't want them around and they ask us to help them move the Jews out. Yet when we asked for protection from the Turks, they ignored us. If they had listened to us, they never would have let the Jews come and none of this would have happened. That is why no one will respond to their call for Jihad. No one ever responds to them. Not among our people. They are Turks. We are Arabs."

What he learned from the Arabs took Jabotinsky's story in a different direction from the one he'd planned, but it was interesting nonetheless. He wrote an article for Vyazemsky summarizing what he'd learned so far and filed it from Algiers, then traveled to Tunis and took a ship across the Mediterranean, past Alexandria, to Port Said.

At Port Said, he encountered a group of Jews who'd recently fled Palestine. From them he learned something of what conditions were like in Palestine. He also learned that the British were housing most of the Jewish refugees—as many as fifteen thousand—at a camp in Alexandria.

Jabotinsky was infuriated that Jews were forced to abandon their property—property for which they'd paid the rightful owners—and were now living as refugees in a foreign land. Egypt, of all places.

On the spot, he decided to travel to Palestine to see conditions for himself and to encourage Jews still remaining there to stay and fight, even to the death. But an initial inquiry about transportation from

Port Said to Tel Aviv met only with frustration. Ships captains and ships agents were reluctant to take him, a Russian Jew, as a passenger for fear the Turks and Arabs might damage their ships. And he found no one traveling into Palestine from the Egyptian side of the border. "Everyone is coming here," they said. "No one is going there. Certainly not by land."

When entering Palestine proved more difficult than he'd expected, Jabotinsky decided to travel to Alexandria and talk with the refugees. But first he prepared another story for Vyazemsky and sent it by telegraph to the office in Moscow. Then he boarded a train and headed down the coast.

✦ ✦ ✦

The following day, Jabotinsky arrived in Alexandria and made his way to the refugee camp in Gabbari. After some difficulty at the gate, he was allowed inside and walked past the rows of barracks. It was the middle of the morning, a time between meals, and not much was happening but he found a group of men sitting in the shade at the end of a building. Jabotinsky introduced himself and struck up a conversation.

Most of them had come from an area around Tel Aviv and Haifa, but some were from as far away as Galilee. Most had been forced to leave by Ottoman soldiers but a few had left on their own after being attacked by Arab gangs.

"But the worst part," someone said, "is they won't let us return."

Jabotinsky had a perturbed look. "You mean the British won't let you leave?"

"No," the man explained. "It's the Turks. They've said that even after the war, we will not be allowed to return and that we must find a new place to live."

"Where could we go?" another asked. "Who would have us?"

Jabotinsky was incensed. "This is unacceptable," he fumed.

An older man looked over at him. "Why would someone do such a thing to us?" His voice was filled with sadness. "They sold us the land. We bought it from them at the price they demanded. Now they have taken it back." He shook his head. "It's not right."

"They stole it," another interjected. "They didn't simply take it back. They stole it."

Nisei Rosenberg was with them and after the others had spoken he said, "We are in a difficult place. The Turks see us as friendly with the British. Especially now that we have come to them here for help. They also know that the British are courting the Arabs with a fever— and making some headway at it, I might add. The Turks don't want to lose control of the region, but they don't want to divert troops from other areas to fight here. So they are trying to convince the Arabs to join them and rid the region of all foreigners—us and the British."

"I am Jewish, too," Jabotinsky offered.

"I thought you said you were a reporter."

"I am a journalist," Jabotinsky explained. "And I am Jewish."

"Where are you from?"

"Russia."

One of the others spoke up. "We all are from Russia."

Jabotinsky looked over at Rosenberg. "That is a very perceptive assessment of the region. How do you know these things?"

"I listen," Rosenberg replied.

The first one spoke up again. "So if the Turks are trying to convince the Arabs to join the war on their side, and the British are trying to convince the Arabs to join on their side, that means we are caught in the middle."

Jabotinsky nodded. "That's about where we are."

"What can we do?" someone asked.

"We can't do anything," another offered. "We're stuck."

"No," Jabotinsky replied sharply. "We're not stuck. We *can* do something. We can stand and fight."

"With what?"

"With whatever we have."

"They would kill us all."

"Not all. And if you resist, the Arabs will run."

"That is easy for you to say. You would not be the one doing the fighting."

"But I have," Jabotinsky argued. "When I was a teenager in Odessa, mobs attacked our neighborhood. At first no one did anything out of fear of provoking an even worse attack. But the attacks continued and finally some of us organized a gang ourselves. We knew the ones who attacked us and so we went to their neighborhood and attacked them. And when they came again to attack us, we were ready and waiting."

"And what happened?"

"After one or two more attempts—each of them rebuffed by our own people—they stopped attacking us."

"Are you sure of this?"

"Ask others who know," Jabotinsky said. "Surely you have some here from Odessa. Pogroms in other places continued to terrify our people—even now—but not in Odessa. And it was because we fought back and made them leave us alone. That is how we solved our problems *there* and that is how we will solve our problems *here*."

Rosenberg spoke again. "You should talk to Joseph Trumpeldor."

"Who is he?"

"Come on." Rosenberg stood. "I'll introduce you."

# CHAPTER 6

foz

AMOS AND I were sitting with Trumpeldor when Nisei Rosenberg arrived with Jabotinsky in tow. Rosenberg introduced him and said, "He's been talking about Palestine and how we ought to return and fight to take back our land. I thought you two might enjoy talking."

Trumpeldor looked up at Jabotinsky. "You lived in Palestine?"

"No," Jabotinsky replied. "Not personally. But I—"

Trumpeldor cut him off. "Where are you from?"

"Russia."

"What part?"

"I was born in Odessa."

"And now?"

"Moscow. And you?"

"Petrograd."

"Interesting city," Jabotinsky commented. "I have been there many times. But as I was saying before—"

Again Trumpeldor interrupted. "Who do you know in Odessa?"

"Only my family, mostly." Jabotinsky was growing tense, but working to control his emotions. "I have a few friends there as well."

"You are a journalist, correct?"

"Yes." Jabotinsky's expression turned suspicious. "They told you?" he asked, gesturing to Rosenberg.

"No," Trumpeldor answered. "I have read some of your articles in the *Russkiya Vedomosti.*"

A smile turned up the corners of Jabotinsky's mouth. "You read that paper?"

Trumpeldor ignored the question and asked one of his own. "So, what is your interest in Palestine?"

"I am a Jew," Jabotinsky explained. "And I know something about handling those who hate us and wish to destroy us."

"And you learned this in Odessa?"

"Yes. And what we learned there can be done here."

Trumpeldor was silent a moment. "I heard of the resistance in Odessa," he said finally. "But Palestine is not some otherwise peaceful city on the Black Sea. Life in Palestine, even at its best, has never been as idyllic as it might seem to outsiders."

"Perhaps not," Jabotinsky conceded. "But just because it was bad before doesn't mean it can't change. We can make it better than it was if we stand and fight and don't give up."

"Easier said than done," Trumpeldor noted with a dismissive tone.

"I thought you were interested." Jabotinsky shoved his hands in his pocket and sighed. "Perhaps I was mistaken."

Trumpeldor nodded. "I am interested, but I'm interested in results, not the idealistic talk of a Russian journalist."

"I'm interested in results, too," Jabotinsky argued. "Results like not just taking back farms and houses and lands that were owned before, but in taking control of the entire region. Totally removing the Arabs. Creating a Jewish homeland that stretches from Egypt to

Syria. Reaching from the Jordan to the Mediterranean Sea. A nation taking its rightful place among the nations of the world."

"What you are describing cannot be accomplished in a single life-time," Trumpeldor cautioned. "If that were really our goal—control-ling the entirety of Palestine and not merely retaking our homes and property—it would require a life of conflict for us and a legacy of war for our children. And not just for our children, but for their children, too, and after them for generations to come."

"Perhaps so," Jabotinsky conceded. "But fighting is the only way we will survive. We must respond with force."

"Yes," Trumpeldor agreed. "As I have said many times. But we must face reality and the reality is, we must have an objective that we can achieve in our lifetime. And give the next generation a place to start that is better than ours but one that knows relative peace and safety. Let them decide if the fighting must continue."

Jabotinsky looked away, a bored expression on his face. As if he suddenly lost interest in the conversation. "I'm not sure we can solve these questions today."

"Neither am I." Trumpeldor stood. "But in the short term, I would be interested in working to create a Jewish fighting force to return to Palestine and retake our farms."

"Well," Jabotinsky nodded reluctantly, "that would be a start."

For the next several days, Amos and I followed Jabotinsky and Trumpeldor as they asked around the camp to see if others were willing to return and fight. Others were willing and Jabotinsky was encouraged, but Trumpeldor was not convinced. "We will never be able to raise enough men or supplies to fight effectively."

"That is not a concern," Jabotinsky replied. "We must do it anyway. What we lack we can find as we go."

"And in the meantime," Trumpeldor argued, "people will die."

"It's better than living in a refugee camp the remainder of their lives. And anyway, this was your idea before it was mine. Now you are taking the opposite side of your own argument."

"No," Trumpeldor countered. "I am suggesting we need help."

"Help? From whom?"

"We need the help of the British. They can provide us with training and equipment."

"And which British officer should we see?" Jabotinsky asked sarcastically. "Do you know such a person?"

"The general in charge of British forces in Egypt is a man named Maxwell."

"And how do you suggest we arrange a meeting with General Maxwell?"

Trumpeldor smiled, "We don't. You do."

"Me?"

"You're the journalist. Use your connections."

Jabotinsky grinned. "Okay."

As Trumpeldor suggested, Jabotinsky used his press credentials and arranged an appointment with General Maxwell. Trumpeldor went with him. Amos and I were standing near the central alley and saw them as they started toward the gate. I wanted to go with them but Trumpeldor said no.

Amos was with me as they left to meet with Maxwell and I suggested to him that we should follow and see what happened. When Amos didn't answer immediately, I glanced at him and saw his head was turned in the opposite direction. I followed his stare and saw Dalia two huts down. "Why do you keep staring at her?"

"You wouldn't understand," he replied in a flat tone.

"You like her?"

"Yeah," Amos sighed. Then he glanced at me. "You do, too."

"Yeah," I admitted, suddenly uncomfortable. "But I don't stare at her. Come on. Let's follow Trumpeldor."

"You go. I'll catch up with you later."

Amos started toward Dalia and I watched for a moment, but as he drew near I saw her reach out and take hold of his hand. At first I was angry but then I saw the smile on her face and the look on his and knew—they didn't just like each other, they *liked* each other.

After a moment I turned away and glanced toward the front gate in time to see Trumpeldor and Jabotinsky leave the camp. When they were far enough away not to see me, I walked down near the gate and waited. Not long after that, a truck arrived and after an inspection the guards opened the gate to let it in. As the gate moved out of the way and the truck started forward, the guard's line of sight was temporarily blocked by the passing truck. I slipped out on the opposite side, unnoticed.

+ + +

By the time I cleared the gate, Trumpeldor and Jabotinsky were well ahead of me. I caught up with them, though, and followed at a discreet distance. As they entered the British army compound, I expected they would encounter trouble, but no one seemed alarmed by their presence and they passed through without confrontation. Even more to my surprise, I did as well and trailed them to a barracks building much like the ones at the camp. This one, however, was nicer and cleaner and a sign over the door identified it as Egyptian Expeditionary Force HQ. Trumpeldor led the way inside. Jabotinsky followed. I remained outside and found a place in the shade from which I could watch for them to leave and though I wasn't in the building when they talked, I know what happened.

General Maxwell was seated at his desk when they arrived. Thinking he was addressing a journalist, he directed Jabotinsky to a seat. A second chair was nearby and Trumpeldor pulled up to the desk and took a seat himself. With everyone in place and prepared, Jabotinsky launched into an interview, asking Maxwell about British operations and strategy.

As the conversation neared an end, Maxwell gestured in Trumpeldor's direction and asked, "Who is he?"

When Jabotinsky hesitated, Trumpeldor spoke up, telling Maxwell of his military service. Jabotinsky explained, "I brought him with me because he has a proposal for you."

Maxwell gave Trumpeldor a perplexed look. "What sort of proposal?"

"To recruit and train a Jewish fighting force," Trumpeldor said confidently. "A Jewish Legion to return and fight for control of Palestine."

Maxwell looked amused and intrigued, then skeptical. "You wish to fight with the British army?"

"Yes."

"I'm afraid that would be impossible."

"Why?"

"Only British citizens are allowed to serve in the army."

The news caught Trumpeldor and Jabotinsky off guard. They'd never heard such a thing and were astounded that a country engaged in a war of attrition would decline the service of anyone. They talked about it awhile, then Maxwell said, "You could form a transportation corps—a mule corps—instead. We organize those as separate, auxiliary units. Strictly speaking, not a fighting force, and not an official part of the army, but the men would be armed and play a vital role in the war effort delivering supplies to the front."

"In Palestine?" Jabotinsky asked.

"Not immediately. We have no immediate plans to take Palestine."

"Then what would we do? Where would we go?"

"We're preparing for potential operations in other regions. Not at liberty to say exactly where. I suspect you would be sent there, should you choose to form such a corps."

Jabotinsky had a displeased scowl. "We were interested in Palestine."

Maxwell nodded his head slowly. "I understand. And we should get there eventually, but right now we're planning a major assault on the Turks in another area."

Jabotinsky was obviously displeased. "A suggestion that we should serve in a mule corps is an—"

Trumpeldor tapped him on the knee to distract him. It had the desired effect of interrupting Jabotinsky, and Trumpeldor spoke to Maxwell, "This mule corps, it would have its own officers? Jewish officers?"

"Well. Yes," Maxwell said slowly. "I suppose it could."

"And how would the unit get supplies and equipment?"

"We would supply you, equip you, and train you. And you would operate at our direction."

"So we would have British officers?"

"I suppose we could have both," Maxwell opined.

"British officers ultimately in charge, our own officers directing the men?"

Maxwell nodded. "Something like that. British officers giving direction. Your own officers directing the men. That's usually how it works with these things."

Jabotinsky took a breath as if to speak, but once again Trumpeldor cut him off. "This is an interesting proposal. We'll need a few days to think it over."

"Certainly," Maxwell said. "Take as much time as you like for now. The operation I mentioned is still in the planning stages."

✦ ✦ ✦

As they came from Maxwell's headquarters, I followed after them, though this time I didn't need to worry about following closely to hear what they were saying. They were talking loud with arms flailing and angry looks on their faces. I could hear every word they said.

"It's an insult!" Jabotinsky fumed.

"No," Trumpeldor countered. "It was an offer."

"It was an arrogant, anti-Semitic insult."

"They have rules, you know. Everyone does."

"They let Arabs serve with them."

"Well," Trumpeldor shrugged. "Then there's that."

"But because we are not so many in number, they think nothing of casting us aside."

"The Arabs *are* greater in number."

"So, what are you saying? That they are worth more because there are more of them than us? Is that how *you* think? Do we have to make more babies for you to think our cause is worthy?"

"I'm saying," Trumpeldor countered, "the British are fighting a war. With more people, the Arabs are of greater strategic value. That's all. To get what we want, we can't offer the British numbers. We have to offer something else."

"Like what?"

"Service."

Jabotinsky's voice took a scoffing tone. "Service?"

"They obviously have a problem," Trumpeldor explained. "We can offer them a solution."

"A problem? What problem do the British have, other than ignorance, arrogance, and racism?"

"Just what he said," Trumpeldor explained. "They have a problem getting matériel to the front. Transporting supplies. We can help them solve it."

"With a team of mules," Jabotinsky groused. "I can't believe this. You of all people."

"How else would we supply the front?"

"Let the Arabs do it," Jabotinsky roared.

"So we refuse to help the British because they wouldn't give us what we want. The Arabs cooperate fully, help the British solve their problems, and win the war. Then you expect the British to help us defeat the Arabs and win back our land?"

"Well..." Jabotinsky couldn't bring himself to admit the truth of what Trumpeldor had said, but his voice dropped and his tone softened. "I'm not leading a team of mules into battle. He as much as called us mules."

"I don't think he called us that."

"I think he did," Jabotinsky grumbled.

"So," Trumpeldor rejoined, "if I say you are a Russian, am I also calling you a Cossack?"

Jabotinsky dismissed the point with a wave of his hand. "That's different."

"How?"

"It just is. He couldn't have insulted us more by asking that we supply them with swine."

Trumpeldor glanced around, suddenly aware that others were listening. "Maybe we should talk about this elsewhere."

"Why?"

"Too many people are listening."

Jabotinsky glanced around but seemed not to be bothered by the attention they'd attracted. I hadn't noticed it, either. Jabotinsky raised his voice, "I don't care who hears. They all should hear."

"Not the British," Trumpeldor cautioned in a hushed tone.

Jabotinsky had a questioning look. "What do you mean?"

"I mean we can't fight the Turks and the Brits, too. We need the British to help us. Concentrate on the matter at hand."

"I am concentrating."

"Let's talk elsewhere."

They kept walking in the same direction, but when I heard Trumpeldor suggest they continue the conversation somewhere else, I knew what he meant. When he wanted privacy, one of his favorite places to gather was in a storeroom near the canteen where the British provided our meals. Rather than continuing to follow and risk being seen, I turned away and followed a different route.

When I reached the storeroom I found it empty except for the supplies that were kept there. I crawled into a space near the back and hid behind a barrel of flour. Not long after I was in my place, a door opened behind me, and Amos appeared. "What are you doing in here?" he asked.

"Waiting. Get out of sight."

"Waiting for what?" he asked as he knelt beside me.

"Trumpeldor and Jabotinsky." The space where I hid was cramped already, and with Amos beside me we were both visible from the front entrance. "Move over there. Behind those crates." Amos glanced in that direction, then moved behind two shipping crates, slipping into place just as the door opened and Trumpeldor appeared with Jabotinsky close behind.

As they stepped into the room, Jabotinsky repeated what he'd said before, "It's an insult. All the British are anti-Semites—certainly all the officers—and Maxwell among them."

"Maybe so, but changing their minds is not our goal, is it?"

"Accepting their insults is not our goal, either."

"Serving in a transportation corps is honorable work. Someone has to do it. Every army has a mule corps or a camel corps or some sort of transportation unit. I've served in the army. I've seen them in action. The men of the transportation corps are as brave and courageous as any. And equally as vital."

"We want to invade Palestine, the British don't. We should hold out for the creation of a Jewish infantry unit and for an all-out invasion of Palestine."

"Even if it means never returning to Palestine?"

"Yes."

"So, you're saying we should hold out for the means we demand, even if it means never achieving our ultimate goal."

"If we do what they ask and form this mule unit, they'll send us to work somewhere else and that's all they'll ever do with us. Send us somewhere else and never to Palestine. If the Arabs on the Arabian Peninsula side with them, as I think they will, the British will do all in their power to keep us out of the way. We'll never have a homeland in Palestine."

"If we side against the British, we'll never have a homeland, either."

Jabotinsky looked away and sighed. "I just think this whole idea of a transportation corps serves their purposes and not ours."

"Perhaps, but defeat of the Turks anywhere helps everywhere.

And that means it will help us. If the Allies lose this war—and from what I hear, the outcome is far from certain—any Jews remaining in Palestine will die a painful death."

Jabotinsky was quiet a moment, then finally said, "Well...I...I just can't do it. I just can't join a mule corps."

"Then what are we going to do?"

"I suppose you'll have to remain here. Unless you have somewhere else to go."

"And what about you?"

"I'm going to England. I know a few people there. I'm going to do my best to find someone who will listen and see if we can create a *real* fighting force. A Jewish Legion. Not some mule corps."

They talked a moment longer, then the two men shook hands and Jabotinsky left. When he was gone, Trumpeldor called over his shoulder, "You can come out now." When no one responded, he turned to look in my direction. "I know you're back there, Yoel. Come on out. I saw you following us before."

I came from my hiding place and made my way toward him. "How did you know we were there?"

"I know things," he said with a smile.

"So, are you really doing it? Are you forming the mule corps?"

"Yes," he said after a moment. "I think I will."

"Good," I replied in an eager voice. "I'll help."

Trumpeldor looked down at me with kindness in his eyes. "How old did you say you are?"

"Sixteen," I announced, doing my best to sound convincing."

"Ha," Trumpeldor chuckled. "Not a day over fourteen."

"But I can handle a mule."

"Have you ever *seen* a mule?"

"Of course."

By then, Amos came from behind the crate and stood with us. Trumpeldor looked over at him. "We could use you, though."

Amos beamed with pride at the affirmation of being wanted for duty, but he put his arm around my shoulder, "We're together. Get one, you get us both."

Trumpeldor's eyes shifted to me and a smile slowly spread across his face. "Okay, but you have to do your part. I catch you slacking off, you're out."

"You won't have to worry about me."

+ + +

For the next several weeks, Trumpeldor and I worked our way through the camp, speaking to as many men as possible, trying our best to recruit them. I functioned as Trumpeldor's aide. He did most of the talking. Amos tagged along with us some of the time.

One of the first people we talked to was Nisei Rosenberg—he was easy. Some of the others were more difficult. Rosenberg helped as much as he could, but there wasn't much he could do about some of it.

For one thing, Ashkenazi Jews didn't want to work with Sephardic Jews. Sephardics didn't want to work with them, either. I asked Amos which kind we were, but he didn't know. Others we talked to were more intrigued by the prospect of escaping conditions in the refugee camp than by fighting. We took them anyway. When I asked Trumpeldor about whether they would actually work together and if this was going to be a problem, he acted like there was nothing to it. "We can work all of that out."

Rosenberg said things had been that way since the beginning. "Pharisees and Sadducees. Ashkenazi and Sephardic. Rabbi party. Party that preferred no rabbis. Synagogues, no synagogues. These might not be those same groups but they carry on the same fight."

"But we aren't fighting each other. This war is about the Turks."

Rosenberg responded with a good-natured grin. "They'll work together once we get where we're going and the bullets start flying. Right now they only have each other to fight. So we let them fight to keep them motivated."

FRIENDS OF ZION: *Patterson & Wingate*

# CHAPTER 7

foz

A MONTH OR TWO after we began recruiting, John Patterson arrived in Egypt and met with General Maxwell. They were old friends but Patterson arrived unannounced. Maxwell was glad to see him but surprised nonetheless.

At first they talked about family, chatting amicably over tea as they sat around Maxwell's desk, then moved on to the latest news and gossip about colleagues in the army. Finally, Maxwell said, "So, what brings you all the way out here? No one informed me you were coming."

"Actually..." Patterson began hesitantly, "I was wondering if you had a place for me."

"Oh." Maxwell's eyes opened wide. "I see." Slowly, an amused smile spread across his face. "I assume London doesn't know you're here."

Patterson's eyes darted away. "Not officially."

Maxwell's smile became a grin. "I take that to mean they have no idea where you are."

"Ahh...no," Patterson replied. "They have no idea where I am at the moment."

Maxwell scooted his chair closer to the desk. "Well, can't let a little thing like that get in the way, now, can we?" He shuffled through a stack of papers and files on the desk, as if searching for something. Then his face lit up with a look of realization and he pulled a file from the stack. "Actually, I might have just the thing." He leaned back in his chair and opened the file. "As I recall, you were quite the amateur Old Testament scholar. Still interested in that sort of thing?"

"Very much; I think it was one reason I was attracted to this region. That and our friendship, of course."

Maxwell resumed reviewing the file.

Patterson continued. "Since I was a young boy, most of my free time has been spent reading and researching the history of the Jews. One of the few hobbies I've enjoyed as an adult."

"Then this is exactly what you're looking for." Maxwell leaned forward and handed Patterson the file. "Take a look at this. I think you are precisely the right person for this job."

Patterson glanced at the file, then looked up with a puzzled expression. "A mule corps?"

"I know it's not exactly a command to which either of us aspires." Maxwell leaned back in his chair again. "But this unit is not like the typical transportation corps."

"Oh?" Patterson said skeptically. "And how so?"

"This unit is comprised entirely of Jewish refugees."

Patterson's puzzled look turned to one of interest. "Jews?"

"Yes," Maxwell nodded. "They've been forced out of Palestine by the Ottomans and Arabs and are being held in a camp here. We're feeding about fifteen thousand. Some of them came to me recently and wanted to form a unit to take back their land."

"I heard they were moved out."

"Well," Maxwell explained in a more serious tone. "They weren't exactly *moved out*. They were *forced* out. Driven out. By gangs of Arab thugs and units of Ottoman regular soldiers. The Americans brought them here on one of their ships and we took them in as a humanitarian act."

Patterson closed the file and laid it in his lap. "So they came to you to form their own unit and now they're being organized as a transportation corps?"

Maxwell changed positions in his chair. "We can't accept them as regular soldiers. Regulations being what they are and all. You understand these things."

"We have Arab units working with us all across the Arabian Peninsula," Patterson noted. "Don't you have a man—Lawrence or something like that—actively courting their participation?"

"Yes," Maxwell conceded. "But that is an exception. I assure you, a Jewish lancer division will never gain approval or acceptance. Besides, we have no immediate plans for taking Palestine."

"But we will one day."

"I suppose we will." Maxwell leaned forward and propped his elbows on the desktop. "So, are you interested in the unit?"

"Who's organizing it?"

"That would be your job, from our side. One of the Jews—a man named Trumpeldor—is recruiting men for it. Former Russian soldier. A bit of military experience but unfamiliar with our procedures. He'll get you the men you need, but you'll have to get the unit into shape."

"Trumpeldor," Patterson said, repeating the name. "Never heard of him."

"As I said, he's a former Russian soldier. Lost an arm fighting the Japanese."

"Is he any good?"

"To be honest, he's better than most of the men in my unit. I'd accept him in an instant, but London will never approve an all-Jewish fighting unit and I don't think they would take him in his condition—missing an arm and all." Maxwell looked over at Patterson. "If you want to command this unit, it's yours. Otherwise, I'll have to put you on the first ship sailing for London and find a way to explain your visit as official business."

"Do Trumpeldor's men know anything about mules?"

"I doubt it. Some of them were farmers before the war caught up with them. A few of them might know how to use one for plowing and that sort of thing, but I'm sure they know nothing of how we use the animals. The work is absolutely necessary, though, for the operation we're planning."

"What operation is that?"

"Gallipoli," Maxwell said, his eyes darting away. "But we're not supposed to talk about it. Nothing official yet." He rapped the desktop lightly with his knuckles. "What do you say? Are you in, or out?"

Patterson grinned. "I'll take it."

"Good," Maxwell said with a satisfied look. He stood and reached across the desk to shake hands. "Glad to have you on the team. I'll straighten things out with London." He came from behind the desk to usher Patterson out. "You'll need a staff. I'll let you choose your own. One of my men will help you."

"That would be most appreciated. And I think I'll go over to the refugee camp and have a look around on my own, before they know who I am."

"Not a bad idea. I'll get someone to point you in the right direction."

❖ ❖ ❖

Amos and I were sitting in the shade at the end of the barracks when we first caught sight of Patterson. Tall, lean, and standing straight, he looked strikingly handsome in his uniform with all the buttons shining and his medals and ribbons in place. Shoulders square, hat set just so atop his head. He cut a remarkable figure. I saw him first and asked Amos who he was.

"I have no idea. Never seen him before."

"He's not one of the usual soldiers."

"No, he's not."

As Patterson continued down the alley away from us, I pushed myself up and went to find Trumpeldor. He was sitting with Rosenberg near the canteen. I described the new soldier we'd seen, but neither of them knew any more than we did. Then, while I was talking to them, Patterson walked past.

Trumpeldor glanced up for a look and shook his head. "Never seen him before. But you're right. He's not one of the men we regularly see. Too many ribbons and medals."

Rosenberg wasn't helpful, either. "All I know is he's a colonel in the British army."

"How do you know that?" I wondered how he knew even that much.

Rosenberg pointed, "Insignia on his collar."

In the week that followed, I saw him on three separate occasions. Which, in my analysis, changed him from curious visitor to something else. If he was around that much, I reasoned, he wasn't just passing through and I wondered if major changes were on the way. To satisfy my curiosity, I convinced Amos to go with me to the British encampment where the soldiers stayed.

✦ ✦ ✦

The next morning, we slipped past the guard at the gate and made our way to where the soldiers lived. They were housed in tents set in rows that seemed to run as far as we could see. We wandered among them, ducking out of sight when anyone came near, and watched as they moved past, hoping to catch a glimpse of this new colonel.

At first we saw only soldiers as they went through their daily routine, but after poking around awhile we saw him in a command tent like the ones the British use in the field. The top of the tent was in place, providing shade beneath it, but the sides were flipped up to let the breeze pass through, and we could see him seated at a portable wooden desk. Across from him was a young lieutenant. They were engaged in an intense discussion, but I couldn't hear what they said and Amos refused to sneak up any closer.

Frustrated at not hearing, I gave up and said, "We might as well go back."

Amos whispered, "We never should have come in the first place. If they find us here they'll arrest us."

"I'm sure they saw us when we arrived from the camp. They know we're here."

"Yes, we do," a voice said from behind us and I wheeled around to see a man from the camp. I wasn't sure of his name but I once heard Rosenberg refer to him as Yehuda. He lived in the barracks next to ours and worked as a common laborer for the British, hauling away garbage and cleaning up in the canteen. "What are you two doing over here?" he demanded.

"Just looking around," Amos said lamely.

I could see we were headed for trouble, so I spoke up. "There's a new guy in camp." I pointed toward the tent, "That man. Rosenberg said he was a colonel. We wanted to find out who he is."

A puzzled look clouded Yehuda's face. "You want to know who he is?"

"Yes."

Yehuda still had a perplexed frown. "Don't you know? He's Colonel Patterson. John Henry Patterson. They brought him from England to lead the mule corps you and Trumpeldor are forming. Didn't Trumpeldor tell you?"

"No," I was too astounded to cover it up. "Does Trumpeldor know?"

"I assumed so," Yehuda replied. "But I don't know. I assumed everyone knew. Patterson is recruiting British officers for the unit." He pointed toward the tent. "That's what he's doing now." His voice changed. "Though I hope he doesn't take that one."

"Who?" Amos asked.

"That lieutenant."

"Why?" I asked, turning back to look at the tent. "What's wrong with him?"

"He hates us," Yehuda snarled.

I glanced over at Yehuda. "The lieutenant hates Jews?"

"Yes."

We watched a moment longer, then the expression on Patterson's face turned serious. They said something to each other, and the lieutenant stood. He saluted and came from the tent, obviously upset by whatever just happened. I heard him muttering as he passed us, "Lots of luck with your *kikes*, colonel."

"Good," Yehuda grinned. "I think Patterson turned him down."

"Why?"

Once again, Yehuda looked down at me with a puzzled frown. "Didn't you hear what he said?"

"I heard him say something, but I didn't know what it was."

"Kike," Yehuda said. "He said, 'Good luck with your kikes, colonel.'"

Now it was my turn to frown. "What's a kike?"

Yehuda's puzzled expression turned into a condescending look. "Don't you know anything?"

"I know lots of things, but I don't know what that word means."

"Kike," he repeated. "As in kikel."

*Kikel* was a Yiddish word for the English letter *O*, and I felt the creases deepen in my forehead as I tried to understand. "He called us a circle?"

"No, not literally," he said in a frustrated tone. "It's the latest Gentile word for us. The British got it from the Americans."

"So, it's not a good word."

Yehuda shook his head. "No, it's not a good word."

I continued to stare in the direction of the tent, waiting to see what would happen next and hoping to find out more about the man Yehuda said would be our leader. "Is Patterson a good man?"

"I think he's as good as we'll get."

"We?" I grinned at Yehuda. "You are joining us?"

"Beats taking out the garbage for the British." Yehuda watched with us in silence a moment longer. "They say he spends most of his time reading the Old Testament," he added after a moment.

"Torah?"

"Yeah. I heard some of the men talking about it. They wondered why he was here and not in a university somewhere, teaching."

Just then, Patterson rose as if to leave the tent, and Yehuda turned to us. "Okay, you gotta go now." He put his hand on Amos' shoulder and steered him away. "Come on," he said over his shoulder in my direction. "Get moving."

As we made our way toward the front road I thought about all we'd seen and learned. If Patterson was as Yehuda described him, the transportation corps might turn out like Trumpeldor thought and not

FRIENDS OF ZION: PATTERSON & WINGATE

at all like Jabotinsky had feared. A Gentile leading a Jewish unit was an odd mix, but having a leader who understood our history—as much as any non-Jew could—would be more than we ever hoped possible. I still had questions—in some respects more questions than I had before—but I also had a sense of peace that things were going to turn out alright, no matter how difficult it might be in the process.

✦ ✦ ✦

When we returned to the refugee camp, we located Trumpeldor and told him about Patterson and the things we'd learned. He seemed intrigued but not totally surprised and I wondered if he already knew who Patterson was—and maybe knew even on that first day when I asked. My suspicion was bolstered a week or two later when he received a message from Patterson telling him to assemble the volunteers in a field near the fence, so we could meet our new commander. Trumpeldor read the message and handed it to me. When I asked what it meant he said simply, "Pass the word."

Three days later, the men gathered and not long after that, Patterson arrived. General Maxwell was there, too, and gave a short talk along with one or two others. Then Maxwell introduced Colonel Patterson. He spoke to us for ten or fifteen minutes. I don't remember all that he said, but some of it still sticks in my mind. Especially when he reminded us of our ancient heritage as warriors and told us, "This is an historic day. For today you become the first Jewish fighting force to assemble in over two thousand years."

The first Jewish fighting force since the destruction of the temple in Jerusalem! Even then the thought of such a thing, and that I should participate in it, was almost overwhelming. To think that I—still a teenager—stood in a line of succession that ran back to David, the mashiach king of Israel.

Afterward, we were sworn in as soldiers and Patterson introduced Trumpeldor as our ranking Jewish officer. Officially, we were known as the Zion Mule Corps, an auxiliary transportation unit assigned to the service of the British army. We would have our own officers and command structure—Trumpeldor would hold the rank of captain and command us from the top, but ultimately we would all be accountable to Patterson. Then he introduced half a dozen British officers and a much larger group of sergeants who would assist in training us.

When the speeches ended, we were led by one of the officers to the British army facility and directed to a field not far from where Amos and I saw Patterson that day when we sneaked away from the refugee camp. We arrived to find tents lying in bundles on the ground, the canvas covering wrapped around wooden support poles and tied up with the ropes. They'd been laid out with more or less even spacing and arranged in rows, but none were assembled.

As we learned that day, we were to sleep four men to a tent but rather than assigning places for everyone, Trumpeldor let us decide for ourselves. I made certain Amos and I shared a tent. We teamed with two other men from our barracks, both of whom slept in bunks across from ours and were agreeable fellows. Then we spent the remainder of the afternoon driving the poles into the ground and laying the canvas in place.

By the time we finished with that a truck arrived with cots and wooden footlockers. Amos and I positioned our cots next to each other. With so much happening, I didn't want to lose contact with him and thought if we shared a tent and our cots were together we could at least see each other at the end of the day.

Finally, as the sun was sinking toward the horizon, we all trekked back to the refugee camp and gathered our belongings. It was almost dark when we returned to the tents and collapsed on our cots. I was tired but not with the wearisome exhaustion that came after spending a day doing nothing, as our days had been when we loitered around the barracks. Instead, this was the kind of tired that comes from work—the kind of tired that reminded me of life on the farm with Papa. As always, I wondered whether he was alive and, if so, where he might be. But I didn't think about it for long as I quickly drifted off to sleep.

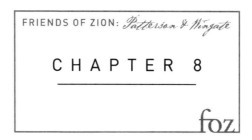

FRIENDS OF ZION: *Patterson & Wingate*

# CHAPTER 8

foz

FOR THE NEXT FIVE DAYS we marched—all day long. But they fed us morning, noon, and night, and though our legs throbbed and our backs ached from nonstop drilling, we were glad to finally have enough to eat. No one complained.

In the second week, the mules arrived. Each of us received an animal and one of the sergeants gave instructions on how to care for it. Since Amos and I came from a farm, some of the men thought we knew all about them. We did know how to care for them, but that didn't come from having owned one. Papa didn't like mules. He used a horse instead, but feeding and watering a horse is about the same as doing it for a mule.

When we weren't feeding and watering them, we led them around by a lead rope attached to the bridle that fit over their head. Trumpeldor said we had to get used to them and they had to get used to us. "Only way to do that is to spend time together." So when we weren't taking our meals or sleeping, we had our mules with us at all times.

Sometime later, a truck arrived with pack saddles and mule tack— blankets for a pad on the mule's back and leather straps for holding the saddles in place. Colonel Patterson joined us that day and watched while a group of British sergeants showed us how to place the gear on the animals' backs and how to make sure it was comfortably fit to the bone structure. We spent two days doing nothing but making certain the frame of the pack was shaped and formed to our animal. "If the animal isn't comfortable, you won't be, either," they said over and over.

Once the fit was right, we spent countless hours putting the saddles in place and tightening the leather straps, doing it in the cool of the morning, the heat of the afternoon, and the dark of night. Interrupting lunch for it and delaying dinner to get it done. "You have to be able to do this under every circumstance," they told us.

Not long after that, another truck arrived, this one with bales of hay, canvas, ropes, and burlap sacks filled with grain. It was a curious sight but I didn't ask about it. I'd learned by then to keep most of my questions to myself. Anyway, I didn't have to wonder long. One of the sergeants arrived and announced with a toothy grin, "Today we learn the fine art of loading freight on a mule's back."

At first we learned how to tie knots—not the jumbled kind that a schoolboy might tie, but the ones that won't come loose by themselves no matter how hard you try, but can be easily loosened with one simple tug on the correct end of the line. Then we learned how to wrap the canvas around the hay bales and lash it in place with the ropes. It was a challenging exercise for some, but Amos already knew most of the knots and I was pretty good at helping.

After that, we learned how to attach the canvas packs and boxes that were specially designed to fit on the rigging. That part was easy, then they turned our attention to the bales of hay we'd wrapped with canvas. Learning to load irregular-sized freight was a challenge to everyone.

Amos and I worked together loading first his mule then mine. Amos had difficulty getting his mule to mind, but when we changed places so that I stood near the head, things worked much better. I talked to the animal while I held up my side of the load and Amos tied it in place. Speaking gently into the mule's big, floppy ear seemed to have a calming effect on him and whether that's how it worked or not, he didn't move much after that or swish his tail in a circle.

By then we'd been living in the tents almost a month and I hadn't seen anyone else from the refugee camp except for the men who were with us. With so much to do, I hadn't thought about anyone from the refugee barracks, or even from home, either.

Then one night, after lights-out and when everyone was asleep, I was awakened by the sound of Amos as he turned back the covers from his cot. I glanced in his direction and was startled to see he was fully dressed. Part of me wanted to speak up but the other part was curious, so I lay quietly with my eyes almost closed, watching while he picked up his boots and tiptoed from the tent.

When he was gone, I rolled off the cot, slipped my feet in my boots, and went after him. I caught up with him two tent-rows away. "What are you doing?"

"Nothing," he answered as he struggled to slip his feet into his boots.

"It must be something," I responded. "You wouldn't be sneaking off like this for nothing."

"You wouldn't understand," he said in a sullen tone.

And that's when I knew. "You're seeing Dalia, aren't you?"

"Hush," he said sharply. "You're talking too loud."

"Is that what you're doing?" I continued.

"I told you, you wouldn't understand."

"I understand you could get in a lot of trouble if they catch you."

Amos smiled. "Then I'll have to make sure they don't catch me." He didn't bother to lace his boots but stood and stomped his heels against the ground to make certain they were all the way on. Then he glanced over at me, "It's late. Get back in the tent. I'll be back in a few minutes."

Without waiting for me to respond, he turned in the opposite direction and made his way between the tents. I watched until he disappeared from sight, then started back to our own tent. For much of the remainder of the night, I lay awake on my cot, worrying, but after a while my eyelids refused to cooperate and I slowly drifted off to sleep.

✦ ✦ ✦

When I awoke the next morning, Amos was sprawled across his cot, fully clothed with his boots still on his feet. I watched him sleeping soundly and thought of all the things I could do to awaken him. But before I could do anything, the bugle sounded reveille and Amos bolted upright.

After breakfast, we picked up where we left off the day before—working with the mules. If it sounds boring to read about, you should have been there with us when we were doing it. After the first couple of days, we all understood the procedure. And after a week of repeating it, we had the task down to rote memory. Removing the saddle once more, just for the sake of doing it, then reattaching it and loading it all over again taxed our patience mercilessly.

That day, however, just before lunch, one of the sergeants came to me and said Colonel Patterson wanted to see me at his headquarters tent. I left the mules and went there straightaway. When I arrived, he was seated as usual at his desk and offered me a cool drink of water, which I readily accepted. Then he refilled my glass and watched while I emptied it again. I didn't know much about polite social interaction back then and was thirsty from a morning in the hot sunshine.

After I finished the second glass of water, Colonel Patterson directed me to the wooden chair where I'd seen the young lieutenant sitting before. When I was seated, he returned to his chair behind the desk. When he was comfortably in place he looked over at me, "I've been watching you while you work with the mules."

"Yes, sir," I replied. "I've seen you out there."

"You're doing a good job."

I was somewhat embarrassed and unsure. ""Thank you, sir. I'm trying."

"And it's because of how hard you're working that I've made a decision about your future."

*Oh, no!* I thought. *You can't separate me from Amos. Not now. Not after all we've been through.* The horror of being separated from him was...too great to consider. "Please don't take me out of the unit," I blurted. "Please don't, sir."

"I'm not going to remove you," Patterson answered calmly. "I'm going to reassign you."

"Reassign me?" I knew what the word meant but right then it sounded like a military way of getting rid of me, just the same.

"I'm assigning you to be a member of my staff. You'll serve as my aide."

At first it sounded great. I would spend my days working with him and the other officers, most of it out of the sun. Then I realized I wouldn't get to work with Amos during the day. I protested lamely, "But my place is with the animals."

"As I said," Patterson repeated with a nod, "I've seen you with them. You have a natural gift with the mules. And I suspect you have that with all animals."

"I understand them."

He nodded once more. "And I think you understand people even better. At any rate, I need an aide and I want you for the position. You will sleep in a tent over here, on this side of the camp. So you'll need to move your things."

This was the thing I'd feared the most. We wouldn't be together during the day or night. "I don't want to sleep over here. I want to sleep with the men. I can work here during the day and spend the nights over there. In the tent where we...where I've been."

Patterson had a kind smile and seemed to understand the real issue. "You will see...the men often enough. And you can go back and forth between here and there as time allows, but I need you here so you are available to me at a moment's notice. Night and day."

The news was upsetting to me, but I did my best not to show it. Serving as aide to Colonel Patterson was an honor and I had little choice but to accept it. So I quickly nodded my ascent. "Yes, sir."

He smiled, then stood, reached across the desk, and shook my hand. "Good. Welcome to my staff. Collect your things and report back here. When you return I'll show you to your quarters."

I ran back to the tether line where we kept the mules, only to realize the men were eating lunch. I made my way quickly to the tent where we gathered for meals and found Amos sitting alone.

"Where have you been?"

"Colonel Patterson sent for me."

"I heard. You've been with him all this time?"

"Yes."

"What did he want?"

"He wants me to be his aide."

Amos' mouth dropped open, then his face lit up with a smile, "That's a promotion."

"I suppose. But I have to sleep over there by his tent. He wants me available at a moment's notice."

Amos seemed to understand what this meant to me. He set aside the plate he was holding and stood. "Look," he began with his hand gently on my shoulder. "I know you've wanted us to be together as much as possible, but I think this is a good thing for you."

"I don't want to sleep over there." Suddenly my eyes were full. "I want to sleep over here. With you." My voice quivered and I sounded so much like a little boy.

"But over there, you'll be out of the sun. Your duties will be much lighter. And when we go to the battlefield wherever they're sending us, you'll be in the rear with Colonel Patterson instead of packing the mules up to the front."

"I *want* to pack the mules to the front," I argued, much too loudly.

Amos slipped his arm around my shoulder and guided me away from the tent. "I know you like it now," he said when we were out of earshot, "but when we're on the battlefield I think you'll be glad you're a colonel's aide and not leading a string of mules. Besides," he continued, "this is the perfect job for you and a great opportunity."

"But who will look after you?"

"I'll be fine," he chuckled.

A sergeant appeared and ordered everyone back to work. Then he looked over at me and said, "You better get moving, too. Colonel Patterson is waiting for you."

Reluctantly, I said good-bye to Amos one last time, then walked over to our tent to collect my things. When I arrived back at headquarters, Colonel Patterson was seated at his desk, studying a map. He glanced up as I entered and said, "Good. Perfect timing."

As he rose from his chair, I glanced down at the map and saw sitting on the corner of the desk was a framed photograph of a woman with a young boy sitting. "Your family?" I asked, pointing.

He turned to see what I was staring at and said proudly, "Yes. This is my wife, Frances." He took the picture from the desk and held it in his hands. "And this," he beamed, pointing to the boy, "is my son. Bryan."

"He looks like you," I said, remembering the comments I'd heard others make.

"Thank you," he held the photograph a moment longer. Then he returned it to the desk and guided me out the back of the tent. "Your quarters are right over here," he explained. "Just a few steps away."

A space wide enough for a truck to pass separated the back of the headquarters tent from a smaller tent pitched just behind it. About half the size of the tent I shared with Amos and the other two men, it was only a few steps away from the chair where Colonel Patterson spent most of his time working from his desk.

We reached the front flap with little effort and Colonel Patterson lifted it aside for me to enter. "This is your tent," he announced as I moved past him. "You'll have this one all to yourself, though I dare say when we reach our destination you may be sleeping in the head- quarters tent. And then only in intermittent naps." I didn't know what intermittent meant but I assumed he was telling me not to expect much rest when we were in the field.

Beneath the tent was a standard-issue cot with a locker at the foot. A table stood beside it with a kerosene lamp and next to the lamp was a pen and inkwell. A wooden folding chair sat in the corner beyond the table.

After glancing around a moment to survey the space, I set my things on the cot and waited, expecting Colonel Patterson to leave me to myself. When he lingered, I began stowing my extra uniform in the locker. While I did that, he moved to the table and fiddled with the lamp. "I suppose they checked this to make certain it works."

I glanced at it, "It seems to be in order."

He gave me an amused smile. "Do you have anything to read?"

"No, we could only carry a few things when we left the farm in Galilee. The books we owned were left behind."

He smiled, "Well, then, we'll have to correct that. I'll be right back." Then he stepped toward the tent flap and disappeared outside.

A few minutes later, Colonel Patterson returned holding a book. I closed the lid to the locker and stood beside the cot. "Here," he thrust the book toward me. "You might like this. I did when I was younger." The book was a collection of stories by Rudyard Kipling. I'd heard of him but never read anything he'd written. "My father introduced me to his works when I was about your age," Colonel Patterson added. "I found that copy in a shop in Alexandria the day I arrived. I'd intended to take it home, but who knows when that will be. You should have it."

And right then I realized why he'd selected me to serve as his aide. He probably did need someone to deliver messages, sort through correspondence, and keep things straight, but a British soldier would have been the logical choice—someone who already knew the way the army liked to have its business handled. Even a private would have been better equipped than I. But that wasn't what Colonel Patterson was thinking of when he chose me. He wasn't thinking of efficiency or proper organization. He was thinking of his son, Bryan. I was the youngest person in the unit—less than half the age of most of them, except for Amos. When he saw me, he saw his son.

At first I was unsettled by that. I didn't want anyone but Papa to think of me as his son. And I didn't want to think of anyone but Papa as my father. But the gesture of the book felt good. It felt kind. I felt... noticed. Someone took an interest in my well-being—like that first day when Rosenberg talked to me about standing up for myself, and then with Trumpeldor as I followed him through the camp. I wanted someone to treat me as his son. I *needed* someone to look after me, but I would never admit it. Not then. And so I just said, "Thank you, Colonel. I'm sure I'll enjoy the book."

FRIENDS OF ZION: *Patterson & Wingate*

# CHAPTER 9

foz

WHILE WE WERE SETTING up the tents, marching around the army camp, and working with the mules, Jabotinsky was living in London. When he arrived there, he took a room at the Guardian Hotel on Church Street. The bill was paid by *Russkiya Vedomosti*, his newspaper. He also received a stipend for his expenses and a salary that went to his home in Russia.

Jabotinsky enjoyed writing and worked diligently as a reporter, filing articles for the newspaper in Moscow, but he spent most of his time talking to anyone who would listen about the need for a fighting unit—a Jewish Legion—to return to Palestine and restore the land stolen by Arab gangs and Ottoman troops. Though he would talk to anyone on the subject, his first effort to organize serious support for the cause was among established Jewish leaders. Some were interested, but others were not and much of his time was spent arguing rather than organizing support. After one particularly acrimonious encounter in a back room at a store in Spitalfields—his friend Alfie Lipmann asked about Chaim Weizmann's position on the matter.

Weizmann, a noted biochemist and ardent supporter of Zionism, had been instrumental in the formation of the Palestine Land

Development Company, an organization that promoted the settlement of Jews in Palestine by raising money, purchasing land, and training settlers as farmers. He also was involved in establishing the Israel Institute of Technology, one of the first Jewish schools of higher education in Palestine. And he was a prominent figure in the British Zionist Federation.

Jabotinsky knew of Weizmann but the two were not well acquainted and after the trouble he'd already encountered with Jewish leaders, he was not enthusiastic about involving one more.

"They all have their agendas," he said. "Weizmann, I'm sure, is no different. I am a member of the World Zionist Organization and I see him at many of the meetings. The WZO is splintered and fractured by politics and infighting. Surely the British Zionist Federation can be no different."

"Yes," Lipmann agreed, "but the Federation is quite large. Most prominent Jews in England are members. Weizmann has almost as many friends as the entire Federation. He could put you in contact with practically anyone in the country."

"If he were so inclined."

"You won't find out unless you ask."

Jabotinsky looked away and sighed. "I think there must be another way."

"You mean you intend to ignore Weizmann?"

"Not ignore him. Or the WZO. Just work around them." Jabotinsky looked over at Lipmann. "I need to talk to British officials. Talk to them directly. Face-to-face. Without attempting to gather intermediaries for support."

"And how do you propose to do that without the help of people who know them? You can't just show up at their offices."

Jabotinsky had a mischievous smile. "I'm a journalist. Surely they will talk with a reporter from one of their ally's most prominent newspapers."

Over the next several weeks, Jabotinsky used his credentials as a journalist to gain access to cabinet ministers and influential officials of the British government. As Jabotinsky had suggested, he was a reporter for one of Russia's most influential newspapers, and the Russians were a critical ally in the war effort. No one refused his request for an interview.

Although he gained access and conducted insightful interviews, he ran into a wall of opposition when he turned the discussion to the topic of Jewish involvement to win control of Palestine. No one supported the idea. "No need to take on trouble in Palestine now. It will fall under our control after we take Constantinople. Once the Turks surrender we can deal with the issues of the region in a time of peace and stability."

At first, Jabotinsky allowed the sessions to end with that response, but as the interviews continued and he met with similar results from other officials, his level of frustration grew, so did his anger. As a consequence, all of the later interviews ended badly. So badly, in fact, that when Jabotinsky tried to arrange an appointment with Herbert Kitchener, the secretary of state for war and last remaining minister yet to grant an interview, he couldn't even get in the door to discuss the matter with the ministerial staff. Apparently, others who'd already met with Jabotinsky tipped him off to the Russian reporter's real interest and purpose.

Frustrated by the response of British officials, Jabotinsky reluctantly turned once again to the Jewish community and approached Chaim Weizmann for help with his idea for a Jewish Legion. They talked over tea at the table in the kitchen of Weizmann's home.

To his surprise, Weizmann was in favor of forming a Jewish

Legion. "We must do something to take back the land. And if no one else will do it, we must do it for ourselves. We will never have a Jewish state in Palestine unless our people move there, buy the land, and demand a state for themselves. But," he cautioned, "I'm afraid others do not share our concern."

"I know," Jabotinsky agreed in a downcast tone, "but I don't understand."

Weizmann paused to take a sip of tea. "It's rather more complicated than it might first appear."

"It doesn't seem complicated to me," Jabotinsky responded. "They just don't want to do it. But why don't they want it?"

"You must realize, many of our key leaders are Russians," Weizmann explained. "They fled to England to escape the atrocities fomented against us by Russian authorities."

"As am I Russian," Jabotinsky argued. "And I know very well the troubles we faced there—and continue to face."

"Yes," Weizmann said patiently. "But unlike them, you see a much bigger picture. A picture of the future. They can only see the horror of the immediate past. They hate the czar. Yet Russia is one of the Allied Powers fighting with the British in this war. Many Russian Jews in England think that by joining the Allies in the war, they are also aligning themselves with the czar, whom they see as their enemy. The idea of a Jewish Legion to take control of Palestine probably appeals to many, but the thought of somehow being in agreement with the czar— though only tacitly—is more than they can countenance."

"I'm not sure it's that political."

"I assure you for many that is precisely the obstacle you face. It is the topic of discussion in most of the coffee shops and synagogues in London."

"And what about the others?" Jabotinsky asked.

Weizmann looked puzzled. "The others?"

"The wealthy ones who have a more sophisticated understanding of world affairs. Why are they opposed to forming a Jewish Legion?"

"Ahh," Weizmann smiled. "Yes. The wealthy ones." He shifted positions in the chair once more. "As aliens and refugees living here in England, they are exempt from military service. They can live here in safety, develop their fortunes, and bear none of the responsibility for ensuring the security they so readily enjoy."

Jabotinsky's expression grew tense and he tapped his finger on the tabletop. "That is exactly the attitude and thinking we have to change."

Weizmann nodded. "I agree, but we cannot change their minds and hearts overnight."

"But a gradual approach to educate them will take too long. It'll be too late." Jabotinsky threw up his hands in a gesture of frustration. "By the time they get around to seeing the truth of what we're saying, Palestine will be lost. We, the Jewish people, will be lost. The dream of Herzl and all the work that our forebears did in years past will have been for nothing."

Weizmann reached across the table, patted Jabotinsky's arm and smiled, "Perhaps not. I have championed many causes that seemed hopeless at first but later proved quite successful."

"Then you'll help?"

Weizmann responded, "Yes, although I can't say what good will come of it, I will help."

✦ ✦ ✦

The next day, Weizmann rode with Jabotinsky down to Whitehall, where he introduced Jabotinsky to Jan Christiaan Smuts and Alfred Milner, members of the prime minister's war cabinet. Smuts and Milner listened attentively as Jabotinsky described the problem in Palestine and his notion of forming a Jewish Legion within the British army as a means of solving the Palestinian situation.

"How have you pursued this idea," Milner asked. "Who've you been talking to?"

"I've talked to a number of private individuals," Jabotinsky explained. "And I've spoken with every minister and many lesser officials in every department. I've seen all of them except Kitchener."

"And I would surmise you've received not a drop of support from any of them," Smuts commented.

"They will hardly allow me to finish my explanation before they say no." Jabotinsky shook his head. "I don't understand why."

"Forget about approaching the ministers directly," Smuts said. "They will never support such a cause without a groundswell of support."

"Or some catastrophic event that makes it necessary," Milner added.

"Why not?" Jabotinsky asked.

"It's too risky," Milner replied.

"Too politically risky," Smuts added.

"These are risk-averse men," Milner continued. "They might be bold enough to move forward on their own to address much smaller matters—questions of personal staff or a request for help from the field—things that would attract little or no attention, but not on something like this."

"Far safer to stick with big, obvious issues," Smuts noted. "Things that won't attract a lot of popular opposition."

"So, what should I do?" Jabotinsky asked.

"You need to find British officers who support the idea."

"But why can't the ministers support my idea?"

"For one thing," Milner said, "they see themselves making big, strategic decisions. In reality, the true decisions they make are quite small. Most of the time, they only implement the decisions made by the prime minister and the generals who run the army."

"Milner is right," Smuts added. "We work at this level every day and see this sort of thing from the inside out. If you want to make headway with the Jewish Legion idea, you'll have to approach it from the tactical level, not the strategic level, and build support from the bottom up."

Jabotinsky frowned. "The ministers will listen to lesser officers?"

"The prime minister will," Smuts said.

"Under the right circumstances," Milner added.

Smuts nodded. "Yes, under the right circumstances. Gather support from officers in the field. The higher the rank, the better. Then we'll have to hope for an event that changes the nature of the strategic discussion regarding plans for the Middle East region. Something that makes it an advantage to have a Jewish Legion participate."

"A situation that presents a problem that Jewish soldiers can solve."

"That's where you'll make headway," Smuts continued. "With the officers. Generals and officers who do not work at the ministerial level. The more officers from the field who find the Legion a tactical advantage, the better."

Jabotinsky had a perturbed scowl. "Your ministers are shortsighted."

"Perhaps so," Milner said with a nod, "but as we have said, right now there is little support strategically for an assault on Palestine."

"Precious few soldiers for the European front as it is," Smuts noted. "We're doing all we can to maintain our position in Egypt with the minimum number of troops in order to free as many as possible for the European front."

"Right," Milner agreed. "Difficult to persuade the ministers and others of the need to take on the Turks in Palestine while the Germans are at the front door here in Europe."

+ + +

Not long after the meeting with Milner and Smuts, Jabotinsky received a telegram from Nikolai Vyazemsky, his editor in Moscow at *Russkiya Vedomosti*. The telegram came to him at the Guardian Hotel. Vyazemsky had heard rumors about an Allied operation supposedly planned for Gallipoli. He'd tried all the usual Russian sources but came up with nothing. The telegram directed Jabotinsky to check with sources in London, determine as best he could whether the rumors were true, and file an article on the nature of the planned operation.

Because his previous interviews proved to be little more than an opportunity to promote his ideas about a Jewish Legion, many of Jabotinsky's regular sources were suspicious of his stated purpose. He was just a reporter working on a story, and reluctant to discuss anything of importance with him. That changed when he disclosed the few details he'd managed to gather. Seeing that he was diligent in uncovering the facts, and not wanting to lose control of the story, several key officials at the sub-cabinet level were willing to talk. From them Jabotinsky learned that an Allied operation was indeed planned for later in the year, most likely in Gallipoli, though no one would say exactly when or who might be in charge.

Using information from those sources, Jabotinsky prepared a report that contained enough detail to satisfy Vyazemsky. He could have stopped right there and transmitted the report to Moscow. But with a serviceable article in hand, Jabotinsky realized questions about a proposed Gallipoli Campaign might provide one more shot at reaching Kitchener. *An interview with him,* Jabotinsky thought, *might establish a direct connection to the war secretary's office and a way to avoid the long, plodding strategy Milner and Smuts outlined.*

One more time, Jabotinsky contacted Kitchener's office and requested an interview. And once more, Kitchener's staff denied the request. The following day, Jabotinsky was outside the War Department building and noticed Milner and Smuts coming down the steps, followed by other members of the prime minister's war cabinet. Seeing them all together reminded him that Kitchener must leave the building that way, too.

Hoping to catch Kitchener in an unavoidable moment, Jabotinsky waited by the steps until long after dark, but Kitchener never appeared. Not to be outdone, he returned the following day followed the same tactic, waiting by the steps until after dark, again without so much as a glimpse of the secretary of state for war.

Finally, late in the afternoon of the fourth day, the doors opened at the top of the stairs and Kitchener appeared. He was surrounded by staff who did their best to shield him from curious onlookers, but he was there nonetheless and Jabotinsky moved in closer to make his approach.

Positioning himself on the sidewalk, between the bottom step and a long black car parked at the curb, Jabotinsky waited as Kitchener approached. He expected a cold, aloof brush-off, but instead Kitchener broke into a smile.

"Ah, yes," he said as he came to a stop at the car. "Mr. Jabotinsky."

The journalist nodded. "Mr. Secretary, I have a few questions."

"None about your Jewish Legion, I hope."

"I have many questions about that, but right now I'm wondering what you can tell me about the proposed Gallipoli Campaign."

Kitchener seemed taken with surprise by the question and staff members moved to end the conversation, but Kitchener waved them off, squared his shoulders, and said, "Tell me what you know and I'll decide what I can say on the topic."

Jabotinsky summarized what he'd learned so far and for the next five minutes he and Kitchener engaged in a fast-paced, intellectual repartee. Kitchener seemed to take delight in the verbal jousting match and Jabotinsky, much to his consternation, found the war secretary far more likeable than he'd imagined.

Had the conversation ended there, Jabotinsky might have actually accomplished what he wanted—an end run around a much more elaborate political strategy to gain acceptance of the Jewish Legion. But Jabotinsky found the opportunity of the moment irresistible and as the interview concluded, he returned to the issue Kitchener had broached when they first began and asked a follow-up question about the possibility of action against the Turks in Palestine.

Suddenly, Kitchener's face turned to stone and he replied coldly, "We are holding that matter for later consideration. Certainly, we would consider making it a part of the peace agreement at the conclusion of the war, but right now we have other, more pressing, priorities." Then he pushed his way past Jabotinsky, took a seat inside the car, and slammed the door shut.

FRIENDS OF ZION: *Patterson & Wingate*

# CHAPTER 10

foz

AS THE MONTHS WORE ON, correspondence and memos crossing Colonel Patterson's desk pointed increasingly toward Gallipoli as the site for the Zion Mule Corps initial deployment. General Ian Hamilton, whose career had involved mostly administrative positions rather than field command, was seen as the most likely choice to lead the effort. I read most of the correspondence, often before the colonel, but as much as I wanted to tell Amos, I kept the information to myself.

Near the end of the month, Patterson and I went out to where the corps was training. Trumpeldor was there, as usual, and we reviewed the men with him while they continued their daily routine. In the midst of that, Colonel Patterson folded his arms across his chest, leaned closer to Trumpeldor, and said very calmly, "We sail next week for Gallipoli."

Trumpeldor nodded thoughtfully. "I think they're ready."

"Yes," Colonel Patterson agreed. "They've accomplished all they can accomplish here."

That night, after we'd concluded the day's business, I walked from the headquarters tent over to where the men were billeted and found Amos. "We're leaving for Gallipoli in a week," I said as we walked among the tents together.

"To join the fighting?" he asked eagerly.

"Yes, as part of a major campaign for control of the peninsula."

"Good," Amos said resolutely. "It's time."

"Good?" I asked with surprise. "You think deploying to combat is good?"

"We're tired of training," he said dourly. "Most of us were ready two weeks ago."

"They say it could be as bad," I continued. "Some think as bad as the fighting in Europe."

"This is what we wanted," Amos replied in a matter-of-fact tone. "To fight the Turks."

"Yes," I agreed, "but we wanted to fight them in Palestine, not Gallipoli."

"Palestine would be ideal," Amos conceded. "But Trumpeldor is right, fighting the Turks anywhere is still fighting them, even if it's not in Palestine."

We walked in silence a ways, then I said in a soft voice, "I'm worried."

"You'll be with Patterson," Amos responded, patting me on the shoulder. "Not at the front."

"But you will have to deliver supplies to the front," I lamented. "You'll be right there in the midst of it."

"It's okay," Amos assured. "I will be fine."

A week later, men of the Zion Mule Corps disassembled their tents, broke down their cots, and loaded them on the mules. For a few, it was a monumental task but most had little trouble. When everything was ready, we all marched over to the docks in Alexandria, where we found a ship, the HMT *Hymettus*, awaiting our arrival.

Loading animals, gear, and men was a torturously slow process, but for most of it I stood with Colonel Patterson as he observed the men in their first action away from the camp. That proved less stressful than handling the animals but far more boring. It did, however, allow me to watch as Amos came aboard.

Getting everyone aboard took most of the day but late that afternoon, when all the animals were in place and the equipment was stowed, we manned the rail to watch as the ship slipped away from the dock. As we stood there watching, I saw Dalia on the dock with her father. Seeing them surprised me and I wondered how they were able to get away from the camp to be there, then I noticed Amos down the rail. He caught their eyes, waved to them, and they waved back. I figured from their exchange that Amos had arranged for them to see us off, though I wondered how he managed to do that, because I hadn't seen a memo or message about it.

At first I was jealous—seeing the obvious affection between them, though not as intensely as before—then I wondered if their interest in each other would survive the deployment to Gallipoli. For a moment I entertained the notion—perhaps even the hope—that it might not, and if not, then I might have a chance with her. Instantly, however, I was consumed with guilt for thinking such a thing. *Amos is my brother,* I thought, castigating myself. *I'm supposed to want the best for him.* I did want the best for Amos, but as I stared down at Dalia I was unable to avoid noticing how pretty she was. Thinking maybe she would—

Colonel Patterson nudged me and when I looked over at him I saw he had a sly grin, as if he'd seen me staring at Dalia and wasn't at all displeased. He chuckled, "Come on, we have work to do."

Late that afternoon, I returned to the rail with Amos in time to watch as the Egyptian coastline faded from view. In a while we saw nothing but open water in every direction. The air was damp but cool, much more pleasant than afternoons at the camp, and we enjoyed it in silence.

As we leaned against the rail, I thought of Papa, Mama, the farm in the Galilee, and how much had transpired since that night when the Arabs attacked us. Surely, I reasoned, Papa must be dead. If he were alive we'd have heard from him by then. The refugee camp was a long way from Kinneret but our location was no secret. Finding us might have taken a while but he would have come looking and any number of people would have told him where we were. That he still was missing told me he must be dead. But I said nothing of this to Amos and kept my thoughts to myself.

+ + +

At first, the trip was smooth, but sometime in the night after we'd departed Alexandria, a strong wind came up from the east. With it, the waves grew taller and more powerful. Though a storm never developed, the ship rocked from side to side and the motion of it made me nauseated. I resisted the urge to stand at the rail and vomit, as some of the others did, but I was sick and very uncomfortable. By midmorning of the next day, the waves calmed and I grew accustomed to the ship's rhythmic motion, but any affection I might have had for the sea was lost. I had no desire for a sailor's life.

Colonel Patterson spent the first morning at sea reviewing and updating our plan of action that the men would implement once we reached the Gallipoli coast—designations for where the tents went, the tether lines, the staging areas for supplies destined for the front. Work teams were assigned to each task in each area to make certain the transition from ship to land went smoothly. Then we developed a schedule for coordinating our arrival with troops already operating on the beach. We did that work from his stateroom in a session that lasted until noon. Though we still had more to do, we took a break for lunch.

In midafternoon we toured the ship, checking on the condition of our men. From the beginning, Colonel Patterson put me in charge of bunk assignments for the trip and I made sure Amos had a comfortable location. For that reason, I followed Colonel Patterson that afternoon as he wound his way through the ship, hoping for a chance to make certain Amos had whatever he needed.

Two days later, we entered the Aegean Sea and not long after that we arrived off the Gallipoli coast, due south of Alcitepe. However, rather than sailing immediately to shore to unload, we lingered at sea, just in sight of the shoreline, waiting while British forces cleared a landing area. Apparently the fighting was fiercer than anyone expected. Even from a distance we heard shore artillery and battleship cannons firing. We stood near the bow of our transport and watched through binoculars to see the puffs of smoke and dust as the shells reached land and exploded on targets inland from the coast.

One day, while we waited, I found Amos and took him up to the top of the ship's superstructure. Using the binoculars, we spent a few minutes watching the action on the beach. At that height, the glasses gave a remarkably clear and detailed view of what happened there. Amos watched with rapt attention.

"I see men dying," he said finally with a note of dismay. Then he looked over at me with the strangest expression. "I see them dying right there on the beach." The look on his face told me the reality of what lay ahead finally reached him. I'd tried to tell him this was a dangerous situation, that day when the men first learned we were going to Gallipoli. Now, perhaps, he realized his younger brother was correct.

Amos watched through the glasses awhile longer, then handed them to me. As I took them and we started down to the main deck, he looked over at me, "No matter what happens, you must stay with

Colonel Patterson. Don't even think about taking a string of mules to the front."

+ + +

After ten days loitering along the coast, a beachhead was finally secure at Cape Helles and the Zion Mule Corps, the first Jewish fighting force assembled in more than two thousand years, went ashore on the Gallipoli peninsula. Amos was with the men and animals. I remained at Colonel Patterson's side.

Artillery shells exploded on the beach, blasting large holes in the ground around us and we were peppered by small arms fire, but though a few men were wounded no one was killed. I spent most of the first hours checking the lists of injured to make sure Amos' name wasn't among them.

In the afternoon, Colonel Patterson gave the order for the men to saddle the mules. Boats arrived, ferrying our tents and other gear from the ship. The men unloaded it and stacked it on the sand, then lashed the bundles to the saddles as we'd practiced over and over again back in Egypt.

When everything was squared away, we all hiked a mile or so beyond the beach where we came to a flat but well-drained grassy meadow. There the men set tether lines, secured the mules to them, and erected the tents. I helped with setting up the headquarters tent and my own personal one. After that, it was time to feed and water the animals. Then we took a break for our evening meal and life slowed to a normal, though tense, pace.

During those first days, fighting lay ahead of us, farther ashore, and from what we saw it must have been horrible. Casualties coming back from the front were in terrible condition. Confusion seemed the order of the day. Not among us—the Mule Corps was more or less organized—but it seemed to be rampant among the infantry units.

Over the next several days, as the volume of wounded continued unabated, Colonel Patterson sent some of our men to help with the wounded. I was designated to accompany them and direct their effort to see that they cooperated as much as possible.

Beyond our compound, demolished equipment was strewn everywhere—both ours and that of the Ottoman army. Bodies littered the ground, too, and burial crews sorted through them, but the process seemed slow and rather haphazard. In a few places we saw trenches—abandoned by our troops as the fighting moved on, but they were a stark reminder of what life at the front was like. When I described all this to Colonel Patterson, he seemed unaffected by it and said without emotion, "This is nothing like conditions in Europe."

FRIENDS OF ZION: *Patterson & Wingate*

# CHAPTER 11

foz

ABOUT A WEEK AFTER we went ashore, supply ships arrived. The first ones ran aground while still well out in the bay, forcing us to unload them using smaller craft to ferry the freight to the beach. Colonel Patterson gathered everyone on the beach and explained the process. Some of us would unload the smaller boats, stacking the freight in an area above the high-tide line. While that continued, others were to prepare the mules and bring them down to the shore where they would be loaded with supplies and packed to the staging area near the tether line. A third group would man the staging area to assist with off-loading the mules.

When he'd explained the system thoroughly and answered a few questions from Trumpeldor, Colonel Patterson directed me to signal the ship that they should begin. Not long after that, a boat appeared on the waves with oarsmen rowing it toward us. In a few minutes, it reached our position and the men went to work.

Unloading that first boat proved a challenge, with men stumbling over each other and falling into the water, but they soon sorted it out and with Colonel Patterson directing them they fell into a rhythm. Gradually, the cargo moved from the boat to the beach, and our stack grew larger. By the time they finished, the mules arrived and that part went smoothly just as the men had practiced it many times in Egypt.

When the first string of mules started up from the beach toward the staging area, a second boat appeared on the water, making its way toward us. The craft we'd just unloaded was ready to return and the oarsmen took their places. As they were about to shove off, Colonel Patterson stepped into the boat and looked over at me. "I'm going out to the ship to supervise the unloading. You shall remain here and keep the men working, Yoel." He had a proud grin. "I'm counting on you. If the men won't mind, have Captain Trumpeldor deal with them."

"Yes, sir," I called as the boat moved away from shore. "I'll do my best."

"I'm sure you will."

I'd never seen an operation this complex, much less attempted to coordinate it. All the people, and pieces, and tasks. It seemed over-whelming. But as I gazed after Colonel Patterson the second boat neared us and there was nothing to do except do my best to make sure the unloading went smoothly. So that's what I did. I stood near the bow, out of the way of those who did the heavy lifting, and encour-aged them. And when someone raised a question, I answered it before anyone else could speak up. Most of them realized I was doing the bid-ding of Colonel Patterson and if they caused trouble he'd make them answer for it, so they did as I suggested.

The greater distance from our position to the ships, and the need to use the smaller craft to deliver the cargo, made the process longer and more cumbersome than it might otherwise have been. Everyone worked hard and we encountered fewer and fewer obstacles with each load. Sadly, the same could not be said for the ships.

With the supply ships sitting helpless in the water, and the boats we used for unloading equally vulnerable, it wasn't long before the

Turks realized the bay was filled with targets of opportunity. An hour or two into the unloading work, artillery shells began splashing into the water around us, both near the beach and farther out to sea. The lighter craft, being smaller and more agile, proved elusive but the ships were quite large and more easily hit. After one or two shells dropped harmlessly short of the ship closest to shore, and another two harmlessly long, a fifth went down the ship's smokestack and exploded.

The concussion of the explosion startled us and we stood at the water's edge watching a giant fireball rise into the sky. Though we were some distance away, we saw men falling from the superstructure and diving from the decks. Someone cried out, "Colonel Patterson is gone!" and for an instant my heart sank. Tears came to my eyes and I was filled with despair.

Just when I thought all was lost, Trumpeldor spoke up and said, "That's not his ship." He pointed and we saw the ship we'd been unloading, the landing boats moored to its side, waiting to be filled with cargo.

In response to the attack, the unloading craft still out by the ship were redirected for the rescue of survivors who were in the water. We quickly emptied the boats at shore and dispatched them to assist.

As the boats made their way into the bay, Trumpeldor called for me and I hurried to his side. He was standing next to a stack of ammunition boxes with a map spread over the top. "We need to direct our own fire on their artillery positions," he said as he traced across lines on the map with his finger. "Our cannons should be here," he added, pointing.

He studied the map a moment longer and said, "From the way the shells are falling, I'd say the Turks have their artillery over here." He indicated the location on the map. "I need you to get up to our artillery and tell them where to hit the Turks."

Managing the unloading of boats was one thing, but telling a captain or colonel of an artillery unit where to train his guns was...most unusual and very much out of order. "You expect me to tell the artillery what to do?"

"I expect you to deliver a message from me."

"Do you think they will believe me?"

"They'll believe the message you give them."

"Don't they know where the Turks have their cannons?"

"I don't know, but I'm not standing around here waiting to see." He looked over at me. "Listen," he explained, "telegraph and phone lines are not yet operational for us. The only way to get a message to them is for someone to carry it up there to them." He scribbled coordinates from the map on a note and handed it to me. "Get this to them. Go quickly. And be careful."

From the beach I made my way up to the tether line and untied a mule. One of the men, a slender fellow from Haifa who wasn't much bigger than I, gave me a curious look as I mounted the animal's back, but he knew I was Colonel Patterson's aide and did nothing to stop me.

Three hours later, I reached the British artillery position. They were surprised to see me—a young soldier riding a mule—but I ignored their jeers, located the captain in charge of the battery, and handed him Trumpeldor's note. He read it with a frown, "That's quite a distance down the coast."

"Yes, sir," I replied with a nod. "But we're in a desperate situation."

He found a map and laid it atop a gun carriage to check the position. "Rather far for our guns."

"Yes, sir, but you're the nearest battery and they've already destroyed one of our ships."

"We noticed," he answered wryly, then turned back to the map. "Well," he said after a moment, "might as well give it a go."

The captain turned to a crew manning one of the artillery pieces, and I watched with fascination as they turned it to point down the coast. It was an involved affair—dislodging the cannon from its position facing inland targets, turning it forty-five degrees to the left—and a task that required the assistance of my mule, but they repositioned the cannon without undue delay.

When it once again was secure and stable, they loaded the first shell in the breech and closed it for firing. The captain nudged me with an elbow, "Put your fingers in your ears." As he said it, he pressed an index finger against each ear and I did the same, somewhat hesitantly, though, not realizing why. Moments later, the cannon fired and I knew in an instant what he meant. A sudden concussion struck my chest with a heavy blow and the ground shook beneath my feet. In spite of my fingers, the sound of it caused a painful ringing in my ears.

After several rounds of artillery fire, I mounted the mule and made my way back toward the beach. Before I was halfway there, the Turkish guns fell silent.

It was almost dark when I arrived at the base camp. While I was away, the men had transferred that day's cargo to the staging area and were busy tending to the animals. The ship we'd been unloading was still lying in the bay, but Colonel Patterson had returned and I found him seated at his desk in the headquarters tent.

As I entered, he looked up at me with a smile. "You're back. Good, you've had a day of adventure."

I wanted to say something in response that sounded mature and confident, but right then I was overcome with emotion and choked back tears. "I thought you were dead."

Colonel Patterson rose from his chair, came from behind the desk, and put an arm around my shoulder. "It's okay," he said in the kind of painfully detached manner men often use in times of deepest emotion.

"It's okay to be afraid, especially when you conduct yourself with the kind of bravery and determination you displayed today."

In my heart I wanted to rest my head against his chest and cry, but I refrained. Instead, I stood up straight and squared my shoulders, "Captain Trumpeldor gave me a message and I delivered it."

"And the guns went silent," Colonel Patterson beamed. "Good job."

✦ ✦ ✦

The next day, our men prepared to pack supplies to the front. Water was in high demand as springtime on the peninsula was quite warm, but so was ammunition, as the Ottomans proved to be much better at holding their ground than we'd been led to believe. We had no specific orders for what to transport and Colonel Patterson reasoned, "If they have no water, they may die in a few days. But if they have no ammunition, they may die in a few minutes." Most of the mules in that first string were devoted to the heavy boxes of rifle cartridges, with only a few carrying water containers.

Colonel Patterson wanted to go with them on that initial trip, to observe conditions for himself and to make certain our route was as efficient as possible, but Trumpeldor and I prevailed upon him to remain at the rear. When that proved difficult, Trumpeldor offered to go in his place. I wanted to accompany him.

After further discussion, Colonel Patterson relented and agreed to let Trumpeldor go in his place. When I raised the question of accompanying him, Trumpeldor was against it but Colonel Patterson agreed with me. "You will go with Trumpeldor as his aide, to help him discharge his duties and to report to me about conditions at the front."

As Trumpeldor and I walked toward the tether line to join the others, he looked down at me with a disapproving scowl, "You should not have come."

"You really think I should have stayed with Colonel Patterson?" I asked.

"No," Trumpeldor said. "You should have stayed in Egypt."

"In Egypt?" The suggestion astounded me. "Why?"

"You're too young to be out here. Too young to see all this," he added, gesturing to our surroundings. "This is not something people your age should witness."

"Then why did you allow me to join and why didn't you object when we received orders to embark?"

Trumpeldor's voice softened. "Because I didn't want you in the refugee camp alone, without your brother."

The thought that Trumpeldor would have left me behind was disappointing, but a warm sense of acceptance swept over me as I considered the depth of consideration he'd given to me and to my situation. I didn't want to be anywhere without Amos, either. Not in the refugee camp and not at the rear base camp, either. But I was glad Trumpeldor had thought of me that way.

More than anything, I wanted to be accepted as one of the men, to be regarded by them as a man. While on the one hand, Trumpeldor's view that I was too young for combat was an affront to that desire; on the other it was a wonderful affirmation that I was part of the group—that my best interest was worthy of his consideration. He had thought of me and had made a decision based on his estimate of what I needed, regardless of how he felt about it. That was something Papa would have done.

At the tether line, Trumpeldor and I watched as the men loaded the mules. Amos saw me and came over to where I was standing and smiled. "Glad you came out to see us off. Our first trip to the front on this *grand* adventure." He spoke with a humorous tone but I knew from the look in his eyes that he was worried.

"It *is* our first trip, but it's not good-bye."

A frown wrinkled Amos' forehead. "What do you mean?"

"I'm coming with you," I answered boldly, knowing he would not like it. "Colonel Patterson is sending us to review conditions on his behalf."

"No!" Amos snapped. "You cannot come to the front."

"Colonel Patterson is sending me," I repeated.

"You can't go," Amos insisted. "I won't allow it."

"I have no choice."

"Yoel is right," Trumpeldor said, interrupting us. "Colonel Patterson assigned him as my aide. We're going to the front with you for this trip."

Amos was angry at my inclusion but there was little he could do except glare at me. After a moment, he turned away, trudged back to the mules, and secured his load, but I could tell by the way he walked that he was upset.

When the mules were ready, we started out from base camp and a few hours later reached the trenches. Unlike the shallow ones near the coast, these were deeper than the height of a man and well fortified—some sections reinforced with sandbags and others with timbers.

Beyond the trenches lay a barren wasteland and I could see what appeared to be soldiers in the distance. Someone said they were men of the Turkish line. It seemed serene enough, though, and I wondered if we were to simply walk up to the British positions from the seaward side and hand over our cargo as if delivering the mail. Then a bullet whizzed past my head. Another struck the ground a few meters away and after that, Trumpeldor adjusted our route to a path that ran along a ridge just behind the trenches, out of the line of direct gunfire.

Eventually we reached a command position—an underground bunker dug into the side of the trench. It had the British flag flying above. The mules remained on the path, below the ridge, while Trumpeldor and I scurried up to the trench, dropped down inside, and went in search of someone who could tell us where to deliver the supplies.

We were met by a private who was not much older than I. Trumpeldor told him what we were about, and he pointed us toward Colonel Hackett, a stocky fellow with a distinctive mustache. He directed us to unload our freight right there at his position and dispatched some of his men to help.

At first the work went well. Men in the trenches were glad for ammunition and even gladder for the water. As word of our arrival spread, others volunteered to assist. We had more than enough help. But half an hour into the process, an artillery shell landed on our position and we learned the hard way that we were out of danger from the Turkish riflemen but not out of range of their big guns.

The shell they lobbed on us exploded with such force that one wall of Colonel Hackett's bunker collapsed, briefly trapping several of his aides and assistants beneath dirt and timbers. For us, the consequences were much worse.

When the artillery shell exploded, it killed two of our mules and wounded several of our men. The sound of it scared the other animals and they bolted. Our men reacted quickly and brought them under control but in the melee of the moment, one of the mules leaped atop the collapsed bunker, then somehow managed to scramble up the opposite side of the trench into the expanse between the British position and enemy lines. The cargo strapped to its back—cartons of ammunition vital to the soldiers—remained in place. At first we held out hope that the mule might return close enough to the trenches to allow us to recapture it. That hope was dashed when moments later a barrage of gunfire brought the mule's life to an end and it collapsed in a bloody heap twenty meters out.

Before anyone could speak, Moshe Beilin, a man from our unit who had lived at Degania, charged from the trench and crawled toward the felled mule. He reached it without much trouble but when he raised himself up to undo the straps on the pack frame, a bullet ripped through his skull and he died immediately.

It was a brave act but ill-advised, and I said so to Trumpeldor. He agreed but as we were exchanging opinions, someone called out, "There goes Amos!" I looked in horror to see Amos clawing his way up from the trench and out toward Beilin and the mule. Without hesitation, I started after him.

When I reached the top, I instinctively spread myself as flat as possible against the ground and crawled quickly toward the mule. Amos, with a head start and taking more chances, reached it first and moved Beilin's body aside. There was a gaping hole in the back of Beilin's head and no hope that he was live. I saw the hole as I arrived at Amos' side.

"Oh," I gasped, unable to contain my reaction to the sight of so much blood.

Amos jerked his head in my direction. "What are you doing out here?" he yelled in an angry, demanding voice.

"Helping you," I shouted in response, more to be heard over the sound of gunfire than anything else. Just then a burst of machine-gun fire struck our position, ripping into the mule's carcass. We ducked low behind it and stared at each other.

"You could get killed," he continued to argue.

"You could, too," I retorted.

"It doesn't matter if I die," he growled. "But you can't die."

"It matters to me if you die," I blurted out. "And why can't I die?"

Then he looked at me with tears in his eyes and stammered, "Be... because...Papa told me to look after you."

His emotion caught me off guard and for a moment I forgot the trouble we faced. "I can die if you can," I said as tears streamed down my cheeks. "You can't stop me!"

Amos looked at me for a moment, then a grin spread over his face. "Okay," he chuckled. "I guess if I can die, you can, too. Come on." He rolled on his stomach and reached for the ropes that held the mule's cargo. "Help me untie this."

Using the mule's carcass for cover, we managed to unfasten most of the cargo without getting hit by enemy gunfire. Two ammunition boxes, though, were trapped beneath the mule's body and we were forced to leave them. The others we pushed and pulled toward the trench.

That's when the lunacy of our actions became apparent to me and I was certain we would be killed at any moment. But just when I thought all was lost, men appeared at the top of the trench and laid down a covering fire. Amos and I hustled toward them with the boxes and when we reached them they greeted us as heroes.

Trumpeldor, however, was not amused. "That was a brave thing you did, but it was incredibly stupid."

Amos and I wanted to go back for Beilin's body, but Trumpeldor declined. "It's too risky. You've done enough. We'll get the body later. There's nothing we can do for him now."

"But the body must be buried before sundown," I protested.

"I'm sorry. I understand your concern, but I'm sorry. We can't risk another foray for a man who's already dead."

"We'll see to his body later," Colonel Hackett added.

While we argued, Harry Schoenthal and Aaron Ben Joseph, men who shared a tent with Beilin, quietly climbed out of the trench and crawled toward his body. The private who'd greeted us at the bunker when we first arrived now appeared at Hackett's side to tell him the news. Hackett moved to a position from which he could observe our men and watched with great disapproval.

He glared at Trumpeldor. "Can't you control your men?"

"I can guide them," Trumpeldor replied. "Controlling them isn't altogether an option."

"Patterson's Jews," Hackett groused. "I tried to tell them this would be difficult."

"But I'm sure you're glad for the supplies," Trumpeldor responded. I could see the veins pulsing in his neck and knew he did not like Hackett's comment. "Your men certainly are glad for it," Trumpeldor added.

Hackett looked back at him and nodded. "Yes, we are glad for that."

When Hackett turned again to watch, Trumpeldor looked down at me and winked.

✦ ✦ ✦

We arrived back at base camp with Beilin's body strapped across the back of his mule. As it turned out, the animal that had been shot in no-man's-land wasn't even his. Beilin simply wanted to complete the task the corps had been assigned and did his best to make sure the delivery was complete.

Everyone at base camp was sad to learn that Beilin was dead but news of our actions at the front heartened most of them. Most—but not all. We prepared Beilin's body for burial, then dug a grave and as the sun was setting we placed him in the ground. But all the while, a faction of our men grumbled and murmured about leaving and returning to Egypt. I didn't like it and I talked to Colonel Patterson about it. He said I shouldn't worry. "They're only reacting to the loss of a friend and comrade. Things will be better tomorrow. You'll see."

However, the next day some of the disgruntled corps members refused to take deliveries to the front lines. "The Turks shoot at us," one of them protested. "And their artillery shells explode at our feet."

"This is war!" someone responded. "What did you expect?"

"No," another said. "It's not war. It's hiding in trenches and executing the man who sticks his head up over the edge."

Trumpeldor was perturbed but unemotional. "You can't go home," he said in a flat, even tone. "If you try, you'll be punished. If you refuse to carry out your orders, you'll be punished. If you attempt to recruit others to join you in your dissent, you'll be punished."

One of them said defiantly, "And who will do the punishing?"

Trumpeldor looked him in the eye. "I will."

Faced with the prospect of confronting Trumpeldor, the men reluctantly acceded to his order and took the next string of mules to the front. That night, though, three of them left camp, slipping away into the darkness. The following morning, when their absence was noticed, Trumpeldor reported them to Colonel Patterson.

Colonel Patterson sent a party to find them, which didn't take long—there was nowhere to go except the areas secured by British troops. Before breakfast, the men were returned to camp bound at the wrist and roped together like criminals to prevent their escape. Colonel Patterson questioned them, then assembled all the men of the Zion Mule Corps and made us watch as the three escapees were flogged by a British sergeant.

After that, no one talked about leaving, but many of our men were uneasy about their circumstance and for some the obedience was but a hollow gesture.

# CHAPTER 12

foz

THOUGH RESISTANCE was much stronger and fighting far more difficult than expected, British troops slowly pushed forward into the interior of the peninsula, steadily making progress after those first difficult weeks. So much so that sentiment swung from the first month's despair that we would be driven into the sea, to the notion that the campaign would succeed beyond original expectations. Those hopes were woefully premature.

After our initial incursion from the coast, the Turks regrouped and pressed hard with a counteroffensive. Though our lines held and prevented them from driving to the coast, the slaughter of British troops was horrible. Our mule teams were pressed into double duty, ferrying supplies to the front and returning with wounded soldiers. Fighting, disease, and poor physical conditions took a toll on our men, too. Though we incurred more sick than wounded, our men did not escape the plight of modern warfare.

As the fighting intensified and our work with it, Colonel Patterson was forced to delegate more and more of the details. He assigned me the task of obtaining medical attention for our men. Though I was the youngest man in the unit, it was my duty to see that any who were wounded or ill were delivered to the British hospital tent and properly enrolled for care.

If the assignment had come to me earlier in our service on the peninsula, I might have been intimidated by being thrust into daily regular contact with the British. They were generally condescending to everyone and particularly ill-tempered to those of us in the Mule Corps, their physicians more so than most. By then, however, I had been thrown into so many uncomfortable positions that I hardly noticed the challenge and plunged headlong into the task of caring for our men.

The British—being ever British—had not changed as much as we and remained as reticent as ever to do much on our behalf, even when our men faced obviously life-threatening injuries. Instead, they offered excuses and complaints about how they were short on medical staff, supplies, and tents. Too short, I learned, to give attention to injured members of a transportation corps. Especially one who was Jewish.

When I pointed out to them that our men were in as much danger as anyone in the trenches, and that the men in the trenches—whom they seemed so intent on lavishing with all manner of care and attention—would all die if we weren't able to do our job, the medical staff became enraged. Lionel Vaughn, the chief physician, was particularly incensed by my remarks and threw me out. "I'll not be dressed down by some impudent little Jew boy," he snarled.

Their calloused disregard for us sent me away that day, but it did not stop me from returning with the sick and wounded. Our men worked hard and endured as much peril as any soldier on the front line. They deserved to be treated on an equal basis and I said so as often as possible. Still, our men received far less attention than British soldiers with similar maladies.

Colonel Patterson complained to the medical corps himself, going above Vaughn to General Hamilton. When that proved futile, he contacted generals and friends in London, lobbying for their assistance. "Men who are sick need to be cordoned off from the others," he argued. "The wounded need proper and immediate attention. They need the treatment and expertise of doctors, not the passing review of an untrained private with a first-aid kit." Colonel Patterson was convinced our men were being treated shabbily because they were Jews and he continued to complain to any who would listen.

When the letters and complaints brought no immediate results, we took matters into our own hands. Colonel Patterson dispatched six men to find a tent large enough to serve as a medical center and sent me to locate cots to fill it. In only a matter of hours, I found a stack of unused cots in a British camp up the beach from our position and commandeered a horse and wagon to carry them.

The men who went in search of a tent returned to base camp about the same time as I. They brought with them a huge canvas roll and a large number of wooden poles, which they hauled using a rope sling rigged between two mules—the mules walking side by side with the load of fabric and poles bundled between them. It was an odd sight and some of the men greeted it with laughter, but they were glad to have the tent and proud of the ingenuity displayed in hauling it. No one asked where they found it, not even Colonel Patterson, but the markings indicated it had been the property of an ANZAC unit—a unit from the Australian and New Zealand Army Corps. I took charge of erecting it and called for volunteers to assist. We had more than enough help, both with the tents and the cots, and were ready for operation by nightfall.

Colonel Patterson continued to send letters and messages about our situation but in the meantime he went over to the British facility and met with Lionel Vaughn to see what arrangements could be made for staffing our facility. A few days later, they sent a meager cache of medical supplies and detailed a doctor to visit our men once each week.

✦ ✦ ✦

As fighting continued to intensify, many of our men were forced to fight to defend themselves as they moved back and forth from the coast to the front with the mules. We'd been armed with rifles since leaving Egypt but had little occasion to use them. That changed as the Ottoman counteroffensive pressed our troops harder and harder. Often when our men arrived at the front they were pressed into duty covering the unloading of the mules and sometimes simply to shore up a position along the British line to keep the Turks from storming through. It wasn't the sort of duty auxiliary units were created to fill, but many of our men had originally wanted to be infantrymen anyway, so they didn't mind the opportunity to stand and fight.

Midway through our campaign on the peninsula, we received reinforcements from Egypt. Most of them were volunteers from the refugee camp but a few were from the United States. They had heard of our exploits and wanted to join us. With our ranks depleted from disease, injury, and death we were glad to have them. At the time of their arrival we were operating at less than half our original strength.

Not long after the reinforcements arrived, I noticed the color of Colonel Patterson's skin had developed an eerie orange cast. He was feverish, too, and often weak. Before long, he was forced to conduct afternoon business from a cot I set up near his desk—a stark contrast to his usual gallant demeanor and can-do attitude. His condition worried me and after a day or two with no improvement I slipped away to the British hospital tent and located Lionel Vaughn.

Dr. Vaughn was in the midst of treating a soldier when I arrived and not at all glad to see me, but as I had brought none of our sick or wounded with me he listened while I described Colonel Patterson's condition. In spite of their difficult introduction, he and Colonel Patterson had become friends and he seemed genuinely concerned.

"Jaundice," he commented as I finished.

That term was new to me and I felt a puzzled frown wrinkle my forehead. "What does that mean?"

"Liver damage, I would imagine," he explained. "Not uncommon for conditions like those we are facing—poor food, excessive heat, not enough water." He turned back to the patient he'd been treating. "Keep him comfortable as best you can. I'll take a look at him when I have time."

I returned to our headquarters tent and reported to Colonel Patterson, telling him what Dr. Vaughn had said. We had little means of making anyone comfortable but I made sure he had plenty of fresh water to drink and gave him a damp cloth to wipe his brow.

Late that afternoon Dr. Vaughn arrived. Colonel Patterson was still reclining on the cot and when Dr. Vaughn saw him the expression on his face turned even more serious than usual. "Jack," he said as he approached Colonel Patterson. "You don't look so good."

Colonel Patterson managed a smile, "Thanks for the encouragement, Lionel." For the first time I noticed how weak he sounded and realized his condition was not good.

Dr. Vaughn remained with him for almost an hour that evening, conducting a thorough physical examination and chatting amicably when he was finished. I brought them tea and did all I could to make their time together as pleasant as possible. We needed Dr. Vaughn's help and I wanted to encourage cooperation between them. They talked at length about acquaintances they found in common, and once or twice I heard them laugh.

As he departed the tent, Dr. Vaughn took me aside, "His condition is serious but if it is as I think, it is also treatable. I'll arrange to have him moved to one of our hospital ships where he can be properly diagnosed. Until then, do your best to see that he remains right where he is. On that cot. No moving around. And keep him as quiet as possible."

I nodded. "Yes, sir. I'll do my best."

Dr. Vaughn stood there a moment, as if thinking, then smiled at me in a gesture much softer than I'd seen from him before. As he turned to leave, he patted me on the shoulder and headed off into the darkness.

The next day, a boat arrived from the *Grantully Castle*, a hospital ship anchored just out of range of the Turkish artillery. Members of the ship's medical staff helped Colonel Patterson onto a stretcher and carried him down to the boat. I grabbed a few things we might need and followed after them, not waiting to be invited. If he was going to the hospital, I was going with him and let myself aboard the boat. No one asked why I was there and Colonel Patterson didn't object.

A crowd of men gathered at water's edge to see us off. Trumpeldor was there, as was Amos and some of the others. They watched while Colonel Patterson's stretcher was secured in place, then gave a salute as the crewmen picked up their oars and prepared to shove off. Moments later, we started across the bay.

On board the ship, Colonel Patterson was taken immediately to an examination facility where he was able to shower and change. Then the doctors began working with him, drawing blood samples and checking his bodily functions. The ship was well-equipped for its purpose but space was tight and there wasn't enough room for me to remain at his side. Consequently, I was left to myself.

142

Because of his rank, Colonel Patterson was also assigned a state-room. I took his belongings there to deposit them, then realized he would not be using it for quite some time. So I availed myself of the facility and took my first shower in what seemed like years. One of the orderlies located clothes for me and I sent my uniform to the laundry. It hadn't been cleaned since we arrived. Later that day, I went to the dining hall and ate a meal the men ashore could never imagine, with fresh bread, real butter, and meat that tasted like meat.

Tests conducted by the ship's doctors confirmed what Dr. Vaughn had suspected. Colonel Patterson's problem was with his liver. No one ever told me exactly what the issue was but they made plans to send him to a hospital in London, so I assumed it was quite serious. I knew how much he valued the men of our corps and was certain that if he were not in grave danger he would have insisted on returning to command them.

After the doctors announced their plans to send him home, I met with Colonel Patterson to discuss the matter and to ask if I might accompany him on the journey. If he wasn't going to return ashore, I didn't want to go back there, either.

"No," he said with a genuine hint of sorrow. "I'm afraid that will be impossible. We must part company for a time." He noticed the tears forming in my eyes and patted the back of my hand. "But don't worry. I will do my best to get back as soon as possible."

The thought of not having him with us weighed heavily on me—almost as heavily as the day when the ship blew up and I thought he'd been killed. I was, however, less emotional this time and managed to choke back the tears without shedding them—a characteristic I attributed to a growing sense of maturity. That evening, I busied myself making him ready for the trip and preparing myself to return ashore to the men.

The next day, I watched as Colonel Patterson was brought from the examination area on a stretcher, then lowered slowly down to one of the small craft and transferred to the SS *Assaye* for the trip to London. As he was taken aboard that ship, I gathered my things and climbed down to one of the boats used for going ashore. When I was seated, the oarsmen manned the oars and we started toward the beach.

As we bobbed across the bay, the reality of Colonel Patterson's absence became more real and intense than I'd allowed myself to sense when he was leaving. From the water I noticed how bare and desolate the peninsula had become. The vegetation we'd seen upon arrival was stripped away and the ground beneath it churned to a dusty brown by our constant activity. Seeing it so sparse and naked, with the great expanse of water surrounding us, my heart was filled with sadness and I longed for our home, the Galilee, and the peaceful farm we'd once known. Knowing that we may never see it again seemed more apparent to me that day than at any time since we'd left.

About halfway to shore, I noticed two sacks of mail lying near the bow or our tiny boat. Months had passed since anyone in our unit received correspondence and I was glad to bring it to them. When we reached the beach and I stepped out to the sand, one of the oarsmen tossed the sacks in my direction and I quickly dragged them out of the reach of incoming waves.

Two men passed by and I directed them to carry the sacks to the headquarters tent. They dutifully obeyed, as if the order had been given by the colonel himself, and I liked the sense of acceptance it gave. Still, I didn't want to seem out of place, so I trudged along after them, my hands full of the gear I'd brought with me to the ship.

The headquarters tent was just as we left it, only now it seemed all the more empty and lifeless without Colonel Patterson there to energize it. I pushed aside the temptation to sit and brood and, instead, turned to the task of sorting the mail. I knew the men would be glad to receive it, so I worked as quickly as possible to prepare it for them.

As I sorted through the envelopes, I noticed three of the letters were addressed to Amos, all of them in the same handwriting. At the sight of it my heart sank. A glance at the return address on the back flap told me what I already knew. The letters were from Dalia. I set them aside, gave the others to a private for distribution to the men, and took Amos' letters for delivery myself.

Amos was delighted to see me and greeted me with a genuine hug. I was glad to see him. News of Colonel Patterson's departure already had reached the men and he was sad to see the colonel go, though not as sad as I. We talked a moment longer, then I handed him the letters from Dalia. His face lit up with a smile and he eagerly ripped open the one with the earliest postmark. I waited while he read it and couldn't help but notice he was grinning from ear to ear.

When he finished with the first letter, I inquired about what she had to say, expecting some news of the camp or of her family. Instead, he brushed me aside with a dismissive wave of his hand and tore open the second envelope. He was immediately absorbed in reading it and from the expression on his face I surmised she was not telling him about the weather or the latest gossip. I lingered a moment longer, hoping for some bit of news or mention of me, then drifted away and started back to the headquarters tent.

As I walked in that direction I realized any hope I might have harbored for Dalia was lost for good. Or at least until this thing she had with Amos had run its course. Whatever feelings I might have for her would have to wait. Amos was my brother. Dalia obviously cared for him in a way she did not for me. In my heart I resolved to keep quiet about my own desires and let the two of them pursue matters between them in peace. And that was that.

✦ ✦ ✦

With Colonel Patterson gone Trumpeldor took command of our unit. I continued to serve in my former position, working as his aide. The men of Zion Mule Corps continued the trek from coast to front, delivering supplies that were sorely needed by the men in the trenches. On one of those trips, some of our men reached the front, unloaded their cargo, and were detained for work as a corpse detail—removing the bodies of dead soldiers and burying them downhill from the trenches. A few of our men were offended and refused. Dead bodies are unclean for us and they took the assignment as an insult.

An argument ensued and the captain in charge of the infantry became infuriated at the supposed insubordination. When he struck one of our men with the back of his hand, a fight erupted. Infantrymen rushed into the fray and when it was over a number of our men were in custody, held at gunpoint on pain of death. They weren't killed, but they were forced to gather corpses from the trenches while others were sent to dig graves.

When they returned, word of their ill treatment spread quickly and reignited the earlier dissatisfaction that had been left simmering since Colonel Patterson's flogging of the men who'd tried to desert months before. Some who joined the corps only to escape conditions in the refugee camp now found new cause to leave.

"The British treat us like slaves," one of them complained.

"I won't go back to the front," another said resolutely. "I'm not leading a string of mules all day only to face humiliation."

"Let them get their own supplies."

"Or die from the lack."

That night, a number of our men disappeared from camp. Trumpeldor sent a squad to search for them, but conditions were far worse than when they'd tried before and the search party returned empty-handed. A month later, we received news that several of the men were back in Egypt. I asked Trumpeldor whether we should request that they be returned to us, but he declined. "Let them go. They wouldn't make it to us in time to be of much help anyway."

His comment struck me as odd and I knew things were not right. Colonel Patterson would never have allowed that sort of conduct to go unchecked and neither would Trumpeldor a few months earlier. That he tolerated it now told me something had changed about our operation. Not long after that I found out just how right I was.

After almost a year of struggle with no real effective result, General Charles Monro arrived on the peninsula. Stern and businesslike, he was a general's general with a blunt, plain-spoken manner that valued honesty and fact, rather than optimism and opinion. In the weeks that followed, General Monro and his staff conducted a thorough review of the Gallipoli Campaign, examining the situation from coast to front line. Shortly thereafter, a major shakeup in British command structure occurred.

As a first step, General Hamilton, who'd held overall command of the operation, was relieved of his position and recalled to London, where his military career quietly came to an end. General Monro took his place.

Not long after that, Monro's responsibility was expanded to include command of all troops operating in the Mediterranean, including those of us from Egypt who'd been under General Maxwell. General Maxwell was sent to Ireland, where he was appointed governor general. No one attributed his removal to poor performance on the peninsula. The campaign wasn't his idea and he'd remained in Egypt the entire time. As I reflected on it later, I wondered if it were not more of an apologetic gesture—tacit acknowledgment of a mistake someone else made at his expense. At any rate, the move to Ireland was seen by everyone as a promotion and Maxwell was supposedly glad to go. Those of us who served in Egypt and on the peninsula could readily understand why.

Almost immediately after taking command, General Monro gave the order for us to withdraw from Gallipoli. News of it came to us one morning as our men prepared for the day's work. A shout went up from them and several broke into a spontaneous dance. Trumpeldor calmed them down long enough to explain that withdrawal would take time to implement and that we would likely be one of the last units to leave. Still, the men were overjoyed with the prospect of returning to Egypt and the refugee camp. The irony of their attitude was not lost on me. Months earlier they'd been eager to leave such squalid conditions. Now they were eager to return.

The operation on Gallipoli was largely a disaster. In the aftermath, some suggested it at least staved off further advance of the Turks in other regions, but while the Turks might have been distracted by our actions, the Germans paid it little attention. While the British were pinned down on Gallipoli, the German army invaded Poland. As troops began to depart the coast, conditions in Europe and the future of the war looked bleak indeed for England and her Allies.

An understanding of that, however, came later when we had time to reflect on our experiences and receive news from other parts of the world. Right then, we were just glad to finally be leaving the peninsula.

For the next two months we continued to supply the front, but our return trips were devoted to hauling back unused arms and light equipment. Some of our men were assigned to wagons and hauled cannons and helped drag the heavy guns. Since that first day when we unloaded the ships at the beach, a temporary harbor had been created that allowed ships to unload with greater ease and efficiency. Now the process was reversed and we assisted with transferring men, equipment, and matériel to much larger ships for the trip home.

Shortly before we were to leave, Trumpeldor assembled the Zion Mule Corps at the base camp and outlined our departure schedule. When he concluded his remarks he ordered the men to slaughter their mules and set fire to the remains. Most were sad for the animals, having grown fond of them after such long and close association, but they understood the need to conserve space aboard the ship. Mules were expendable. Berths on the ships were in short supply. That afternoon, the animals were systematically killed, then cremated in a dozen large fires.

Once the remains of our mules were properly disposed of, we marched in formation to the temporary harbor and boarded a transport ship. Amos and I were together as we made our way up the gangway. When we reached the top, we paused a moment to stand at the rail and gaze one last time at the landscape we were leaving behind.

As we stood there on deck, with the remainder of our men still coming aboard, I thought of how much the past year had changed me and how much we'd all been made different by the experience. And at the thought of that, a sense of pride welled up inside me.

The Gallipoli Campaign had proved a disaster for the British, but it was not a disaster for those of us who served in the Zion Mule Corps. Quite to the contrary, our experience had worked in the opposite direction, creating a core of Jewish men who were trained in fighting, endowed with brilliant leadership skills, and thoroughly at home with army life. Men like Trumpeldor, Nisei Rosenberg, Harry Schoenthal, and Aaron Ben Joseph—all of them able soldiers who'd proved their mettle in the heat of battle. They'd seen the value of military force when properly applied and the weakness of it when woefully used. Yet they'd come through this year of service and its overwhelming challenges with a sense of indomitable determination and a wealth of invaluable experience.

Colonel Patterson had reminded us of our historic fighting heritage—a tradition all but lost in the past two millennia. He had revived it in us and called to mind images of Joshua and David—warrior kings whose bravery knew no bounds—and reminded us of our place in that great and mighty heritage. His confidence in us gave us confidence in ourselves that we could, with God on our side, shape our future and become once again true men of Israel. And though I was the youngest of them all, I was determined to use the things we'd learned to continue Colonel Patterson's work of keeping that tradition alive for our men.

# CHAPTER 13

OUR RETURN VOYAGE across the Mediterranean took three days. The days at sea passed slowly and made the trip seem much longer than it really was, but finally we reached the port in Alexandria. Dalia was there to meet Amos at the dock. I greeted her with a polite smile and a hug, then found a reason to excuse myself and stepped away. Trucks were there to take us back to the army compound and I started toward them. A few paces farther, I glanced over my shoulder for one last look and saw them embrace. I shouldn't have turned back to look—the sight of them wrapped in each other's arms brought only pangs of jealousy deep inside me and made the realization of how alone I really was all the more apparent.

From the docks, we were transported back to the training camp in Gabbari. This time, however, we were assigned to barracks. They were located on the far side of the compound and in well-worn condition but much more comfortable than the tents we'd lived in on the peninsula and the ones we'd known at the camp before. Trumpeldor was given a private building that served as both his quarters and an office. I continued in my role as his aide and assistant.

Most of the men assumed we would be sent to Palestine next, but a week or two after our return to Gabbari, Trumpeldor received a note from General Arthur Lynden-Bell, chief of staff to General Monro, summoning him to Lynden-Bell's office. I went with him.

At that meeting we learned that the Zion Mule Corps was being sent to Ireland to assist Governor General Maxwell and the British army in putting down a revolt by Irish rebels. Trumpeldor was pleasant while we were in General Lynden-Bell's office, but as we left I could see he was rather disconcerted.

"What's happening in Ireland?" I asked.

"Ireland is a British possession. They want to be independent."

"What's wrong with that?"

"Nothing, I suppose. Except the British don't want them to go."

"That's what they're fighting about?"

"It's a little more complicated," he explained. "Religious, mostly."

My forehead wrinkled in a frown. "Religious?"

"Ireland is divided. Half the people are Protestant, half are Catholic."

"What's the difference?"

"I'm not sure."

"Aren't they all Christian?"

"Yes," he nodded with an amused grin. "They're all Christian."

"Then what are they fighting about?"

"I don't know," he shrugged. "Maybe you should talk to someone who can answer your questions."

"Like who?"

"I don't know," Trumpeldor shrugged again. "Maybe a priest."

"A priest? A Catholic priest?" I'd never even *seen* a Catholic priest, and the thought of talking to one seemed strange. "Where would I find one of those?"

"I don't know, but I think the British have a chaplain with their army. Maybe he could help you understand."

"He would talk to me?"

"I suppose so," Trumpeldor laughed. "He's a chaplain, not one of their regular army officers."

This was still a strange notion to me. "So, they don't mind? I can just walk up to him?"

Trumpeldor grinned. "Yes, you can just walk up to him."

We walked in silence a little farther, then I returned to the conversation to the topic I knew would be on everyone's mind. "I don't like the idea of going to Ireland. I'm not even sure where it is. We should be going to Palestine instead."

"We have orders to Ireland," Trumpeldor said in a resolute tone. He was an army man, thoroughly versed in the army way and committed to the army life.

"Do *you* like the idea of fighting the Irish?"

"No. But we took an oath."

"We signed up to defend Palestine," I argued. "To take back our land. To regain our farms. Not travel around with the British army, carrying their luggage for them. If we go off to Ireland, we'll *never* get back home."

Trumpeldor didn't reply but I knew he felt much the same way. Going to Ireland was a bad idea. Our home was in Palestine.

When we arrived back at the office, Trumpeldor directed me to assemble the men for a meeting. I passed the word down the chain of command and we gathered in the same field where we used to march when we were in training. Though our unit had expanded to as many as six hundred fifty during the campaign, we now were down to less than three hundred. Assembled in groups of fifty, they looked lean and weathered but disciplined and orderly. I was terribly proud of them.

Trumpeldor stood in their midst, with me at his side, and in a short statement announced the decision to send us to Ireland. "Right now, we are scheduled to depart Alexandria in two weeks. Make your plans accordingly."

The men were silent but I could see from the expressions on their faces that they had many questions. Before anyone could approach him, however, Trumpeldor turned away and started toward the office. I was left to field questions.

Most of the men felt the same as I about going to Ireland and it was difficult to deliver the British position with authority, but I did my best even though it was horribly inadequate. When I couldn't answer their inquiries with the definiteness they wanted, the men turned away in disgust, murmuring among themselves. That evening, more than a few disappeared from camp and never returned.

+ + +

Trumpeldor had been an important figure in my life—the first of several whose influence would set the course of my future—and I had learned from Patterson the necessity of loyalty and honor. I wanted to serve Trumpeldor faithfully, but he was thoroughly committed to following the army's rigid structure of command and control. Had he been present, Colonel Patterson would have echoed that same sentiment. An order had been given from our commanding officer directing us to deploy to Ireland. That order had to be obeyed. I, however, was convinced in my heart that we should be headed for Palestine, not Ireland, and that we should avoid going elsewhere at all costs.

Still, I didn't understand much about the situation in Ireland and so, while we reluctantly worked on plans for deployment, I followed Trumpeldor's earlier suggestion and went in search of a British chaplain. I found Rev. Neville Stuart in a makeshift chapel near the British officers' quarters and introduced myself, hoping to learn from him more details about the conflict to which we were being sent.

Rev. Stuart responded to my bumbling question about the Irish rebellion. "It's a rather complicated affair. But I'll try to simplify it for you." He paused to clear his throat. "The Irish were once a free and independent people. Then about the year 1100, King Henry II led an army that invaded the island, and after that we've pretty much controlled it, top to bottom, until recently."

"What happened?"

"From the beginning, the Irish didn't like being ruled but there wasn't much they could do about it. Lately, they've been able to muster strong local support for independence."

"Is that a bad thing?" It didn't seem so to me.

"Not really, I suppose," he answered in an honest but tentative way. "Except that the Irish are divided among themselves. Half of them are Catholic and half are Protestant."

"That's another part I don't understand. What's the difference?"

"Well," Rev. Stuart smiled, "when you boil it down to the nub of the matter, there's not much real difference. Primarily, it's a disagreement about tradition."

"Tradition?"

Rev. Stuart nodded. "They favor one tradition. We favor another."

His response left me puzzled. "What does that have to do with independence?"

"The ones who favor the Catholic tradition want to be free. The ones who favor the Protestant tradition want to remain part of the United Kingdom."

I finally understood. "Oh, that's a lot like what we face in Palestine. Some of us are Jewish. Some of us are Arab."

He nodded, "Yes, I suppose it is. After a fashion."

What I learned from Rev. Stuart convinced me we should have nothing to do with the fight in Ireland, and by the time I reached the barracks I'd made up my mind. Duty or no duty to serve Trumpeldor, I would do my best to convince the others not to participate.

+ + +

With the windows and doors open, our barracks enjoyed a cool breeze most of the day. As a result, many of our men spent their free time inside, seated on their bunks, talking or playing cards. After their long and arduous service in Gallipoli, everyone needed time to relax, recover, and heal.

When I returned from meeting with Rev. Stuart I found Nisei Rosenberg playing Skat—a card game we picked up from the British, which they picked up from German prisoners—on a bunk with Harry Schoenthal and Aaron Ben Joseph.

Rosenberg glanced up as I approached. "What's bothering you?" I assumed the look on my face gave away the thoughts in my mind.

"We can't go to Ireland."

Rosenberg looked perplexed. "I thought Trumpeldor said we were going?"

"He did. And he says we have orders and those orders must be obeyed. But I just talked with one of the British chaplains, and he told me more about what's going on over there. This fight in Ireland is not something we want to get involved with."

Joseph looked up from the cards he was holding. "Why not?"

"For one thing, if we go over there, we will never get back to Palestine."

"I've been saying that since they made the announcement," Schoenthal said sarcastically. "Fighting the Turks, yes. Fighting the Irish, no."

"What convinced you?" Rosenberg asked. "What did that chaplain say?"

"He said the Irish are fighting the British only because the Irish want their independence from the United Kingdom. They just want the right to determine their future for themselves rather than having it dictated to them by officials in London."

"He told you that?"

"Yes," I nodded.

"Rather strong language coming from a member of the British army," Schoenthal noted.

"Sounds like the same thing we want," Joseph added.

My eyes opened wide. "Exactly."

Rosenberg glanced down at the cards that had been played. "Aren't the Irish fighting among themselves over religious issues?"

"Yes," I replied. "And that is also very similar to the situation we face at home."

Schoenthal had a mischievous look. "So, you're saying if we went over there and helped the British, we'd be fighting against a group of people who are a lot like us?"

I knew he wasn't completely serious but I used the moment to say what I was thinking. "I'm saying, as far as fighting for their freedom goes, they may not be Jewish, but they are our brothers in the cause of freedom. We can't fight them."

"Listen to him," Joseph chided. "Spends a few minutes with a Protestant chaplain and the kid becomes a Jewish radical."

I hated that reference—calling me a kid. They noticed my reaction and Schoenthal nudged me on the shoulder. "Relax, live a little longer. Then tell us what we need to do."

"Yoel is right," Rosenberg said in my defense. "We are a lot like the Irish."

Schoenthal arched an eyebrow in a skeptical expression. "How do you figure that?"

"Look around." Rosenberg gestured with a sweep of his arm. "We've come to the British for help, for protection. We begged them to let us participate in their war, hauled freight for them on the most forsaken scrap of ground of earth, and now we are sitting in a British army camp waiting for them to send us somewhere else. The British might yet help us reclaim some portion of Palestine, but if they do, they will be right there with us the entire time. And eventually we will have to struggle against them ourselves, just as the Irish are attempting to do. One day, we will have to fight to break free of British domination."

Joseph seemed unconvinced. "You think if they help us take back our land in Palestine, they will somehow get control of Palestine for themselves."

"They have a history of occupying an area and not leaving until forced out," Rosenberg elaborated. "Just look at what happened in the United States. And India. And all those ports they control in Asia. Their colonies in Africa. They come with a friendly smile but then forget to go back home."

Schoenthal looked over at him. "So what do we do?"

"We should refuse to deploy to Ireland," Rosenberg said as he played a card. "Keep ourselves organized but remain in Egypt. See what we can do from here."

"That won't be much," Schoenthal growled.

"Would be more than we could do from Ireland," Joseph noted.

"You have a point," Schoenthal conceded. "But what about the oath we took?"

"We'll have to resign," Rosenberg replied.

"But stay together," I added quickly. "We'll have to stay together."

"They'll run us out of here and send us back to the refugee camp," Joseph commented.

"We can still train and march on our own," I suggested. "Everyone knows the drill."

Rosenberg looked over at me. "Okay, we'll talk to the rest of the men about what to do. But you get to tell Trumpeldor."

"The others might not all agree," I cautioned.

"We can put it to a vote." Rosenberg threw down his cards and rolled off the bunk. "Let's get to work. We don't have long to make a decision."

From the barracks, I walked over to Trumpeldor's office. He was seated at his desk when I entered. He looked over at me as I took a seat across from him.

"Something on your mind?" Again I realized the look on my face gave away far too much.

For the next few minutes I recounted the things I'd learned from Rev. Stuart, then I told him about my conversation with Rosenberg and the others. He wasn't pleased that I went to them without coming to him first.

"You would have told me not to do it," I explained.

"Perhaps. But maybe not."

"Rosenberg and the others are polling the men," I added. "To gauge their sentiment."

Trumpeldor cut his eyes in my direction. "The men are in rebellion?"

The suggestion of a rebellion caught me off guard. "No, they are simply asking around to find out how the men feel."

Trumpeldor turned away and sighed. "I suppose as an auxiliary unit they have that right."

We sat in silence a moment with Trumpeldor staring out the window and me quietly in the chair across from him. Then I said, "When I told you before I didn't want to go to Ireland, you said we had orders."

"Yes," Trumpeldor nodded. "I did say that."

"But that's not how you feel, is it?"

Trumpeldor picked up a pencil from his desk and absent-mindedly drummed it on the desktop. "Working on plans for actual deployment makes it less...attractive."

"So, what do we do?"

"Give the men a day or two to decide. Then we'll gather them together and let them decide."

+ + +

After breakfast two mornings later, we gathered on the field and Trumpeldor explained our predicament. "Some of you want to follow our orders and go with the British army to Ireland. Some of you object. Enough of you have objected that I think we should vote. We'll do that now, by show of hands."

"No!" Rosenberg shouted from the back of the group. Everyone watched while he shoved his way to the front, then in a strong voice said, "We should do it by secret ballot." Laugher teetered through the crowd as everyone had expected a long speech.

"Okay," Trumpeldor chuckled. "We'll do it by secret ballot." He dispatched me to the office to prepare paper for the vote, while everyone else waited in the hot sunshine.

A few minutes later I returned with paper and pencils and we passed them among the men. "Mark your vote yes or no," Trumpeldor directed. "'Yes' if we should go. 'No' if we should refuse and stay here."

One by one, each man marked his vote and brought the paper to me. I gathered them in a pile until everyone had finished, then began sorting them into two stacks. Very quickly it became obvious, the vote against going to Ireland was going to prevail.

We counted the votes, then recounted them to make sure, and made a final tally. Trumpeldor announced the results. "The 'no' vote won. We stay here." A cheer went up from the men. Almost everyone had voted against going to Ireland.

After the votes were counted and the results announced, Trumpeldor and I went to see General Monro. He was standing near his desk as we entered, but after he and Trumpeldor exchanged salutes he took a seat. Trumpeldor sat across from him. I stood near the door, listening and watching while Trumpeldor told him about the sentiment among our men and the vote they'd taken.

General Monro's response was predictable. "Captain Trumpeldor, you and your men have your orders. You are expected to obey them or suffer the consequences."

"Sir, the Zion Mule Corps is an independent unit. We are not British conscripts."

General Monro didn't like that response. "May I remind you, your unit was expected to serve for the duration of the conflict?"

"Yes," Trumpeldor noted, "but Ireland is not a member of the Central Powers. Going to Ireland is an internal civil matter for the United Kingdom. And, if I might add, sir, a religiously charged one at that. Having Jews present among a conflict between Protestants and Catholics would only make matters worse."

General Monro gestured with a wave of his hand. "Very well, very well. If your men don't want to go to Ireland, their only option is to resign and be deactivated from service with the British army."

"We would prefer to remain a unit and return to Palestine to retake the land seized from us by the Arabs."

"I'm afraid that is not possible," General Monro argued. "At the present time, we have no plans for taking Palestine. Your choice is Ireland, or deactivation."

"Very well, then." Trumpeldor stood. "I shall inform the men that they are released from service to the British army." He offered General Monro a salute, then reached across the desk and shook his hand. "Thank you for the opportunity to serve."

"And thank you for your service," General Monro replied without bothering to stand. "I didn't see you in action but I've heard and seen numerous reports of your work. Your men did a fine job."

And just like that, our time in the British army came to an end. I had expected it to be a moment of great elation, but as we walked away from General Monro's office I felt hollow and empty, as if a part of me were missing. Trumpeldor assured me it was only natural. After all, we'd been doing this for almost two years and life with the British had become part of us. Still, I was sadder than I expected.

Late that afternoon, Trumpeldor assembled the men one more time and told them of General Monro's decision. Deployment to Ireland was our only option. Otherwise, our service with the British army was ended.

Some of the men were glad to be released and departed immediately for the refugee camp. Others prepared to travel north in hopes of crossing the border and making their way back home. A number of us remained behind, satisfied at the decision not to go to Ireland but dissatisfied with any of the available options. Returning to Palestine seemed all but impossible, in spite of the determination of a few to try. Disbanding and returning to civilian life seemed like a waste of the training and experience we'd received. And still there was the problem of our land. It was taken from us by Arabs and occupied by them against our will. We wanted it back and were eager to do something—anything—that might bring us closer to making that a reality.

Sometime during the next week, we were ordered to vacate the barracks. Those of us who were still there packed our belongings and started up the road to the refugee camp. By then our places in the barracks had been assigned to others, but Amos and I found a bunk that was empty and took it for ourselves.

A day or two later, after everyone was settled in the refugee camp, Trumpeldor assembled the remaining members of Zion Mule Corps and we began training together as a unit. I was no longer content merely to be an aide and requested a position in one of the platoons. Trumpeldor agreed and I began working as one of the men. Amos and I were in the same platoon, though different squads.

As we trained, we talked among ourselves about what would happen next. Some wanted to slip away from camp and make their way to the border, then sneak across to Palestine on our own. Our ranks were severely depleted, numbering less than two hundred fifty on most days. Even so, sneaking that many men across the border, unnoticed, would have been a monumental task the reality of which gradually became apparent.

Finding no means within ourselves of reaching Palestine, someone raised the question of whether there were people outside Egypt who might help. Rosenberg looked over at me. "Have you heard from Colonel Patterson since he left Gallipoli?"

"Only a letter to say that he reached London and was feeling better."

"I think it's time to contact him," Rosenberg said.

"Maybe Jabotinsky could help, too," Schoenthal offered.

"He's too arrogant," Trumpeldor grumbled. "Probably sulked his way back to Russia by now."

"I don't think so," Joseph said. "Last I heard, he was still in London stirring up trouble. We should write him."

"We don't have an address," Schoenthal said.

"What about Patterson?" Rosenberg turned in my direction again.

"Do you have an address for him?"

"Yes," I replied. "I think it's on the letter he sent me."

"We would need some help with writing a letter," Trumpeldor said. "I'm not good at that sort of thing and my handwriting is terrible."

Amos, who'd been listening quietly, spoke up. "I'll help write it if someone will tell me what to say."

While they worked on the letter, I ran back to our barracks and searched through a backpack for Colonel Patterson's letter. I found it without much difficulty and returned to find that writing the letter had become a group effort with everyone offering their suggestions. It rambled a bit, but talked about our desire to remain together as a fighting unit and return to Palestine to reclaim our land. We were not interested in continuing as a transportation corps but as a fighting unit. At the insistence of Schoenthal, we told him about Jabotinsky, that he was in London, too, and went there to advocate for the creation of a Jewish Legion—the kind of fighting force we wanted to become. Finally, we suggested the two of them might work together and, regardless of whether that collaboration proved profitable, asked if Colonel Patterson would help us achieve our goal of reaching Palestine.

The return address on Colonel Patterson's letter to me was a general address the British used for civilians sending mail to soldiers whose exact location was not known to the public. I folded the letter, sealed the back, and wrote the address on the front. Then I posted the letter with the outgoing mail, and we resigned ourselves to awaiting a response.

FRIENDS OF ZION: *Patterson & Wingate*

# CHAPTER 14

foz

UPON HIS RETURN to London from Gallipoli, Colonel Patterson spent several weeks in a hospital receiving treatment for damage to his liver. When he recovered enough to move around on his own he was discharged to a convalescent facility to continue healing. Frances, his wife, and Bryan, their son, visited him regularly but were not able to remain at the facility on a permanent basis. He would rather have recovered at home, surrounded by family and friends, but understood the need for more immediate care than could be obtained under those circumstances.

If his physical needs were apparent to him, the irony of his situation was not lost, either. He had gone to Egypt in part to avoid the horrors of the fighting in Europe. Instead, he ended up in Gallipoli, where he participated in some of the worst fighting, under the most intolerable conditions, of the entire war. Images of what he saw there were etched in his mind and continued to trouble him long after the fighting ended.

For much of his time in the hospital, when he closed his eyes all he saw were the wounded—some of them men from the Zion Mule Corps—as they returned from the front draped over the backs of our mules, straggling on foot, carried along by their comrades. Awful wounds with blood oozing from limb and abdomen. Those with the least injury groaning for help. Others too far gone to raise a whimper.

As his physical strength returned, he had wanted to talk to Frances about the fighting, to tell her what he'd seen and describe it for her in great detail—to let her know just how awful it was everywhere and not just in Europe—but each time he thought of speaking, the images returned with such force and effect, he had been unable to tell her how he really felt.

After his transfer to the convalescent facility, he grew more at ease with the memories and he found that he could mention one or two incidents at a time without becoming upset. At the same time, the emotional release he found in talking about the campaign produced a positive effect on his recovery and encouraged him to talk more, which he readily did.

During one of their regular visits, while Bryan played on the floor, Colonel Patterson looked over at Frances and related with no particular prompting, "The Zion Mule Corps served well in Gallipoli. All of the men rose to the task in a most commendable way, but some of them distinguished themselves in bravery. They did all they were asked to do and more."

"I'm sure they gave their best," she said, hoping he would continue.

"We had a few who were a bit of a disciplinary problem, I suppose." His voice trailed away as images of flogging the deserters came to mind and he relived each lash as it struck their bodies. Of all the things he'd seen and done, that was one of the most difficult to accept. "But," he continued after a moment, "most were as brave as any soldier with whom I've ever served. And even the ones who...gave us trouble made good soldiers in the end."

"I'm sure you did only as much as you had to do."

"It was a difficult time under..." He hesitated, wanting to say more but wasn't sure he should. "Under...difficult circumstances. I think we all...did our best."

"But?" she urged in a voice that anticipated there was more.

Colonel Patterson looked her in the eye. "The intelligence was... completely erroneous. The planning was wrong." The words came easier now. "And from the action I saw at the front, the strategy was as flawed as any we've attempted in this war. The enemy was ten times stronger than reported. Their cannon were better placed. They were better-equipped and far better supplied. We couldn't even disembark when we arrived because a beachhead hadn't been established."

Frances, who'd encouraged him to talk, now looked concerned. "Have you spoken with anyone about this?"

"No, of course not."

"You mustn't, you know."

"Yes. I know," he agreed. "But I must tell someone and for now that someone is you."

She smiled, "Good. That is as it should be." She reached over and took his hand. "Now tell me about the day you arrived."

For the next thirty minutes, Colonel Patterson related some of what happened. How we waited off the coast in the ship for ten days and even when we went ashore and were bombarded by enemy artillery. He told her about the ship that exploded, how he narrowly escaped it, and the trenches. The awful trenches that saved lives and yet were such miserable holes.

✦ ✦ ✦

A few days later, Colonel Patterson received a visit from Edward Davis, the man who accompanied him earlier on his tour of the western front in Europe. By then promoted to the rank of Major, Davis worked at the Committee of Imperial Defense, a vital part of the War Office.

Colonel Patterson was glad to see him and at first thought Davis' visit was merely a social call, a friend dropping by to wish him well and encourage him in his recovery.

"Oh?" Colonel Patterson responded, sitting up straight. "What's the matter?"

"We've just received word that Lord Kitchener has been killed."

The news struck Colonel Patterson hard. Lord Kitchener, the first Earl of Kitchener, was Herbert Kitchener, a young officer in the Royal Engineers, when Patterson met him. He'd been serving with a mapping expedition in Palestine and had returned to London only briefly following a spate of unrest in the region. Patterson had been enthralled by Kitchener's tales of life in Jerusalem, Joppa, and Jericho.

"What happened?"

"Lord Kitchener was on his way to Russia for a series of diplomatic meetings when his ship struck a mine. He and six hundred others who were on board perished at sea."

"At sea?" Patterson's brow was furrowed in a frown. "You mean they weren't killed in the explosion?"

"If that were only so," Davis sighed. "I'm afraid they were not so lucky as to die that quickly." He paused to take a breath. "It seems they all drowned." He glanced away, his eyes darkened with a look of anguish. "The water must have been terribly cold."

"What sort of talks was he attempting to conduct?"

"Diplomatic discussions. You know. The kind that are all hush-hush if one inquires directly on the matter, but later you learn everyone has known all along."

Patterson nodded. "The Russians want out of the war."

"And they may very well get what they wish." Davis gave the colonel a tight-lipped smile. "But you didn't hear that from me."

"Has his body been found?" Colonel Patterson asked, returning to the subject.

"No. A few who were on board the ship managed to survive. Though I have no idea how. One of them reported seeing Lord Kitchener floating for a time, but the water was too cold for them to last long and after a short while he simply slipped from sight." He looked over at Patterson. "I doubt he'll ever be found."

Colonel Patterson was silent a moment and then said quietly, "I knew Kitchener."

"Yes." Davis nodded. "I remembered you were acquainted with him, which is why I came to tell you in person—before you heard it in the news. We haven't released it to the papers yet."

"I appreciate that. You were always very considerate."

"I heard you were here," Davis continued. "Been wanting to see you, just never seemed to have the time." He had a sheepish look. "Army life, you know. Sorry my visit has to be under these circumstances."

"Would that no one ever receives such news again. But in as much as that is not likely to occur, I should always be glad to receive the news from a friend, rather than a stranger."

The room fell silent again. Then Davis spoke up. "How was your duty with the Zion Mule Corps? I saw that you were seconded to them, but that campaign wasn't part of my responsibility, so I didn't see any of the reports. I heard the campaign went rather badly, though."

"My service with the Zion Mule Corps was an honor and a privilege. They performed far beyond all expectations. And not merely in hauling freight. Many of them were pressed into combat on more than one occasion and they fought with honor, dignity, and bravery."

"I heard the fighting came to just about everyone over there."

Patterson looked over at him. "It was bad, Edward. The worst I've ever seen."

"I understand General Monro took one look at it and ordered a withdrawal."

Patterson wanted to continue on the topic, to tell Davis all he had seen and how angry he felt over the way the situation had been handled by his superiors, but he remembered Francis' warning and chose to avoid saying more. Instead, he took a deep breath and said, "I'm not sure what happened after I left. I haven't received much news since they brought me here. I know they departed from Gallipoli, of course, and arrived in Egypt where they were disbanded. But as to the details, I have not heard."

"There was talk at one time about sending them to Ireland."

Colonel Patterson shook his head. "That would have been a bad idea. There's enough trouble in Ireland with the Catholics and Protestants. No need to add a Jewish transportation unit to the mix."

"Perhaps that's what others concluded," Davis suggested.

"Yes," Patterson nodded. "Perhaps so." Then it was his turn to change the subject. "Who will replace Lord Kitchener?"

"Looks like Lord Derby will get the appointment. Do you know him?"

"Met him once. What do you think of him?" He was certain Davis cared little for the man but wanted to hear his response.

"I'm...I'm not sure," Davis replied awkwardly.

Patterson glanced over at him with a smile. "Not much support for the appointment among the ranks?"

"To be blunt, most think he's rather...weak. But we'll see. He may surprise us all."

"Let us hope he does."

✦ ✦ ✦

The conversation with Davis left Patterson in a brooding, down-cast mood that lasted into the afternoon. Unable to endure it any longer, he did what he'd always done for relief and went out for a walk on the grounds of the convalescent facility. As he strolled across the well-manicured lawn with its neatly trimmed bushes and towering trees, he thought of Kitchener, the sinking of his ship, and imagined what it must have been like as he fell into the water, knowing he would not survive.

In many respects, his friendship with Kitchener had been an odd association. One man born of privilege and on his way to the heights of military command. The other, a young man of much lowlier means, working to make his own way. Back then, when they both were young men and Kitchener still was early in his career, the differences hadn't seemed so great and in spite of their unlikely meeting, they'd become quite good friends. As they grew older, however, and the disparity of their positions became more pronounced, they drifted apart. They remained in contact, never completely losing touch, each watching the other from a distance as their lives unfolded.

Remembering those days from so long ago brought to mind Patterson's childhood and with it came memories of his father. The irregular relationship they had...weathered. The checkered past they shared. The mother he never knew. And the mystery that enshrouded them both.

One good thing that came from his earliest childhood years was the stories his father told. Stories from the Old Testament that made heroes of the faith come alive in a form as vivid as any he'd ever known. It was those stories that had ignited an interest in the ancient history of Israel and given him a deep and abiding affection for the Jewish people. An affinity that sealed his commitment to Christianity and made him a thorough-going, though nonpublic, Christian Zionist.

As he continued his stroll around the grounds, Colonel Patterson's mind moved on to memories of the Zion Mule Corps. He thought of how he'd decided to go to Egypt to hit up his old friend Maxwell for a position in the war. He'd gone not knowing of a specific opening and had found the Zion Mule Corps ready and waiting. As if God had destined him as their leader. Because of his obedience in making the trip, he'd been in a position to assume command of the unit. And not just any unit, but a Jewish unit—a Jewish army. The first assembled for combat in over two thousand years. *Not many men in human history have had the opportunity to command the army of Israel.* And none of them Gentile Christians.

Remembering the corps and the men who served it filled Patterson with a sense of pride. Not in himself and his own accomplishments, but in the men—the way they'd grown and the things they had accomplished together. No, they had not singlehandedly driven the Turks from the Gallipoli peninsula and brought the Ottoman Empire to its knees. But they had applied themselves completely to the task at hand and in the process had been transformed from a band of civilians with only dreams of military exploits into a military unit capable of making those dreams a reality.

The men of the Zion Mule Corps had come far, much further than anyone had thought possible, and by the time Patterson had completed a circuit of the grounds, his thoughts had moved on to the future. By the time he reached the steps to return to his room, his mood had changed. The gloom that lingered over him before was gone and he was wondering what would become of the men he'd trained and whether there was more to their story than had yet been told.

✦ ✦ ✦

A week or so later, Colonel Patterson received the letter from Trumpeldor. He read it with excitement, glad to hear the men still were together, and with interest, especially the part about continuing the Zion Mule Corps as a fighting unit. The suggestion that he contact Jabotinsky, however, left him wondering what to do.

Patterson had heard of Jabotinsky—anyone interested in Jewish history and affairs would have known his name—but he had never met the man and hadn't a clue how to locate him.

"London is a big place," he whispered aloud. "How could one find someone in such a place?"

Then he remembered Edward Davis. As a major and member of the War Office staff, he had access to hundreds of directors and countless intelligence reports. Surely he or someone in his office would know how to locate a man like Jabotinsky who, by reputation, was an outspoken advocate of Zionism.

That afternoon, Patterson placed a call to Davis and told him what he was trying to do. Davis, like Patterson, knew very little about Jabotinsky. "I can't promise anything," he added, "but I'll see what I can turn up."

Two days later, Davis arrived at the convalescent facility. Patterson ushered him to a chair in the building's front parlor, then took a seat across from him.

"Jabotinsky," Davis began, "is a Russian Jew who works as a journalist for a newspaper in Moscow. The paper is known as *Russkiya Vedomosti*. As you probably know, he is an ardent Zionist advocate."

"I was aware of that," Patterson nodded. "Why is he in London?"

"He was in Egypt covering the Turkish call for Jihad. General Maxwell, however, mentioned him in several reports filed regarding his meetings with Joseph Trumpeldor. I believe you know Trumpeldor."

"Yes." The mention of the name brought a smile to Patterson's face. "I know Captain Trumpeldor quite well, but I didn't realize Jabotinsky was associated with him, too."

"The reports indicate the two of them—Trumpeldor and Jabotinsky—originally came up with the Jewish corps idea as a unit that would return to Palestine and fight to reclaim their land."

Patterson nodded again. "They all wanted to do that."

"General Maxwell informed them we had no current plans regarding Palestine and offered them a slot as a transportation corps. Trumpeldor was interested and went to work recruiting volunteers. Jabotinsky rejected the idea and came here to agitate for a legion of Jewish soldiers that would serve as a genuine fighting force."

"Has he made any progress here?"

"Not that I can tell."

"Any idea where he's staying?"

"The Guardian Hotel on Church Street. Are you interested in seeing him?"

"Seems like an interesting man. Thought it might be a good idea to contact him and see what he has to say. Any reason why I shouldn't?"

"As I think you know, the Zion Mule Corps has been deactivated."

"Yes, we discussed that the other day. But apparently the idea of a Jewish fighting unit remains alive."

"We have not flagged Jabotinsky as a problem," Davis noted, "but be careful. There is very little support for a Jewish corps of any kind and strong opposition to an armed fighting unit."

"I'm sure I could give you a list of most of the opponents."

"And they know you, too."

"What does that mean?"

"You've become known in certain circles as a troublemaker."

Patterson was perplexed. "Troublemaker?"

"Yes."

"How so? All I've ever done is simply perform the duties of my assignment."

"Not everyone sees it that way."

"And why not?"

"Those requests you put in from Gallipoli for hospital equipment and supplies did not set well here. Your suggestion that the delay in response was due to Whitehall's anti-Semitic sentiments made you some enemies."

"I never accused anyone of anything," Patterson argued. "I merely raised a few questions. If they'd done a better job planning the logistics of that campaign, I wouldn't have been forced to ask."

"Well, no one cared for the remarks. And I wouldn't allow myself the luxury of commenting on the Gallipoli Campaign, either. Most in London want to simply forget it ever happened."

"Which only proves my point."

"I understand," Davis nodded. "But I'm your friend, and as a friend I'm saying go slow on the idea of a Jewish Legion."

Patterson was thoroughly angry by then. "The Jews still are God's chosen people." He looked toward the window, avoiding eye contact with Davis as he spoke. "He hasn't forgotten them."

"I know," Davis agreed. "We've discussed it many times. But none of that matters to the people in power at the War Department. Some would trade half the colonies for a victory right now."

Right then Patterson couldn't have cared less about the war. His mind was only on the Jews and the issues that mattered most to them. "The Jews have been trying to return to Palestine now for almost fifty years. And not a single nation has helped them."

"I suspect they've been trying longer than that," Davis noted.

"Yes, but I mean this latest concerted effort," Patterson explained.

"Look," Davis said in a tone of finality. "I understand your point of view. I respect your point of view. I agree with most of it. But at the War Office, returning the Jewish people to Palestine is not a priority. Most of us are focused on surviving this war. And I will tell you, Colonel, that outcome is by no means certain."

✦ ✦ ✦

When Davis was gone, Patterson wrote a letter to Jabotinsky introducing himself, describing the letter he received from Trumpeldor, and asking Jabotinsky to come to the convalescent center for a visit. Four days later, Patterson and Jabotinsky met in the lobby of the main building, then went for a walk around the lawn at the center.

"I understand you are interested in forming a Jewish Legion."

"And I am sure you know there is no support for such a unit among your ministers and officials in the War Office."

"They seem to see no need for it."

"That is because they have no strategy for Palestine. They are focused only on Europe, the traditional site of their wars."

"It's also the place where they live."

"And Palestine is the place where we live," Jabotinsky added.

"I thought you were from Russia?"

"I am. But Palestine is where my heart lives." They walked a little farther, then Jabotinsky continued, "When I was a teenager, living in Russia, the Russian gangs attacked our neighborhood. The older people did nothing and forbid us from responding, but we were angry and wanted to fight back. When the gangs returned, we ignored what we had been told and met them in the streets. The next night, we went to the neighborhood where the gang members lived and attacked them. After that, they didn't come to our neighborhood anymore." He looked over at Patterson. "That is the life of a Jew in Europe. And it will be the life of a Jew in Palestine. We only want to reclaim the property seized by Arab gangs. That is all. And if we do that...if we fight back, they will leave us alone."

"That certainly is the way Israel did it in the past."

"You are familiar with the stories of the Torah."

"Yes."

"I have heard that about you. Some of our people have relatives who served in the Zion Mule Corps. They gave a good report of you."

"I was honored to serve them." Patterson looked over at him. "I understand you and Trumpeldor came up with the idea of the corps together."

"We had the idea for a Jewish fighting unit. A Jewish Legion. General Maxwell was the one who turned it into the Mule Corps."

"And you didn't care for that idea."

"Asking a Jew to serve in a mule corps is an insult."

"How is that?"

"In Yiddish, the word for mule is very close to the word for donkey, which is an insulting term to us."

"But every army has a transportation corps that relies on animals of varying kinds."

"Trumpeldor made that argument." Jabotinsky gestured dismissively. "I still want nothing to do with the mules."

They talked through the afternoon and as Jabotinsky prepared to depart, Patterson asked if he was free to meet again the following day. "I am glad to talk with you, Colonel Patterson, but coming here takes me away from my primary task."

"I'm not talking about meeting here."

"Then where?"

"I'd rather not say just yet, but if you are free and the idea I have works out, could I pick you up at your hotel?"

"I suppose."

"Good. I will call you at the hotel by midmorning to let you know whether things can be arranged."

# CHAPTER 15

foz

THE NEXT DAY, Patterson collected Jabotinsky at the Guardian Hotel and rode with him to Parliament, where they met with Leo Amery, a member of the House of Commons. Amery was seated at the desk in his office when they arrived. He stood as Patterson and Jabotinsky entered.

Amery and Patterson first met in Africa during the Boer War, where Amery worked as a war correspondent for the *London Times*. He mentioned that as he introduced Jabotinsky, telling Amery that Jabotinsky was a fellow journalist. The two of them chatted a moment on the topic of reporting and journalism, then Amery inquired of Patterson's health. He was aware that Patterson had recently returned from the Gallipoli Campaign and that he continued to deal with the physical toll that tour of duty had taken. He nodded politely as Patterson deftly responded, then said, "Well, all that is past us now." Amery moved behind the desk and took a seat. "Not much point in dredging it up again. Please," he said, pausing to direct them. "Have a seat."

Patterson was tempted to tell Amery right then and there just how much of an unmitigated disaster the entire Gallipoli affair had been, and how many of their men had died because of it, but that was not his purpose in arranging the meeting, so as he and Jabotinsky took a seat, he chose to avoid the topic. Instead, he used the moment to turn the conversation toward the reason they had come. "One very bright spot in that campaign," he began, "was the exemplary service of the Zion Mule Corps."

"Your battalion?" Amery asked.

"Yes. Joseph Trumpeldor and I commanded them."

"That was a transportation unit, I believe," Amery noted.

"Yes," Patterson acknowledged, "but they were armed and fought with bravery on numerous occasions."

"Perhaps they should have been more engaged in the fighting," Amery noted with a hint of sarcasm. "Things might have turned out differently if they had."

"Perhaps so. Which brings us to the reason we wanted to see you."

"Yes." Amery leaned back in his chair and crossed his legs. "I was wondering what you were up to. Your message was rather...cryptic."

Patterson gestured in Jabotinsky's direction, "Which I'm sure you'll understand once you hear our reason." He paused a moment to gather himself, then began again. "As you are no doubt aware, the Turks have increased their military presence in Palestine where they have colluded with resident Arabs in an attempt to solidify their control over the region. In the course of that, they declared a Jihad against all foreigners—including us and the Jewish settlers who have moved into the area."

Amery gestured to Jabotinsky. "A situation you wish to remedy by raising a Jewish army to return to Palestine and retake the land they seized from you."

"I am glad to see you are well informed on the matter," Jabotinsky replied.

"I should think everyone knows of your name and your work, though I dare say most misunderstand it."

"That appears to be the case," Jabotinsky conceded.

Amery placed both feet on the floor and scooted closer to the desk. "Well—as a way of cutting even more directly to what I believe is your point—allow me to say, gentlemen, that I am supportive of both the theory and the effort to form a Jewish Legion, arm it, and incorporate that unit in an overall strategy for dominating Palestine. But there is not enough support in Parliament to do much to effect that by way of direct legislation. However," he said with a wisp of a smile, "I hear the winds of change are blowing through the War Office. You might fare better there."

"Oh?" Patterson was surprised, especially in light of his recent conversations with Davis. "I was not aware they'd changed their position."

"Not so much regarding a Jewish unit," Amery explained, "but regarding the war in general. They're putting the best face possible on the Gallipoli Campaign, but behind closed doors everyone admits it was an absolute and total failure. Acknowledgment of that fact has led to a complete review of our strategy."

"That would be quite useful," Patterson noted, resisting again the temptation to vent his frustration with the army, the War Office, and the entire mess.

Amery leaned forward and lowered his voice. "I understand some have broached the possibility that Palestine might be a good place to make gains against the Turks. Attack them from the underbelly, so to speak."

Jabotinsky spoke up. "Anyone we should speak with about that?"

"Let me ask around. I'm sure I can find someone who might be able to help." Amery pushed his chair back farther and stood, a signal the meeting was over, then stepped from behind the desk. Patterson and Jabotinsky stood and the three of them started toward the office door. "The other thing that's pressing us," Amery added, "is the tremendous loss of life in Europe."

"I should imagine it would," Patterson noted.

"Yes," Amery agreed. "Both sides are desperately in need of bodies to stand at the line."

"What about the Americans?" Patterson asked. "Will they ever enter the war?"

Amery smiled. "We're working on it. Tough group to convince, though. Sitting way over there as they are. Isolated from events over here. Difficult to persuade a man in Chicago to send his sons to die at the Marne when there appears no real threat to North America."

They were at the door by then and Amery reached to open it. "By the way," he added almost as an afterthought, "our mutual friend General Chaytor deployed to Egypt with the Australian and New Zealand Mounted Division. I believe they helped protect the Sinai and the Suez Canal. Did you by chance see him when you were over there?"

"No," Patterson replied. "I did not. My time was entirely consumed preparing our men for Gallipoli."

"Pity you didn't," Amery remarked. "He might be of assistance. I think he would be sympathetic to your cause as well. Perhaps you should contact him."

"That is a very good suggestion," Patterson responded. "I think I shall." And with another round of thanks and well-wishes, Patterson and Jabotinsky departed.

+ + +

As they made their way from the office, Patterson could see Jabotinsky seemed upset. He said nothing about it until they reached the sidewalk outside, then Patterson turned to him, "That did not go as you planned?"

"We hardly even talked about the Jewish Legion," Jabotinsky protested. "We spent most of the time talking about *you—your* friends, *your* health, and that Gallipoli Campaign."

Patterson responded with an amused grin. "Welcome to British politics, my friend. That is how we do it."

"What do you mean that is how we do it?" Jabotinsky's voice grew louder "We didn't do *anything*. I expected a discussion about ideas, conditions in Palestine, the plight of our people. We did none of that."

"Leo Amery knows all that already," Patterson assured. "He said so while we were talking."

"But does he know the *truth*?"

Patterson stopped and turned to face him. "Listen, I understand you have deeply held opinions on these topics and you are keenly interested in talking about them and equally interested in convincing others that you are right. But that is not what we are trying to do."

"That is *precisely* what we are trying to do," Jabotinsky countered.

"No," Patterson corrected, his expression serious and his voice firm. "We are attempting to raise British support for a Jewish Legion to fight the Turks in Palestine. And that is very different from convincing them to agree with you about your views on the needs and aims of the Jewish people."

Once again Jabotinsky had a puzzled frown. "I do not think—"

"This is England," Patterson interrupted. "The men we need to win over are not Jewish. They are, for the most part, Anglo-Saxon Protestants. Their primary motivation, their primary focus, their all-consuming goal is winning this war for the United Kingdom. In protecting her possessions and extending her global reach. To win their support, we must craft *our* goal in those terms. We must show them how a campaign in Palestine benefits their cause and how a Jewish Legion can aid them in that effort. They will not be persuaded by an emotional appeal to assist the Jewish people in returning to their homeland." Patterson placed his hand lightly on Jabotinsky's shoulder and gestured with the other. "Now come. Let us enjoy luncheon together. Perhaps we can come up with a strategy over a light meal."

"I think this will take more than a light meal."

"Yes," Patterson chuckled. "Perhaps you are right, but we can begin with tea and see where it goes from there."

✦ ✦ ✦

The following week, Jabotinsky returned to see Patterson at the convalescent facility. Patterson was lying in bed. Jabotinsky was taken aback to find him that way.

"The staff would prefer I remained here all the time," Patterson explained.

"How were you able to meet me last time?"

"I ignored their orders."

"Have you heard from Leo Amery?"

"No. Not yet."

"I think we should go see him again."

"I don't think so. These things take time. He's only had a week, and I'm sure he's attempting to inquire on our behalf without raising too much suspicion."

"What about the man he mentioned? The general."

"Chaytor?"

"Yes. Did you attempt to contact him?"

"Not yet," Patterson hedged. "He is supportive of a Jewish Legion, but he is still in Egypt. Not sure how much help he can be, and there is some risk in contacting him by letter."

"Risk?"

"An assistant will see the letter before he does and there's no way to determine ahead of time how that assistant might feel about what we are attempting to do. It would be best to talk with him in person."

"I doubt he can actually help. Lord Smuts and Milner suggested the same thing."

"Smuts and Milner? You know them?"

"Yes."

"They are members of the war cabinet."

"I know."

"How did you meet them?"

"Chaim Weizmann introduced us."

"Were they supportive?"

"Yes. They seemed to be."

"Were they willing to help?"

"I think they would be if we could get the idea raised at their level."

"Did they have any suggestions on how we could do that?"

Jabotinsky had a sheepish look. "They said we should recruit generals and other officers who support us. Build support for the idea from the bottom up."

"You've been hearing that a lot," Patterson laughed.

"Yes," Jabotinsky sighed. "I know."

"Perhaps we should give it a try."

✦ ✦ ✦

Two days later, as Patterson was preparing to contact General Birchwood—a general whom he knew would support a Jewish Legion and was more accessible than Chaytor—a note arrived from Amery asking Patterson to bring Jabotinsky to Amery's office for a visit. Patterson collected Jabotinsky from the Guardian Hotel and they rode over to Amery's office.

"There are two members of the war cabinet who are particularly supportive of a Jewish Legion," Amery explained. "Jan Christiaan Smuts and Lord Milner." He looked over at Patterson. "Are you familiar with them?"

Jabotinsky, looking somewhat embarrassed, spoke up. "I have talked with them previously."

Amery was surprised. "Oh, how did you meet them?"

"Through Chaim Weizmann."

"Ahh," Amery nodded. "Chaim is a good contact to have. I forgot about him for some reason. Saw him not too long ago. Knows more people than the prime minister."

"Yes," Jabotinsky agreed. "He has many contacts."

Amery seemed rather deflated, having had the wind knocked out of what he assumed would be big news. Nevertheless, he recovered well and looked over at Patterson again. "So tell me, what is the status of the Zion Mule Corps?"

"They returned to Egypt but were instructed to deploy to Ireland."

"They are in Ireland?"

"No. They refused to go."

"Oh," Amery frowned. "That's not good."

"Why not?" Jabotinsky asked.

"The people you must convince are rather sensitive to things like duty, country, obedience."

"They are an auxiliary unit, not British conscripts," Jabotinsky clarified. "They did not join the war to fight the Irish. They joined to fight the Turks. We would have preferred to fight them in Palestine, but the British had no strategy for attacking them in Palestine. The corps was sent instead to Gallipoli, but the men were willing to participate since it was an operation against the Turks. But fighting the

Irish is an affair among British subjects. Addressing that dispute does not take us closer to our goal of reclaiming the land that is rightfully ours in Palestine."

Amery seemed rather put off by Jabotinsky's last comment. "Rightfully yours?" he asked with an empirical tone.

"They purchased their own farms. They did not simply arrive unannounced and squat on someone else's property."

Amery turned again to Patterson. "What happened when they refused?"

"General Monro understood their reasons for objecting and released them from further service."

"So, they have been decommissioned."

"No," Patterson replied. "I don't think so. They were not created by the army. They were accepted for service with us by General Maxwell and seconded to the Gallipoli Campaign, but they were their own unit. At least, that's my understanding. They had their own officers, under my command, of course."

"So, you are under the impression they still exist as a unit."

"Yes," Patterson answered. "I have heard there is a core of about one hundred twenty men who are still together. Training, drilling, preparing. Hoping for deployment against the Turks—ideally in Palestine."

"I'm wondering if we shouldn't get them involved in this some way."

"Involved?" Patterson had a curious expression. "In the effort to gain approval for a Jewish Legion?"

"Yes, I think it would strengthen our argument if we could show that we have a core of trained, seasoned soldiers ready for service in the Jewish Legion we are proposing."

"Ahh," Patterson nodded approvingly. "To show that we are not starting from scratch, with nothing more than raw recruits."

"Precisely."

"Well," Patterson continued, "if they were actually here, in England, where they could be seen marching, training, conducting drills—that could be very helpful. Any suggestions as to how we could bring them here?"

Amery pointed to Patterson. "If they are still a unit, and you are still their commander, perhaps you could ask General Monro to transport them."

"Joseph Trumpeldor is their commander, strictly speaking," Patterson noted.

"But you were the British officer in charge."

"Right."

"I'm sure you could find a way to use that to your advantage."

"Perhaps so," Patterson said.

After the meeting, Jabotinsky again was less than satisfied. Patterson sensed his mood. "You didn't care for this discussion, either?"

"It wasn't the discussion," Jabotinsky replied. "I think the suggestions Amery made were good."

"Then what is it?"

"Trumpeldor."

Patterson frowned. "Trumpeldor? What about him?"

"As we discussed, the idea for a Jewish Legion began as a discussion between myself and Trumpeldor. When General Maxwell offered us the position, I wanted to refuse right there in his office. Trumpeldor interrupted me and told Maxwell we needed an opportunity to consider the offer."

"Then you and Trumpeldor argued."

"Vehemently," Jabotinsky sighed.

Patterson had a kindly smile. "I know Joseph. He's big enough to get past all that. He'll understand. The only question is whether you're big enough to get past it, too."

"I suppose we have no choice."

"We really don't."

"Then what should we do? How do we reach him?"

"I contacted you because Trumpeldor sent me a letter suggesting I should. Perhaps we should contact him the same way."

"With a letter?"

"Yes. But not from me." Patterson pointed at Jabotinsky. "The letter should come from you."

"I don't think so," Jabotinsky replied.

"Why not?"

"I don't think he trusts me that much. You write the letter. I'll talk to Trumpeldor when they arrive."

That evening, Patterson penned a letter to Trumpeldor inquiring about the Mule Corps, summarizing his work with Jabotinsky, and asking if the remaining men would be willing to come to London. A few weeks later, Trumpeldor replied that the men were willing to make the trip but had no means of doing so.

Patterson contacted General Monro, reminding Monro that he was still the British commander of the Zion Mule Corps, and asked that the corps be transferred to a suitable location near London so he could continue to work with them. Monro responded that the corps was unwilling to deploy to a location other than Palestine, and their subsequent deactivation from service to the British army, made it impossible for him to transport them anywhere.

Again Patterson responded, inquiring as to whether the corps might be reactivated for special service and transported to England to undergo training for that purpose. "We need all the bodies we can get, regardless of where they ultimately go, and neither of us knows what the next operation might bring."

After another round of correspondence and several telegrams, Monro reluctantly agreed to send the remaining members of the Zion Mule Corps to London. They were transported by ship within the month.

When Jabotinsky heard the news, he was elated. "How did you do that?"

"It's the army," Patterson shrugged. "Talk to the right people and things can happen quite rapidly."

# CHAPTER 16

foz

OUR LETTER to Colonel Patterson brought a prompt reply, followed by a series of correspondence between us as he kept us informed of the latest developments in London. His news to us about the desire to bring us to London was met with excitement and anticipation. There was, however, one problem. In order to make the trip, we had to rejoin the British army—this time not as an auxiliary unit but as regular soldiers.

Not wanting to refuse Colonel Patterson or the British, Trumpeldor took the matter to General Monro, who agreed that we could enlist without committing to an extended term of service. Our men would be free to resign after a single year of enlistment. That accommodation resolved the issue for all but a few, who chose to stay in Egypt. One hundred twenty-five of us were sworn in as soldiers in the British army, moved once again to the military barracks, and prepared to leave for England.

A few nights before we were to depart, I noticed Amos was missing from his bunk. I waited for him to return but around one in the morning I went out to look for him. I didn't have to go far. He was sitting on the steps outside the door.

"What are you doing out there?" I asked.

"Thinking."

"Did you see Dalia?" I asked in a whisper.

Amos nodded his head in response. "For a little while."

"Is she worried about us leaving?"

"Not too much."

"That means she's worried a lot, right?"

He smiled. "Yeah, she's worried a lot."

"Well," I noted, "at least we aren't going into combat right away."

"That's not what's bothering her."

"Then what is it?"

"Her father is talking about leaving."

"Leaving? The refugee camp?"

"Yeah."

"Where's he going?"

"He wants them to go back to Galilee."

"All of them?"

"Yes."

"Can they do that?"

"Of course. We aren't prisoners. We can leave anytime we like. The problem is, it's not easy to get across the border. And once they're across, they still have to travel all the way north. And then the farm they owned might be occupied."

"Occupied? The house burned to the ground that night when the Arabs attacked."

"I know, but someone else might be there now. They might have built a new house on it."

"Oh. Yeah," I suddenly remembered the Arabs who attacked us that night.

"If their farm is occupied by someone else. What's he planning to do?"

"He thinks he can get them off the property."

"And if not?"

"They'll go to the settlement at Kinneret, or somewhere like it until they can find something else to do. They'll probably have to live there anyway at first, until they can build a house."

"You think they'll be in danger?"

"Not any more danger than we'll be in if we get to Palestine."

"We're closer than we've ever been."

"Yeah."

"What?"

"Nothing."

"It's not nothing. I can tell when you're thinking about nothing and when you're thinking about something. You're thinking about something. What is it?"

"The problem with Dalia isn't that she and her family are going back to Galilee. Or that I'm going to London."

"Then what is it?"

Amos looked over at me. "I'm thinking about going with them."

The suggestion that Amos might return to Galilee alone hit me hard. Since the night we walked away from the house I had assumed we would one day return to the farm and rebuild it together. The notion that we might not caught me by surprise and I responded to him with silence.

A few moments later, Amos asked, "You upset?"

"No," I sighed. "Just...disappointed."

"Yeah?"

"Yeah," I said in a somber tone. "I had assumed we'd go back together."

He patted my knee with his hand. "Well, we may yet. I said I was thinking about it. I didn't say I was going to do it."

✦ ✦ ✦

Not long after that, we marched down to the docks in Alexandria and boarded a ship for the trip to England. Amos was with us and I was glad he decided to come, but he was sad at the thought of leaving Dalia behind. Seeing him like that made me think of abandoning the Jewish Legion idea altogether and going with him.

Dalia was at the pier to see Amos off. Her father was with her, and I took him aside to talk while Dalia and Amos said a long good-bye. Even then, after time had passed and I had become reconciled to the fact that she cared for him and not for me, I still felt jealous at the sight of them together and so obviously in love. But I pushed that aside and concentrated on my conversation with David, asking about his plans for the farm and what he might do if that didn't work out.

Twenty minutes later, Trumpeldor ordered us aboard the ship. I waited while the others shuffled up the gangway, then nudged Amos and told him we had to go. He gave Dalia one last kiss and promised to find her wherever they might go, then shook David's hand and turned to leave. At the last moment, just as we were starting up toward the ship, Dalia reached over the handrail and took hold of Amos' arm. "I love you."

Amos leaned over and kissed her. "I love you, too."

If Amos had said, "That's it. I'm not leaving," and walked away, I would have joined him. Enlistment commitment or not, if he had wanted to go, I would have left with him and taken my chances at the border, crossing Galilee, and finding the farm. But he didn't. Instead, he squeezed her hand and started up the gangway. I tossed a wave in Dalia and David's direction, then started up after him.

✦ ✦ ✦

When the ship carrying the Zion Mule Corps reached England, it docked at Portsmouth. Patterson was there to greet each of us as we disembarked. He was friendly to everyone, smiling and laughing, and he became even more animated with those whom he remembered for some particular incident, but when he saw me coming down the gangplank his eyes opened wider and his smile grew deeper.

As I drew near, he reached out to shake my hand, but I avoided his grasp and lunged for him, wrapping my arms around his waist in a hug. He responded with an embarrassed chuckle and rested an arm across my back, but I could feel the distance between us. Seconds later, he gently pushed me away and greeted Amos, who was standing behind me. Others were waiting to get past us, and I stepped aside to let them through, then lingered nearby, hoping for a moment to talk to the colonel, but he seemed distracted and unusually remote.

Trucks were parked nearby to take us to an undisclosed destination. Most of the men were already loaded and ready when, finally, Colonel Patterson turned to me. "You should get on one of the trucks. We have arranged a place for all of you to stay."

"They told us we should reaffirm our oath," I ignored what he had just said. "But they didn't tell us the operation we were recommitting to." The question in my statement was implicit but obvious just the same.

"That has not been fully determined," Patterson replied. He rested a hand on my shoulder, much the same as he had in the past, and guided me away from the dock. "Our hope is that we can undertake a campaign in Palestine, but no decision has been made." His voice sounded thinner than before, and I noticed for the first time that he had aged since I had last seen him. Or maybe it was the war and we all had aged, the effects of it only now becoming noticeable. In any respect, he was different from the man I had known in Egypt and Gallipoli—not in a bad way, just different—and I wondered how different I had become.

"So," I continued in a less than appreciative tone, "we are once again at the disposal of the British army? Obligated to go wherever they tell us?"

"It was the only way to get you here," Colonel Patterson explained. By then we were away from the gangplank. He gestured toward the trucks, "We will talk more, but right now, you should go with the men. The drivers are ready to take you to a facility in Winchester where you will be housed for the time being. I'll be around to explain things."

Reluctantly, I started toward the trucks and saw Amos seated in back of the closest one. There was an open space beside him and I climbed up to take it. I was disappointed at the way things had turned out with the colonel so far. I had hoped for more—for us to pick up where we left off or...something, but not this.

As we sat there, waiting to leave, I watched Colonel Patterson escort Trumpeldor to a car, then the two of them got in back and drove away. Amos saw them, too, and noticed the look in my eyes. He gave me a nudge, and seemed to sense how I felt. "Don't worry about it. I'm sure Colonel Patterson will straighten everything out eventually."

"He *was* glad to see us," I conceded.

"No," Amos corrected. "He was glad to see *you*. The rest of us were merely window dressing."

"I thought he would have included me in the car," I whispered, hoping no one else heard.

"Trumpeldor is an officer. Just give it time. Don't get discouraged. Don't you like being away from the front?"

"Yes."

"And don't you like being away from Egypt?"

"Yes."

"Then relax. Let things run their course."

The truck lurched forward and we moved away from the docks. "I really enjoyed working with the colonel," I continued.

Amos nodded. "And he enjoyed working with you." He leaned against the wall of the truck and closed his eyes. "This will all work out. You'll see."

✦ ✦ ✦

About an hour later, we arrived at an army training facility near Winchester and were met by four or five sergeants. They divided us into groups and assigned us to barracks that were well-lit, pleasant buildings equipped with electric lights and indoor toilets. We had standing lockers that were located along the walls next to our beds, and all of us were given individual cots. Back in Egypt we had been sleeping on wooden bunks that we shared with two or three others. Glancing around the building, we were certain we'd landed in the lap of luxury.

A mess hall was located nearby and we were provided with a mealtime schedule that gave us three meals each day. "Snacks are available between meals," our sergeant offered. "You can help yourself if your duties permit the time. But we do not allow food inside the barracks."

Three meals...and snacks! Whatever happened next, I hoped from that moment forward that we never returned to Egypt.

In a little while, Trumpeldor arrived and told us we were free to relax until the following day, when Colonel Patterson would join us to discuss our status. We lounged around the barracks until dinnertime, then trooped over to the mess hall and ate our fill.

Midmorning the following day, we assembled on a parade ground located at the opposite side of the camp. Not long after we were in place, a car approached and drove right up to where we were standing. The doors opened and Colonel Patterson stepped out. We were surprised to see him arrive in that manner, rather than walking there on foot like the rest of us, but the men knew he'd been under medical care, so no one asked any questions.

Trumpeldor accompanied him to an oversized ammunition crate someone had put on the field for use as a dais. The colonel stood atop it and, speaking in a loud but thin voice, reminded us again of our heroic service in Gallipoli, the hardships we'd endured there, and the success we had attained. "You not only learned to survive the battlefield," he said, "but to persevere, adapt, and overcome every extreme and to do so in a most admirable manner."

"At Gallipoli," he continued, "you were trained as a transportation corps but forced to take up arms out of necessity. Now you will receive genuine combat training from experienced British soldiers." A cheer went up from the men. "Training that will allow you to fully enter into the heritage of your forebears. To take your place among the men of old who have, time and time again, conquered their enemies and liberated the land of Israel. You are the modern version of those ancient warriors!"

When he finished, we all were ready for battle right then and in a frenzy of emotion broke ranks, surging toward him en masse. In Egypt and later in Gallipoli, Colonel Patterson would have disciplined us severely for such a breach of procedure and protocol. But that day, on the field at the training camp in Winchester, he did nothing to stop us, and we all basked in the glory of the moment.

Gradually, enthusiasm waned and the men drifted away. A few of us, however, remained at the colonel's side, wanting to know more of what lay ahead for our unit. Amos and I were among them when Harry Schoenthal asked if we were going to Palestine.

"I don't know," Patterson replied. "I don't know where we are going but I am doing everything possible to see that we are included in a British strategy regarding the Middle East."

"Much chance of that happening?" Schoenthal pressed.

"Hard to say," Patterson answered. "We face a difficult task in convincing officials at the War Office that a Middle East campaign would be beneficial to their cause of winning the war in Europe. They have been reluctant so far to do more than simply protect the Suez Canal and shore up their long-standing position in Egypt."

"So, why are we here?" Amos asked.

"To be quite frank, you are here for two reasons. First, to receive the training necessary for whatever lies ahead. That much is absolutely true. Either you will fight with those of us who are in the British military, or you will fight on your own. I am positive of that. Second, and of equal importance in the immediate sense, you are here to demonstrate to the War Office that there are men of Zion who have demonstrable combat skills and abilities. Skills and abilities that would benefit the United Kingdom in attaining her goals for the war."

"We're part of a publicity campaign?"

"More like politics," Colonel Patterson said with a smile. "But in the Western world, substance and politics are all but inseparable." He glanced around at each of us. "You must show them that the fighting men of Zion can help them with their current effort. The manner in which you conduct yourselves during training will answer that question. So train hard," he added and gestured with his fist for emphasis. "Give it your all. Distinguish yourselves yet again."

More questions were raised and Colonel Patterson did his best to answer them, but slowly the others drifted away until only he and I remained. When they departed, Colonel Patterson turned to me and I assumed he would simply say good-bye abruptly, as he had each time I'd seen him since our arrival. Instead, he looked at me with a kind smile and asked about what I had been doing since we were last together. I told him and he was glad to hear that I had been training with the men, rather than remaining with Trumpeldor in an administrative capacity.

"That is good," he beamed with a sense of pride. "You are older now. The training will serve you well. You are sixteen?"

"Yes, sir," I answered. In truth I had not stopped to calculate my age in quite some time and agreed with him out of convenience, but I was not sure the number was correct.

"You are old enough to serve as a regular soldier," he noted, "but your experience as an aide would make you better suited for duty beyond mere fusilier. The way you managed the men at Gallipoli was far beyond your age. That kind of skill can't be taught and shouldn't be ignored."

This was the Patterson I remembered. The man who paid attention. Who noticed what I was doing and who I was. Who sensed where I belonged before I knew it myself.

"I don't yet know how this whole thing with the War Office will develop," he continued. "We are trying to form a Jewish Legion to help liberate Palestine, but, as I said earlier, the outcome of that effort is not yet certain. Powerful people are opposed to us. And even if we are successful in establishing the Legion, I do not know what my role in that unit would be. But I am looking for a place for you that will give you the best opportunity."

I did my best to ignore the tears filling my eyes as I whispered, "Thank you."

"I know you wanted us to pick up where we left off," he said with a pat on my shoulder. "With things as they were before. But that is not possible right now. Still, I haven't forgotten you or the service you rendered during the Gallipoli Campaign. I just don't yet know the final arrangements here."

Hearing him speak to me that way, my confidence in him soared once again and my commitment to him grew even deeper. He could have told me anything and I would have believed him. Colonel Patterson wasn't simply back in my life. Colonel Patterson, I learned, had never left.

◆ ◆ ◆

The following day, our training commenced in earnest and the sergeants at the camp put us through the same pace given to new recruits in the British army. We were up before dawn for a long-distance run, then formed up on the field for physical exercise until breakfast. An hour later, we trained on the rifle range with live ammunition, followed by instruction in hand-to-hand combat that took us to lunch.

Afternoons were devoted to the obstacle course—which Amos described as more long-distance running, with walls and streams in the way—followed by exercises in surveillance and tracking. Following dinner, we attended a two-hour class, usually something about small-unit tactics or improvised explosives.

Most days, Trumpeldor ran the courses and took the classes with us, shaming us with his ability to best our efforts using only his one arm, but about two weeks into training he left the facility in a car with a driver. Later I learned that he traveled to London for a meeting with Colonel Patterson at the convalescent facility.

◆ ◆ ◆

Colonel Patterson met Trumpeldor at the main building and escorted him to a private room. When they were alone, Trumpeldor asked about Patterson's health.

"I am all but well," Patterson replied confidently. "The doctors have not yet said when I can leave, but I don't think it will be much longer. I heard them the other day debating among themselves about when I would be able to return to active duty."

Trumpeldor remained concerned about Patterson's circumstance but let the issue pass and turned to more pressing matters. "I assumed from your letter and subsequent exchanges with General Monro that you met with Jabotinsky."

"Yes, he and I have been working together."

"How is he?"

"He is well," Patterson answered. "A little apprehensive about seeing you again, but otherwise well."

Trumpeldor glanced away. "Yeah, I suppose we should talk about that."

"I understand the two of you parted on less than friendly terms."

"Jabo and I came up with the idea about the same time—of recruiting men to go back to Palestine and retake our land. But he didn't want to form a transportation corps. I thought it was at least a place to begin."

"And your decision was a good one," Patterson acknowledged. "But the two of you should talk. If this idea of a Jewish Legion is to work, it will take both of you to make it happen. So you need you to resolve whatever remains between you."

Trumpeldor looked over at him. "How do we do that?"

"We go see him."

✦ ✦ ✦

Trumpeldor spent the night in London, and the following day he and Colonel Patterson went to the Guardian Hotel. Jabotinsky was waiting for them in his room. Almost instantly, and without

Patterson's intervention, the former animosity melted away and the two men mended their relationship. The past resolved, they turned to the details of what needed to be done to promote the Legion. They spent most of the morning on that.

As they broke for lunch, Trumpeldor handed Jabotinsky a note from Nisei Rosenberg. Jabotinsky read it quickly, then stuffed it into the pocket of his jacket.

Trumpeldor looked over at him. "Nisei told me what it said."

Jabotinsky nodded. "I'll have to think about it."

Patterson injected himself into the conversation. "Well, Rosenberg didn't tell me. What was in the note?"

Jabotinsky turned away, "It was nothing."

Trumpeldor answered, "Some of the men knew Jabo from when he was in Egypt. They want to see him and get reacquainted."

"That's a great idea," Patterson said enthusiastically.

"I don't know," Jabotinsky sighed. He put his hands in his pockets and stared down at the floor. "I wasn't there with them for any of the things they experienced. While they were in Gallipoli, I was here." He removed one hand from his pocket and gestured to the room. "Eating three delicious meals and sleeping on a comfortable bed."

Patterson ignored the comments. "The men of the Zion Mule Corps owe their existence as a military unit to you, at least in part. They fought with distinction. Many won the Distinguished Service Medal. And those men are the product of *your* ideas." He pointed with his index finger for emphasis. "You ought to go see them."

"I suppose." Jabotinsky looked over at Trumpeldor. "But Trumpeldor was the one who led them on the battlefield. Not me." He glanced over at Patterson. "I just don't know what I could say."

"Tell them how proud you are of the way they fought!" Patterson roared. "How proud you are of the way they conducted themselves.

Tell them they acted like true men of Israel. Like men who stand in the line of a great and powerful heritage. Speak to them from your heart."

After lunch, they talked awhile longer and Trumpeldor extended his visit yet one more night.

The following morning, they traveled to the camp at Winchester, where Jabotinsky watched us train. That evening, after dinner, he spoke to us in the mess hall, reminding us again of our historic heritage—as Patterson had earlier—and how proud he was of our accomplishments on the battlefield. We were excited by what he said and I think he was, too. The following day, he joined the Jewish Legion and moved into the barracks to train as one of us.

FRIENDS OF ZION: *Patterson & Wingate*

# CHAPTER 17

foz

MEANWHILE, WAR IN EUROPE reached a stalemate and, according to some, it came at a good time. After more than two years of fighting with extremely high casualty rates, both sides were running out of conscription-aged men. Moreover, Germany was running low on supplies of every kind.

From the beginning of the war, the United States sought to avoid the conflict in Europe by following a noninterventionist policy. It was common knowledge, however, that sentiment for the Allied cause ran high among the Americans, as it did among most US neighbors. Wilhelm II, the last of the German Kaisers, knew it, too, and he was infuriated. Any action he might take to prevent the transfer of goods between them, however, bore the risk of antagonizing the United States, and so he refrained.

At first, that policy of German restraint against nonaligned nations made sense. There was little advantage to antagonizing nations such as the United States and every reason not to. They were on the opposite side of the Atlantic, the war did not concern them, no point in adding another country to the enemies list—especially one with a manufacturing base like the United States. But as conditions in Europe changed and Germany's situation became more desperate, the advantage accorded the Allies by the imports it received out-weighed the risk of provoking the Americans. As a result, Kaiser Wilhelm issued orders expanding German submarine attacks to include all shipping bound for Allied countries.

Rear Admiral Alfred von Tirpitz, German secretary of state for the navy, received those orders with concern and took the matter to Wilhelm directly. They met in a drawing room at the kaiser's palace in Berlin.

"You realize, sir," von Tirpitz said cautiously, after a lengthy discussion of naval policy, "this will mean sinking ships from the United States."

"I understand that." Wilhelm stood at the window as they talked, gazing out on the flowers below, with his back to von Tirpitz.

"And such an action might very well bring them into the war," von Tirpitz continued. "Some think they were very close to entering with the *Lusitania* incident."

"They are already in the war," Wilhelm noted dryly. "But they are too cowardly to take up a rifle at the front line."

"This may push them to that."

Wilhelm placed his hands behind his back. "So be it. We cannot allow our fear of the Americans to set German policy."

Perhaps in a concession to von Tirpitz, Wilhelm ordered that the change in policy be publicly announced to the world, and for a very short time many in the world understood the new policy as merely an attempt of one nation to defend itself. However, shortly after the announcement was made, British intelligence officers intercepted a telegram sent from German foreign secretary Arthur Zimmermann to the German ambassador to Mexico, Heinrich von Eckardt. In that telegram, Zimmermann instructed Eckardt to offer an alliance to

Mexico, with German funding and support, as an encouragement to mount a Mexican operation against the United States to retake Texas and the Southwestern portion of the U.S. The contents of the message were relayed to the American ambassador in London, who cabled the news to Washington. Sentiment in the United States against entering the war changed overnight.

A few days later, that rising sense of indignation toward German aggression was magnified when German submarines began sinking US merchant ships, sending seven to the bottom in short order. That spring, the United States entered the war as an associate of the Allied Powers.

✦ ✦ ✦

With America's entry in the war, the mood in England changed dramatically. A renewed sense of optimism swept the country. Until that time, most people in Europe had little regard for America, and even less for American foreign policy, but with the war in a desperate state and England feeling threatened, everyone was enthralled at the prospect of access to the untapped potential they saw in the United States—especially the potential in her great reserve of young men.

The implications of American involvement were not lost on anyone, least of all the British prime minister, Lloyd George. Most apparent to him was the additional troops, of course, but beyond that, American entry into the fray meant additional armaments, equipment, and supplies. Things that were lacking at the front now wouldn't be in six months and that presented all sorts of new possibilities.

Bolstered by the prospect of new life and fresh energy to the war effort, George met with his newly appointed war secretary, Lord Derby, to discuss their options.

"With Americans entering the war," Prime Minister George asked, "I wonder if there are other ways to expand the war effort. Something beyond the standoff we've reached at the western front."

Derby seemed less than enthusiastic. "Such as?"

"I suppose we could open a new front in Europe," George offered, "but that would require us to open it from the east, which is what we contemplated when we began the Gallipoli Campaign."

"Yes," Derby conceded. "That was the ultimate goal of that operation."

"Is there another location besides Europe that might tip the strategic balance?"

"I'm sure there is, but what purpose would it serve?"

"I think it would—"

Derby interrupted. "If I may, Mr. Prime Minister, you seem to have something particular in mind. This might go better if you tell me what you are thinking."

George cloaked his irritation with Derby at being interrupted with a tight, thin smile. "I'm thinking," he continued tensely, "we should pursue the alliance with the Arabs in a more aggressive manner."

"We're already—"

George cut him off. "I know we've had liaison officers working with them, and I understand one of those officers has made quite a bit of progress in this regard."

"Yes," Derby replied. "Lawrence, I believe."

"Right," George nodded. "T. E. Lawrence. From all reports, he's done an excellent job. But I think the time is right for us to prevail upon the Arabs to undertake action against the Turks in a much broader manner."

Derby had a puzzled expression. "An Arab uprising?"

"Precisely."

"I see the logic of it," Derby agreed, "but even if we did that, there would be little tactical or strategic benefit to us. The Arabs supply very little in the way of support to the Ottoman Empire and haven't much to contribute to our war effort, either."

"But," George countered, "if we turned the Arabs in our favor, we could shrink the Turkish Empire considerably. That would force them to divert attention to their southern flank."

"I'll take it up with the cabinet," Derby said. "But I—"

"No," George said coldly, cutting him off yet again. "I don't want you to *take it up* with them. I want you to do it."

"Very well, sir," Derby agreed, still not emotionally engaged in the conversation. "But may I raise one other point?"

"Certainly."

"Any new effort to encourage the Arabs to join us will prompt a new round of agitation by the Jews for similar facilitation on their side. They've been arguing for quite some time for our help with a Jewish Legion to retake their farms in Palestine. Chaim Weizmann and Ze'ev Jabotinsky have been to my office so many times I have issued standing orders to decline any requests for meetings with them."

"Well," George spoke slowly, "we do need all the bodies we can muster."

"Yes, Mr. Prime Minister." Derby looked away. "I suppose so."

George frowned. "You seem dissatisfied by the notion of including the Jews, too."

"Their presence among our troops might be rather...disruptive."

"And the presence of armed Arabs would not?"

"Well, you have a point." For the first time in the conversation, Derby showed a smile. "But that touches on another sensitive topic."

"Which is?"

"I assume any effort in the east would require the use of our forces currently in Egypt."

"It would seem so," George nodded. "Is there a problem with that?"

"Perhaps." Derby shifted in the chair uncomfortably. "I know that you are partial to General Monro, and he did a great job cleaning up the Gallipoli Campaign, but I think someone...with a...different approach might work better—if we're going to expand our operation in that region."

George was impressed by Derby's candor. "I'm glad you brought that up. I've been thinking for some time that a change in leadership there might be good. Do you have anyone you would suggest?"

"Edmund Allenby would be my choice. Aggressive, forthright, able to formulate a plan and make it work."

George smiled again, only this time it was a genuine smile and not a guise for seething anger. "I think Allenby would make an excellent choice. I'll give him due consideration."

After Derby left the office, the prime minister called for an assistant, "Send a message to Arthur Balfour. "Tell him I would like to meet with him in my private study."

"Mr. Balfour is out of the country today, sir."

"Tell his office I should like to see him immediately upon his return."

"Certainly, sir."

✦ ✦ ✦

The following afternoon, Derby convened a meeting of the war cabinet and conveyed to them the prime minister's interest in a Middle East campaign. "He wants that operation to involve an alliance with the Arabs."

Jan Christiaan Smuts spoke up. "This will seem as if we support the Arabs, but not just against the Turks."

Derby had a questioning look. "What do you mean?"

Smuts explained, "I mean, Arabs and Jews already are engaged in a struggle against each other over control of Palestine. They've asked for our help repeatedly and we have turned them down. If we choose to align ourselves formally with only the Arabs now and specifically use them in the region, it will appear as though we've chosen sides."

"Is that a problem?" someone quipped, only half joking.

"We're protecting thousands of Jews right now, in Egypt," Smuts sniped. "Jews who were forced from their homes in Palestine by the Arabs."

"Yes, but with the Turks helping and provoking them," someone added.

"This is war," another noted. "We are obliged to do those things that further our own best interests. We can't be limited by attempting to please everyone."

Lord Milner spoke up. "Perhaps we can." All eyes turned to him. "Perhaps we can do both—convince the Arabs to help, while at the same time using the Jews to help as well."

"And what about the problem between the Arabs and the Jews that we've just been discussing? Are you suggesting we ignore that?"

"They can serve in separate units," Milner suggested. "The Arabs already are serving with us in segregated units that are deployed in other regions. We'll just continue that same policy with the Jews, rather than integrating them into existing units comprised solely of non-Arabs."

"That still leaves us with our central problem," someone elaborated. "After the war, when we have defeated the Turks, we'll be left with Arabs and Jews still fighting each other over who should control

Palestine. Only then they'll be equipped with *our* training and *our* arms."

Someone else spoke up. "That's an easy issue to resolve."

"How so?"

"After the war is over and we have won, *we* will control Palestine. We can simply impose our will on them." Everyone laughed in response.

Another person joined the discussion. "We could always save the resolution of this issue for later. For any of this to matter we have to win the war, and the reality of our situation in Europe is we need all the men we can get. Englishman, Arab, *or* Jew."

"And in the final analysis, the region's problems aren't necessarily ours to resolve. We can defeat the Central Powers, then withdraw from Palestine and let them have at it."

"Perhaps we should return to the issue at hand," Derby added, attempting to bring the discussion under control. "We know there are major groups of Arabs who will join us in a Middle East campaign. Will the Jews join us? And more to the point, will they join us against the Turks knowing the Arabs are with us, too?"

"The enemy of my enemy is my friend," someone offered.

"Maybe," Smuts answered. "If we work with the men who were with us in Gallipoli."

"What would we have to offer them to get them to fight?"

"A homeland," Milner suggested.

"We had Jews helping us in Gallipoli?" someone asked.

"Patterson and his Zion Mule Corps." Everyone chuckled in response.

"Don't laugh," Milner countered defensively. "They fought well."

"With mules?" the joke continued.

"They were armed," Milner explained. "And they took up the

fight when necessary. Several were awarded the DSM for their acts of bravery."

"They wanted our support for a fighting unit earlier," Smuts added. "A unit to return to Palestine and retake their land, but General Maxwell turned them down."

"Perhaps we should find a way to say yes this time," someone added soberly.

"That fellow Jabotinsky's been working for a Jewish unit, too."

"And he's found considerable support for it," Milner offered.

"Support?"

"From whom?"

"General Chaytor supports the idea. General Birchwood as well."

"That's all fine and well, but another issue we should consider is how this will appear to the British people—British troops taking control of Palestine on behalf of the Jews." A murmur went around the room. "Arabs they would understand. We've been over there for quite some time with archaeological explorations and the like. And they have oil. But Jews—that's not going to sit well with many."

"Don't tell them."

"Be serious. This would be a major undertaking. How do you propose we do all that without the people finding out?"

"Tell them we are protecting our interests around the Suez Canal," Smuts suggested. "Then simply expand our operations northward as a matter of necessity. Vital to our military and economic concerns and all that. Cast it in that light rather than in the vein of returning the Jews to Palestine."

"Okay," Derby said. "The question remains. Would either of these groups actually go for the idea of serving amicably together in a Middle East campaign?"

"I suppose we can find out."

Derby looked over at Smuts. "You have contacts among the Jews, don't you?"

"Yes."

"Think you could sound them out?"

Smuts nodded. "Certainly, I would be happy to."

✦ ✦ ✦

That evening, Smuts and Milner met with Chaim Weizmann at Weizmann's home. Milner summarized the cabinet discussion, then Smuts asked, "Is Jabotinsky still interested?"

"Yes," Weizmann replied. "He's training with the men now."

"Training?" Smuts asked in a perplexed voice. "With what men?"

"Patterson and the men from the Zion Mule Corps."

"Jabotinsky left to join them?"

"No," Weizmann replied. "The men are here. Patterson convinced General Monro to transfer them here. They're training at a camp in Winchester."

"Who's training them?"

"Men from your army."

Milner and Smuts were floored. "How did he do that?"

"I don't know how he convinced General Monro," Weizmann shrugged. "But Patterson thought it would be good to have the men here. So others could see that they are serious about forming a Jewish Legion and so they could demonstrate that we have capable men who are willing to fight."

"This is news to me," Smuts said, still astounded.

"News to both of us," Milner added. "Can we see them?"

"I'm sure Colonel Patterson would be glad to arrange a visit for you."

"This is amazing," Smuts marveled. "That he was able to put this together and we not know it."

"Yes, but the cabinet had a question they wanted answered."

"Very well," Weizmann said. "I will tell you as best I can."

"If we undertook a campaign in the Middle East, it would most likely be comprised of both Jewish and Arab units. Would the inclusion of Arabs in the operation prevent Jewish participation?"

"I can't speak for Jabotinsky, or Colonel Patterson, or any of the others," Weizmann said. "But for me, it makes no difference so long as we drive the Turks from Palestine and the Arab units don't use the battle as a pretext for destroying more Jewish homes."

"What about after the war?"

"What about it?"

"Will the Jews return to their land?"

"Of course they will return," Weizmann assured. "That is their desire now. That is what they want to do. Most of them would leave the refugee camps of Egypt this very minute if they thought they could get across the border."

"But what about the Arab question? Will the Jews who settle in Palestine work cooperatively with the Arabs to settle their differences amicably?"

"You should ask the Arabs that question. We have never been the aggressor. Our people went there peaceably to farm. They purchased land from the Sultans of Istanbul who sold them the worst land in the area. No matter. Our people did not protest. They purchased the land that was offered and went to work to make it produce a harvest. They irrigated the desert. Drained the marshes. Wherever they were given space, they made it flourish. It was the Arabs who attacked our people. Not the other way around."

"Will Jabotinsky cooperate?" Milner asked.

"And we only ask," Smuts added, "because in his effort to recruit people to fight in Palestine, he often describes it as liberating Palestine from the Arabs."

"You must understand," Weizmann explained. "Jabotinsky arrived at his inclination to fight out of necessity. When he was a young man, Russian thugs attacked their neighborhood. The elders of the neighborhood preferred to do nothing, trusting that the matter would pass over. When it did not, Jabotinsky organized a group of men and they resisted. As a result, the attacks stopped. If there had been no attack, there would have been no need to resist and Jabotinsky would not have chosen that path as the solution."

"You're saying the only reason he's recruiting fighters for Palestine and describing it as a war against Arabs is because Arabs joined with the Turks in attacking Jewish settlements?"

Weizmann nodded. "Precisely."

"You are certain Arabs were involved?" Smuts asked.

"Right now, in Egypt," Weizmann replied, "the United Kingdom is feeding and housing eleven thousand witnesses to the truth of what I say. Go and ask them for yourself."

# CHAPTER 18

foz

A FEW DAYS LATER, Arthur James Balfour, the British foreign minister, returned to London and went immediately to Lloyd George's office. They met in a sitting area on the opposite side of the room from George's desk, Balfour at one end of an overstuffed sofa, George in an armchair situated to the right of him.

"I'll get straight to the point," George began. "We would like to launch a new operation against the Turks. This one in the Middle East, probably moving up through Palestine from our bases and camps in Egypt. In support of that operation, we intend to solicit the help of Arabs living in the region. I understand we are working with them already but we mean to take that sense of cooperation beyond merely a flirtatious relationship. We would like to gather the Arabs into a trained, disciplined army and apply the force of that army to suit our strategic and tactical purposes."

"I understand," Balfour answered with an approving nod. "Excellent idea."

"And," George continued, "we want to offer that same opportunity to the Jews. Those who are already living there and those who wish to return to Palestine and secure the lands that were recently seized by the Turks."

"Excellent idea as well," Balfour added enthusiastically. "There will be a slight complication, however, regarding the seizure of Jewish land."

"What is that?" George asked.

"Some of those seizures occurred at the hands of Arab residents in Palestine."

"At the instigation of the Turks, I understand."

"The Turks were involved," Balfour acknowledged.

"You understand, Arthur, we have no interest in engaging the Arabs in a war. It doesn't suit our purposes, or theirs. The Ottoman Empire is our enemy and this operation must be framed for the public in that context. We must be seen as simply rallying the local population—an oppressed local population, both Arab and Jew, I might add—to throw off the yoke of Ottoman rule."

"I'm sure we can work through any Jewish-Arab issues once the Turks have been ousted."

"And you think this strategy will succeed?"

"If you're asking whether the Jews will join us in the fight, then my answer is yes. I have every confidence a substantial number of Jews will agree to assist us and that they will make exemplary soldiers."

"So I am told by many. What about the Arabs?"

"We've already seen examples of what they can do. Our man Lawrence has a cadre ready to go, even as we speak."

"For this to work, we need to reach some sort of understanding with the Jewish constituency about how things will turn out."

"You mean, an understanding of what things might be like after we win."

George nodded. "Yes. Precisely."

Balfour's expression turned serious. "That part could be a bit tricky."

"Why is that?"

"With the Arabs, Hussein bin Ali controls a strong core group and the various Arab factions even in remote areas at least have tribal leaders with whom one might conclude an entente. The Jews, no matter how sympathetic one might be to their cause, are not a sovereign nation and have no unifying leader. They have no head of state who might enter into a binding agreement or understanding of the sort I think you are suggesting."

George smiled knowingly. "Which is why we're having this conversation."

"I suppose," Balfour added, thinking aloud, "we could always tout someone as that unifying Jewish leader, whether he is or not."

George seemed puzzled. "I'm not sure I follow."

"When the man on the corner says William Smith is a leader in Sussex, his voice carries no more weight or force than that of any man common in casual conversation. It certainly bears no imprimatur of official policy. But when the prime minister refers to Mr. Smith in those terms, suddenly Mr. Smith is elevated to heights of public awareness and stature he might very well never attain by his own effort."

George grinned. "I see I made an excellent choice in selecting our secretary of state for foreign affairs."

"Excellent indeed," Balfour acknowledged. "So, how would you like to handle this?"

"As discreetly as possible," George noted. "And as far from this office as possible."

"Well," Balfour mused. "There are any number of prominent organizations here that represent large Jewish constituencies."

George looked interested. "Any one of those organizations come to mind as of particular strategic importance over the others?"

"The World Zionist Organization," Balfour announced confidently.

"I've heard of it."

"They have chapters throughout the country but the central office for the United Kingdom is here in London. Run by Chaim Weizmann. Respected biochemist. Knowledgeable man. Rather deft at handling delicate situations. It's the strongest single Jewish group and represents the largest number of people."

"Then perhaps you could work out the details with them."

"I'm sure we could," Balfour responded. "But any understanding we reach with them would be rather ambiguous at best."

George smiled. "All the better, and it would be good if we could claim they approached us with the idea."

"Then I shall see to it." Balfour pushed himself up from the sofa. "Consider it done, Mr. Prime Minister."

George stood and they shook hands. "In spite of my confidence in you, Arthur, I shall consider it done when it is finally done and put to rest. But I appreciate your enthusiasm."

✦ ✦ ✦

Later that evening, Leo Amery received a phone call from Balfour asking Amery to meet Balfour that evening in his office. When they were together, Balfour said apologetically, "Sorry to drag you away from home at such short notice, but I'm afraid a matter has come up that can't wait."

"I am always delighted to be of assistance. How may I help you?"

"As you are aware, the Americans have finally entered the war."

"A most welcome development."

"Yes," Balfour agreed. "And it comes at a most helpful moment."

"Quite so."

"Their entry into the fight has not only presented us with new resources, it has opened up the possibility of new and different strategies. The hope is that we can finally put an end to this thing, once and for all."

"May it happen soon," Avery added.

Balfour nodded, "By all means. To that end, we are considering several options that might benefit our...associated constituencies. Groups of...marginalized peoples who have an interest in the outcome of the war but have not been aggressively...managed heretofore."

"I think I follow."

"Then I'll get on to the point," Balfour said. "I believe you are acquainted with Chaim Weizmann?"

"Yes, he and I get along quite well."

"You see him often?"

"As often as either of us might need. Is there something you would like for me to do?"

"Well," Balfour hedged. "Yes. There is. For some time now, Weizmann has been agitating for support of the Jewish cause in Palestine."

"Yes, Mr. Secretary. Both he and Ze'ev Jabotinsky have pursued that cause with marked passion."

"Jabotinsky," Balfour chuckled. "I think he's been to this office more often than have I."

"Yes, sir." Avery nodded. "He is persistent."

"In the past, this office has turned down all such proposals, dismissing them out of hand, as we had no strategy that might usefully employ them. However, things have changed, as you well know, and the suggestion has been made that we should reconsider Weizmann's... ideas."

"Regarding a Jewish Legion?"

"Yes."

"Are you asking me to relay some sort of message?"

"I'm wondering whether you think Weizmann might like to discuss these matters...with me."

"I'm sure he would be glad to talk you. Overjoyed, in fact."

"Just the two of us." Balfour shot Amery a look. "At his suggestion, of course."

"Certainly," Amery said, acknowledging the implication.

"Do you think he would be open to once again asking for a meeting on this topic?"

"I can't speak for him directly, sir, but I would be glad to...sound him out on the matter."

"Informally," Balfour added. "You understand."

Amery nodded in agreement. "Certainly, just two friends discussing the possibility of finding a mutual...raison d'être."

"Precisely," Balfour smiled.

✦ ✦ ✦

Though it was late when Amery left Balfour's office, he went straight to Weizmann's house. They met in the den. "Things are changing," Amery said.

Weizmann looked puzzled. "What do you mean?"

"Things at the prime minister's office. Things at the War Office. This entry of the Americans into the war has thrown the entire government into a frenzy. Everyone's abuzz with all the *possibilities* that American involvement present. Old strategies are being questioned. New strategies are being proposed."

"You came to my house in the middle of the night to tell me this?"

Amery gave Weizmann a knowing look. "I think this is the time to approach Balfour again about a definitive statement of the British position on establishing a Jewish homeland in Palestine." It sounded rehearsed but Amery didn't care.

Weizmann's face wrinkled in a confounded expression. "Leo, are you drunk?"

"No, not in the least."

"Then tell me, what has happened?"

"I have a source," Amery said with the excitement of someone who knows the inside story. "I've spoken to him within the hour. And that source says the time is now."

"A source?"

"Yes," Amery nodded. "Aren't you friends with Arthur Balfour?"

"Of course...everyone knows that. I mean, we aren't great friends or anything like that, but we get along quite well."

"Good. That will make this all the easier."

"Make *what* all the easier?"

"Your approach to him."

"But I didn't approach him," Weizmann replied with a sense of frustration. "What is going on with you?"

"I'm talking to you about the approach you're going to make."

Weizmann frowned. "You think I am going to approach Arthur Balfour?"

"Yes, I have good reason to believe he would be pleased to hear from you."

"What makes you so sure of that?"

"As I said, I have a source."

"And this *source* thinks I should simply call on the foreign minister of my own initiative?"

"Yes," Amery nodded with a grin.

"The first Earl of Balfour?"

"Yes."

"Merely present myself and say, 'Here I am, old chum. What's say we have a chat?'"

"A letter would be more fitting as a first step," Amery suggested.

Weizmann's forehead was deeply furrowed. "Are you certain?"

"Trust me, Chaim." Amery rested a hand on Weizmann's shoulder. "Write Balfour a letter. Tell him you think it is time for his office to make a definitive statement of British policy regarding the return of Jews to Palestine and the establishment of a Jewish state. Tell him you think the two of you should sit down together, alone, to discuss the matter."

"I'll have to think about this."

"No, Chaim." Amery's expression was serious. "Write the letter. Have it delivered to Balfour's office tomorrow morning before lunch."

✦ ✦ ✦

At Amery's insistence, and in spite of his own personal misgivings, Weizmann penned a letter to Balfour asking, as he often had already, for a definitive statement from the British government in support of Jewish efforts to resettle Palestine and the establishment of a Jewish state, as well as a meeting to discuss the matter. The letter was delivered to Balfour's office before lunch. That afternoon, much to Weizmann's surprise, he received a reply from Balfour stating that he was willing to meet with Weizmann the next day.

As arranged, Weizmann appeared at Balfour's office and found the secretary of state was away for a moment. An assistant ushered Weizmann to the same chair where Amery sat two nights before and left him alone in the office. Weizmann took a seat and Balfour entered shortly thereafter.

For the next three hours they discussed the desire of Jews to return to their historic homeland, the issues they faced in Palestine, and the possibility of a British effort to secure the area as a Jewish state. It was a wide-ranging conversation about dreams and aspirations, ideals and realities—the kind of discussion for which Weizmann had hoped and prayed most of his adult life. Not only that, Balfour made copious notes and, as they concluded their time together, proposed that he draft an official statement along the lines of their mutual understanding expressed that day. "I'll send it to you for review before we do anything with it."

The moment seemed too good to be true and Weizmann left the meeting both elated and wary. In the years since Theodor Herzl first proposed the idea that Jews should return to Palestine, there had been other occasions when sovereign powers seemed ready to announce support for the Jewish cause, only to be deterred at the last minute by some unanticipated problem or angry constituency. This time the British appeared to be closer than ever. *Perhaps*, Weizmann thought, *we shall at last receive tangible support from a legitimate international power.*

✦ ✦ ✦

Later that week, Balfour asked Weizmann to return to his office and showed Weizmann the letter he drafted, written along the lines of their earlier conversation. At first glance, the content seemed appropriate and posed few problems. Weizmann, however, was caught off guard by the fact that it was a letter.

"I thought this was to be an official statement."

"It is official," Balfour replied.

"Yes," Weizmann said slowly, not wishing to press the matter too harshly. "But correspondence conveys opinion. Not the pronouncement of official policy."

Ever the diplomat, Balfour responded, "It seemed best to handle the matter this way. You understand. These things must be made to work at many levels."

"I see." Weizmann sensed the all-too-familiar anti-Jewish roadblock he'd encountered in the past. "Well," he continued, determined to get something from the opportunity. "Let's have a closer look at the language."

For the next hour they pored over the document, changing, deleting, and refining the language. Honing it until finally they agreed on a text, which Balfour read aloud.

"'His Majesty's Government view with favor the establishment in Palestine of a national home for the Jewish people, and will use their best endeavors to facilitate the achievement of this object, it being clearly understood that nothing shall be done which may prejudice the civil and religious rights of existing non-Jewish communities in Palestine, or the rights and political status enjoyed by Jews in any other country.'

"Now," Balfour pronounced when they'd finished with the statement, "we must decide how to issue it."

"Perhaps a speech would work best," Weizmann offered, still hoping for an authoritative, public pronouncement. "Or a paper giving a statement of policy—a clarification perhaps—released to the press, of course."

Balfour shook his head. "Too incendiary. We want to reach an understanding on the matter without making too much of it."

"Anything you say in this regard will incite a response from all concerned," Weizmann countered. "From those who are for us, and those who are against us. I'm afraid there is not much of a way to say the things we're saying without everyone finding out."

"Still..." Balfour pressed hesitantly. "What about issuing it the way it is—as a letter?"

"I suppose you could send a letter to me," Weizmann offered. "Making a statement as follow-up to a discussion we held. That would have the advantage of aligning with the facts. We met. We talked. You wrote me to summarize the British position on the things we discussed. That might work."

"I was thinking of something a little less..." Balfour was inviting Weizmann to finish the sentence.

"Something more circumspect?" Weizmann offered.

Balfour agreed. "Yes, more circumspect. Precisely."

The reality of what was happening struck Weizmann with full force. The British wanted Jewish support without supporting the Jews. They wanted Jewish participation in a military campaign—a full and complete commitment from the men on the ground, doing the fighting—while making no lasting commitment in return. It angered Weizmann to know they would treat the Jews this way, and that they thought him vulnerable to such obvious deception, but this was as close as he ever had come to getting a clear statement from the British and he didn't want to turn it down, though he felt like it. Instead, he asked, "Wouldn't a letter dilute the effect?"

"Not the effect of the statement," Balfour suggested. "Merely the effect of issuing it."

"I see," Weizmann said. *Just get the letter,* he told himself. They could always publicize it themselves and make of it whatever they chose, once it was released.

"What about a letter to a prominent public figure?"

As head of the British Zionist Federation, and a leader in the World Zionist Organization, not many Jewish figures were more prominent than Weizmann. Still, if Balfour asked the question, he must have someone in mind. "I assume you are thinking of someone in particular."

"Well, as a matter of fact," Balfour noted, "I was thinking of Walter Rothschild."

"He's associated with our organization but he is not an officer."

"Exactly, I could write him suggesting a clarification, as if this were a point he and I had discussed, and ask that he convey the letter to the various organizations."

This was the point Balfour had been driving at for days. Weizmann smiled broadly. "Very well, I am glad we have reached this understanding."

"As am I." Balfour rose and the two men shook hands. "I look forward to working with you as we continue to develop our friendship and that of our peoples."

# CHAPTER 19

foz

FOLLOWING HIS MEETING with Balfour, Weizmann contacted Colonel Patterson and asked him to bring Jabotinsky from the training facility to a meeting in London. They gathered at Weizmann's house and he handed them each a copy of the statement Balfour prepared.

The Colonel read it quickly, "How do they propose to issue it?"

"In a letter addressed to Baron Rothschild."

"I see," Colonel Patterson replied.

Jabotinsky laid the paper on the table. "It's soft, and issuing it as a letter makes it even softer."

Weizmann bristled at the comment. He'd accomplished far more than Jabotinsky ever could have hoped for. *Huh,* he said to himself. *Jabotinsky couldn't even set foot in the foreign secretary's office, much less convince him to issue a statement of this nature—yet he had the nerve to criticize the statement as soft.*

Still, it seemed important for the three of them to remain united, at least in pursuit of the Legion. So once again Weizmann pushed aside his emotions and said tersely, "If Balfour issues the letter, it will be the most definitive statement of pro-Zionist support we have ever received from any bona fide, recognized national government."

"If Balfour issues the letter," Colonel Patterson said, "we should press them to take action as quickly as possible."

"What sort of action?"

"Something consistent with that letter. Force them to act on the statement. That would certainly bolster it and negate any indefiniteness that some might perceive."

"But what should we press them to do?" Weizmann asked.

Colonel Patterson looked over at Jabotinsky. "If Balfour issues the letter, you should petition the prime minister for a Jewish Legion. That would give him an opportunity to act on what his foreign minister has said."

"We've asked many times," Jabotinsky said in an irritated tone. "And every time we've asked, they've turned us down."

Colonel Patterson spoke in an authoritative voice, leaving little room to doubt the suggestion wasn't really a suggestion at all but an order. ""Ask again. Reference Balfour's letter—"

"Declaration," Weizmann interrupted.

Colonel Patterson had a questioning look. "What declaration?"

"Don't refer to it as a letter. Call it a declaration."

Colonel Patterson turned back to Jabotinsky. "Good idea. Reference Balfour's declaration and ask again for the establishment of a Jewish Legion within the British army. I assure you, this time the answer will be different from the ones you've received in the past."

✦ ✦ ✦

A week later, Baron Rothschild met with the British Zionist Federation leadership committee and showed them the letter he received from Balfour. Rothschild, who knew Balfour better than any of the others, had held many discussions with him but none so recently as to necessitate such a response. Still, he presented the letter as the culmination of his long-standing work with the foreign office. Weizmann, who as president of the Federation was in attendance, forced himself to sit quietly and watch while Rothschild took most of the credit for the breakthrough.

Everyone was delighted at the news that, finally, the British government appeared to have turned a corner toward a more amicable and supportive relationship with its Jewish constituency. But not everyone agreed on what that statement meant or what action the Federation should take in furtherance of it. Weizmann moderated the discussion, allowing it to run its natural course without getting too far afield, all the while moving them gently toward referring to the statement as a declaration, not a letter.

In the end, the committee decided to release Balfour's statement to the press as a Federation press release. Weizmann, primarily responsible for the language of the release, made certain the press referred to the letter as the Balfour Declaration.

✦ ✦ ✦

While the committee worked to release the Balfour Declaration to the press, Colonel Patterson, Trumpeldor, and Jabotinsky sped to the camp in Plymouth to tell us the news before it reached the papers. They assembled us outside the barracks and read Balfour's statement to us. A cheer went up from the men, followed by an impromptu version of "Hatikvah," a song adapted from a poem by Naftali Herz Imber. Written to commemorate the founding of Petah Tikva, one of the earliest settlements in Palestine, it quickly became associated with the Zionist dream of founding a Jewish state there as well.

We were still dancing and singing long after Colonel Patterson left, but then I noticed Amos wasn't with us, so I went looking for him. I found him sitting on the steps of the mess hall and took a seat beside him. "Wasn't that great news?" I asked, still grinning from ear to ear. "We're getting closer to the day when we can return home to the farm."

Amos stared down at the ground. "I suppose."

"What do you mean you suppose?"

"I mean," he grumbled, "we aren't there yet."

"Maybe not, but we're closer than we've been before. And you're closer to getting back to Dalia."

"Right."

"What's the matter?"

"Nothing."

I rolled my eyes. "Let's not go through that conversation again."

"What conversation is that?"

"Just tell me," I insisted. "How is she? Have you heard from her lately? Did they make it to the farm?"

"It's only been a few weeks."

"Have you received any letters from her?"

"No." He propped his elbows on his knees and leaned forward. "Not a one."

"And that's bothering you? Why?"

Amos glared at me. "Because I'm wondering if she still feels the same way," he snarled. "Why do you *think* it bothers me?"

"Write to her at the refugee camp. Maybe they haven't even left yet."

"It would never get to her," he groused.

I sighed. "You're probably right. And if she's at the farm already, mail delivery would be difficult."

"She could post from Kvutzat Kinneret."

It always irritated me when he did that. We argue, I finally take his side, then he argues against me, but I pushed it aside that night and took a different approach. "How many times have *you* written to *her*?"

Amos looked over at me. "Me? I'm not talking about *me* writing. I'm talking about *her* writing."

"How many times have you written to her?" I repeated, unwilling to concede the point.

He sighed again. "I haven't," he said in a resigned tone.

"Did it ever occur to you that she was waiting on you to write first?"

"No," he said indignantly. "Why would she do that?"

"I don't know. Perhaps she doesn't know how to reach you by mail. Maybe most soldiers who are lonesome for their girlfriends write to them. Some of these guys write home every day."

Amos ignored what I said about writing and instead focused on Dalia. "What do you mean how to reach me?"

"The address," I responded loudly. "Did you give her an address where she could write to you?"

"We didn't know an address when we left."

"Then you can write to her."

"How?"

"Pencil and paper."

"No. Not that," he retorted. "How do I know it will get to her?"

"Post it to her in care of Kvutzat Kinneret. They'll see that it gets to her."

"Yeah, maybe so."

✦ ✦ ✦

When reports of Balfour's declaration reached the newspapers, Jabotinsky did as Colonel Patterson insisted and filed a request with Lloyd George seeking the establishment of a Jewish Legion as a combat unit within the British army. Three days later, Lord Derby, the secretary for war, sent Jabotinsky a note at the camp in Winchester requesting his presence at a meeting. Jabotinsky showed the note to Patterson and Trumpeldor.

"This is great!" Colonel Patterson exclaimed.

"I'm not sure of that," Jabotinsky demurred.

Colonel Patterson looked perplexed. "Why not?"

"What does he want?"

"You asked the prime minister about establishing a Legion, right?" Jabotinsky answered. "Yes, but this is not a request to meet with the prime minister. This is from the War Office."

"As it should be," Colonel Patterson insisted.

"I don't know," Jabotinsky hedged. "I'm not sure this is a good thing."

"What do you mean you don't know?" Colonel Patterson blurted. "This is what you've been working for. This is what we've all been working for."

"I'm not a person of high enough stature to meet with such a high-ranking government official."

"Didn't you interview Kitchener?" Trumpeldor was irritated by what he perceived as Jabotinsky's false sense of piety.

"That was different. That was as a reporter. And we were on the steps of his office. This is not like that. I would not be interviewing him as a reporter."

"You correspond with the prime minister, but you're afraid to meet with the war secretary?"

Jabotinsky glanced at him. "You go."

Trumpeldor shook his head. "No, my English isn't very good and besides, you are the one who has been pushing for the Legion. You have to go."

"Joseph is right," Colonel Patterson added. "You have no option.

You *must* take the meeting. To decline it would be an affront to Derby and the end of the Jewish Legion."

"It would be the end of everything we've been working for," Trumpeldor added.

Jabotinsky looked over at him again. "You'll go with me?"

"I will accompany you," Trumpeldor agreed. "But strictly for moral support. *You* must do the talking."

The following day, Jabotinsky and Trumpeldor met with Lord Derby, who informed them that the prime minister had received Jabotinsky's request to create a Jewish Legion. "And," Derby continued, "it is my duty to inform you that your request has been approved."

Trumpeldor smiled. Jabotinsky seemed unmoved. "We not only want a Jewish Legion, we also want that Legion to be sent to Palestine to reclaim the land that was seized from us."

"That strategy is being considered," Derby said, somewhat ruffled by the tone of Jabotinsky's response. "But this is a first step. Forming an actual fighting unit. Preparing that unit for combat."

Trumpeldor nudged Jabotinsky's foot and gave him a nod. Jabotinsky took a deep breath, squared his shoulders, and forced a smile. "We are grateful for the approval, and delighted to be of service to His Majesty's army."

Darby replied, "Good, we would be pleased to receive your recommendation of a suitable officer to take command of the men."

"Without question," Jabotinsky said. "We want Colonel Patterson to command us."

"Excellent choice," Derby replied approvingly. "I am certain we shall have no difficulty obtaining approval of Colonel Patterson's appointment."

After the meeting concluded, Jabotinsky and Trumpeldor located Weizmann and Colonel Patterson. They told them of Derby's announcement that the Jewish Legion had been created and of their request that Colonel Patterson command the unit.

"I'm flattered," Colonel Patterson replied. "But not altogether confident Derby will consent, much less forward the nomination for formal approval."

"Quite the contrary," Trumpeldor argued. "He seemed to agree wholeheartedly and indicated there should be no difficulty obtaining official approval."

Colonel Patterson looked surprised. "Really? I didn't know he and I got along that well."

"He seemed to think it was all but done," Jabotinsky added. "It's a good thing, too. We could not think of going into battle with anyone else."

They stood there soaking up the realization that finally, after years of work and months of frustration, they had reached their goal. The Jewish Legion was officially a unit of the British army. And for the first time that anyone could remember, Colonel Patterson appeared on the verge of tears.

✦ ✦ ✦

A few days later, Colonel Patterson was called to a meeting with General Archibald Wilson, Royal Army attaché to the War Department. Wilson began, "I've been directed by Sir William Robertson, chief of staff to Field Marshal Haig, to inform you that we are appointing you to command the Thirty-Eighth Battalion of the Royal Fusiliers."

Colonel Patterson, of course, knew the appointment was in the works and was overjoyed to receive it. But if his experience in the army had taught him anything it was that one could obtain more at the time an appointment was made than at any time thereafter, so he took care to make certain the details were addressed. "The Thirty-Eighth?" he asked with a skeptical tone. "There is no Thirty-Eighth."

"There is now. Thanks to your Jewish colleagues. They've won the day and convinced the prime minister to give them their Jewish Legion. We've assigned it the designation of Thirty-Eighth Battalion."

"Is there any objection to referring to it as the Jewish Legion?" Colonel Patterson asked.

"I suppose not," Wilson responded. "Many of our units have...colloquial titles apart from their official designations."

"Excellent."

"They requested you as their commander," Wilson continued. "I assume your physicians will consent."

"Yes." Colonel Patterson nodded confidently. "I assume they will."

"Good." Wilson took a file from his desk. "Is there anything else?"

"As you are aware," Colonel Patterson continued, "members of the former Zion Mule Corps are now in training at Winchester."

"So I am told."

"We will use them to form the core of the unit."

"Recruitment is your responsibility," Wilson noted, laying the file aside.

Colonel Patterson agreed. "And I am glad to do that, however, most of our men are interested in returning to fight in Palestine. To regain control of the land that was seized from them."

Once more, Wilson glanced down at the papers on his desk. "Nothing is certain yet, but the general consensus is that they are to be used as part of a new strategy in Palestine."

"In conjunction with General Monro's troops now in Egypt?"

"No doubt, our troops in Egypt will be part of any undertaking in the Middle East. It has not been announced yet, but the feeling is that

General Allenby will take over for General Monro as commander of the Egyptian Expeditionary Force, regardless of the overall strategy."

"And I would report to General Allenby?"

"Yes. Of course."

"Good. I know General Allenby. He is a great man and an excellent leader."

Wilson looked up from his desk. "So, are you in?"

"Yes, sir, I accept the position of commander for the Thirty-Eighth Battalion."

"Good." Wilson pushed back his chair to stand.

"There is one more thing, sir," Colonel Patterson added. "If I may."

"What is that?" Wilson seemed impatient.

"Joseph Trumpeldor was second-in-command of the Zion Mule Corps—the ranking Jewish officer in the unit. I would like him with me for this, also. As ranking Jewish officer for the Jewish Legion."

"Can't help you with that one," Wilson said coolly. "I'm afraid Trumpeldor is out."

Colonel Patterson was astounded. "Out? Why? He's an excellent soldier. One of the bravest men I've ever known."

"Perhaps he is," Wilson said, his expression unchanged. "But our rules do not permit one-armed soldiers."

"He was fine for Gallipoli," Colonel Patterson argued.

"Entirely different unit," Wilson countered. "That was an auxiliary transportation unit. This is regular infantry. Different rules apply."

Colonel Patterson could see the decision was final. "Has Trumpeldor been told?"

"We intended to leave that task to you."

"Then I'll take Jabotinsky as my Jewish officer," Colonel Patterson said boldly.

"Very well," Wilson agreed. "But he cannot hold officer rank."

"Why not?" Having been denied Trumpeldor, Colonel Patterson wasn't about to give in on Jabotinsky without a fight.

"You know the rules, Colonel. Foreigners are not allowed officer rank in His Majesty's army."

"The czar of Russia holds the rank of colonel."

"That is purely an honorary gesture."

Colonel Patterson smiled, "That will do for Jabotinsky."

Wilson's shoulders, normally square and angular, collapsed. "Very well," he sighed in a defeated tone. "I'll pass along your request." He glanced up at Colonel Patterson. "But only for the rank of lieutenant. He must not be seen as your equal."

When the meeting was over, Colonel Patterson walked out to the street, where he found Weizmann and Jabotinsky waiting. "It's done," he announced with little fanfare.

"The Jewish Legion?"

"Officially the Thirty-Eighth Battalion, but it will also be known as the Jewish Legion." He looked over at Jabotinsky. "You and I are to share command."

Jabotinsky looked surprised. "What about Trumpeldor?"

"I requested him, but General Wilson denied the request."

"Why?"

"Apparently army regulations do not allow one-armed men to serve in the infantry."

Jabotinsky's eyes narrowed and the veins in his forehead bulged. "I don't like it."

"I know," Colonel Patterson replied. "And I don't think Joseph will care for it, either."

"You haven't told him?"

Colonel Patterson gestured over his shoulder. "I just came from the meeting. I just now walked out. You two are the first people I've seen."

"This is a good day," Weizmann offered, attempting to interject a more jubilant mood. His eyes were fixed on Jabotinsky. "We have the Jewish Legion and we have Colonel Patterson."

"I think I should resign," Jabotinsky responded, still angry.

"Why?" Weizmann blurted out. "Why would you resign now?!"

"Because this is not the way I wanted things arranged. I wanted Colonel Patterson *and* I wanted Trumpeldor. And I don't like having an *official* designation and an alternative *permissible* name. I want *Jewish Legion* to be the official designation."

For Weizmann, months of frustration with Jabotinsky suddenly boiled over. "How can you be so blind?!" he railed. "We've obtained almost everything we wanted and you would throw it all away because you didn't get *your* way. Never mind about what anyone else might want or how much work *they* put into it. Did you think the British army would bend hundreds of years of tradition and experience just to accommodate *your* view?"

"You should listen to him," Colonel Patterson added. "Think about the bigger picture and primary objective. We are attempting to restore Jewish settlers to their land in Palestine. We are not trying to reeducate the entire United Kingdom or force the kingdom to conform to the will of Ze'ev Jabotinsky."

"I suppose you're right," Jabotinsky mumbled. "But British officials make me so angry."

"Yes," Colonel Patterson agreed. "They can be quite infuriating."

✦ ✦ ✦

That same afternoon, Colonel Patterson and Jabotinsky rode to the camp at Winchester. Jabotinsky rejoined us in our training exercises while Colonel Patterson called Trumpeldor aside and the two of them went for a walk. As they strolled across the parade grounds, Colonel Patterson told Trumpeldor the Legion had been approved and that he had been named the unit's commander.

"I am glad to have you in charge," Trumpeldor responded. "It will be like old times."

"There is one thing I must tell you, though," Colonel Patterson said in a downcast tone.

"What is that?"

Colonel Patterson looked over at him. "You cannot serve as my second in command."

"Oh." Trumpeldor was taken aback but did his best to recover. "Well, I was a foot soldier before. I can be one again. Who will you name instead? I can give you several recommendations."

"I'm sorry, Joseph," Colonel Patterson said with a heavy voice. "They will not admit you to the unit at all."

Trumpeldor frowned. "Not at all?"

"No."

"Why not?" The hurt in Trumpeldor's voice was obvious.

"General Wilson says we are now a regular army unit," Colonel Patterson explained. "According to him, regulations do not permit one-armed soldiers in the regular army."

"I heard something about that rule the other day," Trumpeldor nodded. "But I did not think it would be a problem. Not after Gallipoli. I assumed no one would object."

"Look," Colonel Patterson said in a friendlier tone. "We are required to recruit our own soldiers. You would be excellent at that, as you were in Egypt finding men for the Zion Mule Corps. Can you help us recruit men for the Jewish Legion?"

"I don't think so," Trumpeldor said, declining the offer. "That would be awkward, recruiting men for something I'm disqualified from doing. And it would be difficult for the men we already have, too. Seeing me here, but not one of them. I think the best thing I can do is leave."

Colonel Patterson knew that would be Trumpeldor's decision and already had chosen not to oppose him. "Where would you go?"

Trumpeldor shrugged. "I don't know...return to Russia, I suppose. I've been thinking of home lately anyway. Perhaps I should go there and search for a way to return to Palestine."

"Well, you'll need somewhere to stay until you can arrange the trip back home, if that is really where you want to go. So until you do, you can stay at my home. I will arrange it for you."

✦ ✦ ✦

Trumpeldor packed his things while we were still completing that day's training exercises. He left before dinner without saying good-bye to anyone and that day, when Colonel Patterson came to find him and took him for a walk, was the last time I ever saw him. He was a man among men and much later, when I learned he'd been killed defending his farm near Degania, I was neither surprised nor sad. I could see him standing among the rubble of his home, rifle in hand, defending his ground, fighting to the very end, and I knew for certain he wouldn't have wanted his life to end any other way.

✦ ✦ ✦

When Colonel Patterson received official notice of Jabotinsky's promotion to the rank of lieutenant, he assembled us on the parade grounds—the place where we gathered when we first arrived from Egypt. Most of us were Zion Mule Corps veterans and were familiar with how the organization worked. Colonel Patterson announced it anyway, describing the dual command we would follow, with Jabotinsky as our ranking officer and all of us accountable to him, but with British officers alongside us, too. Then he pinned Jabotinsky's rank insignia on his uniform and we all gave a salute.

Afterward, Amos and I went forward to congratulate Jabotinsky. As we were leaving to return to the barracks, Colonel Patterson called me aside and informed me that I had been designated his chief of staff. I could not have been happier.

# CHAPTER 20

foz

FOR THE NEXT SEVERAL MONTHS, Jabotinsky, Colonel Patterson, and I plied the neighborhoods of London and the coffee shops of surrounding villages, recruiting men to fill the ranks of the Jewish Legion. It was a difficult task. Most people knew the truth about the conditions troops from both sides of the war endured in Europe. Everyone knew of the horrendous loss of life that occurred there. As a result, the mention of service in the army met with almost immediate resistance. No one gave up, least of all Jabotinsky, and gradually we convinced more and more young men to join us. As the weeks went by, membership in the Legion grew and our ranks swelled closer and closer to capacity.

Even as our work went forward with the men in the street, however, influential Jewish businessmen and civic leaders—men who never would have been required to serve in the military under any circumstance—rose up to oppose us in our recruitment effort and government backing for the Jewish Legion we were creating.

Those who opposed us the most claimed they were worried that calling the unit "Jewish" would inflame Muslims in Palestine and that deployment of such a unit would only increase the number of attacks launched against the Jewish settlers who remained in Palestine, having stubbornly refused to leave their farms as ordered by the Turks. Official support for a Jewish state in Palestine, they argued, would do the same but on a much broader scale.

Opposition from officials in the British government and from upper crust Protestant elites was predictable. They had a long history of deep disdain for Jews. But opposition from our fellow Jews was hard to take.

Colonel Patterson tried to explain things to me, telling me the Jews who opposed us came from families who for generations had endured persecution in Europe. Because of that, he argued, they learned the value of avoiding any activity or association that drew public attention to them. "Their reaction to us and to the Legion is merely an extension of attitudes that are generational in nature." I understood what he was saying, but it didn't make the opposition any easier to accept.

As the opposition became more pronounced, Colonel Patterson proposed a meeting with the Jewish leaders who were working hardest against us. By then I had decided there was nothing we could do to make them stop and that any attempt on our part to change their minds would be futile, but he insisted that we try and instructed me to arrange the meeting.

A week later we gathered in the basement of Bevis Marks Synagogue with two dozen of London's most prominent Jewish businessmen. They listened attentively as Colonel Patterson explained the current strategy, one born of the British desire to protect its interests in the Suez and that furthered the aims stated in Balfour's declaration.

"Yes," they argued, "but your proposal would have Jews fighting as a designated Jewish unit of the British army."

"It wouldn't simply be a unit of the British army," someone clarified. "It would be a unit known specifically as a *Jewish* unit."

"The unit already has been formed," another commented.

"Is that true?" someone asked.

"Yes," Colonel Patterson replied. "The unit now exists. It has been formally requested by the prime minister and approved by the War Department. We are currently working to enlist a full complement of soldiers to fill out the unit's ranks."

"And it is known as the Jewish Legion."

"Yes," Colonel Patterson acknowledged. "That, however, is not the official designation."

"What is the official designation?"

"The Thirty-Eighth Battalion of the Royal Fusiliers."

"We can't possibly participate in that," someone opined.

"Participating in the Jewish army is not an issue," another argued. "Many young men from right here in this synagogue are members of regular British army units. But creating a special one and labeling it the Jewish Legion within the British army puts us in alignment with Russia."

"It makes us look like we're allies with Russia, too," another added.

"The Russian government for years has followed a policy of systematic persecution against us," someone called out from the back of the room. "They persecuted us, our relatives, our neighbors, and our ancestors. We will *not* be seen as an ally of the czar's army."

"Hear! Hear!" the crowd called out.

"Besides," another commented, "in England we are exempt from military service. The government doesn't conscript us or force us to volunteer and we don't want them to start."

"Many of our children would have to fight," another lamented.

"We get all the benefits of freedom and security without having to serve in the army."

Colonel Patterson spoke up. "It is true, European Jews have been persecuted since the day they arrived on the continent. Much of that persecution came at the hands of the Russians. Many of you and your ancestors have been forced to live in excluded areas, prevented from entering many of the professions, and unable to stand for elected office. I understand your feelings against the Russians quite clearly. But one thing is equally apparent for us here in the United Kingdom: She cannot win this war alone. She must have allies. Like it or not, Russia is one of those allies. And, I would add, many Protestant citizens are as uncomfortable with that arrangement as you are. But the United Kingdom cannot go it alone against the Central Powers. You can be offended by that, but you cannot deny the truth of it."

"And this Jewish Legion will somehow remedy both our historic situations?"

"The only real remedy for the Jewish situation in Europe," Colonel Patterson replied, "is through the creation of a homeland—a Jewish homeland—and the only place for a Jewish homeland is in Palestine."

"Many have already returned," someone countered. "Without the need of some Jewish Legion."

"Yes," Colonel Patterson responded. "They returned on their own and they were driven out on their own. They are right now living as exiles in Egypt. Forced from the land they lawfully purchased in Palestine."

"And they would have been in a better position if they'd had this Jewish Legion to defend them?"

"Few of them fought back effectively," Colonel Patterson responded, "because they didn't have the means to fight back. They weren't trained for it and they weren't equipped for it."

"And fighting back is the answer?"

"Historically, yes," Colonel Patterson responded. "The only safety Jews have ever found has come from resisting, from fighting back. And the only way you'll ever have a state anywhere is to fight for it.

But in order to do that, you must have a collective force capable of a quick and decisive military response. If the Jews of Palestine had that capability two or three years ago, you and I would not be discussing the matter because there would be no matter to discuss."

In many ways it was a remarkable meeting. A Gentile officer from the British army telling a room full of Jews they had lost their heritage. He said it, without saying it, but the message was clear as ever. Then he offered a way to recover that heritage. They argued with him. They attempted to refute his position. But no one threw him out of the building. Colonel Patterson was eloquent, passionate, and obviously convinced of the rightness of our cause, but though we stayed there in the basement of the synagogue until almost midnight, he managed to persuade only two or three to agree with our position.

When it was obvious to everyone that the Jewish Legion was going to succeed, several of the Jewish opposition leaders—all of them wealthy, influential people—went as a group to see Lord Derby. In a meeting that lasted far longer than was appropriate, they raised the same objections as they had voiced in the meeting with Colonel Patterson.

At first Derby resisted, saying his hands were tied. The decision to form the Legion had been made by others. The prime minister was in favor of it. It was he who requested it in the first place. But as the meeting wore on, Derby's strength began to fade and by the time the meeting ended he backed down, agreeing to issue orders rescinding the name of the unit and the commitment to deploy the unit to Palestine.

Word of Derby's decision reached Colonel Patterson while we were on a recruitment trip to Liverpool. The colonel was outraged and immediately ripped off a written protest to Field Marshal Haig lampooning Derby's order as despicable. "Based on Derby's prior representations, and on statements from your chief of staff," he wrote.

"I already have promised hundreds of recruits they would fight in Palestine. Former members of the Zion Mule Corps have been deceived into enlisting and I, myself, have been deceived as well, and in the event Lord Derby's ruling stands, I shall resign my commission immediately in protest."

At the same time, Weizmann complained to Lord Milner, who was equally outraged. To vent that anger, he paid a call on Wickham Steed, editor of the *London Times* and explained in great detail all that Derby had done, including the identity of the men who had pressured him to do it. The following day, the *Times* issued an editorial calling Derby out for his actions and accusing him of caving to a group of arrogant plutocrats. The article also urged Colonel Patterson to reconsider his decision and remain with the Legion.

That morning, Lloyd George read the *Times* alone in his office, as was his daily custom. When he came to the editorial article he, too, was incensed. "Who does Derby think he is?" his voice boomed out to no one in particular. An assistant rushed into the office to see what the shouting was about.

"This is not what I wanted!" George continued. "Recruiting Jewish soldiers and forming this unit is part of a well-laid strategy. A strategy Derby helped create. Get him in here now!"

The assistant retreated quickly to her desk and placed a call to Lord Derby's office. Within the hour, Derby arrived to find George still in a fit.

"They're right!" George shouted as Derby entered the room. He held up the *Times* and pointed to it. "For once they are absolutely correct. You caved to a small group of plutocrats. A tiny group of wealthy businessmen who think they can tell this government what to do. Why did you do that?"

"They made some good arguments."

"I know what they said," George scoffed.

"Someone told you?"

"No one had to tell me," George retorted. "I know. They offered the same pitiful excuses they've offered since the war began. 'The Muslims might be enflamed,'" he said in a mocking tone. "'We're foreigners living as refugees. We're not required to serve in the military and we don't want the government to change that policy.' We let them live here as refugees, protect them while they grow rich, and then they cower when it's time to serve this great nation."

Derby shrugged. "Well, I've issued the order. It's done now."

George was beside himself. "No!" he shouted, pounding on the desk with his fist. "It's not *done*."

Derby looked surprised by the outburst. "What do you mean?"

"I mean, you'll fix this."

"But how?" Derby lamented. "I told them my decision already. I agreed."

"You'll recant and give Ze'ev Jabotinsky, Chaim Weizmann, and Colonel Patterson precisely what you promised." George glowered at him. "You'll give them what *we* promised. A Jewish Legion, deployed to fight in Palestine."

Derby frowned. "Is that still our strategy?"

"Yes!" George shouted again. "Why do you ask?"

"It puts me in a terribly uncomfortable position."

George came from behind the desk. "How you *feel* is not important. Not to this country and not to me. The important thing is that we seize control of Palestine at the earliest possible moment. And to do that we need every able-bodied soldier we can find. Get the Jewish Legion formed, trained, and ready for deployment. As soon as possible!"

Before the day was over, Derby recanted. Colonel Patterson decided not to resign and our unit was transferred to a much more elaborate facility at Plymouth, where we began training in earnest for deployment to Palestine.

WITHIN HOURS of Lord Derby's announcement, news that the Royal Army had formed a Jewish Legion reached New York. Rumors that the Legion was to be used as part of an Allied Palestinian campaign quickly followed. One of those who heard the news was David Ben-Gurion, who learned of it from an article in *The New York Times*.

Ben-Gurion was an interesting man. I had met him when he arrived in England to train with us and continued to see him later during his time in office as Israel's prime minister—a post he held jointly with that of defense minister. He was smart, quick, and decisive, though by no means infallible, and remained that way throughout his life, valuing the practical over the ideal—but never fully surrendering the ideal. A quite unassimilated man.

The last time we were together was at a rally in Jaffa, long after the colonel was dead and all the things we'd yet to do had been done. By then, Ben-Gurion was retired from politics for the final time—he had announced his retirement on at least one prior occasion, only to come back from the sidelines as the next election approached—and though we both were older and not quite as energetic as we once were, it still was easy to see how he came to be known as the Founding Father of our country. He was a man with considerable personal force.

When war broke out between the Allies and the Central powers, Ben-Gurion was living in Jerusalem. Back then, he was certain the future of a Jewish state in Palestine lay with the Ottoman Empire and recruited a group of Jews to fight with the Ottoman army. Unimpressed by his sentiment or his effort to help, the Ottoman government deported him to Egypt along with the rest of us. I never saw him in the refugee camp and learned later that he had quickly moved on from Alexandria to the United States, where he settled in New York.

Inspired by news of the Jewish Legion, and realizing from his time in the United States that the Ottoman Empire would not prevail in the Middle East, Ben-Gurion went to work recruiting volunteers to join the Legion—this time hoping to find Jews who would join the war on the British side. Interestingly, he encountered some of the same opposition as we did, though to a much lesser degree.

Ben-Gurion began his recruitment effort among American Jews— children of second- and third-generation Jewish families who were well established in the United States. However, most of them who were of fighting age were subject to US conscription. With mandatory military service looming in their future, they were hesitant about join- ing the army of a foreign nation, even that of an ally, for fear of being prosecuted by American authorities for evading the draft or worse— being prosecuted for treason. Others were wary of being labeled a draft dodger.

They were also quite Americanized—having a greater sense of loyalty to their adopted nation than did the Jews who chose to live in England. They were inspired to take up arms for the Allies but less inclined to fight for a distant Jewish homeland, as they'd found one that suited them right where they lived. Most were eagerly awaiting service in the United States Army.

A few—mostly recent arrivals to America—were not intimidated by any of those concerns and readily chose to volunteer. "I would rather be labeled an American deserter than a deserter of my native Israel," they said. Seeing the reaction of Jews who had yet to become Americanized, Ben-Gurion turned to Russian immigrants, a large group of whom lived in Brooklyn, and found in them a ready source of able-bodied manpower. Not yet US citizens—or only recently so— they had less loyalty to America and fewer inhibitions about joining a foreign army, even if it was the British army. They also had not tasted the prosperity of Western life to the same degree as their relatives in England. With less to give up they found the prospect of fighting in Palestine a welcome adventure. The notion of building a country from the ground up suggested a much quicker route to the life they sought than did slogging out a daily existence on the streets of New York.

"Where do we sign up?" they asked.

"We'll travel to London and join up there," Ben-Gurion explained.

"But we have no money," they protested.

"I'll raise the money," Ben-Gurion promised.

"And what if we get there and the British don't let us join—what then?"

"We'll make certain everyone knows the British refused us and we'll find a way to bring you back here."

✦ ✦ ✦

Several months after we moved to the facility in Plymouth, Ben-Gurion arrived with the recruits from America. Almost immediately it became obvious to everyone that although Jabotinsky and Ben-Gurion were acquainted with each other from prior associations, they rarely ever got along well. It would be a pattern of relationship that followed them the remainder of their lives—and even beyond—but I digress...

The recruits from America were, as a general observation, louder and bawdier than the Mule Corps veterans or the men we recruited from England. During the Americans' initial month at the camp, discipline was an issue. Colonel Patterson, ever mindful that he was a Protestant Gentile in a racially and religiously charged environment, did his best to impose order without appearing unduly harsh while avoiding even the appearance of being prejudicial. I think he remembered with regret having flogged the soldiers in Gallipoli and was determined to head off a repeat of that situation if at all possible. Lack of discipline, however, wasn't our only problem.

With the influx of volunteers from America, our numbers rose to almost twice that of a single battalion. The facility could easily handle the extra men. Our command structure, however, was strained to the breaking point. To address that situation, Colonel Patterson turned to the idea of creating a second battalion. "I'm not sure how that will go over in London," he mused aloud as I entered the office on my way to the filing cabinet.

"Maybe you shouldn't ask," I offered.

"What do you mean? Just keep going the way we are? We can't possibly manage this many men ourselves."

"I didn't mean give up on the idea," I explained. "I meant, maybe you should just do it without asking."

Colonel Patterson's eyes opened wider as he pondered the idea. "Well, they admitted the extra men to our ranks because they need all the soldiers they can get. And having accepted them, one could argue they tacitly approved the structure necessary to manage them." He smiled at me. "That is a brilliant idea. I think I'll give it a try."

That afternoon, we prepared a report informing London of the latest developments with the Jewish Legion, including an official total for the number of men in camp and news of our action in dividing the Legion into two battalions—one under Colonel Patterson's direct command, the other under the command of Eliezer Margolin, with Colonel Patterson having a supervisory role. Margolin was a Jewish soldier who served with the British army and whom we met in Gallipoli. As a citizen of Great Britain, Margolin was unaffected by the regulations that excluded Jews and held the rank of major at the time. He was already at Plymouth when we arrived.

In the final paragraph of the report, Colonel Patterson attempted to soften any otherwise negative reaction to his actions by requesting an official designation of the second battalion as the Thirty-Ninth Battalion of Royal Fusiliers. We sent the document by courier to the War Department and assumed we'd receive an official response in a week or two, as was the custom with routine matters.

In London, officials of the War Department who opposed formation of the Jewish Legion from the beginning were outraged by Patterson's unilateral decision to create a second battalion and by his request for an official designation of that unit. They protested the action through memos to their superiors and fulminated against it in departmental meetings, attempting to raise the matter sufficiently to obtain a review by the war cabinet.

When that failed to produce the desired result, the disgruntled faction lobbied Lord Derby directly, bombarding him with memos and personal entreaties from related officials and one or two cabinet officials urging him to disband the entire project.

Much to their chagrin, Derby, chastened by previous attempts to curtail the Legion, refused to get in Colonel Patterson's way and authorized formation of the Thirty-Ninth Battalion, extending to them the designation of Jewish Legion as well. But those who opposed us were determined to work against us. They didn't have to wait long for their first opportunity.

Many of our recruits, particularly those from the United States, were orthodox Jews and not long after they arrived at Plymouth they voiced an objection to the food in the mess hall. They wanted kosher food. The camp had neither kosher food stocks nor kosher facilities from which to prepare it.

At first the issue was one the men attempted to solve on their own. Orthodox recruits ate regular food during the week and fasted on the Sabbath. After a month went by and kosher food still was not offered, they grew tired of the make-do arrangement and began to murmur among themselves, asking whether they should continue to serve in the Legion. When their private discussions turned hostile, Aaron Ben Joseph brought the matter to Colonel Patterson's attention.

The colonel listened attentively but shook his head. "I'm not certain the War Department can accommodate meal requests like that."

"Why not?" Joseph asked.

"For one thing, it would require special treatment and I'm not sure they're set up for it. They would have to requisition kosher food and create a kosher kitchen. It's not as simple as changing an item on the menu. Do you know if they supply kosher meals to Jews serving in other regular units?"

"No, sir, I don't."

"I don't know that, either."

"But I know the British supply Muslims with halal food," Joseph argued.

Colonel Patterson frowned. "You are certain of this?"

"Yes, sir, I've seen them eating it."

"How many men are we talking about? The ones in the Legion," Colonel Patterson quickly added. "How many men do we have in the Legion who want a kosher diet?"

Joseph reached for his hip pocket and produced a list. "These are the names."

"Very well," Colonel Patterson replied. "I'll see what I can do."

For some, the response of "I'll see what I can do" would have been a sure sign they intended to do nothing at all, but Colonel Patterson wasn't like most men. Instead, he immediately put me to work preparing a requisition order to London asking for kosher food.

When the request arrived in London, an aide showed it to Colonel Ogilvie, one of the officers in charge of supply coordination and a key staff-level figure in the opposition against our unit. He took one look at the form and denied it on the spot. Then he asked to see our training schedules. The aide produced them the following day, and Ogilvie noticed we didn't train on Saturdays.

"Why doesn't Patterson train his unit on Saturdays like every other unit in the Royal Army?" Ogilvie asked the aide.

"Saturday is the Jewish Sabbath," the aide reminded him.

"Well," Ogilvie snarled, "we'll put an end to that. If the Jews want to serve in the army, they can serve under army rules. We have Jews in almost every company. They train on Saturdays like everyone else. Patterson's Jews will be no exception."

In an official memo to Colonel Patterson, Ogilvie informed us that the request for kosher meals had been denied and that a review of our training schedule showed an unauthorized deviation from Saturday drills. Ogilvie ordered us to discontinue this practice immediately and conform all training to standard army practice.

Colonel Patterson responded by filing an immediate protest with Lord Derby at the War Department. He also sent a message to Leo Amery informing him of the matter. Four days later, Lord Derby once again found himself in the prime minister's office, facing the wrath of Lloyd George.

"Is this true?" George demanded, waving a copy of Colonel Patterson's protest. "Do we provide special meals to Muslims who serve in the army?"

"Well...yes, Mr. Prime Minister. That is our current practice."

"Meals that fit their dietary restrictions?"

"I believe the understanding at the time was that they wouldn't serve if we didn't."

"And do we give them Friday off from training and other duties so they can pray?"

Derby glanced down at the floor. "It was a necessary concession."

"Then why not do the same for the Jews?!" George demanded.

"Our officers think it would be...too much."

"Too much?!" George's face was red and the veins in his temples pulsed. "It wasn't too much to do it for the Arabs, even though it had never been done until now. It wasn't too much to provide them with special meals and a special schedule. Yet when the Jews—who've asked repeatedly for permission to help with the war, even *begged* us to allow them to participate—when they ask, suddenly it's *too much*."

Derby, who'd been out of the loop on Ogilvie's decisions and orders, easily could have said so and laid the matter at someone else's feet, but he was not that sort of man. Instead, he said lamely, "We've never done it that way."

"Obviously we have," George retorted. "In fact, we're doing it right now by the very practice of accommodating the Muslims, which you just admitted is the current policy of the Royal Army."

Derby looked up at him. "I meant, we've never accommodated Jews, sir."

"Until this war, we'd never accommodated Muslims, either, but we made space for them. Give the Jews equal treatment. Give them what they need."

"I'm not sure—"

"I didn't ask for your excuses!" George shouted. "I asked for *action.* Provide the Jewish Legion whatever they need to function properly and get them to the field as quickly as possible. General Allenby needs all the help he can get!"

Derby rose from his chair. "Yes, Mr. Prime Minister," he said, and he turned toward the door.

"And, Derby," George said in a calmer voice, "I'm expecting you to handle this sort of thing in accordance with my wishes—*before* it reaches this office."

Derby turned to face him. "Yes, sir."

"I don't think I need to remind you that there are many in this government who think you're in over your head."

Derby nodded meekly. "Yes, Mr. Prime Minister. I shall see that they have all they need."

✦ ✦ ✦

Less than a week after Lord Derby's meeting with the prime minister, orthodox rabbis arrived at the camp and established a kosher cooking facility complete with a Jewish chef in the mess hall. When the first kosher meal was served, I noticed Amos avoided the regular serving line and got in the one for kosher. After I went through, I took a seat at the table with him. I was curious about why he was eating that way—neither of us had ever eaten anything but *treif,* or non-Kosher, for as long as we could remember—but it seemed rude to ask, so I talked about other things and waited to see what happened.

"Did you write to Dalia?"

"Yeah."

"What did she say?"

He put down his fork, reached into the pocket of his shirt, and took out an envelope, which he tossed toward me. "Don't open it," he snarled.

I caught the envelope just before it landed on my plate and glanced at the front. Scrawled next to the address was a note written in Hebrew that said simply, "Gone to the Galilee."

"Hey," I smiled. "At least now you know."

"Yeah," he answered glumly. "Now I know." He reached across the table and snatched the envelope from my hand. "But I still haven't heard from her."

I watched as Amos stuffed the letter into his pocket and shook my head. "You don't know how lucky you are."

"What do you mean?"

"You have Dalia. Any guy in this room would die to have a girl like her."

"How do I know I have her?"

"Did you see the look in her eyes when we were at the dock, right before we left?"

His eyes flashed at me. "You were looking at her eyes?"

"You weren't?" I retorted.

"That's different for me, but you're my brother."

"You think I don't notice when a pretty girl goes by?"

"Yes," he admitted. "I suppose so. But we're not talking about *any* girl."

"You noticed she was pretty, right?"

"What are you getting at?"

"If you noticed her, what makes you think a thousand other guys won't, too? She's not wearing a sign that says, 'I'm Amos' girl. Look the other way.'"

It sounded so stupid to hear the words, but it was true. No one was going to stop noticing Dalia just because Amos had kissed her a few times. He realized it was stupid, too, and a smile spread over his face. I grinned at him and seconds later we were laughing.

When he paused to catch his breath, Amos said, "I'm sorry I was upset. It's just tough not seeing her."

"I know, but if you write to her now through the farm in Kinneret, maybe she'll have the letter when she gets up there. Might already be there now."

"I'll know in a few days."

"Why?"

"When the letter to the refugee camp came back, I did what you said and wrote her at Kinneret."

I wanted to slug him for arguing with me, but Amos seemed oblivious to the moment. He leaned over his plate, took a bite of food, and swallowed. Then he pointed to the food, "You should get this next time. It's pretty good."

✦ ✦ ✦

A few weeks later, Colonel Patterson received a request for a report on the Legion's condition for combat. He glanced over the document, then brought it to me at my desk. He took a seat across from me and laid the document between us on the desktop. "This is important." For the next twenty minutes he explained the report to me, line by line, describing in detail the information needed to properly prepare our response.

"London wants to know if we're ready to deploy," he said. "And we must be very careful how we respond."

"They're looking for another reason to keep us from going?"

"Perhaps," he acknowledged, "but this is also standard procedure. Even units engaged in combat must periodically file these reports as a way of permitting a commander to express his opinion about his troops."

I frowned. "So, is this a problem?"

"Not for the Thirty-Eighth Battalion. That battalion has a strong contingent of former Mule Corps members and is ready for deployment right now."

"But the Thirty-Ninth?"

"They're mostly American and British civilian volunteers. Very few of them have any military experience whatsoever and none of them understand how the British army operates. And," he continued, "they did not arrive in very good physical shape."

"They need more time," I observed.

Colonel Patterson agreed. "Yes, they need more time."

"If that's the case, should we ask Major Margolin to prepare a report for them?" There was a hint of doubt in my voice. I didn't think that was what he wanted.

Colonel Patterson shook his head. "I don't think so. If we turn in separate reports for each battalion, London might use the Thirty-Ninth's lack of readiness as a pretext to deny deployment for the entire Legion."

"And if we file a single report?"

"It runs contrary to the argument that we are two battalions, but it would allow us to merge some of the numbers and fudge on the overall condition of the group."

"Well," I suggested, "we *are* a single Jewish Legion."

Colonel Patterson's face brightened in a look of realization. "Yes," he smiled. "A single Legion made of two battalions." He looked over at me and pointed to the document. "Another of your brilliant ideas. Do that. Prepare a single report covering both units. Refer to it as a Jewish Legion report. I'll write a cover memo to accompany it."

"And this will be sufficient?"

"We'll have to hope so."

When the report was ready we forwarded it by courier to London and waited. If the request for the report really was a matter of standard procedure, Colonel Patterson said we could expect a response in a week or two. If it was a search for a reason to stop us from going, the response might come much sooner.

Five days later, an envelope arrived for Colonel Patterson from the War Office. I delivered it to him, unopened. He ripped the seal off and took out a single sheet of paper. As he glanced over it, a smile came to his face, then he handed it to me and waited while I read. The document was an order directing us to deploy to Helmieh, Egypt, where we would prepare to conduct operations in support of General Allenby's campaign to gain control of Palestine. The Jewish Legion was expected to depart before month's end. Tears filled my eyes as I read it again.

Those of us who served in the Zion Mule Corps at Gallipoli knew how terrible combat in the mechanized age could be. Yet when news of our pending deployment was read to the men, they responded with a cheer, elated at the prospect of finally returning home.

A MONTH LATER the Thirty-Eighth Battalion departed from the camp at Plymouth, boarded a ship at Portsmouth, and sailed for the eastern Mediterranean. Five days later, we landed at Port Said, Egypt, and were trucked to a camp at Helmieh, near Cairo. Our first task was to establish our own encampment, then we went to work preparing a place to accommodate the arrival of the Thirty-Ninth Battalion.

By the time we arrived, General Allenby's forces already had entered Palestine, where they quickly captured Gaza. Driving rapidly north and east, and with the help of a company of Arabs led by a young British colonel named T. E. Lawrence, who charged northward from Aqaba, Allenby's forces solidified their hold on southern Palestine and seized Jerusalem without great difficulty.

News of Allenby's progress and of the assistance rendered by Arabs, left our men excited, disappointed, and anxious. Excited that Jerusalem was liberated from Ottoman control and that the campaign might be over much quicker than first expected, but disappointed to have been left out of the early stages of the fighting. Many of the men— particularly those who served in the Zion Mule Corps—had dreamed of fighting in the campaign from border to border, Egypt to Syria. They also were worried that Arabs who joined with the British and obtained early success might steal the spotlight they hoped would be the Legion's stepping-stone to legitimacy. It was a fear that would find substance very soon.

Shortly after we arrived, Colonel Patterson contacted General Allenby at his Jerusalem headquarters and asked for a meeting to discuss details of the Legion's duties in the campaign. Allenby's chief of staff, Lieutenant General Louis Bols, responded and summoned Colonel Patterson to a meeting at Be'er Ya'akov. I went with him.

At the meeting, Bols informed Colonel Patterson that Allenby did not intend to deploy the Jewish Legion for combat duty in Palestine. Colonel Patterson was outraged and argued vehemently that his men had been promised deployment to Palestine as a condition of their enlistment. Bols, however, was unmoved. "Deploying a Jewish Legion to Palestine would be too disruptive to the Arabs—both to Arabs living in the region and those serving with the Royal Army. We can't campaign against the Turks and endure disagreement among ourselves. Not of the sort that exists between Arabs and Jews."

"Then talk to the Arabs," Colonel Patterson argued. "Tell those who serve with us the kind of conduct you expect. My men won't cause trouble. We worked all this out months ago."

"I'm afraid it would be too risky to introduce your men now," Bols replied. "And on top of which, adding armed battalions of Jews to the fight will only inspire resident Arabs to side with the Turks and provide even stronger opposition than we've already incurred. None of which does us any good."

"You're assuming the—"

"Our decision is final," Bols interrupted in a curt tone. "Your men may continue to train and recruit in Egypt, but deployment to Palestine is simply out of the question."

For most of the trip back to Egypt, Colonel Patterson said nothing of the meeting, but as we approached Helmieh he said, "Do not mention the meeting with General Bols to the men. I'm not certain how they will react and I want nothing to distract them from their training."

"Yes, sir."

"We may still have a few options," Patterson added.

"Shall we inform Jabotinsky?"

He shook his head. "No, keep this between you and me for now."

"What shall I say to him if he asks?"

"Tell him to see me. And if you must say more, tell him the meeting was preliminary. The situation is still unfolding. That we're working on details of a strategy."

I glanced at him with an arched eyebrow. "Are we working on details of a strategy?"

"There are many ways to accomplish a goal, Yoel. We don't have to find them all. We only need one."

When we reached Helmieh, Colonel Patterson learned that his friend Major Edward Davis was in Egypt with a group from the Committee of Imperial Defense. They'd made the trip from England in order to review Allenby's progress. Colonel Patterson arranged to meet with Davis the following morning. I went with him and we stayed for lunch, which is how I learned many of the facts about their friendship and the trip they took to review earlier fighting in Europe.

As they talked that day, Colonel Patterson told Davis about the meeting he'd had with General Bols and the decision not to deploy the Jewish Legion to Palestine.

"I should not be surprised," Davis replied.

"Why not?"

"Bols has been steadfastly opposed to the Jewish Legion from the beginning and adamantly opposed to you as its commander."

Colonel Patterson frowned. "Why would he be opposed to me?"

"It's my understanding his sentiment runs back to the Gallipoli Campaign and all those letters you wrote on behalf of your men."

"I was only demanding the support that was rightfully theirs and that we were obligated to provide."

Davis agreed. "And then there's the problem of his sentiment toward the Jews, generally."

"He is anti-Semitic?"

"It would seem so. He and much of his staff. They've opposed you at every turn. Your contacts and friendships in London and elsewhere were too formidable for him to overcome, but now that you're here he is in a much better position to assert himself."

"Is the decision not to use the Jewish Legion also the opinion of General Allenby?"

"I can't quite speak for Allenby, but my understanding is that he is much more sympathetic to your cause. Do you two know each other personally?"

"Yes," Colonel Patterson replied.

Davis concurred. "As it would seem. I rather think Allenby would bring your Legion up immediately but he is preoccupied right now with securing his position in Jerusalem. Consequently, many of the day-to-day details have been left to Bols for the time being. I suspect the decision about your Legion was one he made pretty much on his own."

✦ ✦ ✦

With Allenby preoccupied and Bols steadfastly against us, Colonel Patterson had little choice but to turn again to Weizmann, Amery,

Milner, and Smuts. He contacted them by mail—telegrams seemed too risky—and informed them of the trouble he'd encountered. We posted the correspondence from Cairo and continued looking for other solutions to our situation.

One alternative Colonel Patterson enjoyed and to which he often resorted in the past was that of contacting other generals outside our chain of command. Doing so was a violation of army procedure, but Colonel Patterson felt he had no choice and so he contacted General Chaytor, whose Australia and New Zealand Expeditionary Force was now deployed in Palestine to protect Allenby's rearguard.

At a hastily arranged meeting near Gaza, Colonel Patterson explained the Jewish Legion's predicament and asked for Chaytor's help in getting the unit moved to the Palestinian front.

"You do realize, don't you," Chaytor noted, "that you are risking your entire career by contacting me?"

"I don't care. My men were promised deployment to Palestine. It was a condition of their enlistment. Not only that, most of them are residents of Palestine who were displaced by the Turks. Deploying them in this campaign is not only our obligation, it is our duty, and it is the right thing to do."

Chaytor had a pained expression. "Perhaps so, but you are violating the chain of command. Allenby won't like it. London won't like it." He looked over at Colonel Patterson. "I'm not sure *I* like it."

"I understand that, but listen; the army of Israel hasn't been seen for two thousand years. They are re-forming this very moment at a camp in Egypt, under my command, preparing to battle for what is rightfully theirs. We cannot oppose them."

Chaytor arched an eyebrow in a skeptical look. "You mean we cannot oppose God?"

"Yes," Colonel Patterson said without hesitation. "That is precisely what I mean. This isn't merely the dream of men."

"I see." Chaytor sighed. "Well, as your friend, I'll do all I can to help you, but I fear no good will come of this." He glanced away. "For you, and perhaps not for me, either."

◆ ◆ ◆

Not long after the meeting with Chaytor, the combined effect of Colonel Patterson's advocacy for the Jewish Legion took hold. Letters, cables, and telegrams regarding the issue of our deployment began arriving at General Allenby's headquarters. Members of Parliament, the war cabinet, and various officials throughout government, all thanking Allenby for his foresight in using us and urging him to make full use of the Legion. Lord Derby's correspondence was more to the point, conveying to Allenby in no uncertain terms the prime minister's displeasure with the current status but, curiously, falling just short of ordering him to move us forward.

The nature of London's reaction to his decision regarding the Legion caught Allenby off guard. He had been assured by Bols that no one would respond, one way or the other, and that decisions regarding the precise nature of troop movements on the battlefield were left to the prerogative of the commanding officer. No doubt, that was true in early times when communications were much slower and the consequences of war much different from that of the mechanized age in which we lived, a fact Allenby now discovered.

As the communiqués continued to arrive—and the stack of letters, telegrams, and memos on his desk began to rise—Allenby realized the liability to his reputation and career was rising, too. Not deploying the Jewish Legion was now a greater risk than any of the Jewish-Arab consequences Bols had offered as reasons to withhold them. *Bols got me into this*, Allenby thought to himself. *I never should have listened to him.*

With the rising risk to his career, Allenby now sensed other risks as well. Strategic risks obscured his army's lightning advance, but now more apparent as they paused in Jerusalem.

Allenby's men controlled Jerusalem and the southern half of Palestine. However, a large Turkish force still remained to the north, dominating the Galilee from Ramallah northward to Syria. A force that gave the Turks a decisive advantage over Allenby's much smaller force.

When he and Bols had reviewed their strategy prior to the assault on Jerusalem, the risk of attack from the north seemed low and they focused primarily on defending to the south—Bols and others supposing that a large force would swing around to the west and approach from that direction rather than straight down the Jordan Valley. That assessment was the impetus for Chaytor's deployment to Gaza.

Now that Allenby held Jerusalem and his troops were in a defensive posture, the risk of attack from the north, and from Amman to the east, seemed much more apparent. "If they counterattack from either of those directions," Allenby noted. "We could be easily overrun."

Allenby reviewed his assessment with Bols, pointing out to him on a map the location of their men and each of the Turkish units. "We are not in a good position. We need to make some changes."

Bols took a condescending tone. "You are thinking of changing our strategy?"

"I'm thinking we can't simply stop here. We must hold Jerusalem, but continue forward."

"That would require considerable time in planning and analysis," Bols cautioned.

"We don't have time for that."

"What did you have in mind?"

"Attack!" Allenby's voice suddenly became loud and decisive. "North and east." He jabbed the map with his index finger. "Straight into the strength of the Turkish army."

"I'm not sure—"

"I know what to do," Allenby interrupted. He pointed to the map again. "Put our troops here, here, and here." He indicated locations north of Jerusalem near the edge of their thinly stretched defensive lines. "Use them to convince the Turks we have a much larger force than we actually do and protect the northern flank while the main force proceeds toward Amman."

"That's a rather ambitious plan," Bols noted.

"Yes," Allenby agreed, "but I think we have no other option. If we remain here, in the defensive posture we've assumed, the Turks will reinforce from the north and east and we'll be trapped."

"Yes," Bols said in an imperious tone. "I suppose that is correct, but a plan of this nature would require a much larger force than we currently possess." He glanced over at Allenby. "We are dreadfully short on troops."

"But we have troops in Egypt," Allenby explained with a knowing look.

Bols seemed puzzled. "In Egypt? There's hardly more than—" He stopped short and his eyes narrowed. "You mean Patterson and his Jews."

Allenby noticed the look in Bols eyes. Bols hadn't given him advice based on strategic assessment. He'd given advice based on his personal prejudice against the Jews. Advice that ran counter to the directives he'd received from London.

There was much Allenby wanted to say but the situation they faced on the ground demanded action. "They aren't just Patterson's Jews," he said tersely. "They're *our* Jews, my Jews, the Royal Army's Jews. And we are theirs as well." Allenby gestured to the map. "Deploy Patterson and his men along the Jordan River at the crossing on the road to Amman. Put Margolin's brigade to their south. Position elements of Chaytor's reserve to the west, here and here." He indicated again with his index finger on the map. "We'll use Patterson's men as the fulcrum when we pivot our units to the east."

"This will take time to arrange."

Allenby gave Bols a steely glare. "Do it now. We don't have time for further delay. Patterson's men should have been up here as soon as they arrived."

Three days later, Colonel Patterson received the order to deploy. At last, we were going into battle as a real combat unit!

✦ ✦ ✦

About a week later, both brigades of the Jewish Legion departed Helmieh and traveled by train from Egypt through Palestine to Jerusalem. Upon arrival, we marched down to our designated positions in the Jordan Valley east of Jerusalem; The Thirty-Eighth camping along the old road to Amman, the Thirty-Ninth to our south.

When we left Helmieh I knew our destination and pinpointed the locations for both units on a map. The region where we were to camp and patrol was generally high and dry and Colonel Patterson thought our designated post would be the same. I had never been there but I knew what conditions were like along the river farther to the north and wondered if the place along the road to Amman would be as easily manageable as he assumed. It turned out I was right.

The area we were assigned as our campsite was low, damp, and mosquito-infested. Just to our north conditions were even worse with a bog that covered a large swath of river bottom. Mosquitos outnumbered us a million to one.

The men might have protested—conditions were really bad—but they were tired from the trip and too preoccupied with slapping mosquitos that buzzed around them to put up much fuss. Instead, they shrugged off their packs and went to work putting up the tents.

At the time, we assumed our location was chosen for strategic and tactical purposes. Though it was a miserable location we did our best to take it in stride, attributing any hardship to typical army life. Much later, however, when I learned more about General Bols and observed firsthand the extent of his dislike for us, I came to wonder if he hadn't chosen that location on the river merely to make our lives miserable. Colonel Patterson, who was attempting to learn to limit his battles to essential matters, never really said what he thought.

✦ ✦ ✦

During the day, we hardly ever saw Turkish soldiers but almost from our first night on station we encountered scattered gunfire and more than a few skirmishes. Reports we'd received indicated the Turks were positioned to our north. Our reconnaissance found units across the river directly opposite our position. They were a constant nuisance and on a few occasions a serious threat, but by far our biggest threat came from malaria borne by the mosquitos.

A significant number of our men became ill and once again I was tasked with establishing a hospital tent and locating staff to operate it. As the number of sick mounted, I grew worried about Amos. When I tracked him down to check on him, I found out he was worried about me.

To combat the mosquito attacks, Colonel Patterson put some of the men to work draining the swampy areas around our camp. That lessened the infestation but did not rid us of them altogether. While they worked on that project, two of our companies and several from the Thirty-Ninth were assigned to a different and more unusual task.

Drawing on experience from earlier campaigns and stories of creative tactics from the past, General Allenby instructed men from one of the mechanized units to create a phantom brigade—comprised of cavalry, machinery, and artillery—and deploy it to our west. The Jewish Legion was ordered to assist.

At first I thought it was a crazy idea, but Colonel Patterson told me that fake armies had been used many times with great success—armies with a limited number of canons moving them from position to position around a mountain as an enemy patrol passed by, giving the appearance of an artillery emplacement far more formidable than actually existed. So I assisted in putting the men to work erecting worn-out tents for brigade encampments, positioning cardboard structures that resembled artillery pieces, and draping horse blankets over scrubby bushes to form fake tether lines.

Finally, after weeks of battling mosquitos and tending to props that were "camped" in a location better than our own, orders arrived summoning Colonel Patterson to a meeting with Margolin and General Allenby.

When Colonel Patterson returned that evening, we learned that after months of preparation General Allenby's force was ready to resume its drive northward to gain control of all of Palestine. The first target was to be Amman, which lay to the east of our position, a strategic location that, when secured by the British, would narrow the Turks to the much smaller area between the Jordan River and the sea.

As its part in the attack, the Jewish Legion was to strike at the river crossing and move eastward, breaching the Turk line across the river and opening a way for Allenby and his men.

A smile spread across my face and my chest swelled with pride at the news of what we were about to do. The Jewish Legion—opposed, scorned, ridiculed, and obstructed in every way possible—would open the way for the army that would seize Amman and thus control Palestine beyond the Jordan. It would be difficult to describe the depth of pride I felt at the honor.

✦ ✦ ✦

Two days later, we struck Turkish forces just north of the road, then crossed the river and took positions on the opposite side. Leaving two companies to hold the area, we pressed on with the remainder of our men, moving up the road toward Al Salt. Fighting was fierce at first, but the farther we went the less resistance we encountered and when General Allenby's main force came through they swept up the road at lightning speed all the way to Al Salt and on toward Amman.

Most of us assumed our duty had been done and we would maintain our position in a defensive posture, but as Allenby's units bore down on Amman, we were ordered to attack northward up the Jordan Valley to protect Allenby's flank. In response, Colonel Patterson repositioned us once more, reducing the number of men holding the river crossing to a single company and assigning the second to cover the road to Al Salt. The rest of us pivoted to the left, fought our way into the Jordan Valley, and began the push northward toward Deir Alla on the east side of the Jordan River.

At first, resistance was heavy—the heaviest we were to see in the entire campaign. We took lots of fire and incurred a number of casualties. As the wounded were brought to the rear, I assisted in directing them to a makeshift triage station we'd positioned in a safe area. With each stretcher that appeared, I feared the soldier it bore would be Amos.

During those initial hours I wondered if we weren't going to get bogged down in a long, protracted operation, forced to fight from shrub to shrub. As with clashes along the road, however, once we broke through their initial resistance, the Turks scattered. By late afternoon, a rout was on as Turkish units retreated in disarray. By sunset our mission had devolved into herding their retreat to the west, keeping Allenby safe to the east.

Seizure of Amman and our attack northward from Jerusalem crippled the Turkish army. The collapse that began when our Legion crossed the river and Allenby's men came through, spread across the Middle East. By October, the Ottoman Empire surrendered, leaving all of its former territory under Allied control and reducing the Ottoman presence to an area roughly corresponding to modern-day Turkey.

At the time of the Ottoman surrender, we were camped in a location across the river, opposite Beit She'an, about thirty-five kilometers south of Kinneret, as close to our farm as I had been in a long time. Sporadic fighting continued for several weeks, but then a welcome calm spread over the region as the reality settled in that the Ottoman army was no longer available to defend Arab arrogance.

The men used the time to catch up on personal matters, washing—such as was possible—mending clothes and equipment, and writing home. A mail delivery reached us, too. Our first since arriving in Palestine. I was no longer in charge of sorting and delivering it but I made it a point to observe the process and noticed Amos received ten letters, bound together with string in a bundle. He grinned when a private handed them to him. I assumed they all were from Dalia. I wanted to know what she said but after our earlier conversations about her, I thought Amos needed to enjoy the letters without me pestering him, so I turned away and spent the remainder of the day at Colonel Patterson's tent, tending to the daily reports.

Late that afternoon, with my eyes tired from reading and writing, I stepped outside the tent and watched the sun setting. It was a sunset I had seen many times from our farm at a time that seemed three lifetimes ago. So much had happened since then. So much had changed. Yet so much remained the same. The hills, the golden streaks of fading sunlight across a cobalt blue sky. The smell of cedar, mimosa, and Asteraceae in the cool of early evening.

As I stood there taking it all in, a thousand thoughts flooded my mind. General Allenby's campaign to capture Palestine might have developed without us—from a military perspective, Palestine was an obvious point of Ottoman vulnerability with a terrain naturally conducive to large-scale modern battle. As a practical matter, however, that campaign never would have happened without American intervention and the constant, persistent work of Trumpeldor, Jabotinsky, and the tactical leadership of Colonel Patterson. They were the ones who dreamed it, planned it, argued and cajoled for it, then fought to keep it on track. In essence, it was a simple plan borne solely of our desire to find a homeland where we could live free from prejudice and oppression, but having expected a long and bitter fight, I was astounded at how quickly the end came.

Immersed in thought, I didn't notice Amos coming up behind me until he tapped me lightly on the elbow. "Beautiful view." He glanced toward the sun as it sank below the horizon.

"Yes," I replied. "Reminds me of home."

We watched in silence a moment longer, then he said, "You saw the letters I received?"

"I saw you had a stack."

"Yeah," he grinned.

"How is Dalia?"

"Fine."

"Was that the first you'd heard from her since we left Alexandria?"

"Yes. I put them in chronological order and read them the way she wrote them. Apparently, my letter to her from Plymouth was waiting for her when they reached Kinneret."

"How was their farm?"

"Crews from Kinneret were farming the land, which no one seemed to mind, as it kept it from getting overgrown. The house was gone from the fire that night, so I guess that kept the Arabs from living there."

"Is the kibbutz claiming ownership now?"

"No. Not at all. In fact, as rent for the use of the land, the settlement is helping them rebuild."

"They could stay at our house."

"I thought of that but wasn't sure how you'd like it. They have a cottage at the kibbutz for now."

I looked to the north, "Kinneret isn't far away."

"I thought of that," Amos replied. "But if I go there for a visit now, I don't think I will be able to return. We'll be done in a few months anyway, and I wouldn't want to be labeled a deserter after all we've been through."

I grinned. "We've been through a lot."

Amos put his arm around my shoulder. "Yes, we have, but I think we have much more yet to do." He glanced over at me. "Though I do hope this is it for us and the army."

Suddenly, a sense of sadness swept over me at the thought of no longer being in the Legion. For a moment I imagined my life without the camaraderie, the sense of belonging—of family. Was I to choose between the Legion and Amos? And then it occurred to me that with the war over, the Legion might be disbanded. Gone. No more. Surely that would never happen. Jabotinsky, Weizmann...someone would find a way to keep us together. Wouldn't they?

I said none of that to Amos. Instead, I smiled at him in return, "The Jewish Legion kept us alive." He didn't respond, but I hoped he felt the same.

# CHAPTER 23

foz

NOT LONG AFTER the cessation of armed conflict on the battle-field, Colonel Patterson learned that the British government intended to occupy Palestine for the foreseeable future and, though agreements had not been reached setting the terms that would officially end the war, the decision had been made to appoint General Bols as military governor of the region. Outraged at the prospect of Bols being in charge, Colonel Patterson cabled Amery and Weizmann in London in an attempt to warn them of Bols' anti-Semitic nature. A cabled response from Avery indicated his awareness of the problem and that he was doing all he could to oppose the appointment. Weizmann, he informed us, was in Cairo to negotiate with Bols.

Colonel Patterson read the message from Amery with alarm. "Weizmann has no idea who he's dealing with."

"You don't think he can handle Bols?" I asked.

"Weizmann thinks of himself as a diplomat. Bols is a master at deception."

"What should we do?"

"We must go there right away," Colonel Patterson decided, "before it's too late."

Early the next morning, we rode over to Haifa on a supply truck and boarded a train that took us down the coast to Gaza. There, we crossed the border on foot and boarded a second train for the remainder of the journey to Cairo. We arrived to find Weizmann waiting at the Windsor Hotel. He seemed glad to see us and escorted us to his room for a private talk. I thought things were going well, but Colonel Patterson seemed tense and when he attempted to warn Weizmann of Bols' true nature, Weizmann dismissed his concerns out of hand.

"I've talked to General Bols. I think he and I have reached an understanding."

Colonel Patterson appeared worried. "I've dealt with him before, and I can tell you from experience, he is anti-Semitic to the core."

"I've looked into his eyes," Weizmann countered. "I don't think he's against us."

"If he's appointed governor of Palestine, you will rue the day he takes office," Colonel Patterson warned.

Weizmann looked offended. "Why would you say such a thing about the man? He's your superior officer."

"I saw how he treated the Jewish Legion," Colonel Patterson replied. "I know from experience the man he truly is."

"Well…" Weizmann's voice trailed away and he glanced to the left. "I disagree."

Colonel Patterson leaned forward and propped his elbows on his knees. "Do you remember the issues you discussed when you talked to him?"

Weizmann cocked his head in an imperious pose. "I'm not telling you everything we said."

"I'm not asking you to tell me anything. Do you remember the issues you discussed?"

Weizmann looked indignant. "Of course. I remember them perfectly well."

"Good," Colonel Patterson said with a sardonic smile. "Because once Bols is in office, he will create a government capable of reaching to the bottom of every issue you raised with him. He will announce the creation of laws and offices bearing directly on those topics and he will do it in terms that make you think he's responding to you in a positive way. Then he will fill those offices—and his entire government—with as many anti-Semites as he can possibly find and they will rule against you at every turn."

"Colonel Patterson," Weizmann said in an aloof tone, "I don't know what sort of disagreements you've had with General Bols in the past, but I assure you, he and I will work well together."

Colonel Patterson was thoroughly done with Weizmann, and though we stayed the night just two floors above his room, we saw no more of him. As I lay in bed that night, thinking of the conversation, I found it sad that Weizmann, Jabotinsky, and Colonel Patterson achieved so much together, yet could go no further—for I was sure Jabotinsky would share Colonel Patterson's view of Bols and of Weizmann's decision to work with him.

It wasn't the first time I'd seen friends work together only to part ways. Trumpeldor had been with Jabotinsky in Egypt when they first started to organize a Jewish force, then parted ways over how to do it, only to come together again later as the idea of a Jewish fighting unit entered its third iteration. That gave me hope that one day Colonel Patterson and Weizmann might meet again and work together on the next version of the Zionist dream. As for me, I never saw Weizmann again.

✦ ✦ ✦

On the train ride back to Palestine, I lamented what seemed to be fact—that a significant portion of the British government favored the Arabs—not merely favored them but preferred them to our detriment—and now the most belligerent of those who opposed us were to govern Palestine.

"I understand how you feel," Colonel Patterson said in response. "But you must remember how this happened."

"How the British came to embrace anti-Semitism?"

"No. How the British became *fascinated* with the Arabs."

"Is that what it is? A fascination?"

Colonel Patterson attempted to explain: "As I've mentioned before, when British historians rediscovered Egypt, they found a treasure trove of artifacts wonderfully preserved in the arid climate. Since then, British archaeologists have trekked to the region to find, collect, and record pieces of an ancient past most thought had long since vanished from the earth."

"They've been going there a long time?"

"For the past fifty years."

"Jews have been living in Europe two thousand years," I noted. His argument irritated me and for the first time I felt better informed on a topic than he. "Europeans hated us long before the British became fascinated with Egypt. They've hated us since long before...the British existed."

"Compared to history," Colonel Patterson admitted, "our fascination with the Arabs is a fad. I concede that much. But this is where we are as a society. That's all I'm saying."

"So you're making excuses for them?" I felt compelled to press the point on behalf of the thousands who were about to be subjected to an anti-Semitic governor.

Patterson frowned. "No. And I'm not sure I care for your tone."

"Perhaps it's not my tone you disapprove of," I rejoined.

He had a perturbed look. "Then what is it?"

"Perhaps you disapprove of anti-Semitism." I looked over at him, determined not to flinch. "And the way it seeps into everything. Even into you."

Colonel Patterson's eyes opened wide. "Even me?" he said in a demanding voice. "How dare—"

"I'm not saying you're anti-Semitic." I cut him off before he said too much. "But why are you defending the hatred your colleagues have for us?"

Colonel Patterson did not reply. Instead, he turned away and looked out the window. I stared blankly down the aisle of the train car, listening to the click-clack of the wheels against the rail.

Why I chose that moment to say those things to him would be difficult to say, but they had been building up inside me for a long time. Anti-Semitism was, and remains, a most deceptive beast. Few want to admit they've ever harbored a negative view of a person based solely on their race, but most have. Yet by not admitting the possibility that they, too, have entertained those thoughts, they leave open the door for the thought to return. And when it returns, it always brings a friend. Before you know it, those fleeting thoughts have taken root and become attitudes. I'd witnessed it in many of the British officers who dealt with us in Gallipoli and in many of the men who joined the Legion. I had also seen it in myself. Not anti-Semitism but anti-English sentiment—the tendency to categorize all British people as hating us, which wasn't the case.

That conversation on the train was a turning point for Colonel Patterson and me. Things changed between us after that. I remained his aide and we worked together in the same manner as before, but the personal interaction between us was different. I can't describe it

exactly, but it wasn't the same. Amos used to say Colonel Patterson
had become like a father to me, replacing the father who disappeared
when we fled the farm that night. If he was correct in his assessment,
then that day on the train I became the teenage son approaching
twenty whose independence of mind, spirit, and direction was no
longer avoidable.

+ + +

The period between the end of fighting on the battlefield and the
execution of treaties formally ending the war involved intense diplomatic negotiations. Much of it took place in European capitals far
from the Middle East and required extended discussions. In Palestine,
General Bols used the intervening time to piece together a territorial
government that would be fully functional by the time the documents
were executed. By then, everyone knew Palestine was in for a long
British occupation.

Over the next several weeks, rumors circulated about the people
General Bols asked to serve in key positions. As Colonel Patterson pre-
dicted, the list of pending officials was packed from top to bottom with
rancorous anti-Semites. Their proposed jurisdiction, when imple-
mented, would reach everything from the language of administrative laws used to apportion property for settlers to the language used
for street signs and government forms. Almost everything was to be
printed in English and Arabic, but nothing was to appear in Hebrew.
Government-sponsored schools were to teach in English and Arabic,
but no classes were to be offered exclusively in Hebrew. Muslim holi-
days were set to be officially recognized by the territorial government.
No Jewish feast days were given the same accord.

In spite of the way the meeting with Weizmann in Cairo ended,
Colonel Patterson continued to circulate memos and messages to

Amery and the others in London who'd worked with us in the past, detailing the most recent developments and urging them to redouble their efforts to prevent General Bols from formally taking office as governor of Palestine. As ranking Jewish officer in the Thirty-Eighth Battalion, Jabotinsky had been privy to most of that communication. He kept quiet at first, for once giving Colonel Patterson time to address the matter through regular channels, but as it became obvious that no one was having any success in thwarting General Bols' appointment, Jabotinsky grew increasingly frustrated.

That frustration soon spilled over into Jabotinsky's conversations among the men and in the few public speeches he made during that time. His rhetoric, however, was so harsh and emotionally charged that Colonel Patterson was compelled to confront him directly and called him to our tent for a meeting.

"I know you don't care for General Bols," Colonel Patterson began. "And, frankly, neither do I, but he is still an officer in the Royal Army. A general, who outranks us both."

Jabotinsky had a piercing look. "You're telling me I have to keep quiet?"

"I'm telling you," Colonel Patterson responded, "if you continue to speak out, I shall be forced to discipline you."

Jabotinsky looked surprised. "Discipline me?"

"Yes." Colonel Patterson was serious. "I realize this is an awkward position for us, but as an officer of the Royal Army, I cannot allow you to publicly ridicule a major general. And if I don't tend to it myself, someone in London will dress me down for it and force me to take action."

Jabotinsky lowered his voice, "John, they have created a situation rife with potential for serious and catastrophic violence against us."

"I agree," Colonel Patterson said with a nod.

"Why did they do that? Why did they appoint Bols?"

"I don't know."

"Why did General Allenby allow that to happen?"

"He made the appointment."

"Why?!" Jabotinsky's voice was loud and belligerent. "And why didn't Weizmann or Amery try to stop them?"

"I think Amery tried. But being in London, with Bols and Allenby here, there just wasn't much he could do. I tried to warn Weizmann about Bols."

This was news to Jabotinsky. "You talked to him?"

"Yes. Yoel and I rode down to Cairo to see him and I told him what the man was like."

"What did Weizmann say?"

"He rather dismissed me out of hand. Said he was certain Bols was a man he could deal with."

Jabotinsky scoffed. "No one can deal with Bols. General Allenby can't even handle him, much less Weizmann."

Colonel Patterson shifted in the chair and crossed his legs. "That's all behind us now anyway. We'll just have to make the best of it."

"The British are so arrogant," Jabotinsky was unwilling to let the topic pass. Then his eyes opened wide as he remembered Colonel Patterson was British. "Not you," he corrected quickly. "I mean *them*."

"No need to apologize," Colonel Patterson smiled. "I agree. British officers tend to be particularly stuck on themselves."

"Sometimes Weizmann is just like them. Not in his attitude toward Jews but in his need to always be right, even when he is very wrong."

"He did seem oddly unwilling to listen," Colonel Patterson noted. "I'm not at all sure why."

They sat in silence a moment, then Jabotinsky said, "The British might see their treatment of the Arabs as an act of friendship but the

Arabs will see it quite differently. They will take it as permission, perhaps even authorization, to do as they please against the Jews. Even to the point of attacking and killing our settlers."

"What are you wanting to do?"

"I want to stop them," Jabotinsky declared. "I want someone to stop Bols."

"I don't think we have the means of doing that."

"Someone appointed him to office. Someone can remove him."

"I don't think that will happen."

"Doesn't General Allenby have the authority to do that?"

"I suppose, but he won't. At least, not now."

"Then when? When would he do it? After the Arabs start killing our people?"

"Let us hope it doesn't come to that."

After talking to Colonel Patterson, Jabotinsky appeared to back away from his earlier rhetoric, but that only lasted about a week and then he was at it again, speaking to anyone who would listen, telling them about the persecution he was sure would happen. At the same time, he wrote a letter to General Allenby, expressing his concerns over Bols and British policy toward the Jews and asking for a meeting to discuss the matter.

Whether Allenby would have agreed with the substance of Jabotinsky's argument or not was never clear, but one thing was certain: A junior officer writing to a general officer was so far beyond the British norm that nothing good could have ever come from it. Jabotinsky's letter met immediate and unyielding resistance at every level of Allenby's administrative apparatus and when it finally reached his desk it received a resounding "no."

As I observed the dispute over Bols—with Weizmann doing everything to accommodate Bols, and Jabotinsky opposing him at every turn—it seemed the rift in the coalition that formed the Zion Mule Corps and the Jewish Legion was much deeper than merely a disagreement between Weizmann and Colonel Patterson. Weizmann was committed to the practical, pragmatic path. Jabotinsky was unwavering in a radical approach of fighting against all who opposed the Zionist dream in its purest form. Weizmann saw compromise as inevitable. Jabotinsky saw it as a treasonous offense. I didn't know it then, but it was a division I would see play out in dramatic ways during the coming years and one that marks the history of Israel to the present day.

✦ ✦ ✦

As British rule in Palestine took shape, even before formal agreements and treaties were signed, Colonel Patterson was placed in command of the troops that occupied southern Palestine. The Jewish Legion withdrew from the Galilee to encampments in and around Beersheba. From there, we patrolled the Negev south of Jerusalem to the Egyptian border and westward to the sea. Gaza, which had been occupied earlier by General Chaytor, now fell under our jurisdiction as Chaytor withdrew to Egypt.

Calm prevailed and our work slowed to a much less hectic pace than it had been during the war. That left more time for me to visit with Amos, which I still enjoyed, though we were growing in different directions and I could feel the distance increasing between us. His mind was mostly on Dalia, with whom he exchanged almost daily correspondence now, and on returning to the farm. I was interested in knowing what happened to the property but the thought of leaving the Legion still made me sad, though I kept my thoughts about it to myself.

AS PASSOVER APPROACHED that year, we were looking forward to celebrating in Jerusalem, but a few weeks prior to the feast, General Bols sent a memo notifying us that Jerusalem was off-limits to Jewish Legion soldiers. Our men were more than a little disgruntled and disheartened by the announcement. I expected Colonel Patterson to protest the order and lobby his friends to get it rescinded, but all he said was, "Perhaps it's for the best."

We didn't discuss the matter further but I've often wondered if he thought the order was a good idea and I've wondered, too, if he had reason to believe the Arabs were planning to make trouble for us.

Colonel Patterson, however, refused to let us wallow in disappointment and anger. "We'll celebrate Passover right here," he announced. "Among ourselves. As it should be anyway." Ever the resourceful leader, he solicited donations from friends back home in England and donated his own money to purchase the items we needed for our Seder.

Nisei Rosenberg took charge of logistics and surprised us all by creating a tent fashioned from cotton fabric reminiscent of the material used by our ancestors who first occupied the land. At the sight of it, many thought of Abraham and recounted stories of his arrival in Palestine. When I saw it I thought not of Abraham but of David who lived in the Negev, not far from where we were camped, before he became king.

Though Passover was a holiday, we were not exempt from our duties enforcing security for the region. The men still had to make their regular patrols. To accommodate them, we celebrated multiple Seders, rotating men in and out in a way that met the required duty schedule and allowed them to participate in the formal Passover service.

At each celebration, the men gathered around the long tables and listened while Colonel Patterson reminded us as he had before, "When we were in Egypt as the Zion Mule Corps, I told you that the corps was the first Jewish army to assemble in over two thousand years. In England, I reminded you of that again and that you would be the first Jewish army of combat soldiers. Now we are here. And for the first time in two thousand years, a Jewish army patrols the Negev."

In spite of the solemn occasion, the men responded with a shout, then Aaron Ben Joseph presided over the Seder readings and prayers. The meal quickly became a feast in the truest sense, and for all of us it was the most moving religious service we'd ever attended.

Later we learned that the order prohibiting us from entering Jerusalem during Passover came at the instigation of Kamil al-Husayni, the Muslim grand mufti of Jerusalem. He lobbied General Bols for the order, convincing him that the Jews would use the holiday as an excuse to foment violence against the Arabs. If we had known that at the time, we might have gone to Jerusalem in anger just to create trouble, which might very well have been the response Husayni hoped we would make. I've often thought how blessed we were not to have known how the order came about.

✦ ✦ ✦

Not long after Passover ended, Amos and I sat outside Colonel Patterson's tent, discussing everything and not much of anything at all. In the course of conversation, Amos said, "I hear Jabotinsky is talking about forming a Jewish force to defend all of the Jews in Palestine against Arabs."

"Isn't that what the British army is doing?" I asked, glancing in his direction. "Isn't that what *we're* doing?"

"Jabotinsky says the British are keeping the Arabs safe but doing it at our expense, and the only way we can be safe and free is to resist."

"He's been saying that since he arrived in Egypt, even before we formed the Mule Corps."

"This time he's saying it a little more forcefully."

"Oh? How so?"

"He's telling anyone who will listen that we must fight back and if that isn't enough, we must drive the Arabs from the entire region." Amos glanced in my direction. "And if the British get in our way, Jabotinsky says we should drive them out, too."

"He isn't supposed to talk like that."

"Maybe he misunderstood the directive," Amos quipped.

"Yeah," I sighed. "Maybe so." Jabotinsky's problem wasn't that he didn't understand. He understood perfectly well what Colonel Patterson told him and what he was expected to do. His problem was that he didn't care about any of that, which made him perfectly suited to politics but poorly suited to army life. Especially life in the British army.

We sat in silence a moment, then Amos asked, "When do you think we should return to the farm?"

"I don't know," I replied, avoiding him as he looked over at me.

"Our year will be up soon," he noted. "We could go then."

"I'm not so sure I want to go back," saying at last what I'd been thinking for quite some time. "Not to stay," I added.

Amos frowned. "You like army life?" His voice sounded calmer than I'd expected.

"At first, all I could think of was going home, like everyone else."

"And now?"

"Now the Legion seems more like home than anything we've known since Mama died. And besides, I think Jabotinsky may be right."

"About forming our own army?"

"I don't know about that, but I think he's right that we're going to have trouble with the Arabs. They tolerated us during the war because the British told them they needed us to defeat the Turks, but now that the war is over, that argument no longer applies and the Arabs know it."

"I just want to go home," Amos said resolutely. "I'm ready to get away from all of this and get on with my life." We both knew what that meant—Dalia, the farm, a family.

"That's good. That's what coming here is all about. But someone has to be ready to defend our people."

"And you want to be part of it."

"I don't know for certain what I want to do. I just know that when I think of not being here, of not seeing the colonel every day, and the men, and the thousands of questions they ask, I feel sad."

Amos rested his hand on my forearm and gave it a squeeze. "This has been good for you."

"Yes," I replied as tears filled my eyes. "This has been good."

"I'm glad," he whispered.

As a soldier and, more to the point, as Colonel Patterson's aide, I suppose I should have told him what Amos said about the things Jabotinsky was saying and the way he was stirring up the men to action outside the British military command structure, but the idea of talking to my brother and telling someone else what we said didn't set well with me. I preferred to keep our conversations private, as they had been all our lives. Besides, Colonel Patterson and Jabotinsky were friends. If they had a problem with each other, they should work it out for themselves. I wasn't inclined to tattle on him.

The next day, however, news reached our post of an Arab attack on a Jewish farming settlement north of Jerusalem. Jabotinsky was with Colonel Patterson when the news arrived.

"This is what I warned you about," Jabotinsky railed. "This is what I've warned everyone about. I've been saying all along that this was coming and now it's here."

Colonel Patterson looked unsettled. "You've said this to everyone?"

"Everyone who will listen."

"Others have told me they'd heard you were talking again, but I assured them such reports were merely rumors, as you were told not to engage in that sort of conduct and warned that if you did, consequences would follow."

From my desk across the room I heard Colonel Patterson say this and felt vindicated in not telling him of my conversation with Amos, but I wondered who had told him about the things Jabotinsky was saying.

"Consequences?" Jabotinsky looked astounded. "Arab gangs attack Jewish settlers and you would punish me for trying to warn our people?"

"You weren't talking to villagers," Colonel Patterson countered. "You were talking to men who are members of the Legion."

"They asked, I answered. That is all that happened."

"I think there was a little more to it than that," Colonel Patterson reminded him. "And what you said was inappropriate."

"You British can't stand the truth," Jabotinsky scoffed.

"And *you* must learn to operate within the confines and expectations of the British army."

"But the British army must conduct itself within the boundaries of justice and fairness," Jabotinsky replied in a loud, exasperated voice. "They can't give the Arabs undeserved preferential treatment and expect them to behave like typical Protestant British subjects. They will see it as authorization. As validation for their anti-Jewish position."

Colonel Patterson glanced away with a distant look in his eyes. "Well, we have units in that region. I'm sure they received the same information as we and will respond appropriately."

"I don't think they will. And we can't wait to find out."

Colonel Patterson turned back to face him. "What are you proposing?"

"That we respond ourselves."

"That would be out of the question."

"Out of the question?" Jabotinsky shouted. "We are the Jewish Legion. This is the very reason we worked so hard to get here. To protect our fellow Jews!"

"The village is a considerable distance away," Colonel Patterson explained, "and far beyond our jurisdiction. We can't simply invade another commander's territory."

Jabotinsky snarled, "You British always have a reason for not doing the right thing."

Although he'd held to the standard British line, the exchange with Jabotinsky bothered Colonel Patterson. Much of what Jabotinsky had said was true. There was little in the way of a track record to suggest that army units in and around Jerusalem would respond to the attacks in a way that was favorable to the Jewish settlers. And there was every reason to believe that if they did respond, they would do so on behalf of the Arabs. Still, the notion of stepping into the affairs of another district, where another British officer was in charge, was irregular at best.

Rather than departing immediately, as Jabotinsky wanted, Colonel Patterson radioed General Bols in Jerusalem, responding to the information he'd received, noting our availability for action, and asking for instructions. Major Harold Atwell, a member of Bols' staff, replied promptly indicating they were handling the situation. As a result, Colonel Patterson felt we had no option but to remain at our posts in Beersheba.

In the end, British units garrisoned in Jerusalem failed to respond, doing nothing by way of an immediate defense and even less in follow-up investigation. When Jabotinsky learned the British had refused to act, he once more complained to Colonel Patterson.

Colonel Patterson listened politely, "The village is not within our area of responsibility."

"That's what you British always say."

"This time it is true," Colonel Patterson argued. "Our job is to defend farms and settlers here in the southern portion of Palestine. Not up there. That area is someone else's job. If we leave here to go there, the people we're supposed to protect down here will be exposed and vulnerable."

Jabotinsky left without saying more, but as with every other issue involving the British and Arabs, he couldn't let the matter go. The next night, he and other members of the Legion—with Scholem Baazov, Aaron Gruner, and Mosha Pinsker among them as leaders—took their rifles and equipment and rode up to the settlement. They arrived to find the Arabs were still there, terrorizing the villagers who'd been unable to escape.

Enraged by what they saw, Jabotinsky and his men attacked without warning and drove the Arabs away, mercilessly killing many

of them in the process and wounding many more. Early the following morning, General Bols learned of the Jewish raid and ordered an
investigation. When he discovered Jabotinsky was the leader, he had
Jabotinsky arrested along with several of the men who'd accompanied
him.

Over the next several weeks, Colonel Patterson intervened on
behalf of Jabotinsky and his accomplices, arguing that they were
merely doing what British soldiers from the area should have done.
He was forceful and convincing, but I could see in the way he handled
the matter that he had grown tired of the need to constantly lobby his
superiors on our behalf.

Eventually, after protracted argument and considerable political pressure, Jabotinsky and his accomplices were summarily demo-
bilized, dismissed from the army, and released from jail. Even then,
Jabotinsky remained unbowed. As Colonel Patterson escorted him
from the detention facility, Jabotinsky continued to complain about
their treatment at the hands of British officials. "We were only doing
what the army should have done."

"Just be glad you're out now," Colonel Patterson replied.

"They humiliated us. They ought to apologize."

Colonel Patterson took him by the arm and hustled him toward
the door. "Come on," he urged. "At least they didn't hang you."

"It might have been better if they had."

"Why?"

"Our struggle needs a martyr."

"Your struggle needs leadership," Colonel Patterson countered.

✦ ✦ ✦

Freed from his obligation to the British army, Jabotinsky moved
to Jerusalem and sent for his wife and children. They joined him

from Russia and lived in a small house in the Jewish Quarter where Jabotinsky spent his days recruiting men for a paramilitary defense force. Though he began with a small cadre of volunteers, he hoped to develop a corps in all the Jewish settlements, capable of defending them from Arab attacks.

"The British will never defend us from the Arabs," he argued. "We must defend ourselves. Force is the only thing the Arabs respect."

The group that formed under his leadership soon aligned with Hashomer, an older resistance group with ties to the very first Jewish settlers. Jabotinsky became a leading figure in the organization.

To strengthen Hashomer's ability to fight effectively, Jabotinsky sought the help of former Jewish Legion members who were far better trained in military methods and tactics than typical Palestinian volunteers. He imposed a more formal military organization on the group, and in the months that followed they engaged in a series of firefights and skirmishes with Arab groups north of Jerusalem and into the Galilee.

# CHAPTER 25

foz

BECAUSE OF THE INTERLOCKING treaties in effect at the time World War I began, numerous accords, and side agreements were necessary to formally bring the war to a conclusion. As these were reached between the various parties, they were registered with the League of Nations and submitted for its approval.

As talks proceeded, unresolved spoils-of-war disputes among the Allies became a major sticking point and threatened their unity. One of those disputes involved British and French occupation of the Middle East—a particularly delicate matter as both sides sought to retain areas of influence over oil deposits believed to exist in the region.

With League approval hanging in the balance, an accommodation was eventually reached giving France control of Syria and the United Kingdom control of the Levant south of Lebanon to the Egyptian border. That agreement, however, was held in strictest secrecy for fear of upsetting further negotiations among the Allies and of exacerbating relations with Arabs living in the region.

Having resolved the territorial dispute, the ongoing conflict between Arabs and Jews in the region was the lone remaining risk to League of Nations approval of the anticipated Allied resolution. In order to alleviate that potential threat, General Bols arranged a series of private meetings with representatives of both groups to discuss how they would be treated in a British-administered protectorate.

To address the Arab side, he met with the Muslim grand mufti of Jerusalem, Haj Amin al-Husseini. That meeting took place in Jerusalem. For the Jewish side, he met with Chaim Weizmann. That meeting brought Weizmann to Cairo after we made the trip down to warn him about Bols' true character. I learned all of that much later—after Colonel Patterson was gone and all the things yet to happen had occurred—which helped explain the odd way in which Weizmann seemed to act that day. I assumed it was the reason we didn't see him again after our initial meeting and couldn't help but wonder what the British promised the Arabs. I eventually learned the answer to that, too.

All of these proposed treaties and agreements were presented at the Paris Peace Conference. Weizmann attended as the representative for the Jews of Palestine and King Hussein bin Ali attended as an advocate for the Arabs, but as I have stated, the final agreements had already been determined.

After further protracted discussions, most of it merely for the sake of creating the appearance of a global consensus, the League of Nations accepted the proposed treaties and granted France and the United Kingdom their anticipated protectorates. Those protectorates were formalized as separate mandates to each of the respective governments, charging them to administer the affected regions until those regions were capable of standing on their own.

By its terms, the mandate to the British for the administration of Palestine included a provision designating the World Zionist Organization as the coordinating agency for Jewish affairs in Palestine. The mandate also called for the creation of a Jewish National Council with elected representation for Jews living in Palestine. Within days of the League's approval, Weizmann, by then president of the World Zionist

Organization, formed the council and named its initial members who served on a provisional basis pending election of delegates a few months later. Similar provisions were included for Arabs.

The Jewish provisional council drew up maps of Palestine which were divided into electoral districts. When elections were announced, David Ben-Gurion decided to run for a council seat from Jaffa where he lived with his wife and family after the war. Jabotinsky sought one of the seats from Jerusalem. Both Jabotinsky and Ben-Gurion won their respective races and served as members of the first elected council. Arab violence against Jews was one of the first issues the new council addressed.

Although a wide range of ideas and approaches was presented, discussion slowly divided members into two groups. One favored Jabotinsky's insistence that they pursue a straight-forward confrontation. "We should fight now and get it over with," he proclaimed.

Others, led by Ben-Gurion, preferred to address the matter through cooperation with the British. "If we fight the Arabs in a straightforward battle," Ben-Gurion argued, "the British will always intervene on the Arab side. The only way we can prevail is to keep antagonism as low as possible."

The Council refused to adopt a confrontational policy but in light of obvious threats and the remote location of many Jewish settlements, it authorized the formation of Settlement Police to patrol and defend Jewish communities. That decision became known to the public almost immediately. Less well-known was the decision to create a paramilitary organization known as Haganah to provide coordination and training of Settlement Police and to maintain regional cadres of elite forces capable of responding quickly to attacks where additional help was needed.

✦ ✦ ✦

News of the decision to authorize British administration in Palestine was greeted by most as a foregone conclusion. It caused little stir. Recognition of a Jewish coordinating organization and provisions authorizing the creation of a Jewish council were seen as necessary compromises. But by the time the Jewish National Council was actually formed and election of its members was held, tension between Arabs and Jews had grown far greater than most expected. Having a functioning, politically aware Jewish presence was no longer something the British could ignore or the Arabs tolerate.

When the council authorized the creation of Settlement Police, many Palestinians greeted the action with more than raised eyebrows. Not long after that decision was announced, news of Haganah began to leak. Word spread that a broader Jewish defense force was in the offing.

Alarmed by what was perceived as a military threat to British control, anti-Zionist members of the British government, both in London and in mandatory Palestine, began to discuss the threat Jewish nationalism posed to peace in the region. Military planners went to work determining potential action to tamp down Jewish expectations. One of those who was particularly worried about the situation was Major Atwell, a member of General Bols' staff.

Atwell had come to the Middle East in the years before the war, where he was initially posted to Cairo. There he met a young T. E. Lawrence and the two became quite close friends. In late-night conversations, Lawrence described the natural divisions of the Arab Middle East, which he'd observed from experience. A division, he suggested, that offered a solution to the ongoing violence that plagued the region.

Lawrence's partition of the Middle East along existing ethnic and religious preferences seemed obvious to him. So much so that he proposed it during negotiations among the Allies after the war, even going so far as to diagram it on a well-drawn map. Atwell joined the effort to promote Lawrence's idea, hoping that reasonable minds would see the logic of it.

In spite of their work and in spite of the many alleged promises made by British officials to induce the Arabs to join the Allies against the Ottoman Empire in the first place, at the conclusion of the war Arabs held only an area known as Transjordan, and that under a semiautonomous arrangement. Devastated by the result, Lawrence departed for London, ashamed of what he saw as a British betrayal. Atwell remained in Palestine, determined to do as much as possible to see that at least some of the supposed promises to the Arabs were honored.

As General Bols' administration took shape, Atwell was assigned to the intelligence department, a task he accepted with great relish. Working with contacts he'd established among Arabs, he established a comprehensive network of informants that covered the region from the Negev to the Syrian border.

When Settlement Police appeared at Jewish enclaves around the country, Atwell knew about it almost immediately and filed extensive reports detailing size, strength, and estimated capabilities of each unit. He briefed Bols every day with the latest information, even going so far as to plot the locations on a map to dramatically display the extent of coverage the Settlement Police achieved. Bols listened attentively and appeared interested but not particularly concerned.

Atwell continued to gather intelligence on Jewish activity, hoping Bols would share his sense of alarm at the growing militaristic posture of the Settlement Police, but the reaction was always the same. Bols was interested, but not particularly concerned.

Then rumors spread of platoon-size units training in the more remote Jewish farming communities, followed by news that the group called itself the Haganah. Rather than reporting the latest developments to Bols, Atwell decided to take matters into his own hands.

At his desk in Government House, Atwell pored over maps, plotting the locations to which British army units were posted. When he finished with that, he reviewed a list of the officers who commanded each of those posts and ranked them based on how he perceived their attitude to be towards the Jews. From that effort he determined that most of the commanders inside Jerusalem favored the Arabs. Those in more rural regions favored the Jews. Armed with that information, he contacted Salih Jarallah, a Muslim cleric with whom he had worked in the past, and arranged to meet him at a secluded spot near Ammunition Hill, a British garrison overlooking Temple Mount.

"I wanted to talk to you," Atwell began when they were alone, "because I—"

Jarallah said, raising his hand to interrupt. ""Mr. Atwell, I must say to you, this is a very brave thing you are doing."

Atwell looked perplexed. "What is so brave about it?"

"You, talking to me."

"Why is that so brave?" Atwell still looked confused. "I've known you a long time."

Jarallah nodded. "You British are very good at making friends when you are desperate, but as soon as the crisis passes you think only of yourselves."

"You think I have forgotten you?"

"I think there are many people in this city who would accept such a meeting with you solely for the purpose of killing you."

Atwell was startled. "Killing me? What have I done?"

"You are British," Jarallah explained. "That is reason enough for many."

"Why are they angry with us?"

"You make promises you do not keep."

"Oh," Atwell glanced away. "I know."

"You know?"

Atwell turned back to face Jarallah. "I know very well the promises they made to you. That after the war, the Middle East would become an Arab kingdom and the British would control only the tiniest sliver of coastline here in Palestine."

"And now it is the opposite," Jarallah noted. "We have nothing and you have everything."

"That's why I wanted to see you," Atwell said confidently.

Jarallah frowned. "To make more promises you and your superiors can break?"

"To ask you to help me change things for the good."

"Good for you, or good for us?"

"Both."

"And how is that any different from what your superiors proposed before?"

"The Jews of Palestine are organizing for statehood. Even as we speak, they are arming themselves, training themselves, establishing fully functional military units around the country ready to respond at the slightest provocation."

Jarallah nodded. "We have heard of these activities, but they do not appear to be nearly so ominous a threat as you suppose."

"We don't need them to actually *be* a threat," Atwell replied. "We just need enough evidence to suggest they are."

Jarallah frowned once again. "I'm afraid I don't understand."

"Right now the Jews are working very hard to convince the world that Arabs are the aggressors. That Jews are peaceful, tolerate people and Arabs are the ones causing the problems. We need to change that story."

"How?"

"First we publicize Jewish efforts to create Settlement Police and the paramilitary units that have recently come to light. Then we create a major incident that focuses world attention on the Jews as the aggressors."

"You can do that?"

With a devious smile, Atwell answered, "If you can create the incident, I can create the publicity."

"What sort of incident?"

For the next ten minutes, Atwell outlined for Jarallah the information he'd gleaned about the position of pro-Arab British commanders and the opportunity those commanders afforded. "If an incident occurs in one of these areas, we can control the reaction from our side and ensure that you have enough time to create the kind of crisis we need."

"Where did you have in mind?"

Atwell unfolded his map and showed it to Jarallah, pointing out three contiguous zones, portions of which overlapped Jerusalem's Jewish Quarter. "These zones are controlled by favorable British officers. If you can create an incident there and provoke a Jewish reaction, we can limit outside intervention long enough for the skirmish to grow into a major confrontation. Then we can use that confrontation to portray the Jews as the aggressors."

"And if that does not work?"

"We will repeat it in other similar locations until Jews are no longer willing to risk danger to live here. They fled once because of that kind of threat."

"And the men who participate in this...incident. What will happen to them?"

"As I said, if the incident occurs in this area," Atwell tapped the map for emphasis, "that will not be a problem."

Jarallah thought for a moment. "I like the idea, but we must have the grand mufti's approval for an undertaking of this size and nature."

"Should I meet with the grand mufti?"

"Yes," Jarallah replied. "I will arrange it."

✦ ✦ ✦

Two nights later, Atwell was escorted down a dark Jerusalem alley and into a house where Haj Amin al-Husseini, the grand mufti of Jerusalem awaited him. For the next thirty minutes Husseini listened as Atwell outlined once again his plans for waging attacks against the Jews.

"And you think this will drive them from our midst?" Husseini asked.

"I think it will go a long way toward casting the Jews as the aggressor."

"And what will that do?"

"It will help turn the tide of public opinion in your favor."

"And then what shall we do?"

"Create another incident," Atwell smiled. "And another. Until they really do become the aggressor."

"Provoke them into showing their true nature," Husseini observed.

"Yes," Atwell agreed.

"I am interested, and I have asked another to join me." Behind him, a door creaked open. Atwell was suddenly on alert. "It is okay," Husseini said calmly. "No one will harm you here."

As the door opened wider, a short, muscular man appeared, whom Husseini introduced as Fawzi al-Qawuqji, a Lebanese Druze who once had been an officer in the now-defeated Turkish army. At Husseini's direction, Atwell once more explained his plans, this time for Qawuqji's review.

As Atwell concluded his presentation, Qawuqji glanced over at Husseini who gave him a nod. Qawuqji turned back to Atwell. "I believe we have reached an agreement," and the two men shook hands.

# CHAPTER 26

foz

WITH HUSSEINI'S SUPPORT, Fawzi al-Qawuqji went to work organizing Jerusalem Arabs into small groups, which he hoped would be nimble, agile, and capable of blending into the background if necessary. In a series of meetings, he first trained them in basic tactics for creating confusion and fear, providing instructions for disabling electrical service, disrupting water supplies, and creating street obstructions to prevent vehicle and foot traffic.

Once they'd become familiar with this, Qawuqji moved on to training in the use of rudimentary military equipment such as revolvers, automatic pistols, and rifles. When that was complete, the groups turned to methods for fashioning explosives from gasoline, cleaning solvents, and other readily available items. "We won't have many weapons," he explained. "But we will be able to improvise what we need and in many ways that will work much better. When they see that almost anything can become dangerous in the right hands, they will fear everyone."

From working with those groups, Qawuqji selected a small number of men who appeared capable of learning more and doing more. He formed them into small teams and provided specialized training in hand-to-hand fighting where he taught them to use the dagger and sword. "These are the weapons of our forebears," he said, brandishing one of each. "This is how they liberated themselves from their oppressors. We are resurrecting the ancient arts of our heritage to kill the Jews and or at least drive them away. This is how we shall liberate ourselves from the dogs who threaten to destroy our lives."

At meeting after meeting, he reinforced those words and encouraged his followers, fanning the flames of enthusiasm at every turn by saying things like, "All we have to do is cleanse the Jewish Quarter of their filth and the city will be ours." Arabs living in and around Jerusalem heard his words and understood them as coming directly from the grand mufti, leaving little option except to respond. As the training continued, they could think of nothing but venting decades of frustration on their Jewish neighbors.

Although Qawuqji conducted his work in secluded locations and kept the groups small, making them easier to disguise and hide from public view, news of what he was doing eventually leaked out. Before long, rumors spread among the Arab population that a major effort was underway to prepare for attacks on the Jews.

As preparation among Arabs became more commonly known, some expressed concern about, and even opposition to, such a radical approach. "Those who participate will be known to all who live here," they noted. "The British will easily learn their identity and they will not let such conduct go unpunished."

When Qawuqji learned what they were saying, he let it be known that the British were on their side. "We can kill Jews at will," he told anyone who asked. "The British will not interfere. Everything has been arranged. No one will be punished."

✦ ✦ ✦

In addition to holding a seat on the Jewish National Council,

Jabotinsky had returned to his work as a journalist. To help facilitate that, he maintained a broad network of contacts and sources he used to learn about events before they became known to the public. Access to that kind of information allowed him to file stories with *Russkiya Vedomosti,* which were published long before any of the other Russian or European newspapers. That kept him in good graces with his Moscow editor. It also put him ahead of many in Palestine as well.

One of Jabotinsky's contacts was Yezid Shomali, a baker who lived in the Muslim Quarter. Shomali was born and reared by Arab parents. His grandmother, however, was Jewish, and as a child he was very close to her. She was the one who taught him the art of baking and several of the breads he produced from his shop came from her recipes. He faithfully observed all the Muslim practices, including the prayers and fasts, and he attended mosque each Friday. Secretly, however, he loved the Jewish traditions and had a kindness in his heart for us.

When Shomali heard what Qawuqji was doing, he left a message for Jabotinsky with a rabbi in the Jewish Quarter who was Jabotinsky's neighbor. The following day, Jabotinsky arrived at a coffee shop across the street from Shomali's bakery.

From his shop, Shomali watched through the front window and when Jabotinsky was seated at a table in back, he walked across the street with a delivery of fresh bread. When the coffee shop owner disappeared in back with the bread, Shomali took a seat across from Jabotinsky. "Things are happening," he began in an ominous tone.

"What sort of things?" Jabotinsky asked.

"Evil things. Men are training for attacks on your people, and there is talk that the British are supporting the effort."

"When?"

"I think they will happen soon but I cannot determine when or where."

"Who is leading the effort?"

"A man named Fawzi al-Qawuqji. He is very bad but he is not one of us. He is from somewhere else."

Just then, the shop owner returned. Shomali rose from his chair and started toward him. The owner looked at him suspiciously. "You know this Jew?"

Shomali laughed. "He was asking about the bread. It smelled so good."

The owner was still skeptical.

"You will pay me now?" Shomali asked.

"Yeah," the shop owner replied. "Sure." He turned to the cash box with his back to Shomali as he gathered the money to pay. When he turned around, Jabotinsky was gone and Shomali, with his hand out, had a big smile.

✦ ✦ ✦

Later that day, Jabotinsky caught a ride on a delivery truck and arrived at our camp near Beersheba. He came immediately to Colonel Patterson's tent. The colonel was surprised to see him but Jabotinsky ignored his greeting and got right to the point.

"I have a source who has told me that Fawzi al-Qawuqji is in Jerusalem. He was with the Ottomans when General Allenby fought his way through here. Before we arrived."

"Can't seem to put a face with the name."

"You wouldn't. He wasn't much of an officer back then."

"And now?"

"Hires himself out to the highest bidder. I checked with some other people I know. They say the Haj hired him to organize Arabs for attacks against our people."

"Husseini is behind it? Word is, they're planning to attack the

Jewish Quarter. Probably during the Nebi Musa."

Nebi Musa was a week-long Muslim festival. It began on Easter Sunday and lasted for the next seven days, during which all Muslims were supposed to trek en masse to a place near Jericho that was believed to be Moses' burial place. Only a Muslim would believe that. The Torah clearly says God buried him and only He knows the location. But it was a very big celebration.

"That would be the perfect time for trouble," Colonel Patterson noted.

"Thousands of extra people jammed into the city. They'll fill the Muslim Quarter and once they get started, there's no telling what they could do."

Colonel Patterson nodded in agreement. "I better report this."

"But don't mention my name," Jabotinsky cautioned.

"I won't."

+ + +

The following day, Colonel Patterson and I took a truck from camp and rode to Jerusalem. Jabotinsky rode with us until we reached the outskirts of town, then he got out and made his own way. We continued to Government House, which sat atop a hill just south of the Old City. General Bols' office was there and we arrived unannounced.

Bols listened quietly as Colonel Patterson described what he'd learned from Jabotinsky—without mentioning him by name. When he finished, General Bols looked over at him and very coldly said, "You are stationed at Beersheba, are you not?"

"Yes, sir," Colonel Patterson replied.

"With the Jewish Legion."

"Yes, sir."

"Don't you have enough troubles of your own without spending an entire day driving up here to tell me about rumors you've heard?"

"I would assume that if they've reached me all the way down in—"

"You should assume that if they've reached you all the way down in Beersheba, some of us up here have heard them, too!" Bols glared at the colonel. "We hear rumors every day. All day."

"These are rather ominous and—"

"I don't care how ominous they are. Without the mention of names and dates, they are rumors. Do you understand me? Rumors!" Bols was shouting by then. "You don't have time for them. I don't have time for you to tell me about them. And you've already wasted thirty minutes of my day. Now get out of my office!" He pointed toward the door for emphasis.

Colonel Patterson rose from his chair, snapped to attention, and delivered a crisp salute, then turned toward the door, which I held for him, and we both walked out. We walked from the headquarters building to the truck without a word and when we climbed into the cab we found Jabotinsky curled up on the floor.

"Well," he said expectantly, "what did he have to say?"

"He told us we'd wasted his time with rumors and ordered us to leave."

"He threw you out?"

"Yes, I'd say so." He looked over at me. "Wouldn't you, Mr. Horev?"

"Yes, sir," I replied, amused to hear him call me by my last name. "Threw us out with a flourish."

Jabotinsky looked over at the colonel. "Then that confirms it."

"Confirms what?"

"The British are helping them."

Colonel Patterson frowned. "Helping the Arabs?"

"Yes."

"Why do you think that?"

"I heard it."

"From where?"

"Same place I heard the rest of it. I didn't tell you before because... you know..." He had a sheepish look. "You're British. I didn't want to be offensive."

Colonel Patterson had an amused look. "Since when has that stopped you?"

"I was trying to be nice... to protect you."

"How?"

"If I had told you some of the British officers had agreed to help the Arabs attack us, you would have gone to Bols angrier than you already were. You wouldn't have been able to keep quiet about it. You would have blurted it right out."

"What would be wrong with that?"

"He'd figure out where the information came from." Jabotinsky pointed toward the front of the truck. "Keep driving south and don't go back in there to see Bols about this again."

"I'm thinking about turning around right now."

"I know, that's why I'm telling you. Keep driving."

"What will you do?"

"I don't know. But I can tell you one thing, we will not sit idly by and watch." He smiled over at Colonel Patterson. "One way or the other, we will do as we have always done. We will find a way to fight back." He gestured out the window. "There's a building up there on the right. Let me out in front of it."

Hearing the tone in Jabotinsky's voice that day, I knew things were serious. In times past, he would have been far more animated, shouting and yelling and pounding the air with his fists. But that day he was unnervingly calm and level-headed. Almost resolute. As if he understood one simple fact that clarified all the others. Trouble was coming, and before it was over he very likely would lose his life.

✦ ✦ ✦

When we returned to camp that evening I found Amos and told him what was happening. He gestured with a wag of his finger before I was finished. "I've seen that look in your eye before. You want to fix things. And I'm telling you, there's nothing you can do to fix this. Nothing at all. Jerusalem is large and crowded and we're way down here in Beersheba. Someone else will have to handle it."

"But that's just it," I argued. "No one is handling it."

"And what do you think you can do about it from here?"

"I don't know, but I don't think I can sit around here and do nothing." The words sounded like Jabotinsky's.

"Well, that's all we can do. We've got nothing to give them by way of help."

"We have weapons and ammunition," I countered. "I'm sure they need that to defend themselves."

"We need it, too."

"We have plenty."

Amos shook his head. "We can't give it to them. And more to the point, *you* can't give it to them, either."

"Why not?"

"We're in the British army." His voice rose in volume. "We can't give them British munitions."

"Who would know?"

"Anyone who hears the shooting. Anyone who examines the bodies and sees the wounds." Amos ticked the points off in rapid succession. "Anyone who finds unspent rounds. Anyone who digs out a shell—"

"Okay," I interrupted, cutting him off. "I get the point. But we can't just sit here and wait for the Arabs to attack, then watch our people die."

320

"No one is going to die," he said with a dismissive wave of his hand. "No one ever dies in these things. They just talk about it and then nothing happens."

Amos might have believed nothing really happened when Arabs called for attacks on our people, but I wasn't willing to wait and hope he was right. If trouble was coming, Jabotinsky needed our help, and we were morally obligated to give it to him. We were, after all, the *Jewish* Legion. If we weren't going to help our fellow Jews, we might as well disband and go home right then. That's something I believed that night, and it's something I believe today. We were all each other had back then, and we're still all we have today.

As I came from Amos' tent, my mind was made up and later that night, after everyone was asleep and only the guards were awake, I went to Colonel Patterson's headquarters tent. The key to the munitions storehouse was kept on a ring that Colonel Patterson attached to a loop on his trousers. But a second key was kept inside a locked box behind the desk to be used in an emergency. He thought only he knew about it. The key to the locked box was hidden inside a book on his desk. In short order, I opened the box, took out the munitions storehouse key, and hurried across camp toward the building.

Along the way, I recruited Scholem Baazov, Aaron Gruner, and Mosha Pinsker—men sympathetic to Jabotinsky's cause and who I knew were thinking of joining him—and took them with me. The truck we'd used for the trip to Jerusalem was parked nearby and when I opened the storehouse door, we loaded the truck with rifles and ammunition.

With all four of us helping, we pushed the truck away from camp to make the noise less obvious, then started the engine, climbed into the cab, and headed toward Jerusalem. Gruner drove. We made it to Jabotinsky's house, unloaded the truck, and were back in camp before sunrise.

# CHAPTER 27

foz

ON EASTER SUNDAY, the Nebi Musa festival began in Jerusalem's Muslim Quarter. People who lived on that side of the Jewish Quarter told me the crowd arrived early that morning already in a state of frenzy. Most of our people in the city sensed from the sound of the celebration that something terrible was about to happen.

The grand mufti opened the day with a speech delivered from the balcony of the Arab Club, which overlooked the city square. He began calmly enough with a reminder of the way things used to be back in the days when there were no Jews in Palestine—a time, by the way, that neither he nor anyone else in the crowd ever witnessed and, in fact, had never occurred. Though small in number, Jews had always been in the land of Palestine, ever since the days of Abraham. But that did not stop the grand mufti from telling the people how peaceful and idyllic Palestine had been before we arrived, with families living in safety, free to pursue their dreams and aspirations in tranquil bliss. The land of old, he suggested, was a place where families looked after each other and no one lacked for anything.

About midway through that fantasy, his eyes darkened and his brow, furrowed in an ominous expression, sagged low over his eyelids and he said in a grave voice, "Then the Jews arrived and desecrated our holy land—desecrated this marvelous gift of Allah—by their mangy presence."

Suddenly and without warning, he burst into the most vile and vehement rant anyone ever had heard him give, blaming us for a century of supposed ills. By his account, we were responsible for the droughts that ruined the crops and the floods that swept them away. The Turkish occupation, he said, was a punishment from Allah for allowing even one Jew to live there. "But we have freed ourselves from the godless Turk imposters," he shouted, "and now we must cleanse our land from the filthy Jews!"

The crowd picked up portions of that line and began to chant over and over, "Cleanse our land! Jews must die! Cleanse our land! Jews must die!"

Next to speak was Musa al-Husayni, the mayor of Jerusalem. He picked up where the grand mufti left off and, building on the notion that we were dogs, called on Arabs everywhere to rise up and kill the rabid animals among them "before they infect us all." By the end of his speech, the crowd was chanting a new phrase.

"Jews are dogs! Jews must die! Jews are dogs! Jews must die!"

Over and over they shouted at the top of their voices, and the sound of it reverberated through the narrow streets and alleys of the city.

As the crowd continued to chant, carefully selected gangs of Fawzi al-Qawuqji's most aggressive young Arabs slipped into the Jewish Quarter. Under cover of the noise, they prowled the alleys searching for anyone who might be moving about. When they found the streets all but deserted, they turned their anger on the buildings, smashing windows until they'd worked themselves into a rage, then they began kicking in doors, dragging people into the streets, and beating them with clubs.

Back in the Muslim Quarter, Aref al-Aref, the editor of Palestine's largest Muslim newspaper, rose to address the gathering. Shouting at the top of his voice, he recounted supposedly factual incidents of Jewish violence against Arabs, printed accounts of which he claimed to have published in his paper. Only those closest to the front heard him, though, as the crowd continued to chant, drowning out his voice to all but a few.

While Aref spoke, more of Qawuqji's thugs moved among the people, handing out leaflets prepared in the grand mufti's name that said, "Rise up today and celebrate the Nebi Musa with the sacrifice of many Jews. Kill as many as you can. No harm will come to you. You will receive no reprisals. The British are on our side. He who kills a Jew does a good thing. Allah is protecting you."

Over in the Jewish Quarter, the roaming Arab gangs made enough disturbance to attract the residents' attention but their size was small enough that some who lived there thought they could put an end to the trouble by responding in force, as they had on other occasions. Armed with nothing but their hands and improvised weapons, they came from their houses and shops to fight.

Just then, however, the crowd in the Muslim Quarter broke from the square and surged down the streets into the Jewish Quarter. Residents who were in the street defending their lives and property became easy prey, and the crowd set upon them with a vengeance.

The Jewish and Muslim Quarters were located in an area of Jerusalem known as the Old City, a part of Jerusalem that lay within the boundaries of the city's ancient walls. Those walls still existed and the only way through them was by means of eleven gates. That Easter Sunday, as the Muslims entered the Jewish Quarter, British soldiers manning the wall closed each of the eleven gates, cutting off access to the city from the outside and prohibiting anyone already in the Old City from leaving.

Very quickly, things got out of hand as Muslims vented their emotions by destroying property and murdering our people. Rapes and beatings were widespread and by sunset many of our people were dead or wounded.

News of the riot spread quickly throughout the remainder of the city and there were sporadic incidents of Arab violence against Jews all across the country. Men from the newly formed Haganah attempted to intervene but they were blocked by armed British soldiers acting upon orders from General Bols' headquarters. Precisely who gave those orders and Bols' own complicity in them was never established, but most of us were certain it was the work of Major Atwell, if not someone of higher rank.

Using the arms and munitions we supplied, Jabotinsky and his neighbors fought back, doing their best to keep the marauding Arabs at bay, hoping every moment for help to arrive, but they were terribly outnumbered. Fighting from house to house—and sometimes room to room—they managed to confine the Arabs primarily to the eastern sector of the Quarter, but there was damage everywhere and even as they fought, the violence grew worse. Into the night, they heard the screams of anguish from victims and the report of occasional gunfire.

✦ ✦ ✦

Almost as quickly as the riot began, reports of the violence reached Weizmann at his office in Tel Aviv. David Ben-Gurion learned of it as well and arrived at his office insisting they must do something to stop it.

"The gates are closed," Weizmann said solemnly.

"Then let's open them up," Ben-Gurion replied, his fists clinched as if ready to fight right then.

"The gates are guarded by British soldiers."

Ben-Gurion had a pained expression. "You mean British soldiers are preventing anyone from getting out?"

Weizmann nodded. "No one gets out. No one gets in."

"Has anyone tried?"

"Yes. But they have been unsuccessful from either side."

"What does Bols say?"

"I have phoned his office numerous times, but no one returns my calls."

Ben-Gurion turned toward the door. "Then come on, let's go see him."

The drive from Tel Aviv to Government House took less than an hour and they reached it with little difficulty. General Bols, who had not been expecting them, was in a meeting and they were forced to wait outside his office. Ben-Gurion didn't like it and was certain they were being delayed intentionally.

"It's an insult," he said under his breath.

"Relax," Weizmann soothed. "I'm sure he's a busy man."

Ben-Gurion frowned. "And I'm sure he's ignoring us."

Half an hour later, an aide ushered them into Bols' office, where they found him seated at his desk. He did not bother to stand but addressed them from his chair. "What may I do for you today?" he asked in a nonchalant tone.

"You are aware," Weizmann began, "that Muslims have entered the Jewish Quarter and are killing our people?"

Bols' face was expressionless. "I heard there was some trouble up there. Not sure how bad it is, though."

"I'll tell you how bad it is," Ben-Gurion blurted out. "Men and women are dead in the streets. Young and old are being raped at will, some of them two and three times each. Houses have been set on fire.

Property destroyed." He leaned over the desk. "And you know very well what's going on there."

"I assure you, I have yet to receive a detailed report noting anything like what you describe." He looked Ben-Gurion in the eye. "Perhaps you are mistaken."

"I am not mistaken that your men closed the city gates. I am not mistaken that the Arabs are handing out leaflets like this." Ben-Gurion took one of the Muslim leaflets from his pocket and slapped it on the desktop. "Look at that right there." He pointed to the words on the page. "'You will receive no reprisals. The British are on our side.'"

Weizmann was not aware of the leaflets or that Ben-Gurion had one and was startled by the sudden revelation. His eyes were wide as he stared down at the paper. Bols merely glanced at it and shrugged. "Anyone can print a notice like that."

"Shop owners began refusing credit to Jews last week," Weizmann added in a calm, even voice. "Milkmen demanded payment at delivery, in cash—something they have never done before. Christian shop owners marked their stores with the sign of the cross, letting everyone know they are not Muslim."

Bols smirked. "And you think they knew this was going to happen?"

"Your men are guarding the gates," Ben-Gurion retorted. "Preventing us from assisting our people. Trapping thousands inside the city. Watching while Jews die." He pointed his finger at Bols. "And you're sitting here at your desk as if nothing is happening. What are we supposed to think?"

In spite of their protests, Bols waited two more days before ordering his men to respond. When British troops finally entered the Jewish Quarter, it took them three days to put down the riot. A final count showed two hundred fifty people were dead, most of them Jewish. Millions of dollars in property was destroyed.

Of the hundreds of Muslims who attacked our people, only two were arrested. They were held a few hours, then released with no charges ever filed against them.

The following week, however, British officers—Major Atwell among them—convinced one of the Arabs—a man who had been away from Jerusalem during the festival—to lie under oath about seeing Jabotinsky with a firearm. Using his statement as a pretense, they searched Jabotinsky's house, where they found a rifle and ammunition. His neighbors, who were alerted by the presence of British soldiers, quickly disbursed the remaining weapons, hiding them in outhouses and other locations the British would not search.

Possession of firearms was illegal in Palestine—a law enforced by the British only against the Jews—and Jabotinsky was arrested. Having found a weapon at his home, Major Atwell assumed others had them as well and conducted widespread searches of the Quarter. In spite of an extensive effort, they found nothing, but that didn't stop them from arresting a dozen men believed to be Jabotinsky's accomplices.

When Weizmann learned of the arrests and preferential treatment accorded Arabs by the British authorities, he didn't wait for Ben-Gurion to demand action. Instead, he responded on his own and went again to see General Bols.

Unlike Ben-Gurion, who saw himself as an advocate and a man of action, Weizmann viewed himself as a diplomat, preferring to couch his remarks in a conciliatory tone, eliminating as much emotion from the moment as possible. That day, as he talked to Bols, he did just that, calmly laying out the evidence he'd gathered about particular instances when the Arabs were accorded favorable treatment, building his case one incident at a time until he came to the riots from just a few weeks earlier.

When he finished, Bols looked over at him and said coldly, "But you don't deny that Jabotinsky possessed a weapon, do you?"

"I don't deny that one was produced by your men who claimed it came from Jabotinsky's possession. But neither can you deny that more than a dozen Jews were arrested for defending themselves at the hands of Arab attackers, while only two Arabs were detained. And even they have been released without charges."

"There is only so much I can do. The military keeps the peace as best we can."

"Favoring one group over the other does nothing to keep the peace," Weizmann argued. "It only encourages the favored group to vent itself against the disfavored. Your special treatment of the Arabs gives them permission to do as they please against us."

"I will bring the matter up with our commanders, but when it comes to a final decision about how cases are disposed, I have no direct authority over the tribunals. I must allow the judicial process to unfold in as politically neutral a manner as possible."

+ + +

A few weeks later, Jabotinsky and the others arrested with him were summarily tried in a military court, convicted, and sent to prison. Jabotinsky, as the supposed leader of an armed illegal Jewish gang, was given fifteen years and threated with deportation upon release. Colonel Patterson learned of it in a note from Jabotinsky's wife. As he had done before, the colonel went to work immediately organizing an effort to gain Jabotinsky's freedom.

Over the course of the next week, Colonel Patterson met with General Allenby, General Chaytor, and Edward Davis, who'd been promoted to colonel during the war and was fast rising toward a position in the army's top ranks. At the same time, he sent a telegram to Amery outlining the problem.

Amery met with Milner and Smuts and enlisted their help in applying pressure on Lord Derby to intervene. When that didn't produce the desired results, Amery raised the matter with the prime minister in a private meeting.

Finally, after months of incarceration and a dozen more back-office meetings, Jabotinsky's sentence was commuted to one year. Sentences for those arrested with him were reduced to six months. Those men were released immediately. Jabotinsky, however, remained in prison until the full year of his sentence had been served.

A MONTH AFTER the Nebi Musa riots, a court of inquiry, known as the Palin Commission, arrived in Tel Aviv to review conditions and determine the cause for the riots. The commission was comprised of three men, all of them officers in the British army—Major General Sir Philip Palin, for whom the commission was named, Brigadier General E. H. Wildblood, and Lieutenant Colonel C. Vaughn Edward.

As with most official British visits, the commission's arrival was announced in advance, which gave Weizmann and the staff at the World Zionist Organization's Tel Aviv office plenty of time to prepare for their arrival. Golda Meir and Moshe Sharett, two of the younger members of the Agency's executive office, were assigned to accompany commission members through the Jewish Quarter and to assist them in obtaining interviews with the Quarter's residents. The grand mufti, feeling Arabs had been betrayed by the British yet again, refused to cooperate with the commission's work.

After conducting interviews on the ground, commission members interviewed British soldiers in private. Most, if not all, were pro-Arab and did their best to skew the commission's views favorably toward the Muslim perspective. Hard evidence, however, worked against them and made their testimony appear exactly as it was—contrived and disingenuous at best, untruthful and perjurious at its worst.

Once its preliminary work was finished, the commission held court and took sworn statements from selected British officers, Weizmann, and from just about anyone else who wanted to speak.

As I mentioned, the grand mufti—though invited and encouraged to address the commission—refused to participate, which meant none of the Muslim clerics appeared before the commission. Few private Muslim citizens did, either, and those who testified were met with the disdain of their neighbors and, in some instances, physical punishment.

Our people, however, spoke freely with the commission, telling both the good and the bad, including the part about weapons that were smuggled into the Quarter days prior to the riots—though thankfully they left out my name and the names of those who helped. Speaking publicly about that part of the riots was risky, but doing so added credibility to their testimony and to that of others. It was particularly enlightening for testimony regarding the extent to which the public knew, long before the festival began, that trouble was in the offing—all of which made the British administration's claims of ignorance unbelievable.

When its work in Palestine was completed, the commission withdrew to Port Said, Egypt, to deliberate and write its official report. The final draft was finished and prepared for submission by the end of August. Although General Allenby urged its release to the public, the full contents of that report were never made known. Instead, a summary was issued supporting the inescapable conclusion that the riots were instigated by the Muslims, probably the grand mufti himself, with assistance from Fawzi al-Qawuqji. It further noted that the potential for violence during the Nebi Musa festival was well-known to the public; in light of numerous warnings submitted to General Bols and his staff, claims that British authorities were not aware of the rising tension and the violence it portended were without foundation; Palestinian Arabs felt betrayed by the British government's failure to follow through on promises they believed had been made during the war regarding the creation of an independent Arab kingdom; and that Weizmann and others working on behalf of the World Zionist Organization had exacerbated tensions between the two groups by aggressively pursuing Jewish interests at levels beyond the local administration.

The report stopped short of accusing the army of conspiring with the grand mufti to instigate the riots but looked forward to an independent civilian administration, already in the works, that would have the authority to govern the region, including the exercise of control over policy decisions regarding the use of troops stationed there.

Not long after the Palin Commission's report was submitted to London, General Bols and his staff, including Major Atwell, were relieved of their administrative duties. Herbert Samuel, a civilian, was appointed as Palestine's first high commissioner and was charged with forming a civil government to rule the region until a permanent arrangement could be worked out between competing ethnic interests.

As high commissioner, Herbert Samuel, though a Jew, followed a practice that attempted to tread a perilous path between Arab and Jewish groups—slowing Jewish immigration while refusing to give Arabs power to actually stop it, but working to include both groups in the government. It marked a significant departure from Bols' approach but failed to inspire much confidence among us.

For one thing, even though the army officers previously associated with civilian administration of the region were removed from their administrative positions, the permanent civilian staff transferred to

Samuel's control intact. In effect, it gave him a staff as deeply anti-Semitic as Bols' officers had been. He also inherited the policies, rules, and regulations put in place by Bols. Not only that, General Bols and most of his officers remained in Palestine, their roles merely reduced to traditional military authority in commanding the troops. This conflicting arrangement and the fact that the personnel manning the day-to-day operation of government had not changed left us as vulnerable as ever to abuse from mandatory authorities, a condition Weizmann quickly recognized.

Not long after Samuel took office, Weizmann met with him and tried to impress upon him just how corrupt the British officers really were. Samuel listened politely. "You must understand," he said when Weizmann finished. "We face a delicate situation."

Weizmann had a puzzled frown. "We?"

"You, me, the government in London," Samuel explained. "Each of us faces a delicate situation here in Palestine, though perhaps not for the same reasons."

"I understand we have been abused at the hands of British officials," Weizmann retorted, "and we have been persecuted by the Arabs. That's what I and thousands like me understand."

"I know that is your perspective," Samuel replied, trying to show patience, "but the situation is more complex than that."

"I fail to see—"

Samuel interrupted. "Wait! Please allow me to finish." He glanced toward the window as he spoke. "The Arabs have two big problems. One is the presence of Jews in a land they feel is rightfully theirs. The other is the presence of the British. They are angry with the Jews for what they see as an attempted takeover and they are angry with us for what they feel are broken promises made to them during the war. Apparently, from all that I can determine, promises *were* made to the

Arabs in order to gain their assistance in ousting the Ottoman Empire from the region."

"Promises were made to us as well," Weizmann noted.

Samuel nodded in agreement. "Yes, that is true. Which has placed the British government—my government—in the awkward position of having promised two opposing groups things it cannot fulfill to one without denying it to the other."

"The British government put themselves in that position."

"That may be so," Samuel replied, nodding again. "But that is the reality of where we are. You also have one other more practical problem."

"I do?" Weizmann asked, frowning.

Samuel continued, "Strong people, who hold powerful positions in the British government oppose not only the creation of a Jewish state here, but the presence of Jews here at all."

"The United Kingdom is decidedly pro-Arab," Weizmann groused. "We have known that from the beginning."

"Not the United Kingdom," Samuel corrected with a wag of his finger. "Just the government."

For a moment, Weizmann lost his sense of decorum. "They're racists," his voice becoming almost a shout. "They hate us, one and all."

"No," Samuel corrected once more. "They do not hate you and they are not racists. They are colonialists. They have a colonial, almost paternal, attitude toward the Arabs. And," he added, "they also have deeply engrained romantic notions about the simple life of Bedouin Arabs."

"The Bedouin life is not simple," Weizmann replied.

"I know."

"And it's not much of a life, either. For them or any of the other Arabs who live here."

"Perhaps, but that is the situation we face. Which is why there is only so much we can do at the moment. Removing all of the army officers to which you object would be impossible for me without specific charges substantiated with irrefutable evidence. And even then, the task would remain all but impossible."

"So in the meantime, we are supposed to simply take whatever we're given and learn to live with it?"

"I am attempting to guide us past this transitional moment," Samuel said. "I am doing the best I can."

"As are we," Weizmann responded. "But we Jews must survive first. And right now that is still an open question."

✦ ✦ ✦

Later that year, a second commission of inquiry arrived in Palestine. This one, officially titled the Palestine Royal Commission, became known as the Peel Commission after its chairman, William Robert Wellesley Peel, was charged with recommending an ultimate solution to the Palestinian situation. Like the Palin Commission, its members conducted interviews, gathered documents, and held formal hearings. Unlike that prior commission, the Peel Commission was not comprised of army officers. Instead, its members were all men of peerage.

The commission did much of its work in public, holding hearings and official meetings in easily accessible locations in Tel Aviv and Jerusalem. Its deliberative process—the process of evaluating and sifting the evidence it found—was done behind closed doors, most often at the King David Hotel in Jerusalem. Yet as secret and confidential as they tried to be with the private process, news of the commission's progress and of the opinions shared by members soon leaked out.

A few weeks into the work, Weizmann and officials at the World Zionist Organization's office in Tel Aviv learned that commission members favored a division of Palestine along existing ethnic lines, with Arabs gaining exclusive political control of the areas already settled and occupied predominantly by Arabs, and Jews getting control of areas occupied and settled primarily by Jews. The commission reasoned this would give each group a majority from which it could establish its initial government. This suggested scheme posed an immediate problem for us.

"Arabs are in the majority," Weizmann noted. "A majority maintained by a wide margin. If Palestine is divided along existing ethnic lines, they will control most of the land. If we are to obtain a workable area for use as a Jewish homeland, we need to occupy as much territory as possible before the lines are drawn. We need to occupy space on the ground, with our people living there in established, functioning communities."

To do that, Weizmann proposed the implementation of additional programs designed to encourage Jewish immigration from abroad and the establishment of additional farming communities, particularly training farms, to provide space and assistance to the new settlers. Jabotinsky and Ben-Gurion—who worked closely with the Tel Aviv office—participated in the discussion and, in what was becoming an increasingly rare moment, both men agreed Weizmann's suggested policy was a good idea. However, for that idea to work they needed the support of Haganah, the military organization created to coordinate settlement security. Additional settlements would mean an increase in Haganah's security duties, which raised a new set of potential issues.

Although it had been created by the Jewish National Council and operated within the World Zionist Organization framework, Haganah had functioned largely on its own. Most of its operations were conducted without the direct knowledge of council members and without oversight from anyone. Whether Haganah leadership would cooperate with the World Zionist Organization in establishing new settlements was a matter of debate.

Much to everyone's surprise, Haganah's commander, Eliyahu Golomb, agreed to participate and suggested including representatives from key Settlement Police units as well. He arrived at the first meeting with maps of the northern half of Palestine—the area that would offer us easiest expansion, he suggested—and brought with him Yosef Malkin, chief of the Settlement Police from Degania.

At their first meeting, Weizmann showed them a map and said, "We are at a strategic moment in our effort to create a Jewish homeland. The British are realizing that administering this territory could easily become a trap for them and before long, they will be looking for a way out. The group that is in the best position to govern will eventually dominate all of Palestine."

"This is a leadership vacuum begging to be filled," Golomb added. "A country waiting to be filled and occupied."

"Yes," Weizmann agreed. "And if we can do that, we can become the de facto government in waiting, but we have to seize the moment and get our people and systems in place now." He pointed to the map. "We need to create settlements across most of Galilee. You men are here because the new settlements will need security. Settlement Police for each new outpost. Trained Haganah troops to patrol the surrounding region." He looked across the table at them. "Can you do that?"

Malkin nodded. "We are willing to help train and equip Settlement Police for new outposts, but we can't supply the force. We don't have any from among our own people who can do it. We're using every available person right now for our own security."

Golomb expressed the same sentiment. "Haganah doesn't have enough men or equipment to do it, either. Not by ourselves."

"But you could recruit the men you need," Ben-Gurion suggested.

"Yes," Golomb replied. "We could recruit, train, and equip enough men to supply as many settlements as you want to create—if we had the money."

"We can get the money," Weizmann suggested. "That won't be a problem."

"But if we are funding an expanded military role," Ben-Gurion added, "we need clear guidelines of authority."

"We have an established chain of command."

"Yes," Ben-Gurion conceded, "but if we are attempting to create an apparatus reminiscent of a government in waiting, the settlements and outposts we create must be established, manned, and maintained at the direction of this office, not by Haganah's own decision."

"You want us to work *for* you?" Golomb asked. "Not just *with* you?"

"I don't like it," Jabotinsky said before anyone could answer. "Haganah was created as a military organization, not a government department or agency. It has always been afforded a measure of independence." He looked around the room. "Most of you, at one time or another, have been glad for the anonymity that independence has afforded, too."

"We have afforded Haganah tactical independence," Ben-Gurion responded. "Tactical independence is necessary to allow field commanders latitude in executing strategy. But strategy must come from this office." He tapped the table with his index finger for emphasis. "We will make the strategic decisions, from here."

"Why?" Jabotinsky asked with a frown. "What gives this office the right to decide anything about Haganah?"

"We created it," Ben-Gurion replied. "That's what gives us the authority."

"Haganah was created by the Jewish National Council," Jabotinsky argued. "Not this office."

Ben-Gurion agreed. "Yes, Haganah was created by the council and this office was created to execute and administer council decisions. And that is precisely what we are doing."

Weizmann looked over at Jabotinsky and calmly added, "In the most respected nations, militaries are accountable to a civilian government. This is the way it must be here as well."

Jabotinsky slumped against the back of his chair, a look of resignation on his face. With Weizmann against him, there was little he could say or do.

"Well," Golomb said. "How do you want to do this?"

"Let's look at the map," Weizmann suggested, "and see if we can determine the best potential locations for new settlements." He spread the map across the tabletop and everyone leaned forward, studying the lines and dots that filled the page.

"This is an elevation map," Golomb added. "Which is a good way to start our selection process. We should concentrate on the most defensible positions first."

"Which means high ground as opposed to low," Malkin explained for the others at the table. "That sort of thing."

# CHAPTER 29

*foz*

WITH SAMUEL FULLY installed as high commissioner and a civilian government taking shape, life in Palestine settled into a calmer day-to-day routine—not entirely peaceful, as there still were daily attacks on Jews in scattered locations around the country—but life was more stable than before. The Peel Commission continued to move forward in addressing long-term questions about British policy in Palestine, which gave us hope that an ultimate resolution wasn't far off. At the same time, the World Zionist Organization assumed a stronger role through its Tel Aviv office and before long we could see the framework of a potential Jewish government emerging from its work.

Those changes in life did not go unnoticed among members of the Jewish Legion. Most of us had joined solely for the purpose of returning to Palestine and regaining control over the land and property we held before the war. As postwar conditions moderated, our men began to resign their membership and head off to pick up what was left of their lives.

Colonel Patterson shared our sentiment and, though he had not said so, I had known since we celebrated our first Passover in

Beersheba that he was thinking more and more of home and family. He'd been away from them a long time, first in Egypt and Gallipoli, then at the convalescent center recovering from the Gallipoli Campaign, followed by our time at Winchester and Plymouth where we trained, and finally back to Egypt and on to Palestine. Even with brief breaks to return home, that was a long time to be away.

While the Peel Commission was still at work, Colonel Patterson finally spoke openly with me about his desire to return to England and what he planned to do about it.

"I've been away from home too long," he explained. "I need to be with my wife and son. I'm going back to England."

It seemed like an awkward thing for him to say, but I was not surprised. "The army has a post for you there?"

"I'm not looking for a new post."

My forehead wrinkled in a puzzled frown. "What do you mean?"

"I filed papers with the War Office last week. I...I'm asking to retire."

*That* part surprised me. "Retire?"

"I've reached the end of my career and there's no use sticking around."

"What do you mean the end of your career? I don't understand. Has something happened?"

"Nothing has happened. And actually, that is part of the problem... in a way."

"I'm not following."

"I entered the war as a colonel," he explained. "And after all I've done and all we've been through, I'm still a colonel. In the British army, that's not a good thing."

"You should be a general."

"Thank you." He smiled but he was on the verge of tears. "Most men of my age and tenure are. But I'm not going any further in my career. Not now. And not with the enemies I've made."

"Too many letters and telegrams?"

"Yes, at least, that's what they're telling me. But I do not regret for one moment a single one of them. And if I had it all to do again, I would make even more noise on behalf of my men."

We continued to talk about British anti-Semitism, the future for Jews in Palestine, and roadblocks to his advancement, but as we talked he slowly drifted over to a bookshelf near his desk and began sorting through the volumes on the shelves.

He said, handing me a book. "Here, no point in taking this back to England." I glanced at it and saw it was a book about Theodor Herzl. I was still looking at it when he nudged me to take another one. "You should have these, too," he handed me three more. "Perhaps they'll help you understand how we've come to this point—wars in Europe, racial views, the conflicts that separate us." He glanced at me. "Maybe you can find a way to get us beyond all that before the century ends."

"The century has just begun," I chuckled.

He grinned, "Good. You still have plenty of time. So get busy."

✦ ✦ ✦

Colonel Patterson's retirement was approved in record time and by the end of the month he was ready to leave for home. The Jewish Legion threw a party the night before and the men were up at dawn the next day, assembled in formation near the road to see him off. It was a sight to see, all of them standing at attention in ranks perfectly straight.

Amos and I rode with him to Haifa where later that day he boarded a ship for England. As he climbed the gangway toward the first deck, tears filled my eyes.

"It's rather sad to see him go," Amos said.

"It feels like saying good-bye to Papa all over again," I whispered.

Amos put his arm around me and pulled me close. Colonel Patterson moved to the rail and waved at us. After a moment he wiped his cheek with his fingertips, then turned aside and was gone from our sight.

✦ ✦ ✦

Not long after Colonel Patterson left for home, Amos resigned from the Jewish Legion. Suddenly, remaining in the army—without him and without the colonel—didn't seem like such a good idea anymore and I resigned, too.

In spite of the distance, we made the trip north from Beersheba to Kinneret without incident and located our farm without any trouble. The landscape had changed little while we were away.

Our fields, which we'd expected to find overgrown, were planted in neatly laid rows that had been recently cultivated. Amos thought crews from the kibbutz were probably working it to keep it from wasting, as they had the fields owned by the Riskins.

The house, however, was not in such good shape. As we approached the clearing where it sat, I noticed a hole in the roof right above Mama and Papa's room. Amos noticed the yard was overgrown and appeared to have gone unattended since the night the Arabs attacked. We surveyed the damage, speculating aloud how long it might take to put it right, then walked over to the barn.

The animals were gone but a few implements remained and the harnesses for the horses still hung on the wall, right where Papa put them, though the leather was dried and cracked beyond use. Several hand tools were propped in the corner and I walked over to them. An ax was there and I gripped the handle.

"How does it feel?" Amos asked.

"Like work," I replied, then I rested it on my shoulder and walked outside.

A bush had grown near the barn door and I took a whack at it, chopping it off at the ground in one swing. It felt good to finally be working like that again, so I took a swing at another and that's when I noticed Amos still standing there, staring at me.

"What's the matter?"

"I was thinking about finding Dalia."

"Oh. I forgot all about that." It was true. In the rush of seeing the house and the fields and all that needed to be done, I'd forgotten why he really wanted to get back. "Then go. This will all be right here when you get back."

"Want to come with me?"

"Why do you need me?"

"Might be awkward if she doesn't want to see me."

"Why do you say that?"

"I don't know," he shrugged. "It's just...her letters sounded different the last few months. Like something else might be going on."

In the past, back when we first arrived in Egypt, I would have rejoiced at the slightest hint that things might not be working out for them. If Dalia wasn't interested in him, maybe she would be interested in me. But that was then and we'd come a long way since Egypt. I had moved on and was thinking of other things—a life of unlimited possibilities, a life beyond what we'd known in the past.

As Amos headed off to find Dalia, I continued making my way around the barn, hacking away the bushes and saplings that grew there. They were especially thick and plentiful around the chicken coop along the rear wall.

When I finished with that and was all the way back around in front, I went inside the barn and found a wooden ladder Papa kept in the tack room on the far side of the building. It was dusty from lack of use but otherwise in good shape. I dusted it off with a rag and brought it over beneath the access hole that led up to the loft.

With the ladder propped in place, I climbed up to the next floor where I knew Papa kept scrap lumber. Sure enough, it was lying there where he left it. After selecting the better pieces, I slid them down the ladder to the floor below, then climbed down and carried the boards to the house. When I'd moved enough lumber in place, I brought the ladder and some hand tools over to the house, too, and climbed up for a closer look at the roof.

By then I was ready for a break, but the damage to the roof wasn't as bad as I thought. If I kept working I could patch the hole before dark. So I brought the lumber up from the ground and began fitting it in place.

By twilight, the hole was repaired. I returned the ladder and tools to the barn, then walked over to the bench beside the house and sat down, basking in the pleasure of a day's work and watching the sun slowly drift toward the horizon.

A few minutes later I saw Amos coming across the field with Dalia walking beside him. They were holding hands and from their gait and the way he kept looking down at her—and her up at him—I knew they'd gotten along quite well. The sight of it sent a smile across my face.

THE FOLLOWING DAY we walked down to the kibbutz at Kinneret. Several of the people there remembered us. Others we knew from the refugee camp when we were in Egypt. One or two were in the Jewish Legion with us, Scholem Baazov among them, and we were glad to get reacquainted with them. Baazov was good friends with Jabotinsky, and we talked about that awhile.

As we talked, Benjamin Lapid, the settlement chairman, joined us. He confirmed what we'd expected—crews from the kibbutz had worked our fields while we were away. Lapid offered to pay us rent for use of the land and we suggested they pay it in food, as there wasn't anything to eat at the house. They began by offering us breakfast that morning.

We all trooped over to the dining hall, where we sat around a table. Amos and I ate while the others talked. Gradually, however, conversation waned and one by one they left to take care of their farming duties.

In a little while only Baazov remained with us. I'd seen men around in army uniforms that morning so I asked about them. He told me they were Settlement Police. I remembered seeing a notice about them when I was working with Colonel Patterson but it concerned the farming settlements, and that didn't have much to do with me at the time. Baazov seemed to know all about them and didn't mind telling me. I got the feeling he wanted to talk about something else, too, but he never quite found the time.

After we finished breakfast, we came from the dining hall and prepared to return to the farm. Baazov lingered with us, still looking as if he wanted a moment to talk, but just when it seemed he might, Lapid emerged from one of the barns and started toward us. He was leading a mule that had been saddled with a freight saddle just like the ones the Zion Mule Corps used in Gallipoli. I turned to mention that to Baazov but by then he was gone.

"We'll tend the fields until the crop is harvested," Lapid announced as he came near, "but after that you'll need a way to work the land yourself." He handed Amos the lead rope. "You can have this one to get started with. I'll see if I can find another to go with it before plowing starts."

While we talked, three women came from the dining hall with sacks of foodstuffs. They handed them to Amos and he tied the sacks to the saddle with practiced ease.

Half an hour later we arrived at the house. David Riskin was seated with Dalia on the bench in the yard. On the ground beside them was a wooden crate, and through a gap in the slats I saw two chickens. A plow leaned against the barn next to the door and beside it was a shovel.

Amos tethered the mule to a tree near the barn, then we walked over to where they were waiting. He smiled at Dalia. She smiled back. David stood to greet us, and then looked at Amos. "I came to return your property. As I told you before, the plow and shovel were in the barn. Mine were gone, so I used them while you were away."

Apparently they'd talked the evening before when Amos went for a visit.

"Do you still need them? Because the kibbutz will tend the fields until harvest. So if you need—"

"No, no," David replied with a wave of his hand. "I am good. We acquired new equipment."

"Well, if you ever need them again," Amos continued, "they'll be in the barn."

"I appreciate that," David said with a nod. "There were also a few chickens here when we returned. I doubt they were yours but they were on your property. We ate them." He pointed to the crate resting at his feet. "I give you these in return for the ones we took. It is not much and it's not as many as we found here, but they are all I can spare and still have eggs for our family."

"That's fine," Amos told him. "Keep them if you need them."

David waved his hands in protest. "No, no. The chickens are for you."

There was a pause in conversation and when the silence grew uncomfortable I asked David to help me carry the chickens to a coop behind the barn. The coop wasn't in great shape but it was better than the crate and would do until we fixed something better.

As we made our way in that direction I asked him questions about the trip back from Egypt, where they were staying, and how long it would take them to rebuild their house. I didn't care too much about any of that except the house—and Amos already told me it was almost finished. All I wanted was to keep him occupied so Amos could have a few minutes alone with Dalia.

Placing the chickens in the coop took almost no time at all, so I enlisted his help in bringing the plow into the barn, then we walked out back again and I asked questions about crop rotation and the best time to start plowing. The mule had been tethered to the tree all this time, so we walked it into the barn and put it in a stall, then filled the trough with water and watched it drink.

After a while, David and I ran out of things to talk about and we made our way to the house. Amos and Dalia were cuddled together on the bench, so I made enough noise to alert them of our presence. They both stood as we approached and the four of us talked a moment longer, then David and Dalia left.

When we were alone, Amos smiled over at me, "Thanks."

"How is she?"

"She's fine."

"From the look on your face, I guess she's still interested."

"Yeah," Amos grinned. "She's interested." He shoved both hands into his pockets. "You okay with that?"

"Yeah," I shrugged. "Why? What do you mean?"

"You liked her, too."

"That was before," I replied with a dismissive wave of my hand. "She likes you. I knew that before we went to Gallipoli."

"But you liked her, too," Amos pressed, unwilling to drop the subject.

"Yes," I admitted. "I liked her. But that isn't the point."

"What's the point?"

"She likes you, and you obviously like her. Besides, all of that was a long time ago. I've moved on."

"You sure?"

"Yes." I gave him a friendly whack on the back of his head. "I'm glad for you."

✦ ✦ ✦

For the remainder of the year, we worked at improving the

buildings and maintaining the house. In addition to the food they supplied, the kibbutz hired us to work the fields and, as Lapid promised, gave us another mule to match the one we had. Amos saw Dalia on a regular basis, sometimes with her family at the Riskin farm and sometimes alone in a grove of trees near the edge of the field.

There wasn't much furniture in the house and at first we slept on the floor, but eventually we found two beds in a storeroom at the kibbutz, which they let us take, and the Riskins gave us a small table and two chairs. While looking for more lumber in the loft I found one of the original oil lamps that Mama and Papa brought with them when they immigrated. We used it for light when the sun went down.

Late at night, when we'd eaten supper and turned out the lamp, we lay in bed and listened to the sounds of people passing on the dirt road that ran near the house—hoofbeats, sometimes voices, and occasionally the noise of a car or truck. I asked about it at the kibbutz and one of the Settlement Police told me Arab gangs roamed the area at night. "Better be careful," he cautioned. "Attacks are getting worse."

A few days later, that same policeman suggested maybe Amos and I should give up the farm and come to the settlement permanently, but after serving in the Zion Mule Corps and the Jewish Legion, we were no longer afraid of what might happen.

"We've waited a long time to come back," I said in reply. "We're not leaving again."

✦ ✦ ✦

A few months later we were awakened in the night by the sound of gunfire. It was close but not on our property. We pulled on our clothes and I paused long enough to lace up my boots. Amos, who didn't stop at all, was out the door ahead of me. By the time I made it outside, he was twenty meters in front and headed straight for the Riskins' farm. I knew what he was thinking—that they were under attack—but they still weren't living at the farm and I was pretty sure the gunfire was farther away than that.

By the time I caught up with Amos he'd slowed to a trot and it was obvious the trouble was at the Kinneret kibbutz. The Arabs were positioned on our side of the settlement, which meant those defending it were shooting in our direction. As we got closer, I realized we were in danger of being hit by live rounds. I grabbed Amos by the arm and forced him to stop.

"What?" he asked, glaring at me.

"We can't go down there from this direction."

"Why not?"

"We'll get shot."

A frown wrinkled his forehead. "You're scared of getting shot?"

"No, but we're walking straight toward gunfire from the settlement. The Arabs are between us and them. They're shooting in our direction."

Amos suddenly realized our predicament. "What do we do?"

"We need a rifle."

"We need two." He then pointed to the left.

I looked in that direction and saw two men crossing just beyond the stand of trees that grew behind the Riskins' barn. Dressed in loosely fitting shirts, they wore turbans and both were armed with rifles.

Amos nudged me to follow and we moved quietly to the edge of the trees and watched them go by. "We have to take them," I whispered.

"I know."

"Are you ready for this?"

"I think so." I could tell from the tone of his voice that he was worried but I didn't say anything. At that point we were long past talking about it and besides, so much adrenaline was rushing through me that I don't think I could have maintained a coherent conversation much longer.

When the two men were beyond our position, we slipped from our cover, crept up behind them, and grabbed them with an arm around the neck. I took the one on the left. Amos, the one on the right. They put up a struggle at first, but we choked them down until they stopped breathing.

Working quickly but not frantically, we stripped off their ammunition belts, picked up their rifles, and started toward the kibbutz, moving toward the east to avoid the line of fire from the settlement compound. As we did, we picked off some of the Arabs one shot at a time, taking aim, firing, and moving quickly away. No one had trained us for it; we just did it out of necessity.

In a little while, we reached the far side of the settlement and joined a patrol of Settlement Police operating outside the compound perimeter. Thankfully, they recognized us, though when they first saw us they were prepared to shoot in our direction.

Fighting lasted through the night but by morning the gang was gone. Six people from the kibbutz were injured. One was dead. Settlement Police found the bodies of eight Arabs in the field near the compound perimeter, including the two we killed with our bare hands.

An hour after sunup, with no further sign of trouble, we went to the dining hall for breakfast. The Riskins were there and Amos sat with them. I sat nearby at a table with Scholem Baazov. Others were with him, muscular men who looked like they could handle themselves in a fight. Later I asked Amos and he thought they were with Haganah.

On the way back home I could see Amos was lost in thought, so I asked him what was wrong. Without looking at me he said, "Until last night, I'd never killed anyone with my bare hands."

"Me either."

"Where did you learn to do that?"

"At the camp in Winchester." I glanced over at him. "Same place you learned it, too."

"Big difference between practicing in camp and doing it in the field."

"But I think it had to be done."

"I know," Amos said with a quick nod. "But it doesn't make it any better."

We walked a ways in silence and then I changed the subject. "Where's Dalia?"

"I don't know for certain."

"I didn't see her last night."

"They were supposed to move into the house today."

"It's finished?"

"Enough for them to live in it."

"You should go find her."

"I guess," he shrugged.

"You guess?" I laughed. "I think we both know where this relationship is headed. The Riskins will be your family soon. You need to see about them."

"I know..." His voice trailed away and I could tell there was more on his mind.

"What?" I asked in a tone only a brother could manage.

"I don't know," he said with a hint of frustration. "It's just that sometimes I think David and Tzipi would rather I didn't come around."

"Tzipi?" I asked with a doubtful tone.

"Not so much her, but definitely David."

"He's not blind, Amos."

"I know."

"He knows what's going on between you and Dalia. You're about to take away his daughter. Did you expect him to invite you to do it?"

David grinned. "I guess not."

Amos stopped and for the first time since we left the compound, he turned to look at me. "You'll be okay if I do?"

"Help them?" I asked. "Or take her away?"

"Help them."

"Yeah. Sure. And I'm okay with the other, too," I quickly added.

Amos gave me a brotherly shove in response and started toward Dalia's house. I watched him until he disappeared in the stand of trees that surrounded the Riskins' house, then continued on to ours.

An hour or two later, Scholem Baazov came to the farm. Mosha Pinsker was with him. We talked about old times and Mosha reminded me of the time we took arms and ammunition to Jabotinsky in Jerusalem before the riots. The three of us drank a cup of hot tea and when it was time for them to go, I walked out to see them off.

As we stepped outside, Baazov turned to me. "We could use you in our unit."

"Haganah?"

"Yes," he replied.

"Still illegal?"

"To the British, though with Arab violence on the rise, they're looking the other way more and more. You should join us. We could use you."

"I'll think about it."

"Bring your brother, too."

"I think he's committed to this farm."

"Well," Baazov smiled, "we need good farmers, too."

When Amos returned home I told him about Baazov, Pinsker, and the visit we had that afternoon. "They're with Haganah now."

"I figured as much when I saw them this morning."

"They want me to join." I looked over at him. "They'd like you to join also."

Amos looked away. "I'm not interested; I've had enough war. I'm ready to stay right here on this farm." Then he looked back at me. "What about you?"

"I don't know," I sighed. "Sometimes I miss the army life. The guys. The camaraderie."

"So, you're thinking about joining?"

"I think I'd like to find out more about what that would mean."

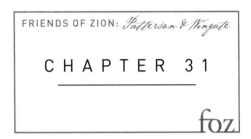

FRIENDS OF ZION: *Patterson & Wingate*

# CHAPTER 31

THE NEXT DAY, I went to the kibbutz to see Baazov. He was nowhere to be found and finally I asked Lapid, the settlement chairman, about him. "He's in and out. If you like, I can let him know you're looking for him." That seemed to be the best I could do so I left a message and returned home.

A few nights later, Baazov showed up at the farm. We sat outside on the bench beside the house and I told him I was interested in finding out what Haganah was like.

"You can train with us one day, but that is all."

"One day," I repeated, considering what that meant.

"Our men serve at great risk to themselves and their families. The British government has threatened to crush us and we are subject to arrest at any moment. Consequently, we do our best to prevent the public from knowing our identities. I will make an exception for you since I know you worked closely with Colonel Patterson and understand how things are for us."

"I appreciate that, but don't you think most of your men are known?"

"They all are known in one way or another. But not all of them are associated with Haganah. At least, not to the public."

It seemed a little extreme but I nodded, "Okay. One day."

"Good." He rose from the bench and stood. "Report to the kibbutz tomorrow afternoon."

"Tomorrow?"

"You have a problem with that?"

"No. I suppose not. But where will you train?"

"The kibbutz."

I smiled at the irony—his insistence on anonymity as a priority and yet they trained right there at the kibbutz in full view of everyone.

+ + +

The following afternoon, I went down to the Kinneret kibbutz at the appointed time. The central courtyard of the compound already was filled with men when I arrived—far more than I expected. Some were from the Kinneret Settlement Police—I recognized them from my previous visits to the farm—but most were men I had not seen before.

We trained for several hours, practicing hand-to-hand combat, demolition skills, and methods for making homemade bombs and weapons from ordinary items. I'd learned most of what we covered while training with the Mule Corps in Egypt and the Jewish Legion in Winchester and Plymouth, but not all the men at the compound that day came from military backgrounds. Some seemed quite awkward, physically, and not used to strenuous physical activity of that nature.

When we finished, Baazov took me aside. "We drill with men in each of the kibbutzim. One day per kibbutz. This is your day. Be here next week." He handed me a single document. "Sign this if you want to come back."

"What is it?"

"A commitment form. For service in Haganah. Sign it and you'll be one of us." I signed it, but all the while I wondered if this really was Haganah, or just something Lapid put together to encourage everyone to stay at the kibbutz instead of leaving for safer quarters in Tel Aviv or Haifa.

✦ ✦ ✦

Over the next month or two, I continued to train with Haganah members at the Kinneret kibbutz once every week. In the meantime, Amos and I worked at the farm, planting small patches of seasonal vegetables in the space around the house and looking after the mules. We rebuilt the coop to give the two chickens space to move around on the ground and learned that one was a hen, the other a rooster. When the hen nested, we made do with other things to eat for a while and let the eggs hatch. Before long, we had half a dozen chickens and more eggs than two men could ever eat.

About six months into the training regimen at the compound, Baazov came by the house again. I knew he wanted to talk in private, so I took him behind the barn on the pretext of feeding the chickens. As I scattered a handful of feed on the ground, he said, "The National Council has decided to build more settlements. Haganah is responsible for security. We need help manning a tower and stockade outpost at Hanita. You interested?"

"Hanita," I said in a contemplative tone. "Isn't that pretty far north?"

"On a hilltop just south of the border."

"With Lebanon."

"Yeah, with Lebanon."

"What exactly is a tower and stockade outpost?"

"Original shape was just what it sounds like. Stockade shaped in a circle with an observation tower in the middle. This one has been added onto since. We have a few settlers living up there, trying to farm."

"How long did it take to build something like that?"

"Constructing the original post didn't take long at all. We hauled it in as a prefab unit. Trucked up there in preassembled pieces, put them up quickly."

"Doesn't sound very sturdy."

"They're strong enough to withstand gunfire, grenades, that sort of thing."

"You have more than one of these?"

"We're putting them up all across Galilee."

"What brought that on?"

"The British are talking about dividing the country between us and the Arabs. Looks like they might do it based on where everyone is already living. Folks in Tel Aviv want to establish details on the ground—so they can say that Jews live in this section or that section—before the division happens."

"To influence the way they draw the lines?"

"Something like that." Baazov had said all he wanted to say on the topic. "Look, you want to do this, or not?"

"Yeah, I want to do it. But I need to talk to Amos first."

"Okay. But don't take too long. We need to get the post fully manned in the next couple of weeks."

Amos and I discussed almost everything that affected our lives, but the offer Baazov made was different. If I accepted it, not only would I move away from the farm and Amos, but into a lifestyle that would likely mark me for the remainder of my days. If I joined Haganah, I was rather certain I would not be returning to the farm—certainly not as a farmer. To make that decision, I needed time to think, so I kept the matter to myself for several days.

✦ ✦ ✦

A few days later, Dalia was at the farm and had dinner with us. Afterward, Amos walked her home. When he returned, I said, "We need to talk."

"I know. I've been meaning to talk to you about it for a while."

I wasn't sure he knew what I meant. "About what?" I asked.

"Dalia."

"Oh."

Amos looked perplexed. "Isn't that what you wanted to talk about?"

I grinned. "No, but what about her?"

Amos glanced away. "We want to get married."

A broad smile spread across my face. "It's about time."

"Yes," Amos nodded. "It is."

"What about her parents?"

"What about them?"

"You said before you didn't think David was comfortable with you coming around."

"He's better with it now."

"Think they'll object?"

"I talked to him tonight."

I was surprised things had gone that far already. "So, this is happening?"

"Yeah, it's happening." The tone of his voice seemed less than exuberant.

"Everything all right?"

"It's just...I'm glad and I want to do it, but it seems more real than I thought it would." He looked over at me. "You know? Like how it felt when we came back here and the place was a mess and the dream of being here ran into the reality of hard work."

363

"I felt that way when we arrived at Gallipoli. It still was what I wanted to do, but it was scary."

"Yes," Amos agreed. "Scary."

I patted him on the back. "It's okay to be afraid. But don't let it stop you. I think you'll find she's worth it."

"She is worth it," he smiled. "I know that. And I love her with all my heart."

Later that evening, after the lamp was out and we were lying in bed, Amos asked, "What did you want to talk about? Before. When I came back from walking Dalia home."

"We can talk about it tomorrow."

"Tell me now. I'm wide awake anyway."

"I talked to Scholem Baazov the other day."

"What did he want?"

"They've offered me a place in Haganah. Full time."

"Oh." Amos tried to sound upbeat, but right away I could tell he didn't care for the idea. "Here? In Kinneret?"

"No."

Amos rolled on his side and looked over at me from his bed. "Where would you go?"

"They want me at Hanita."

"Hmmm," Amos groaned. "That's all the way over by the sea and up near the border."

"Yes."

"That's a long way from here and it's not safe. Not safe at all."

"I know."

"But you want to do it."

I turned in his direction. "I want to do it."

"You still miss the army life?"

"It's something I'm good at. And, yes, I enjoyed the army life."

Amos forced a smile. "Well, then, we'll make the best of it."

"You can manage the farm without me?"

"I'll make it work," he said.

✦ ✦ ✦

A week later, I left the farm, caught a ride with two of Baazov's men in a supply truck, and traveled north to Hanita. I'd never been that close to the border and as I stepped from the cab of the truck the remoteness of the location seemed almost overwhelming. I could not see a single other building in any direction around us.

Meir Weinstein, the Haganah officer in charge of the outpost, was expecting me and took me over to one of the buildings that served as our quarters. A bunk was already assigned to me in the far corner of the room and he led me to it. There was a locker for my gear beside it and I noticed it was larger than most of the others.

"John Patterson and I are old friends," Weinstein said. "I was with you in Gallipoli. You probably don't remember me."

I stared at him a moment, studying the features of his face, trying to account for the years since then and imagining what he might have looked like back then, when I realized he was one of the men who left us, just before the British withdrew. "You left Gallipoli early."

"And Trumpeldor never came looking for me, either," he replied with a tentative smile. "I always thought maybe you had something to do with that."

It seemed a strange thing to say. At the time, I was merely an aide. In any other circumstance I would have been regarded as little more than a servant. To think that I had any sway over anyone's decision struck me as oddly placed analysis, but it didn't seem like the proper time to discuss the matter, or to tell him that I'd suggested we ought to go after them and punish them the way Colonel Patterson did. Instead, I gave him a thin, tight smile and said, "I think Trumpeldor knew we were leaving anyway and there was no point in pursuing the matter of a few men going home early."

"Trumpeldor was a good man." Weinstein grinned. "He also knew Gallipoli was a lost cause."

"Where did you go?" I asked, hoping to move the conversation away from all that.

"We found a fishing boat and took it over to Turkey, then worked our way into Syria and crossed into Palestine from there."

"We?"

"Yeah," he shrugged. "There were a couple of us. We weren't afraid, we'd just finally had enough." A cloud seemed to descend across his face at the memory of it and he glanced down at the floor. "Those boys were dying for nothing."

"Tough trip?"

Weinstein looked up at me. "Not as tough as Gallipoli had been. The British were crazy to try that."

"Yeah," I nodded. "It was...a bit of a longshot." We were silent a moment, each of us gauging our reaction to the other, then I said, "So, you ended up in Haganah."

"Hashomer first," he explained, "then Haganah. Got in it from the beginning."

"I heard of Hashomer as a child. Always wondered if it actually existed."

"Oh," he said with a knowing look. "It existed, all right. And without it, I don't think many of the early settlements would have survived."

We talked awhile longer while I stored my gear in the locker, then we walked outside and made the rounds among the men for introductions. They seemed genuinely glad to see me and I wondered what else Weinstein had told them about me.

Hanita had begun as a tower and stockade outpost but by the time I arrived it had been expanded considerably. A large contingent of Haganah soldiers was stationed there along with the post's own Settlement Police and a smaller number of actual settlers who came to farm the land outside the stockade. Everyone was armed, some with more than one weapon, and it reminded me of images from paperback novels of the American West that I saw once on a shelf in a store in Tel Aviv.

One of the people I met that day was a man from Nahalal named Moshe Dayan. He was second-in-command for Haganah at the post and in charge of training the men. We would become good friends, but when I arrived he was second-in-command and I was the new recruit. He made sure to preserve the distance between us in those first few weeks.

Unlike at Kinneret, the men at Hanita trained every day. However, they almost never went outside the post, and then only in response to attacks on other settlements, not for regular patrol of the region—a practice I was sure they adopted from the British. That was the way they preferred to fight.

All of the men, including the Settlement Police, were far better trained than I'd imagined. And in spite of their defensive posture, their presence reduced the number of Arab raids on surrounding settlements. But I wondered how much more effective we could be if we fought at night, like the Arabs, and went out beyond the perimeter. I raised this issue with Dayan during my first week. His response seemed to reflect the view of all Haganah commanders.

"It's too dangerous."

"No more dangerous than sitting here waiting for the Arabs to attack."

"But here," he argued, "we have the walls to protect us."

"Here," I countered, "we are easy targets and they know right where to find us."

"It's worked well so far."

"Perhaps," I replied, not wanting to prolong the matter. "But one day, they're going to realize that all they have to do is pin us down here with a small force and then they can attack at will across the entire region."

From the look on his face I assumed Dayan had never thought of that, a fact that surprised me greatly. He struck me as a very capable soldier and the notion that he had overlooked the vulnerability of our position left me wondering what else we all might be missing.

The last place Weinstein showed me that day was a tiny closet just off his office. In it was a radio that linked our outpost to Haganah headquarters in Tel Aviv. Seeing it made me feel we were less remote, but Weinstein quickly explained that the radio was almost never used.

"We don't want the British to know we have it."

A frown wrinkled my forehead. "Then how do you communicate?"

"Most of the time we use a light to signal the next station. In code, of course, but it limits the number of people who can know about it. Not like a radio signal that is broadcast to the world."

"How far away is the next station? I didn't see anything around us that looked like a building."

"If you climb up to the top of the tower, the next station in either direction is within our line of sight. All of our posts up here are con-structed on high ground and all have a tower."

"How many are there?"

He avoided a specific answer. "We have a series of them. A line that stretches up and down the border. Rather like the Chinese wall."

"So, you can relay a message from one end to the other?"

He nodded. "Precisely. Down and back in a matter of hours. No trail to follow, as with written communication. No broadcast signal to intercept, as with radio waves. Just the light. And when we are finished transmitting, the signal is gone."

He spoke with satisfaction and confidence in the system, but I was skeptical of how private the signals really were. Anyone who saw them could intercept them, and in a matter of time any code could be broken.

# CHAPTER 32

foz

A FEW MONTHS AFTER I arrived at Hanita, the Peel Commission issued its report. As expected, the commission proposed partitioning Palestine along ethnic lines, dividing the region into separate Arab and Jewish states by assigning each group the geographic territory in which it held a majority. Under that plan, the Jewish state would control Galilee and a narrow strip along the coast that extended south from Haifa, through Tel Aviv, to a point a short distance beyond it toward Gaza.

Almost immediately, the World Zionist Organization announced its acceptance of the plan in principle but asked for further consultation regarding adjustments of the boundary lines. The Arabs, still led by the grand mufti, Haj Amin al-Husseini, with Fawzi al-Qawuqji as his aide, rejected the report without even reading it.

As was their practice, the British appointed a technical commission to review and negotiate revisions to the lines of demarcation between the areas. Officially designated the Palestine Partition Commission, it became more widely known as the Woodhead Commission after its chairman, Sir John Woodhead, a man who'd served previously as an administrator in India. The commission arrived in the spring and worked through the summer taking testimony, gathering evidence, and reviewing the situation on the ground.

Once again, Weizmann and officials at the World Zionist Organization's office in Tel Aviv were prepared for active participation in the commission's work. Written testimony was prepared and witnesses were encouraged to speak. Maps were drawn showing exact locations of every Jewish settlement and presented in a carefully orchestrated manner designed to impress upon commission members the validity of the claims to areas that Weizmann and the others thought should fall under Jewish control.

The Arabs took the opposite approach. Seeing that the British were serious about dividing the country—serious enough to send a commission all the way from London to figure out how to do it—they once again felt betrayed, this time beyond redemption. As a consequence, they abandoned all hope of cooperation, refused to participate in the commission's work, and, instead, increased their attacks on our settlements.

When the attacks proved ineffective in producing the desired result—evacuation of our farming communities—the grand mufti announced a Jihad against us and the British, calling on Arabs everywhere to take up arms against the infidels and cleanse the land of their presence. Attacks against our people increased daily.

With the Arabs in full revolt, the British army did its best to assert its authority, but the general officers remained committed to their traditional practice of safe patrolling. Working from fixed positions, their troops patrolled only during the day and never engaged Arab gangs at night. Having an overwhelming advantage in firepower, the British rather easily controlled the day.

For Fawzi al-Qawuqji, the British choice of strategy was a gift. His Arab gangs ruled the night. Cloaked in darkness, their raids proved far more terrifying than daytime attacks. The nighttime had a way of amplifying everything, creating the illusion of more men, louder explosions, and overwhelming numbers.

At the same time, under Qawuqji's direction the grand mufti purchased arms and ammunition from connections in Eastern Europe, then smuggled them across the border at night from Syria, Lebanon, and Jordan. Once inside Palestine, Qawuqji's men hid them in cartloads of farm goods or in the cargo of delivery trucks and distributed them up and down the Levant. Ready supplies of weapons and ammunition allowed Arab gangs to conduct raid after raid on our villages.

Using a tactic similar to the one I'd warned Weinstein about, the gangs struck quickly, hit hard, then disappeared before any of Haganah's men—who were always behind their stockades—could respond. In only a matter of minutes, these Arab marauders destroyed equipment, set buildings afire, and killed our people with devastating effect, but still they did not break the will of the Jewish people or create the mass panic and hysteria they'd hoped for.

When direct attacks on Jews failed to produce spectacular results, Qawuqji prepared hit lists of British soldiers and key individuals—particularly officers and British dignitaries. He recruited teams of willing young men, many of them the same people whom he trained for the Nebi Musa riots, and turned them loose to execute the people on the lists. After the assassins had been sent out to complete their mission, the grand mufti leaked the hit lists to Jerusalem newspapers, hoping that the combined effort of unrestrained murder and well-armed attacks would succeed in destabilizing the country.

A few months into this aggressive strategy, Arabs began attacking British patrols and the more remote British garrisons. British officers and soldiers traveling through secluded areas became frequent targets for quick strikes. Very quickly, a number of officers and infantrymen were gunned down in what could only be described as massacres.

Far up in Hanita, our region encountered some of these issues, but not nearly as many as occurred in areas closer to Jerusalem, Haifa, and Tel Aviv. Weinstein and our other commanders hoped the escalation in violence would bring a decisive response from the British with the introduction of large forces capable of suppressing the Arab gangs once and for all, but that did not happen.

In typical British style, they did nothing to combat the Arabs but rounded up Jews from every village where an attack took place who were suspected of fighting back and seized their firearms. Instead of providing further training for those brave men and women, they subjected them to public reprimand and the threat of incarceration. Everyone was frustrated.

✦ ✦ ✦

In the midst of all that, I received a letter from Amos telling me that he and Dalia planned to marry early in the summer. I asked Meir Weinstein for permission to attend and received two days leave to return to the farm.

As the wedding day approached, I caught a ride on a supply truck making the return trip south. It took me as far as Tur'an, then I switched to one going to the kibbutz at Kinneret. The driver let me out on the road just across from our house and I walked the short distance to it.

Even before I reached it, I could see the farm was neat, orderly, and well maintained. Amos had worked hard to get the house and buildings in order and keep them that way. I knew his desire to please and care for Dalia was part of the reason, but I also knew Amos was a hard worker, just like Papa.

When I was still crossing the last field, Amos came out to greet me and as I reached the trees that surrounded the yard, I picked up my pace and hurried toward him. We met near the bench that sat near the house. He embraced me with two arms around my shoulders and I kissed him on the cheek.

"I have missed you," he whispered.

"I've missed you, too," I replied, though with all there was to do at Hanita I really hadn't been homesick. Not like when we were in Egypt, anyway.

That evening, we ate dinner at a table by the window near the kitchen—on the opposite side of the room from where Mama always kept one. I pointed that out to Amos, then worried he might think I was being critical. "It works great here," I added quickly. "With the light coming right through the window. I wonder why she didn't put it here."

"Cataracts," Amos replied in a matter-of-fact tone.

I felt my forehead wrinkle in a frown. "What do you mean?"

"She had cataracts. Light from the window bothered her."

My mouth fell open in a startled look. "I didn't know that."

He gestured over his shoulder with his hand. "That's why she set the lamp by the stove when we ate."

"She always said it was safer there."

"I know." Amos smiled. "But the real problem was she had cataracts, and the glare from the lamp—the window...anywhere really—was a problem for her."

"I never knew."

"She didn't want anyone to know."

"How did you find out?"

"I said something about moving the table over here to this side of the room so we could see better, and Papa told me we couldn't. When

I asked why, he told me the problem."

I shook my head in disbelief. "Wonder what else we didn't know."

"No way of finding out now," he replied with a shrug.

We ate in silence a moment before I said, "Any idea of what happened to him?"

Amos glanced over at me. "To Papa?"

"Yes."

"Not really. But I did find one thing."

"What?"

Amos reached into his pocket and took out a watch. He laid it on the table between us and looked over at me. "That's Papa's."

"It was lying between here and the barn," Amos explained. "Half buried in the dirt. I found it not long after you left for Hanita."

"So, he didn't die in the house."

"Probably not. Although I suppose they could have killed him in here, found the watch, left with it, and dropped it before they got away."

"Or they took him with them," I offered.

"Maybe."

"Did you ever wonder why they didn't burn the place?"

"Many times."

"And they never came back to it, either."

"Apparently not," Amos conceded. "Though *someone* was here. Almost all the furniture was gone when we returned."

"And David mentioned there were a number of chickens here when he arrived," I noted. "I'm not sure ours would have survived that long and besides, they were in the coop behind the barn. They would have starved to death before they managed to get out of there."

"Good point."

"Ever ask anyone at the kibbutz about it?"

Amos shook his head. "Not sure I wanted to know all that before."

My eyes widened. "And now?"

"I would like to know what happened to Papa. I mean, if he's out there somewhere, I would want to go get him. I just never think about it when I'm around anyone who might know, and when I think about it no one's around to ask."

"We know he wasn't here the night of the attack. We came back and found Mama's body."

"Right."

"So, if they didn't bury her they probably didn't kill Papa and bury him, either."

"Yeah," Amos nodded.

"So, either they killed him somewhere like over by the barn where you found the watch and something happened to the body, or they took him with them."

"Or someone else removed the body after we were gone."

"But that would mean he died after we were gone. There wasn't a body out there when we came back to bury Mama."

"Well," Amos sighed. "I don't know what happened to him. Maybe we should try to find out."

Silence filled the room again as we continued to eat. When he finished and took the plates to the sink I asked, "Is Dalia going to be comfortable living here?"

David's mouth stretched wide with his happy grin. "Yeah, most of what you see was her idea. Moving the table. Arrangement of the furniture. She has it set up like she wants it, so I think she'll be fine living here."

"Speaking of which, we should talk about the farm—what with you getting married tomorrow and all."

Amos looked perplexed. "Talk about the farm? What about it?"

"You've done so much work to the place. And Dalia needs a home she can call her own. I think it's only right for you two to have it. Outright."

"No." Amos shook his head from side to side. "This farm is your legacy as much as mine. It is all we have left of Mama and Papa. I would not deprive you of it."

"Maybe we should ask Dalia?"

"We've already talked about it," Amos said. "She feels the same way I do. You and I will own the farm."

"Well, I think we'll revisit that issue later."

The following day, Amos and Dalia were married at the Riskin home by a rabbi from Haifa—a cousin of Tzipi, I think. Everyone from the kibbutz attended, and Dalia's friend came up from Tel Aviv. Afterward, we drove them to the farm in a car that belonged to the kibbutz.

Amos and Dalia spent their wedding night at the house. I stayed at the kibbutz. After my conversation with Amos the night before, I had intended to speak to Benjamin Lapid, the settlement chairman, about what he might know of Papa, but he was away on a trip to Jerusalem. I didn't know who else to speak to about the matter, so I kept my questions to myself.

The next morning, I stopped by the farm for breakfast and to say good-bye, then caught a ride on a truck from the kibbutz that was headed to Nazareth. The driver let me off in Tur'an and in a little while a truck came by on its way to Hanita.

# CHAPTER 33

foz

NOT LONG AFTER I returned to Hanita from the wedding, an Arab assassination team murdered Yelland Andrews, the British district commissioner for Galilee, on his way to church in Nazareth. British troops were stationed nearby and responded quickly, only to be ambushed by a second Arab gang that was waiting in hiding. In addition to Andrews and several of his aides, a dozen soldiers were killed before yet another squad of British troops arrived to chase the attackers away.

With a ranking British official now the victim of an Arab attack, the High Commissioner's office sensed the need for a change in strategy. Army commanders sensed it, too, and General Haining, now in command of British troops in Palestine, convened a meeting in Haifa to address the matter. The meeting, which was attended by generals from the army's divisions, along with their staff assistants, was intended to find ways of tweaking existing strategy. Orde Charles Wingate, at that time a staff officer for the intelligence department in Haifa, had other ideas and was looking for a way to express them. The meeting, he was sure, would give him an opportunity to do just that—if he could find a way to attend.

Wingate was reared in an austere British family by parents who were devout in their Christian beliefs. His mother, leery of the socializing influences of public school, educated him at home through the elementary grades but sent him to a boarding school when he was a young teenager—an opportunity made possible with the help of a wealthy and influential cousin.

Upon graduation, Wingate entered the army, where he was known for both his unorthodox tactics as well as his unkempt appearance. More often than not he appeared in formation looking scruffy and unshaven. Even in full dress uniform, his clothes were usually dirty and unpressed. All of which gave him, as one observer put it, a most un-British appearance. He was, however, a highly effective leader. He'd come to Palestine hoping to earn the right to attend Staff College, which he saw as a necessary stepping-stone to reaching the military's upper echelon, but very quickly after arriving, he became immersed in Jewish culture. Before long, he was thoroughly committed to the Jewish cause in Palestine.

Two days before Haining's meeting was set to begin, Colonel Nevil Oliver, Wingate's immediate superior, was called away to Tel Aviv. In his absence, Wingate, as the next most capable man in the office, was assigned to attend the meeting as aide to General Blacker, commander of all British forces operating in northern Palestine.

In addition to General Blacker, the meeting was attended by Generals Fraser, Redman, Stratton, and Simpson. Together they represented the five British army divisions that occupied Palestine. Early in the morning of their first day, they gathered around a conference table at the office in Haifa with General Blacker chairing the meeting.

For most of that morning, Wingate sat quietly to one side, listening as others in the room discussed current British strategy and offered suggestions about how it might be made more effective. Very quickly, however, he realized the meeting was designed to do only one thing—provide political cover for Andrews' death—and had never been viewed as a serious attempt to develop a strategy that would prevent a similar incident from occurring again. It was a colossal waste of time, and he lay in wait for a moment when he could speak up. Shortly before lunch, Wingate could contain himself no longer and, moment or not, decided to act.

"If I may, gentlemen," he said, speaking out of turn. "Perhaps we should consider not merely tweaking our strategy but *changing* our strategy."

General Blacker's face turned red with embarrassment at a member of his staff committing such an obvious breach of etiquette. "Perhaps we should discuss your ideas at another time." His eyes bore in on Wingate. "I can handle this meeting myself."

"Throw it out," Wingate said, ignoring Blacker. "The strategy isn't working and I doubt it ever has."

General Fraser, who was seated on the opposite side of the table, attempted to take up for Blacker. "Are you out of your mind?" he retorted. "You'll be lucky if we don't have you removed from this room and detained for such an outburst."

"You can't seriously defend your current strategy," Wingate continued. "Not men of your caliber who have fought in wars far more serious and threatening than this current... engagement."

"And what would you propose we use as a substitute?" Blacker asked in a belittling tone.

"Night raids," Wingate answered with a smile. "Substitute your strategy for a strategy of night raids."

General Redman, seated to Fraser's left, shook his head and scoffed. "We've never done that sort of thing in all my years of service to the Royal Army. It would be utterly preposterous to do so now."

"You've never confronted this kind of enemy," Wingate countered. "The enemies you fought before formed battle lines and the locations they sought to control were clearly defined. Attack here to reach there. Set your main force here. Attack over the hill there. We've fought so many wars in Europe you could plan the next one now and know already the outcome before it's even fought. But this war in Palestine isn't like that because this enemy isn't like the enemies you've seen before." He scanned the room. "You are all smart enough to know it. You *do* know it. You just don't know what to do about it."

"And what would you propose of these night-raiding parties?" Fraser asked.

"Not *parties*," Wingate explained. "That would imply something akin to an operation of the past—a boarding party, a breaching party—which have been used so often they have their own set rules and procedures. What we need are Special Night Squads. Ad hoc. Unplanned. Roving bands of British soldiers patrolling in the night. No formation. No predetermined routes. Following only what they see and hear."

"But what would they *do*?" Fraser demanded.

"Go after the Arabs," Wingate replied, as if the answer were obvious. "Instead of waiting for them to come to us, we would go to them."

General Redman shook his head. "Young man," he said imperiously, "no one is sure how to find them."

"Because no one has been out at night looking for them," Wingate responded. "If we sent our men out there, allowed them to observe Arab conduct carefully, we would figure out where they are staying. Then we could attack them at their location, rather than waiting for them to come to ours."

"And if you should attack the wrong people?" Blacker asked. "What then?"

"The wrong people?" Wingate asked with a frown.

"Yes," Blacker said. "What if you should attack innocents?"

"He's asking," Fraser added, "what if you attack someone who hasn't done us any harm?"

"Well," Wingate replied with a straight face, "if they shoot back when they see us, we won't reach that question, will we?"

An awkward silence fell over the room and Wingate let it hang in the air a moment, then he continued, "We've been cowering behind the walls of our forts and strongholds far too long. I don't think the Arabs are as fearless as others suppose. I don't think they will be difficult to handle at all. To control them, all we have to do is take the fight to them."

"What makes you think they aren't so much of a threat?" Blacker said in one last attempt to derail the discussion.

"Look at what they do," Wingate said with a hint of impatience. "They never attack by day, always by night. Never occupy and clear a village, merely hit it, inflict damage, and move on before anyone can mount an organized response." He looked around the room once more, making eye contact with each of them. "The Arabs fight that way because they know that if we ever came after them—really came after them, with the intention of engaging them with all our might—we would crush them in short order. So they don't give us that opportunity."

"Still, back to the earlier question, how can you be so sure any of this will work?" Fraser asked. He spoke with a look of displeasure, but the tone of his voice indicated he was intrigued.

"First rule of war," Wingate answered. "Design a strategy that permits you to engage the enemy with your strengths while forcing him to defend with only his weaknesses. We've been allowing them to put us in a totally defensive posture. It's time we do the same to them."

Reluctantly, the generals agreed to let Wingate give his idea a try and authorized him to test his theories in Galilee. Privately, however, many were offended, as much by his proposal as by his uncouth appearance and manner. Almost all of them were certain he would be dead before the end of his first week.

✦ ✦ ✦

Not long after the meeting in Haifa, watchmen in the tower at Hanita sounded the alarm. Weinstein rushed to the top and peered out over the flat plain that lay beyond the foot of our hill. In the distance, a vehicle came toward us, kicking up a cloud of dust behind it.

After a moment, Weinstein borrowed a pair of binoculars from Nahum Ronen, who stood nearby, and focused them on the approaching visitor. He watched for a moment, then said quietly, "I can't believe this."

Coming toward us at a rapid pace was a Studebaker convertible automobile. The top was down, leaving the driver clearly visible. His shirt, standard-issue British khaki, unbuttoned to the waist, flapped in the breeze but even so, the British insignia on the shoulders was plainly visible. "I think he's an officer," Weinstein observed, returning the binoculars to Ronen.

Ronen checked through the binoculars for himself and smiled over at Weinstein. "Yes, sir. He's an officer. Rather unconventional in deportment, but an officer nonetheless."

Weinstein nodded in agreement. "But who is he?"

"I don't know."

Edelman, standing opposite Weinstein, spoke up. "Should we stop him, sir?"

"With what?"

"One of these," Edelman said, slapping the fore-end of his rifle stock.

"Stand down," Weinstein ordered. "He's only one man. We'll find out who he is soon enough. Besides, we don't even know if he's armed."

"Yes, sir," Ronen offered, still following the car through the binoculars. "He's armed."

Weinstein reached for the binoculars. "Let me see those again."

"A machine gun on the front seat beside him," Ronen said as Weinstein focused the glasses. "Bandolier of ammunition on the back seat with a handgun, helmet, backpack, and...several dozen grenades."

Weinstein glanced through the binoculars, then handed them back to Ronen. "Prepare a squad to meet him in front of the stockade," he ordered as he turned toward the ladder. "Keep the gate closed until they establish his identity."

Mosha Dayan grabbed a dozen of us from the barracks and we followed him across the courtyard. As we approached the gate, a guard opened it just wide enough to let us past and we walked out to meet the arriving car.

By that time, the car was less than a hundred meters away and we rushed to form two ranks, six of us on each side. Dayan stood between us and raised his hand high in the air, indicating the place where the car should stop. I wasn't sure the driver would understand and was worried he might run right over Dayan, or us, but moments later the car slid to a stop with the front bumper about a meter from Dayan's legs. Moments later, the cloud of dust that had been trailing behind it swept over us and we held our breath as it passed.

When the dust settled, the driver—a short, muscular man—grinned up at us. "Good afternoon, gentlemen. Do you by chance have a commanding officer?"

"Out of the car," Dayan ordered and the driver promptly complied.

Two of the men searched him but found nothing, then Dayan checked his identity card and that's when we learned our visitor's name was Orde Wingate. None of us knew him but we were amused by the sound of his first name. Orde. We repeated it often among ourselves, smiling and grinning at the sound of it each time we said it.

Dayan detailed four of us to escort Wingate inside the compound to Weinstein's office. The car remained outside the gate, but the men were pushing it aside as we led Wingate away. I assumed it would be thoroughly searched and inventoried.

Weinstein was seated at his desk when we arrived. Pavel Fichman and I remained in the room with them, just in case.

"Orde Wingate," the visitor announced. "Captain Orde Wingate, to be exact, but that is neither here nor there." He extended his hand in a greeting, but Weinstein ignored him. "Out of uniform today?" Weinstein asked in an uncharacteristically condescending tone.

"Hot drive out from Haifa." Wingate buttoned his shirt and tucked it inside the waist of his trousers. "Needed some air to keep cool."

"Do you have some means of identification?" Weinstein asked.

"Indeed I do. But your men took my papers."

Weinstein glanced in my direction with an expectant look, and I stepped forward with the documents Dayan had taken from him at the gate. "I am staff intelligence officer to Fifth Division's headquarters in Haifa," Wingate offered. "Those letters are from your friends in Tel Aviv." He gestured to the documents in Weinstein's hand. "They sent them to you on my behalf as a manner of introduction."

Weinstein scanned the documents quickly. In addition to his military identification card, there was a letter from Weizmann and another from Yigal Yadin, a Haganah officer in Tel Aviv.

The presence of a British officer in the compound was most

unusual, and Weinstein was noticeably tense, as were we all. To the British—at least officially—Haganah was an illegal organization. Not only that, possession of firearms by Jews was strictly forbidden. Most of the men living at Hanita were either Haganah members or Settlement Police. All of them were armed and the outpost had an armory with more weapons and ammunition, some of it purloined from the British army.

"What is the nature of your business?" Weinstein asked in a formal tone.

"I have come here today because you have a problem," Wingate stated confidently. "*We* have a problem," he quickly added. "Multiple problems, actually."

"Oh? And what might those problems be?"

"Recent attacks on Jewish settlements have created a climate of fear among the settlers. The assassination of Mr. Andrews and the appearance of certain hit lists have upset British leadership in Tel Aviv and London. Arabs are smuggling guns across the border, many of them passing right under your nose. That's the sort of problems you and *we* face."

"And how is that of your concern?"

"The British government would like to put an end to it. You and your men have been chosen as one of the units who can help do that."

"Ridiculous," Weinstein scoffed. "We don't have the men for that kind of operation. Neither do the British. Everyone in Tel Aviv and London knows that."

"Precisely what I told them," Wingate replied boldly. "But the beauty of the situation is, we don't need the number of men traditionalists would employ. What we need is a change of strategy and the tactics to execute it."

"What sort of strategy are you suggesting?"

"Raids at night."

Weinstein had a skeptical smile. "At night."

"Yes, sir. Special Night Squads. Men willing to go beyond the perimeter of your fine stockade and take the fight to the enemy."

"And you want my men to do that."

"Not all of them. That would be far too many. They would make an awful mess of it. No. What I'm looking for are a few select volunteers brave enough to ignore their fear of the Arabs and do what is necessary to put an end to these barbarous acts of violence and murder."

They talked awhile longer but it was already obvious Weinstein was more than a little interested in the Special Night Squads strategy. I was, too, and had said as much to Weinstein not long after I came to Hanita. Equally as intriguing was the manner in which they deftly ignored the fact that Wingate was a British officer consulting with the commander of an illegal organization, the existence of which neither officially acknowledged.

Our initial suspicions about Wingate lingered but he persisted in his effort to organize a night squad and met with fifteen or twenty of us to outline his strategy. Not everyone was as interested as Weinstein and I.

"Far too dangerous," someone noted.

"That's because you've been thoroughly indoctrinated in the British way of fighting," Wingate argued.

"Rather an odd statement," someone else commented, "coming as it does from a British officer."

Wingate chuckled. "My superiors think so as well. But the fact remains, one cannot maintain a totally defensive posture and defeat the Arabs at the same time."

Another spoke up. "We can't defeat them if we're dead, either."

"If you sit and wait," Wingate explained, "they will continue to

ABOUT AN HOUR after sundown we gathered in the ready room with rifles and packs prepared for a standard patrol. Dayan was with us, but it was obvious from the moment we arrived that Wingate was in charge.

After a brief orientation about how we should avoid traveling in clusters and formations, and an exhortation about keeping quiet while we walked, Wingate searched through our packs, removing unnecessary gear like maps, compasses, and things of that nature.

He tossed our gear on the table in the center of the room. "All of this extra weight will only slow you down. I have a map. You won't need one. And you won't need a torch, either. Your eyes will adjust to the light and you'll be able to see perfectly well. The thing you should be concerned about is your legs. They will carry you into battle and they will bring you home safely. You'll be using them all night. All of this weight you want to carry will only tire them more quickly."

When he was satisfied we'd jettisoned enough extra items, he led us from the building and across the compound to the gate. Moments later we were outside.

For most of us, roaming beyond the stockade at any time, day or night, was like being set free from a cage. Everything changed. With

Wingate it was even more dramatic. Inside the stockade he was composed, relaxed, and tolerant. Once beyond the gate, he became ruthlessly driven, demanding, focused, and determined.

From the compound at Hanita, we marched west at a quick pace with Wingate in the lead. He seemed to know the terrain as if he'd already been there and paused only once or twice to check the map. Steadfastly avoiding trails, paths, and roads—which he described as nothing but traps for an ambush—we cut across the terrain in a straight line.

We walked for an hour without saying a word, the silence broken only by the sound of him scolding us when we scuffed our boots against the ground. Two hours into the trek, with hardly any break at all, his reprimands became even more severe and took the form of a shove in the back for lagging behind, or a forearm to the chest for not paying attention. And once, when he heard Ronen talking, a slap on the cheek.

After three hours at a steady pace we reached a low hill outside Kafr Bir'im, a village along the Lebanon border well east of Hanita. We paused there long enough to catch our breath, then turned north and traveled at an even quicker pace for another half hour. By then we were well beyond the border into Lebanon and I could tell by the look in the eyes of those who were with me that they were concerned.

Just then, and seemingly for no reason at all, Wingate brought us to a stop and in a whisper ordered us to kneel. As we knelt there, leaning against our rifles, gasping for breath, Wingate pointed into the distance. "See that?" he asked in a whisper.

"Yeah," I replied as my eyes focused on a line of oddly shaped objects about half a mile away.

"That's a line of pack mules," he said with a smile. "They are our targets."

I squinted to see them more clearly against the faint light of the skyline.

"They are Arab smugglers," Wingate continued. "Bringing guns and ammunition across the border. Weapons that will kill your settlers if we don't stop them." He shrugged to one side and slid the strap of his pack from his shoulder. With the bag propped against his knee, he reached inside, took out a hand grenade, and passed it to me. "Here, you know how to use one of these?"

"Yes," I nodded. "Pull the pin and throw it."

"Right." He gave one to the others as well. "We're going to work our way forward about a hundred meters. The trail comes through a spot there that lies between two hills. The caravan will pass right in front of us. When they come through, I'll hit the lead animal." He pointed to me. "You will position yourself farther up the trail to my left. When I throw my grenade, you throw yours." He looked at the others. "The rest of you, clean up whatever's left."

"You mean kill them?" Nahum Ronen asked.

"Yes, of course I mean kill them," Wingate retorted. He shoved Ronen in the chest with both hands. "Did you think I meant to give them a bath?" He paused to take a deep breath, then glanced over at me. "Pay attention," he ordered calmly. "Follow my lead. Go when I go."

As planned, we crept forward a hundred meters and crouched among the rocks, then Wingate directed us to our positions and I moved about fifty meters to the left. In a few minutes, the caravan appeared. Actually, not so much appeared as sounded—we heard them before we saw them. Laughing and talking, they made no attempt at keeping quiet and seemed confident no one was going to intercept them.

Slowly, they wandered forward. Four men on horses, each leading a string of three mules. All of them traveling in a line, talking over their shoulders to each other as they made their way toward us. I'd never experienced combat like that before—the few times I was shot at in Gallipoli the gunfire was indiscriminate and I never saw the shooter. That night, however, as the caravan drew closer, I could see the turbans on their heads and the smiles that turned up their cheeks. And I could hear their voices. Arabic. I could make out every second or third word. They were talking about home. Their wives. Their families. My heart pounded against my chest as I thought of what I was about to do.

Moments later, the caravan was opposite our position. I glanced to the right and saw Wingate already was moving forward. A pang of guilt shot through me for not paying closer attention, for watching the caravan and not watching for him. Moving quickly, I came from my hiding spot and started forward, crouched low, hoping no one noticed me, hoping I would be close enough for my throw to reach the target.

Seconds later, Wingate's grenade exploded to my right and I heard screams and shouts, and animal parts flew into the air. Startled by the noise and bright flash, the mules that still could walk started moving backward, heads high, eyes wild with fear, muscles straining furiously against the ropes.

The lead handler was gone, he and his horse killed by the blast that took out the first mule. The second mule was down and kicking wildly. The remaining handlers fought to keep their mounts beneath them. In the struggle I heard Wingate squeeze off three rounds from a sidearm. Two mules hit the ground, as did the second handler.

All the while I hurried down the hill toward the chaos. Without breaking stride, I pulled the pin from the grenade in my hand, took two more steps, and hurled it toward the last mule in line, which now was less than thirty meters away. As the grenade sailed through the air I dove to the ground and spread my body flat, covering my head with my hands, waiting to hear the explosion.

After what seemed like far too long to be effective, I looked up to see what went wrong. Just then, the grenade detonated beneath the last mule, blasting its carcass into the air and ripping it into a million pieces.

The remaining mules, now startled from the blast behind them, bolted to the opposite side of the trail in a determined stampede for safety, dragging dead mules behind them. Rather than being carried away with them, the two remaining handlers let go of their ropes and held on tightly to the reigns as their horses joined the dash up the hill. That's when Dayan and the others opened up with their rifles and when the shooting stopped, all of the Arabs were dead.

For the next hour, we scampered over the hills for the stray mules. Wingate insisted we find them in order to keep the munitions and arms from Arab hands. An hour before sunrise we'd accounted for all but two and started back toward the post at Hanita. Three hours after sunrise, we arrived at the stockade leading six mules laden with rifles, explosives, and ammunition. Guards opened the gate to allow us inside the compound, and we were greeted like returning heroes.

"This is what I was talking about," Wingate said. "The proper way to defeat the Arabs is to take the fight to them. They are not as brave as others think. They use hit-and-run tactics because they are too weak to stand and fight. A well-planned assault against them in their own positions will overwhelm them every time."

✦ ✦ ✦

Over the next several months, we continued the night raids with increasing efficiency. During that time, attacks by Arab gangs against settlements in our area of northern Galilee declined. On a visit to Haifa, Wingate pointed this out to General Blacker and his staff as proof that his strategy was working.

Having no better strategy for addressing the situation, and being unwilling to argue against success, Blacker agreed to expand the raids using squads composed of both Haganah and British soldiers. Wingate was assigned the task of training the new additions to our unit. Not recognizing us as legal in the first place, no one from the British army bothered to consult with Haganah in advance.

A few days later, Wingate arrived at Hanita with fifteen British soldiers. They were met at the gate by three squads of armed Haganah troops who surrounded them and seized their weapons before escorting them into the compound. Weinstein came out to investigate the trouble and after an extended conversation with Wingate agreed to let them remain, but everyone at the post was nervous.

Wingate, who now understood the well-founded basis for our reaction, did his best to put us at ease. "No one is going to be arrested. The British know you are here. You know they know it. Everyone knows you are well armed and equally well supplied and no one has come to take your arms by force. So relax. Our goal is to combat Arab gangs. That is our common goal. That is all we are doing here. Working together at General Blacker's insistence to expand the Special Night Squads to British units."

New intelligence, which Wingate brought with him, indicated the gang that murdered Yelland Andrews in Nazareth was now staying in Daburiyya, a village east of Nazareth between Nazareth and the Sea of Galilee. He gathered us in the ready room and went over the news. "We have established Special Night Squads at other Haganah locations, but you are the closest. We must attack as soon as possible, before they move to a new location."

Nahum Ronen seemed put off by the idea. "Daburiyya is a long way from here," he said. "It'll be tough to travel that far."

"It's too far for you?" Wingate chided. "Are you worried you'll get tired?" His voice had a mocking tone.

Ronen refused to back down. "It's a long way. Someone will see us before we get there."

Everyone in the room saw the merit of Ronen's comment, but Wingate had a perturbed frown. He jabbed Ronen in the chest with his index finger. "This is the kind of thinking you must purge from your mind. If you want to take the fight to the enemy, you have to go where he is." He looked around the room. "You men are *fighting* men. A remnant of the Maccabees. You can easily cover that distance on foot and still arrive before dawn." He continued talking, developing the comment into a speech that reminded me of how Colonel Patterson used to encourage us, telling us we were part of a long line of great warriors with a rich heritage. Now, it seemed, Wingate was showing us what that meant for the challenges of a new era.

When he finished his remarks, Wingate unfolded a map and spread it on the tabletop. For the next hour we studied it, planning our attack. Finally, after we'd noted the terrain and all its features, he said, "We'll encircle the village using the brow of the hills on either side to shield us from view." He traced the contour lines of the map with his finger. "Position ourselves in groups of two or three here, here, and here." He tapped the map to indicate the roads leading from town. "And the same over here." He moved his finger to the opposite side of the town. "That will cut off the exits. Then we'll send in a small group to fire a few shots to rouse the Arabs." He glanced around the room. "When they come out to see what's going on, the rest of us will ambush them." Wingate's smile was triumphant.

As plans go, it wasn't much different from the plan of attack we used on the smugglers' caravan during our first night with him, but it seemed like a good one to us. No one questioned whether it would work or whether there might be undue danger to us from having men positioned on either side of the village where they would be shooting in the general direction of each other.

Instead, for the remainder of the day we cleaned our weapons, loaded our packs with ammunition, and tried to rest. It was difficult, though. No one wanted to nap. Everyone was ready to leave.

Sometime after lunch, Wingate began sending us from the compound one and two at a time, a method he hoped would avoid arousing the suspicions of any Arabs who might have been watching.

About an hour after the last group slipped past the stockade gate—and perhaps in a tacit acknowledgment that Ronen's concerns were well-founded—Pavel Fichman left the post with one of the supply trucks. He drove west on a road that led toward the coast, then turned south as if going down to Haifa, following the supply truck's usual route.

At al-Bassa, he doubled back to the east and before long arrived at a rendezvous point near al-Samniyya, which was southwest of the post. All of us were waiting for him and climbed into the empty truck as it rolled to a stop.

From al-Samniyya, we traveled east to the outskirts of Daburiyya. It was well after dark when we arrived behind the low hill that lay to the west of town, but we were rested and ready after having ridden instead of walked. Fichman parked the truck in a secluded ravine and we climbed out.

As planned, we divided into three groups. One led by Dayan, the other by Wingate, with a third much smaller force that took directions from Fichman. I was in the group with Dayan.

We worked our way northward from the ravine where we left the truck, following the low hill that rose to our right. At key places along the way, Dayan stationed small groups, usually only two or three men, with directions to make their way to the top and wait there. Then we continued moving north until only three of us remained at the upper end of town with our men strung out behind along the break of the hill.

At the same time, Wingate's group worked its way to the western side of town, across from us, then turned north, likewise leaving two or three men at strategic locations along the way until the final squad reached the northernmost point on that side. They were positioned not far from where Dayan and I were situated.

We held our places a moment, making sure everyone was ready, then Wingate flashed his light, and Fichman's group advanced toward town. A few minutes later, gunfire erupted and before long, Arabs emerged from the buildings. Instead of fleeing in terror, however, the Arabs were riled by the intrusion into fighting, and a full-scale gunfight ensued. Gangs of Arabs, armed and ready, moved from street to street, taking the fight to Fichman and his men, pressing them toward the southern end of town. At the same time, from our position to the north, we could see a group of men advancing on Fichman's flank in an attempt to cut him off from leaving and trap him.

"Come on," Dayan called. "Fichman's in trouble. We have to make some noise." He started down the hill toward town, firing his rifle at anything that moved. I covered to his right and squeezed off rounds every two paces.

Suddenly, to our right, farther down the ridge in Fichman's direction, one of the British squads opened up with a large-caliber machine gun. The sound of it echoed through the night and instantly the town came alive with screaming men, women, and children as they dashed for cover. The Arab gunmen ran, too, only instead of toward us they sprinted to the east, straight toward Wingate's men.

In the confusion, the machine gunner followed them, his rounds kicking up puffs of white dust in an easily traceable track that continued past the last row of houses and up the hill on the far side where Wingate's men were positioned.

Wingate, to his credit, saw the trouble coming from the moment the machine gun fired its first round and started down the ridge to warn the men who were with him. Ahead of him, three rounds struck men from his squad and as he continued, he himself received wounds to his legs from shrapnel that glanced off the rocks that covered the hillside. Still, he continued down the ridge, moving men out of the way, separating them from the fleeing Arabs, and shouting at the gunner to cease fire.

Seeing that Wingate was now in trouble from our attempts to rescue Fichman, Dayan abandoned his advance on the town and ran at full speed along the hill that lay on our side of town, trying to reach the machine gunner before any more damage occurred. By the time he and Wingate had the situation under control a dozen Arabs were dead, but Wingate and three of his men were injured. Two of them mortally.

THE WOUNDS to Wingate's legs kept him in bed a few days but by the following week he was up and moving around, insistent that we return to the night raids. A source had informed him that the Arabs who escaped from the attack on Daburiyya had regrouped and were staying in Afula, a small village to the south. He was keen to go after them and only Weinstein's refusal to permit it kept him on his cot.

After a few more days on his cot, Wingate could wait no longer. "We have to act now," he argued. "Before they move to a new location. Intelligence is only good for a short time." He knew the precise location of each house where the gunmen were staying and was worried they might move to new ones, even within the same town.

Reluctantly, Weinstein relented and the following afternoon we departed for Afula. Once again using the supply truck to transport us, we arrived outside the village in the middle of the night. Pavel Fichman parked behind a hill on the east side and we waited there until dawn. Most of us used the time to nap.

As dawn approached, we roused ourselves from sleep and assembled behind the truck to prepare for the attack. Wingate reviewed our strategy—advance from this side of town, give the Arabs only one way to flee. "Let them escape if they can," he instructed. "But do your best to get them all." Because we were attacking only from one side of the settlement, and given the unusually cautious tone of his voice, I assumed he'd learned a lesson from the confusion we'd experienced at Daburiyya, though he never mentioned it by name.

Wingate accompanied us to the top of the hill, but rather than lead us into battle he turned us over to Dayan and withdrew to a place where he could sit and watch. I liked Wingate but was glad to be with Dayan again. He was an excellent battlefield commander.

As the sun rose over the horizon behind us, the glare obscuring us from view, we raced down the hill toward the village, holding our fire as long as possible. We reached the streets without sight of a single person but as we passed the first house, a door opened and a man appeared. His eyes were heavy with sleep and the expression on his face was downcast—until he saw us. Then the shooting started.

Operating in full daylight, we encountered much less confusion and were able to easily distinguish between mere civilians and those who meant us harm. All but three of the gunmen were precisely where Wingate said they would be and even as I was exchanging gunfire with them I wondered how he knew they'd be there. By the time the fighting was over, we'd killed six Arab gunmen, all of them later identified by village elders as men who'd participated in the raid that led to Andrews' murder. I supposed the elders were Wingate's source for the information—most Arabs preferred us gone but were not given to expressing that preference with violence—but when Wingate sent word for them to come and see the bodies, the men from the village did not seem to know him, nor he them.

Looking back now, with the perspective of time, that raid was an important moment for us. It proved to us that we could do the job. We could plan an operation, carry it out to completion, and return to post under our own direction. Without the need of a British soldier or

402

trained officer or anyone else to tell us what to do when the fighting started. That morning raid, a first for all of us, was a major turning point and one that melded us together as a true fighting force. Many of the men who went on to become some of the best IDF generals ever to serve our nation were there that morning, at my side in Afula.

+ + +

In spite of our success in Galilee, few units in and around Jerusalem adopted our strategy, an error made apparent not long after our attack on Afula when a British mechanized unit became the victim of Arab snipers. Traveling between Tel Aviv and Jerusalem—on an open road, in broad daylight—they came under fire from gunmen hiding in the rocks high above. Two well-placed rounds struck the captain who commanded the patrol squarely in the chest. Two more hit his driver. Both men were killed instantly.

The following day, a similar attack occurred on workmen who'd been tending the Iraq Petroleum Company pipeline, a major conduit for oil that traversed the region. It supplied oil to the country's sole refinery in Haifa and was vital to the survival of all in Palestine.

As a result of those two incidents, General Haining in Jerusalem demanded an inquiry into the reasons why the Arab gangs were not under better control. In response, General Blacker, Wingate's commanding officer, announced a review of the Special Night Squads' strategy and summoned him to Haifa for a meeting. Generals Redman, Stratton, and Simpson—many of the very same men who attended the prior gathering and authorized Wingate to use the facility at Hanita—attended as well. They sat around the table in the room where they'd met just a few months earlier.

"You are aware that one of our patrols recently came under sniper fire," Blacker began.

"Yes, sir," Wingate replied.

"Two of our men died in that attack."

"And the assailants were never found," Wingate added.

"I see you read the reports," Redman noted with a snide tone.

Wingate nodded. "I read all of the reports."

Blacker cleared his throat. "General Haining wants to know why your strategy didn't work against those snipers."

"Were those his exact words, or is that a paraphrase?"

Others in the room bristled at Wingate's brash approach, but Blacker merely smiled. "That's the gist of it."

"Perhaps General Haining should ask a different question," Wingate responded. "Perhaps he should be asking why the patrol was traveling the open road in broad daylight."

General Stratton spoke up. "I thought your strategy suggested they *should* be patrolling."

"Patrolling," Wingate said with a nod. "But not using the roadways to do it. And not during the day, when the Arabs are sleeping."

"If they don't use the roads," Stratton asked with ironic humor, "how are they to get around?"

"Leave the armor at the post," Wingate explained. "Patrol on foot. Never follow the roadways. They're only a trap...an open invitation to ambush. Which is precisely why the Arabs were there that day and precisely where the Arabs will attack once again."

"Certainly," General Simpson noted. "Because they know we must pass that way."

"No," Wingate corrected. "Because Arabs are lazy and they know how lazy men think. Those places are easy for them to reach and easy for our men to use. It's a convergence of propensity."

Simpson looked confused. "Propensity?"

"We have a propensity to take the easy way. They do, too," Wingate continued. "Our men would be far safer traveling in open country on foot rather than by road in vehicles. The Arabs will never go in the open country, except at night and then only traveling to and from some hapless target of opportunity. For attacks on our troops, it is far easier for them to simply wait by the side of the road for us to come traipsing past, then pick us off one and two at a time."

"Some think your so-called strategy is really quite reckless," Stratton commented, changing the subject. "And, I might add, quite cavalier with human life."

Wingate nodded again. "Certainly they do. But one should ask if they really believe that, or are they merely cowards, afraid to do their job?"

"That's out of order!" Stratton erupted.

"What's out of order," Wingate corrected, staring at the others and ignoring Stratton, "is the complete and utter failure of commanders in and around Jerusalem to adopt the practices we use in Galilee. If they'd used our strategy and conducted night raids, the Arab gangs that killed those two fine soldiers would have been long gone when the patrol came through."

They talked awhile longer, with Stratton and Simpson taking exception to almost everything Wingate said. By lunch, it was clear they would never support the Special Night Squads or Wingate's desire to advance further in his career.

What that might mean for Wingate's future was unclear, but things came into sharper focus as they started toward the dining hall to eat when General Blacker steered him aside to a vacant room for a private meeting. General Redman was with him.

"There is one more thing," Blacker closed the door behind them.

"Certainly, sir," Wingate replied, now wary and on guard.

"General Haining also wanted to know if there was anything you could do to find the men responsible for these attacks."

Suddenly, Wingate understood the true reason for the meeting. Blacker was on his side. Redman, too. They believed in the strategy and were glad to have Wingate take the lead in the dirty business of clandestine warfare—to be the "point of the spear," as generals sometimes liked to say. The meeting that day wasn't to dress him down or to blame him for the recent Arab activity. The meeting was called to allow the others to have their say and in doing so to reveal their true positions regarding the Special Night Squads—a warning, as it were, to tell Wingate not everyone was convinced.

Allowing them to do that was also a cover for what Haining really wanted, a solution to the Arab problem that carried too much political liability for a general of his stature to propose forthrightly. A solution many would favor but everyone—including Blacker and Redman—would deny. They wanted him to eliminate the Arabs who killed those soldiers. They wanted him to eliminate as many Arab gunmen as possible. To put an end to the trouble by killing those who caused it. And to make sure no one knew he had anything to do with it.

"That," Wingate said confidently, "is a question that moves us in the right direction."

"You can do something about it?" Redman asked hopefully.

"Yes," Wingate replied. "We can take care of that."

✦ ✦ ✦

When Wingate returned to Hanita, he took me aside with Dayan, Ronen, and Fichman. "We're going on a special mission. Bring only your rifle, one handgun, a few grenades, and two bandoliers of ammunition."

"When do we leave?" I asked.

"Tonight."

"Do we have a target?" Dayan asked.

"Don't worry about the details. I'll show you what you need to know on the way."

Two hours after dark, we left the compound and hurried south toward Ma'alot-Tarshiha. A few kilometers north of the town, we came to a small settlement tucked against the base of a hill with a flat plain beyond. We arrived in the night and took a position that afforded a panoramic view of the area, then settled into place for a rest.

As the sky turned gray with the approaching dawn, Wingate awakened us and we gathered around him, sitting just below the crest of the hill to keep out of sight. "This is where we learn the most effective skill of all. The skill of the sniper." His eyes were wide with excitement. "A shot from far away, striking a target before anyone hears the sound of the rifle, strikes terror in the hearts of even the bravest men. This is where we take the fight to the heart of the enemy."

We followed him up the hill a short distance, then he dropped to the ground and crawled to the crest ahead of us. When we hesitated, he motioned for us to come up and we crawled to where he lay. Prone on the ground, the village seemed somehow closer, as if the buildings were right in front of us, and I felt my heartrate increase. Nothing like that first night—or the night Amos and I killed those two Arabs with our bare hands—but the moment was tense and I felt my skin grow damp with perspiration.

We lay there awhile, watching, but there was no movement at the houses below. Then, as the sun broke the horizon, people emerged from the shadows—first the women to light the cooking fires, then the men looking sleepy and drowsy. Wingate took a pair of binoculars from inside his shirt and held them to his eyes. After a moment, he handed them to me and pointed toward the settlement. "See the tall man by the third hut?"

I trained the glasses on the buildings, focused on the man he'd indicated, and nodded. "Yes, I see him."

"That is Abdul Rahim."

"Who is he?"

Wingate took the binoculars from me. "See if you can hit him from here. One shot."

A glance in Dayan's direction told me he was worried, but Ronen and Fichman grinned from ear to ear—as if to say they didn't think I could make the target. I was reluctant to try, especially without knowing more about why I was being asked to kill someone, but Wingate was a captain and I was not, so I brought the rifle around from where it hung by its sling on my shoulder, rested the foregrip in the palm of my hand, and pressed the stock against my shoulder. Very carefully, I trained the sights on the man's head, held my breath to keep the marks in place, then gently squeezed the trigger.

Instantly, the bullet exploded from the muzzle in a flash of fire and smoke. The sound of it echoed through the hills much louder and far more obvious than I expected. Seconds later, Rahim fell backward, his arms dangling at his side, and collapsed to the ground. That's when I noticed the top of his head was missing and the wall behind him was splattered in red.

A woman who'd been standing nearby rushed to his side and in a moment others joined her. Soon the report of the rifle was replaced by the sound of screaming and crying—an odd confirmation that I'd hit the target and one that sent a smile across my face.

Hitting the target, even though it was a human, was more satisfying than I expected and in the exhilarating rush of success I raised up for a better view. As I pushed up with my arms, Wingate grabbed me by the shoulder and yanked me back to the ground. "Are you crazy?" he scolded in an angry whisper. "Stay down! If they see you they'll kill us all."

"Who was that?" I asked.

"An Arab," Wingate replied, still aggravated with me. "He attacked a patrol not long ago and killed two British officers." We were still lying on the ground, but he turned to me and jabbed me in the neck with his finger. "You're a good shot with that rifle but this kind of work calls for patience. One shot," he again used his finger to drive home the point. "One shot and then out of sight."

Fichman moved closer. "What do we do now? They'll be up here looking for us."

"Lie here and be still."

"Won't they find us?"

"With only a single shot," Wingate explained, "they have no idea where it came from. Two or three more and they'll figure it out. Kick over a few rocks on the way down from here and they might see us. Just lay right here."

Fichman looked dissatisfied. "We have to wait here all day?"

"Not all day. Just long enough for them to look somewhere else."

As we waited and watched, things developed just as Wingate suggested. The women who were with Rahim when he died pointed to the hill where we lay, apparently telling the others the direction from which the shot came. The men, however, seemed not to believe them and spent their time scouring the hills to the north of our position. They found something there that interested them—empty field-ration containers or some other debris, I couldn't really tell what it was—and I noticed Wingate was particularly amused by it, which made me wonder what else he'd been up to. But though they searched for several hours, they never came near us.

The following night, we repeated the attack at another village, only with Dayan taking a turn at the rifle, and over the course of the next several weeks we completed dozens of those missions. Each night, a different member of the team functioning as the sniper. And when he was satisfied we understood what to do, Wingate began training others for the Special Night Squads and sent us out in pairs to multiple targets that we undertook on our own.

IN THE MONTHS THAT FOLLOWED, Wingate was in and out of Hanita as he continued to train new people for additional Special Night Squads that operated from our post and other locations in Galilee. We accompanied the squads from Hanita when he was not with them.

On nights when he was present, Dayan, Fichman, Ronen, and I went out in pairs as sniper teams, targeting specific men identified by Wingate as key leaders of active Arab gangs. Even with Ronen or Fichman at my side, the work was solitary, quiet, and peaceful. Just the two of us out there in the night, slipping into a shooting spot, waiting for sunrise, then locating the target and squeezing off a round.

For all of those missions, we relied solely on intelligence supplied by Wingate. Several times I wondered how he knew the things he knew and many times I wondered how reliable and accurate that information really was. But regardless of those doubts, we did as instructed, carrying out his directions to the fullest extent possible. Not many could resist Orde Wingate's commanding personality and certainly none of us was capable of telling him no.

One night while he was with us and all the squads were in the field, Arabs raided the Jewish Quarter in Tiberias. In that attack they killed a number of adults and a dozen Jewish children. We didn't learn about it until we returned to the post the following morning, but news of what happened enraged us. Wingate vowed on the spot to find out who was behind it and to make them pay dearly for what they'd done.

A week later, one of Wingate's sources traced the attack to an Arab gang that was living in Shaab, an Arab town halfway between Hanita and Tiberias. Armed with that information, Wingate selected the best men from each of our squads and gathered them in the ready room to discuss an attack. Dayan, Fichman, Ronen, and I were with them.

The plan Wingate presented that day—surround the town on all sides, draw the Arabs from hiding with a small force, and finish them off when they appeared—was the same plan we'd used at Daburiyya. A plan that resulted in injuries to him and several of the men who were with us—one of whom died later from those injuries. I pointed that out during the meeting, but Wingate didn't seem to care. "This is the strategy. Remember that we have men on both sides, and don't fire at targets beyond the center of town." Then his eyes met mine and he tapped the table for emphasis. "But this is the strategy."

As before, Fichman drove the supply truck and transported us to the site. We arrived well before sunrise and dispersed in groups of two and three around the town, each team taking preselected positions that cut off all means of escape. Fichman and a team of eight took a place on the west side, in front of Dayan's half of the force.

When everyone was in place, Wingate gave the signal and Fichman's group infiltrated the village, firing randomly in the air in a manner designed to draw the rebels from hiding. All seemed to be going according to plan when suddenly a group of twenty Arab rebels appeared from behind the hill to the east, directly over the position where Wingate's half of our force was placed. Without hesitation, the

Arabs descended on the men with a fury that I was certain would obliterate our eastern flank.

Rather than retreating deeper into the village, where he could have used the houses for cover, Wingate turned his force to face the attackers and ordered them to charge. It seemed like the decision of a madman and the abandonment of all good sense, but the men did as ordered and surged toward their onrushing attackers. Startled by the boldness of the response, the Arabs bolted in retreat back toward the top of the hill, with Wingate and his men in full pursuit.

The rest of us advanced from the west and pressed the fight in the village, cleaning up small groups of Arabs as they emerged from houses here and there until Wingate and his men returned. By then, half a dozen Arabs lay dead.

Frustrated by our inability to get them all, Wingate unleashed his vengeance on the village, sending men down each street with orders to empty all the buildings. Spurred on by Wingate's anger, the men set to the task with zeal, driving men, women, and children from their homes and herding them toward the southern edge of town. Those who resisted were shot on sight and when they were finished, a dozen more Arabs were dead.

With all the buildings and huts emptied of people, Wingate set fire to a row of houses and forced the residents to watch as the fire spread to neighboring structures, then quickly swept through the entire town. As the flames leapt into the air I was certain I saw a smile on his face.

✦ ✦ ✦

Meanwhile, and apparently in a coordinated attack, a much larger gang of Arabs raided the kibbutz at Kinneret. They overwhelmed the Settlement Police and fought their way into the compound. With the property under their control, they set fire to the outbuildings, slaughtered the livestock, and vandalized the equipment. Finally, they routed the remaining police from their defensive positions, killing most of them with abandon, then locked the settlers in the dining hall.

Trapped inside the building, Benjamin Lapid slipped into his office and used the settlement radio to send a distress call. Weinstein, who was in Hanita monitoring the post radio for news that might relate to our mission, heard Lapid's message and learned that no other Haganah troops were available to come to the settlement's defense.

With the distance from Hanita too great to send men to make a timely response, Weinstein was in a difficult position. Revealing our position to anyone under any circumstance was a serious breach of Haganah security. However, with no other force available and Kinneret facing the mass murder of its residents, he had little choice but to take action, no matter how great the risk.

In a message written as cryptically as possible, he told Lapid that we were in Shaab and directed him to send a runner to inform us of his situation. When the messenger reached Shaab, the town already was on fire. Wingate seemed to welcome one more challenge and wasted little time in breaking off our engagement. Within minutes, we were loaded in the truck and headed south.

As we rode toward Kinneret I thought of Amos and Dalia and wondered if they'd been attacked, too. Memories flooded my mind of the night when we were young and Arabs raided our farm. Images appeared—of Mama lying dead on the floor and Papa telling us to leave. Then I thought of the Riskins and the people we knew at the farming settlement.

Somewhere along the way my eyes grew heavy and thoughts of home slipped from my mind. In their place came a flood of images from the fighting early that night at Shaab. It had started well enough, but then quickly seemed to spin out of control. All of it was so completely uncharacteristic of Wingate. The look in his eyes. The sound of his voice. And it was difficult to determine whether we were fighting an enemy or executing the plans of a madman. Little did I know what lay ahead for me.

✦ ✦ ✦

We arrived at Kinneret two hours later and as we drew near I saw thin wisps of smoke rising from Amos' farm. None was visible from the Riskin house. At first I was relieved and thought perhaps both had been spared, but then I saw the charred remains of the trees on the far side of the Riskin compound and realized their house had burned to the ground.

Everything inside me wanted to jump from the truck and run to find out what happened, but there was no time for that now. As much as I would have liked to, I had no choice but to stay with the men until we secured the settlement.

As was often our strategy of attack, Wingate deployed us in a circle around the compound and we advanced toward the center. With each step forward I expected to be leveled by a hail of gunfire, but nothing happened and we saw not a single person.

At the center of the settlement we found the Arabs standing shoulder to shoulder around the dining hall. With their rifles raised to their shoulders, they were shooting randomly through the windows, firing at anyone who appeared in their line of sight. Six people lay dead on the floor and from inside we heard screams and shouts of panic and fear.

No one gave us the order to attack. No one sounded the order to shoot. No one needed to. At the sight of them, we unleashed a torrent of gunfire that felled every Arab who stood before us. None of them escaped.

Having dispensed with the Arab gang so quickly and efficiently, I saw no reason to remain in the compound a moment longer. Against Wingate's rules, and contrary to Haganah policy, I turned away from the dining hall and ran from the compound as fast as my tired legs would carry me.

With no thought of what might await me, I raced up the road toward the farm and arrived to find the house and barn in flames. In the glow of the fire I saw Amos' body lying face down in the yard. I dropped to the ground beside him, lifted his head from the dirt, and cradled him in my arms. Holding him against my chest, I rocked back and forth as tears streamed down my face.

In that moment, voices, as from a distant past, filled the air around me. The laughter of our childhood. The sound of Amos' voice when we were children playing in the dirt as Papa plowed the field. Mama calling us to lunch in the middle of the day. Amos giggling as he tickled me with his foot beneath the table.

Suddenly and without warning, Wingate appeared at my side. He towered over me with an angry scowl on his face, then drew back his hand and struck me with the back of it against the side of my face. "You left your position," he shouted. "You abandoned the men. Your actions endangered yourself and everyone with us!"

I looked up at him, oblivious to the blood that stung the corner of my mouth. "He is my brother," I whispered.

Wingate's countenance dropped and his shoulders sagged. He said something else but I didn't pay him any attention. Instead, I gently lowered Amos' head to the ground and stood. "Where is Dalia?" I asked.

Wingate glanced over at me. "Who is Dalia?"

"Amos' wife."

Wingate had a puzzled look and I expected him to ask a question, but before he could speak Dayan and others arrived. Dayan took one look at the body and slipped an arm around my shoulder. "Your brother?"

"Yes."

"I'm sorry you had to find him like this," Dayan said.

I looked past him. "Did you see a woman anywhere?"

"Dalia?" he asked.

"Yes."

"I'll send some men to search."

"What about the Riskins?"

Dayan leaned around to look me in the eye and noticed blood at the corner of my mouth. A disgusted look came over him and I could see that even without being told, he knew what Wingate had done. He dabbed the blood with his thumb and his countenance softened. "The people in the next house?"

"Yes."

Dayan strengthened his grip on my shoulder. "They are dead, too," he answeree quietly.

While Dayan tended to me, Wingate led a team of men who searched the farm for Dalia. They didn't find her but located tracks that led away from the house toward the north. Wingate returned to inform us, then gathered a dozen men to follow in that direction. I turned to leave with them but Dayan stopped me and suggested I remain at the farm. I insisted on going, and Wingate let me join them.

Half a kilometer up the road we found Dalia's body lying in the weeds. She looked so frail and helpless, but when I rolled her over, her face was as lovely as ever. I bit my finger to keep from crying and used my free hand to brush the dirt from her check.

Wingate stepped aside to check the map. I heard him telling

Fichman of a place to the north where they should meet. "Get the truck. We'll be waiting for you when you get there."

Dayan said something and I heard Ronen respond, but when I looked up, Wingate was headed up the road in the lead with the squad trailing behind him. I assumed they were continuing north in pursuit of the Arabs, but I'd gone as far as I intended to go that night. I lingered behind, watching as they disappeared into the night, then I stooped over, slid my arms behind Dalia's body, and lifted her from the ground.

While everyone else pursued the Arabs, I buried Amos and Dalia behind the barn next to the grave we had dug for Mama. She liked Dalia, and I knew she would be glad one of us married her, even if it lasted only for a short time.

When that was done, I walked down to the Riskins' farm. Their bodies lay at the base of a cedar tree. David's fingers still gripped a pistol. I took it from him and folded his arms across his chest. Tzipi's hand was balled in a fist and when I opened it I found a small locket in her grip. I slipped it loose and flipped the tiny latch. Inside was a picture of Dalia. Tears filled my eyes and anger filled my heart, but I tamped it down and forced myself to remain calm. I was determined not to be consumed by emotion as I had seen it take control of Wingate earlier that evening.

✦ ✦ ✦

In the weeks that followed, I disciplined myself against all emotion, happy or sad, and concentrated on the work of being a Haganah soldier. Weinstein suggested I take some time off to mourn Amos' death. "Go down to Tel Aviv. Spend a few days on the beach, watching the waves." But I refused. Instead, I plunged into the night raids with even greater devotion and joined the next squad leaving from the post. Outside, I appeared as normal as anyone else, but inside I was heartbroken—and wracked with guilt.

Everything was all my fault. The way the attacks came that night—first an ambush from over the hill behind Shaab while at the same time an assault on the farm, the Riskins, the kibbutz at Kinneret—I was certain the Arabs knew I was the one who killed Abdul Rahim. And they must have known I was the one who killed all those others on those nights when we went out in twos and fired a single shot at a single target. They knew. They must have known.

Every time I relaxed, I heard the screams of anguish from the village, the house, the little boy standing beside his father in the field... as the bullet from my rifle ripped through someone's head, exploded in the center of another's chest, instantly changing everything. Sometimes they whispered to me and sometimes they shouted and the only way I could silence them was to do more, to run faster, to charge into one more village, one more town, with guns blazing. The sound of the rifle firing in rapid sequence—*Bam! Bam! Bam!*—silenced the voices and brought peace to my soul. But only for a moment.

As the days moved slowly past, I became convinced the attacks at Kinneret were committed as revenge against me. They could never breach the stockade at our post, but my brother and his wife were easily accessible and if they were attacking there, why not add in all the others to make a statement?

It made sense to me until one night as I was lying on my cot, thinking about it yet one more time, the question came to me—how could they have known about Amos? No one kept lists of our members. There were no diaries, logs, or notes of our actions. No one at the post would talk to an outsider. No one at the post had been anywhere to tell anyone *anything*.

A wave of comfort swept over me and for the first time in a long time a smile came to my face. I relaxed and closed my eyes, then just as I was drifting off to sleep I remembered—the wedding. My eyes popped open and my heart rate increased.

I'd traveled from Hanita to the farm for the wedding. I stayed at the kibbutz on their wedding night.

The trip from Hanita to the farm for the wedding took me a long distance and I had to wait in Tur'an for a ride, going and coming back. Someone saw me. Someone followed me. They knew where I'd been.

As suddenly as it vanished, the guilt returned. Only this time greater than before. It rolled around inside my head telling me over and over, *It was your fault. It was all your fault.* If I'd just been there, working the farm with them, none of this would have happened. If I hadn't gone off on those night raids, killed all those people, destroyed all those villages, the gangs never would have come to Kinneret, never would have attacked the farm, never would have killed the Riskins. Everything still would be just as it was.

A MONTH OR TWO AFTER we returned from Kinneret, while I still was wrestling with all that had happened, Wingate led us on a night raid of a village not far from Hanita where gunrunners from Lebanon were reportedly hiding. As usual, we encircled the village. This time, however, Dayan led the provoking skirmish and took half a dozen of us to the edge of town where we were to create a disturbance to draw the gunrunners from hiding. Because Dayan was in charge, I went with them.

We were supposed to fire random shots, just enough to alert the gang to our presence, but while the others lagged behind at a safe distance, firing into the air, I continued on my own farther into the village. Not far up the street I came to a hut with the door slightly ajar. I kicked it open with the toe of my boot, my rifle at my shoulder ready to respond.

Inside, a woman lay on a sleeping mat with a man on top of her and as the door swung open I heard her protesting. "Get off of me," she cried in anger.

My sudden appearance startled them both and when the man jerked his head around to glare at me all I could see was the face of an

Arab—one of the men who attacked our farm that night when we were young, before we went to Egypt. I blinked my eyes to make sure and saw the woman beneath him was now Dalia. She looked at me with pleading eyes and in a helpless voice cried, "Get him off of me."

Suddenly, the emotion I had been suppressing for weeks swept over me. Anger rose inside me with an overwhelming force. Dalia was an Arab captive and he was on top of her, ravishing her body! It wasn't just an image of my imagination, it was the truth and I knew it as surely as anything I'd ever known in my life.

In an instant, I shot the man in the head. The woman screamed and then I realized she wasn't Dalia at all. She was Arab also with almond shaped eyes, black hair, and—

A man emerged from a back room, eyes open wide, a startled look on his face. He glanced at the lifeless body of the man I'd just shot—a man I now realized was much too young to have been among those who attacked our house the night Mama died. He looked at me in anger and started to say something, but I didn't wait to hear what he had to say. I squeezed the trigger and shot him, too.

With the woman still screaming and crying, I stepped back through the doorway to find men pouring from the houses and huts of the village. Many of them were armed and coming down the street in my direction, shouting and brandishing their weapons. When one of them pointed a rifle at me, I shot him—and the man beside him—and the one next to him—all the while walking backward, retreating the way I'd come.

The villagers kept advancing toward me, warily since I had killed several of their companions but advancing nonetheless. I was down to my last two rounds when Dayan and three men from his squad appeared in an alley to my left. They motioned for me to run, then leaned around the corner of a building and laid down covering fire. I didn't wait around to see what happened next. I turned and ran as fast as I could go.

As I neared the edge of town, Wingate and the men of his squad advanced on the village from the opposite side. I heard the gunfire but didn't bother to look back until I was a safe distance away. When the shooting ended, the six men Wingate wanted us to find were dead—as were dozens of villagers, including women and children.

Wingate thought the Arabs still held a cache of weapons and wanted to search from house to house. Dayan talked him out of it, telling him it would be dawn soon and that we needed to return to post. In reality, Dayan knew what would happen if the search were conducted—more people would die and then Wingate might torch the place. He'd seen enough of that to know that nothing good would come from it.

+ + +

Around midmorning the following day, Dayan took me aside. I could tell by his look he was displeased with something but had no idea what he might be upset about. "That was a pretty scary moment last night."

"Yeah. Thanks for covering me."

"What were you doing out there on your own?"

I tried to shrug it off. "I don't know, just wanted to draw them out like we planned."

"We were supposed to stay together."

"I know."

He looked over at me. "Are you okay?"

I glanced away nervously. "Yeah, why?"

"I don't know." Dayan tucked his arms behind his back. "You just don't seem quite the same. Like something's bothering you."

"No." I shook my head. "I'm fine. Perfectly fine." I gave him a quick glance. "Why would anything be bothering me?"

"You've been through a lot lately," he said with a note of genuine concern. "Your brother is dead. His wife is dead. Many of the people you knew in Kinneret are dead. I just thought—"

The mention of them brought images of that night back to my mind. Vivid memories. Of Amos on the ground. Dalia's frail body. The feel of her in my arms when I picked her up to carry her home. The touch of her body against mine and the realization of what I had missed because she chose him instead of me. I wasn't supposed to feel that, I wasn't supposed to—

"I'm fine," I snapped, trying to get away from the thoughts that filled my mind. "Just, please, don't talk to me about them." I turned away. "You didn't know them. You don't know anything about them." I took a deep breath and stilled myself. "I appreciate your concern." My voice was calmer and I concentrated hard to bring my emotions in check. "But I'm doing fine. Everything is okay."

Only, everything wasn't okay, and after Dayan talked to me, the voices and images returned. Mama seated in the darkest corner of the house, telling us it was time for bed and Amos begging her to read one more story. Papa mumbling to himself as he sat at the table with the lamp behind him on the opposite side of the room. Then the screams of the woman that night when I killed Abdul Rahim.

The voices and images continued to plague me through the day and became even more intense at night when I tried to sleep. I remembered the way the sound of gunfire turned them away and hoped Wingate would take us on a night raid. When he didn't, I arranged to fire a few rounds on a practice range at the post, but it only helped for a short time. Then the voices returned, sometimes louder and stronger than ever. Wingate was away and no raids were planned but I could stand it no more and took matters into my own hands.

Late one night, after everyone was in the barracks and only the guards were on the wall, I slipped from the stockade and went out alone, armed with my rifle, a bandolier of ammunition, and half a dozen grenades.

Two miles east of Hanita, I came to a small cluster of houses. It wasn't really a village, just a settlement, but I knew Arabs lived there and told myself they'd probably been informing on us. Telling Arab gangs and gunrunners where we were and what we were doing. Maybe they helped set up the attack on Kinneret.

Convinced that what I was doing was a righteous act, I took a position on a hill above the settlement, selected a house for a target, and fired a shot through the window. Without waiting to see what happened next, I withdrew behind the crest of the hill and circled around to the opposite side of the settlement, selected another house, and again fired a shot through a window.

As I turned away to change positions once more, I saw a fuel drum standing alongside a utility building. Against all that Wingate had warned us about firing multiple shots from the same location, I raised the rifle to my shoulder, trained it on the tank, and squeezed off another round.

Almost instantly the tank exploded, sending a giant fireball rolling into the sky. People down below ran from their houses, screaming and shouting. The sound of it put a smile on my face and a sense of satisfaction swept over me. I watched a moment, then dropped over the ridge behind the hill and started toward the stockade.

Half an hour later, I arrived back at Hanita, slipped into the barracks, and stretched out on my cot. With the voices in my head now silenced, I quickly fell asleep.

✦ ✦ ✦

A few nights later, the voices returned and I went out again to silence them. Very quickly that became my pattern—complete a sniper mission, sleep well for two or three nights, then, if Wingate hadn't sent us out already, I would do another mission on my own. It was a routine that suited me and life seemed normal with it in place, but when the voices returned they came with the added cries that arose from all those additional shots I'd fired and the people I'd killed.

Before long, I stopped waiting for the voices to return and went out on my own when we weren't busy conducting random sniper operations. Not so much to shoot at human targets—though I cared very little at the time whether anyone lived or died and shot at men, women, and children when the opportunity presented itself—but rather to shoot at anything I chose. I just wanted to hear the sound of the rifle when it fired. That was the thing I needed. That was the part that silenced the voices in my mind.

Then one night, a month or two into this routine, I returned to the post at Hanita to find Moshe Dayan seated outside our barracks, waiting for me. I wasn't sure what he wanted but as I approached he looked me in the eye and said, "You can't do this." His spoke with a matter-of-fact tone. No introduction. No question. Just the bald statement. "You can't do this."

I knew what he meant but refused to admit it. "Can't do what?" I asked in an innocent tone.

"You can't keep going out on your own, shooting into houses, killing people, and blowing things up."

"I have no idea what you're talking about." The door to the barracks was to his right and I tried to move around him toward it.

He moved quickly to block my path. "I followed you."

"You followed the wrong person," I growled, the tension rising inside with every passing moment.

"No, he didn't," Nahum Ronen said, suddenly appearing from around the corner. "He didn't follow the wrong person. I was with him."

"You both followed me?" My tone was growing sharper by the moment but I didn't care.

"You have to stop," Dayan said softly, ignoring my question. He rested his hand on my shoulder and looked me in the eye. "You have to stop *now*."

With one move, I slapped his hand away and stepped aside, trying again to get past him. Once again, he blocked me. "This isn't going away."

My lip quivered as tears filled my eyes and in spite of my effort to stop them they spilled down my cheeks. "They killed my brother," I said in an angry whisper.

"I know," Dayan replied. He put his hand back on my shoulder and pulled me closer. "I know," he repeated.

"They killed his wife."

"Yes," he replied.

"She was young and pretty and never did anything to anyone." I looked up at him. "Who knows what they did to her before they murdered her."

"I know," he said once more.

"It's not right. It's just not right," I sobbed. "They should pay for it."

"The men who did it should pay and they *did* pay. They paid with their lives. We took care of that. But the people you are attacking are innocent women and children. Innocent just like your brother and just like his wife. The people you are shooting at had nothing to do with any of what happened at Kinneret."

I leaned forward, rested my forehead against his shoulder, and cried. I cried for Amos and Dalia, for David and Tzipi, for Mama and Papa. It seemed as though the tears would never stop flowing but in a while I'd cried myself out. I stepped back and wiped my eyes with the backs of my hands. "Does Weinstein know?"

"I don't think so."

"What about Wingate?"

"Who can tell what he knows?"

"He hasn't said anything?"

"No."

With the guilt and anguish gone, the reality of what I'd done hit me hard. Acts of war were defended by officers and governments in every nation. But random acts of violence were condemned by all. "What do I do?"

Dayan pondered my question. "If you stop now, I think everything will be all right."

"You really think so?"

He nodded. "I really think so. No one has complained. There have been no reports filed. Nothing on paper." He reached out his hand and lifted the rifle from my shoulder. "But I think I should hold on to this for now."

Startled by his action, my eyes opened wide and I turned to the right as he slid the rifle and strap off that arm. "I'll need it," I protested. "I need my weapon."

"Not now," he said calmly. "I'll return it to you later, but not now." He held the rifle in one hand and lifted the bandolier over my head. "Let me have this, too."

Without the rifle or the ammunition belt, I felt naked and totally exposed. They might as well have stripped me of my clothes and marched me around the post nude, but Dayan was our executive officer. At Hanita, only Weinstein held a higher rank and even though we often deferred to Wingate, his words were only orders when Dayan said they were. Dayan was the commander of our unit. If he wanted my rifle and ammunition belt, he could have them and I did not put up a fight.

In fact, though I said nothing about it at the time, I was relieved to be free of them. Relieved to see them placed in the hands of one who could control them. One who would not let them control me. One who had my best interests at heart.

✦ ✦ ✦

A few days later, Wingate returned to the compound with new intelligence. He'd been there less than five minutes when he began organizing a squad for a night raid. He expected me to be with them and I was willing to give it a try, but Dayan intervened.

"Yoel is out."

Wingate was immediately angry. "He's not out until I say he's out."

Dayan stood his ground. "I'm the executive officer here. Yoel stays behind."

"We'll see about that," Wingate retorted and charged off to Weinstein's office.

There was a loud commotion from down the hall with shouting and yelling and someone pounding on a desk, but in a little while, Wingate returned with one of the younger men. Nothing more was said about me. While they prepared for the raid, I slipped out the door and made my way to the barracks.

When I reached my cot I found a small book lying there. Tucked behind the cover was a note from Ronen that read, *"This helped me understand what we are doing. Maybe it will help you."* The book was a copy of the Psalms of David.

At first I was put off by it. Books were for women, I thought. Not for men and certainly not for fighting men. Waging war was our business. A dirty business. A tough business. No place for reading or contemplation. Certainly no place for the kind of weakness I'd shown the other night when I broke down in tears.

Then I remembered that David was a warrior. A man's man. A man who learned to fight and when the violence became too much for him he expressed his feelings...in the Psalms. The book Ronen had left for me.

Somewhat reluctantly, I picked it up and leafed through the pages until the book fell open to

May the Lord answer you when you

are in distress;

May the name of the God of Jacob

protect you

May he send you help from the sanctuary

and grant you support from

Zion.

As I read those words it seemed as though David had written them to me and I accepted them as a blessing. I read the verses a second time, just to hear the words, and repeated them to myself as I lay on my cot. Before long, I was sound asleep.

✦ ✦ ✦

In the days that followed, I stayed behind at the post when Wingate assembled the Special Night Squads. I'd had enough of raiding villages. Instead, I spent the time reading. Usually in the book of Psalms that Ronen lent me. Sometimes in a copy of the Torah I found in Weinstein's office.

The voices soon became just a distant memory and when my mind relaxed from concentrating on the work of the day, my thoughts returned to the passages I read from the ancient scriptures. My life took on a normal rhythm. Different from before but normal just the same. Weinstein assigned me the task of conducting daily drills—a far cry from what I'd done the year before—but it eased my mind to know I no longer had to go with the night squads to prove I was a soldier. If anyone needed to know, Dayan was ready to tell them I'd already done that.

All of that helped me understand why Colonel Patterson had spent so much time reading and studying the Scriptures. I think he needed the words he found there to push out the memories and voices of all he'd been through as a soldier. Things I'd never known about at the time and only now came to realize.

Gradually, Wingate's visits to Hanita grew less and less frequent and the flow of intelligence less plentiful. We received reports of his exploits in other regions of the country but for a time saw very little of him.

An uneasy calm fell over northern Galilee, and Dayan turned the attention of our men to interdicting the flow of arms across the border. They were random nighttime patrols, based on nothing more than suspicion or hunch, but Dayan's hunches often proved the equal of Wingate's information and our men seized dozens of caravans bearing rifles, ammunition, and explosives. I took part in some of those patrols and it was good to be out of the post, beyond the stockade, crossing the countryside at night. Life had changed dramatically for me but I was on the mend and getting stronger every day.

WHILE WE WERE BUSY in Galilee fighting Arab gangs, the Woodhead Commission continued its work of revising and amending the plan for partitioning Palestine. As drafts of the commission's report circulated among British officials, rumors suggested the commission planned to drastically alter the Peel Commission's recommendation of a two-state solution. The most popular version of those rumors said the Jews would be left with only a small area along the coast. When a copy of the proposed report fell into Ben-Gurion's hands, those rumors proved to be all too factual.

By then, Wingate had been in Palestine almost two years. Most of that time had been spent with us or with units similar to ours where he led nightly raids on Arab targets up and down the Levant. Outwardly, he appeared fit, rested, and happy. Inwardly, however, he was exhausted and bearing the effects of all the things we'd done. Some of those effects were very much like the things I'd experienced. Those who knew him best could see he needed a rest.

Wingate, of course, resisted all attempts to extricate him from the field. Leading men into battle suited his personality and temperament and it was the kind of difficult work that drew him to the army. Suggestions from General Blacker, however, were more than mere suggestions and at his request, Wingate accepted an extended leave in London.

Before departing, Wingate met with Weizmann, Jabotinsky, and Ben-Gurion at the office in Tel Aviv. By then, Weizmann had learned that Wingate was connected through a cousin, Sir Reginald Wingate—a general and former governor-general of Egypt and the Sudan—to the highest levels of the British government. At that meeting, all three men prevailed upon Wingate to use whatever influence he might have to persuade the British government to reject the Woodhead Commission's report.

"We've already accepted the Peel Commission's report," Weizmann argued. "It's the Arabs who are causing the problem. Not us. If this latest report turns out to be anything like the initial drafts, it will amount to a withdrawal of a hundred years of work. Everything has been moving the region in the direction of a division of the entire area.

"This current administration is very dangerous," Ben-Gurion warned. "They will cast us aside without a second thought for the sake of peace in the region."

"If they cast us aside," Jabotinsky added, "they won't get the peace they think they can attain."

"But don't tell them that," Ben-Gurion warned. "We aren't in a position to threaten them."

"They certainly don't mind threatening us."

"If we issue a threat or an ultimatum, we will only drive them toward the Arabs." Ben-Gurion looked over at Wingate. "Don't threaten them. Be as diplomatic as possible. But do your best to get these latest revisions stopped."

✦ ✦ ✦

As rumors and early drafts had suggested, the Woodhead Commission's report was a scathing review of the Peel Commission's proposal, finding that partition was neither economically nor politically viable. Instead of creating independent Jewish and Arab states, the commission offered Jews and Arabs small areas of autonomous control, leaving the majority of the region in the hands of United Kingdom officials with a federal economic system shared by all three participants.

Weizmann telegraphed his reaction to Wingate, urging him to use any contacts he might have in an effort to have the report rejected. Wingate was all too glad to oblige.

Going over the heads of his superior officers, Wingate contacted his cousin and other family members who obtained appointments for him with cabinet officials and even a meeting with the prime minister, who by then was Neville Chamberlain. To press our cause even further, he persuaded a cousin to hold a dinner party for Winston Churchill. After dinner, Wingate cornered Churchill in the study and lectured him on the finer points of the Jewish-Arab conflict.

Although cabinet members and the prime minister were cordial and indulgent, almost everyone associated with the army found Wingate's actions an effrontery all but beyond forgiveness. A captain... meeting with a cabinet official? Unheard of. A captain meeting with the prime minister...scandalous. Men with twice his rank and five times his experience and ability toiled their entire careers without so much as even a glimpse of a person holding that level of office. What could possess a mere *captain* to think he had a right to leap over all those above him?

It was, however, all for naught. While Wingate still was in London, Chamberlain— thoroughly committed to appeasement as a negotiating technique—adopted portions of the Woodhead Commission's report as the government's official position. In conjunction with that, he issued a white paper, which recanted British support for a Jewish state in Palestine announced years before in the Balfour letter. In its place, he proposed a single government to administer Palestine by majority vote, announced limits on Jewish immigration for the next five years, and enacted provisions making further Jewish immigration subject to majority approval of voters in Palestine.

In Europe that same day, Nazis—now in control of Germany—unleashed mobs on the Jewish population. Thousands were killed. Tens of thousands more were sent to detention camps. And it was only the beginning of what became the darkest period in the history of our people.

✦ ✦ ✦

In reaction to the change in British position, and in response to developments in Germany, the World Zionist Organization held a conference. Weizmann and Ben-Gurion attended, as did others from the World Zionist Organization's office in Tel Aviv. Members of the Jewish Council in Palestine went as well. Retired but still supportive of Zionism, Colonel Patterson accompanied Jabotinsky to the conference.

Weizmann, who supported Chamberlain and pursued a policy of cooperation with the United Kingdom, faced broad opposition. Members of the World Zionist Organization were troubled over the substance of Chamberlain's policy changes and even more so by Weizmann's inability to produce a better outcome. Cooperation, it seemed, had failed to gain British support for the Jewish cause.

Seeing that members were dissatisfied with Weizmann's approach, Jabotinsky sensed an opening to promote his policy of confrontation and strength as keys to a successful strategy, both in Palestine and in Europe. His positions and the force with which he advocated them led to heated public arguments and even more so with Ben-Gurion and Weizmann in private.

As a Gentile and nonmember, Colonel Patterson had no official voice in conference proceedings. I am certain, however, that he did his best to mediate between the factions. The positions—and perhaps more to the point, the arguments made to advance those positions— proved irreconcilable. In the end, the views Jabotinsky expressed were as skewed toward the activist extreme as Weizmann's had been toward cooperation. It was, however, a difference of opinion that divided both the conference and the organization at every level. As the conference entered its final meetings, members took steps to address both the situation in Palestine and in the organization.

The Palestinian liaison office was separated from direct control of the organization and renamed the Jewish Agency for Palestine. David Ben-Gurion, who had proposed and advocated for a more moderate view that fell between those of Weizmann and Jabotinsky, was elected as head of the agency. Haganah and all other agencies created by the Jewish Council in Palestine were placed under his control, as were the office in Tel Aviv and all its ancillary functions. Ben-Gurion was, in effect, head of a Jewish state in waiting.

Thoroughly rebuffed by the conference, Jabotinsky broke from the World Zionist Organization and issued a call for revision of the fundamental tenets of Zionism to include a more militant stand against the Arabs and the British. To promote the goals expressed in those views, he announced the formation of the World Union of Zionist Revisionists. A revised Zionism, he suggested, would have as its goal the establishment of a Jewish state that controlled all of Palestine, including Transjordan. In conjunction with that, he proposed reestablishing the former Jewish Legion as a force capable of driving all opposition from the land. He attracted immediate and influential support.

+ + +

Not long after the conference concluded, Wingate came to Hanita. He arrived as he had the first time we saw him, driving the Studebaker convertible with the top down. This time, however, the swagger and bravado were not quite so evident.

Weinstein assembled the men in formation at the center of the compound, and Wingate, standing atop a truck tire for a dais, announced that he had been recalled to London and would be leaving Palestine within the week. We were sad to see him go, but for many of us it seemed his time had run its course. As I knew all too well, one cannot engage in a life of combat for an indefinite period.

For the next thirty minutes, Wingate gave a sketch of events in the world. Another war with Germany, he said, appeared unavoidable. So obviously, he was to be detailed to the preparation of the defense of England. He also was to be granted a promotion to the rank of major.

Finally, he warned us that many within the British government opposed our very existence and were looking for any excuse to disband the entire Palestinian project. If we wanted to prevent that, he said, we should continue the night raids, no matter what, suggesting that they were the most effective means of change available.

When he climbed down from atop the tire, many in our group swarmed toward him, taking the moment for one last word of encouragement and a final good-bye. Dayan, Ronen, Fichman, and I walked him to his car and followed him out past the gate as he left the compound.

The others wandered back inside but I stood outside, beyond the gate, and watched until the trail of dust that rose behind him drifted away and the last speck of his car disappeared over the horizon. I'd been privileged to know many of the key players in the events of the last forty years. Trumpeldor, Jabotinsky, Weizmann, Colonel

Patterson, and now Orde Wingate. They each had their quirks—their strengths and their weaknesses. Trumpeldor, Jabotinsky, and Weizmann were fellow Jews. That they had differences of opinion, then fought together against a common enemy, then continued disagreements among themselves, seemed perfectly fitting. They were, after all, united in their view that Jews needed a homeland. The thing that divided them was a matter of detail—how to make that homeland a reality.

Patterson and Wingate were different. They weren't Jews at all. Both were Protestant Gentiles. Englishmen. Yet they were as devoted to our cause as any of us.

And for what?

For money? There was no money in it for either of them.

For fame? The infamous were the ones who opposed us.

For the joy of serving a glad and thankful people? I doubt anyone ever said thank you to either of them while they were alive.

Yet it was they who came to our aid without our asking and awakened in us long-misplaced memories of a forgotten heritage—that we were a fighting people. A nation of warriors. A nation of men and women who carved a future out of nothing but a dream.

No. They didn't come to us in the hope of wealth, fame, or self-satisfaction. They came as friends—to the struggling settlers routed from their property, to a nation yearning to be born. Friends to Amos and me. To Dayan, Ronen, and Fichman. Friends to the Jews of Palestine and friends to Jews around the world. Without their help, we never would have made it.

I could have stayed there staring out across the distance for the remainder of the day but a hand touched me on the shoulder, and when I looked Dayan was standing beside me. "Miss him?"

I smiled. "No, but I was sad to see him go."

"Well, get over it quickly."

"What do you mean?"

"We have work to do."

"What kind of work?"

"One of Wingate's sources contacted Fichman. An Arab gang is preparing to hit the pipeline tonight."

"Fichman has Wingate's sources?"

"A few."

"Is it good information?"

Dayan laughed. "I don't know, but I think we're about to find out."

We turned away from the view and started back toward the compound. "Do you think it will ever end?" I asked.

"The fighting?"

"Yeah."

"I don't know. But I think we're ready for whatever comes our way."

"Yes, we have been trained by the best."

ALTHOUGH BASED ON historic incidents, *Friends of Zion: Patterson and Wingate* is a work of fiction. Events have been portrayed as realistically as possible but with an eye toward creating an entertaining and engaging story. Characters, events, and locations are the work of the author's imagination and have been arranged and compiled with the story of Yoel and his brother Amos, fictional characters, in an attempt to provide the reader with a poignant glimpse of the lives of John Henry Patterson and Orde Charles Wingate. Two men who were very much real people and proved to be true friends of Israel and of the Jewish cause.

After leading the Zion Mule Corps during World War I, Colonel Patterson helped organize the Jewish Legion and led its brave soldiers in the fight to liberate Palestine from the Ottoman Empire. Shortly after the close of World War I, he returned to England where he lived with his family to enjoy a much-deserved retirement—but not for long.

The rise to power of the Nazi Party in Germany drew him once more into the cause of Zionism. For the remainder of his life, he traveled the world as an advocate for Jews everywhere, raising money, giving speeches, and doing all in his power to win support for the as-yet undeclared state of Israel.

Later in life, Colonel Patterson settled permanently in the United States where he died on June 19, 1947. On December 4, 2014, in fulfillment of his final request, Colonel Patterson's remains and those of his wife were disinterred from the United States and reinterred at the Avihayil cemetery in Israel, near the graves of some of the men he'd led during World War I.

Speaking at the reburial ceremony, Israeli prime minister Benjamin Netanyahu described Colonel Patterson as a "great friend of our people, a great champion of Zionism and a great believer in the Jewish state and the Jewish people...."

❖ ❖ ❖

After serving in Palestine, Orde Charles Wingate went on to a brilliant, though short-lived, military career. While attempting to adapt his night-raid strategy to conditions in Asia during World War II, Wingate traveled to Burma to check on guerilla teams operating in the region. On March 24, 1944, as he was returning to India, the plane in which he was riding crashed. He and the nine other passengers on board were killed.

The bodies of all ten victims were damaged by fire beyond the ability of medical examiners to determine their identities. As a result, all ten were buried in a common grave near Bishnupur, India. However, seven of the people who died in the crash were US servicemen. After the war, their bodies were disinterred and reburied at Arlington National Cemetery in Washington, D.C.

Both John Henry Patterson and Orde Charles Wingate proved critical in the development of the state of Israel. Patterson for creating the Zion Mule Corps and the Jewish Legion, which became a cadre of soldiers trained in the traditional military role from which Israel Defense Forces leadership sprang. Wingate for instilling in Haganah a can-do bravado that remains with the Israel Defense Forces to this day. To both men, free people everywhere owe a deep debt of gratitude.

ACKNOWLEDGMENTS

This book would not have been possible without the efforts of my writing partner, Joe Hilley, and my executive assistant, Lanelle Shaw-Young, both of whom work diligently to turn my story ideas into great books. And the help of Arlen Young, Peter Glöege, and Janna Nysewander in making the finished product look and read its best. And always, I am thankful for my wife, Carolyn, whose presence makes everything better.

**MICHAEL DAVID EVANS,** the #1 *New York Times* bestselling author, is an award-winning journalist/Middle East analyst. Dr. Evans has appeared on hundreds of network television and radio shows including *Good Morning America, Crossfire* and *Nightline,* and *The Rush Limbaugh Show,* and on Fox Network, *CNN World News,* NBC, ABC, and CBS. His articles have been published in the *Wall Street Journal, USA Today, Washington Times, Jerusalem Post* and newspapers worldwide. More than twenty-five million copies of his books are in print, and he is the award-winning producer of nine documentaries based on his books.

Dr. Evans is considered one of the world's leading experts on Israel and the Middle East, and is one of the most sought-after speakers on that subject. He is the chairman of the board of the Ten Boom Holocaust Museum in Haarlem, Holland, and is the founder of Israel's first Christian museum—Friends of Zion: Heroes and History—in Jerusalem.

Dr. Evans has authored a number of books including: *History of Christian Zionism, Showdown with Nuclear Iran, Atomic Iran, The Next Move Beyond Iraq, The Final Move Beyond Iraq,* and *See You in New York.* His body of work also includes the novels *GameChanger, The Samson Option, The Four Horsemen, The Locket, Born Again: 1967,* and *The Volunteers.*

✦ ✦ ✦

Michael David Evans is available to speak or for interviews.
Contact: EVENTS@drmichaeldevans.com.

# BOOKS BY: MIKE EVANS

Israel: America's Key to Survival

Save Jerusalem

The Return

Jerusalem D.C.

Purity and Peace of Mind

Who Cries for the Hurting?

Living Fear Free

I Shall Not Want

Let My People Go

Jerusalem Betrayed

Seven Years of Shaking: A Vision

The Nuclear Bomb of Islam

Jerusalem Prophecies

Pray For Peace of Jerusalem

America's War: The Beginning of the End

The Jerusalem Scroll

The Prayer of David

The Unanswered Prayers of Jesus

God Wrestling

The American Prophecies

Beyond Iraq: The Next Move

The Final Move beyond Iraq

Showdown with Nuclear Iran

Jimmy Carter: The Liberal Left and World Chaos

Atomic Iran

Cursed

Betrayed

The Light

Corrie's Reflections & Meditations

The Revolution

GAMECHANGER SERIES:
GameChanger
Samson Option
The Four Horsemen

THE PROTOCOLS SERIES:
The Protocols
The Candidate

The Final Generation

Seven Days

The Locket

Living in the F.O.G.

Persia: The Final Jihad

Jerusalem

The History of Christian Zionism

Countdown

Ten Boom: Betsie, Promise of God

Commanded Blessing

Born Again: 1948

Born Again: 1967

Presidents in Prophecy

Stand with Israel

Prayer, Power and Purpose

Turning Your Pain Into Gain

Christopher Columbus, Secret Jew

Finding Favor with God

Finding Favor with Man

The Jewish State: The Volunteers

See You in New York

Friends of Zion: Patterson & Wingate

COMING SOON:

The Columbus Code

The Temple

TO PURCHASE, CONTACT: orders@timeworthybooks.com
P. O. BOX 30000, PHOENIX, AZ 85046